THE SNOWMAN OF ZANZIBAR

GORDON WALLIS

For my long-suffering Mother, with love.

TABLE OF CONTENTS

CHAPTER ONE

– LONDON

My mind awoke before my body. There was the usual deep grumbling sound in the building that was always there. The twenty four hour machine that is London grinding away. One of many annoyances of big city living that the locals didn't seem to notice. More sounds started to filter through. Badly behaved, foul-mouthed children screaming in the street below on their way to school. A siren from a police car or an ambulance on its way to another anonymous drama somewhere in the Seven Sisters area. *Five floors up and still this fucking racket every morning.*

My thoughts went back to the previous evening. There had been beer. Lots of it. I finally opened my eyes and reached for the glass of water and the cigarettes on the bedside. I slowly began the routine of the morning, quietly cursing to myself. As I leant on the sink I slowly lifted my eyes to look into the mirror and the forty nine year old face stared back at me solemnly. *Jason Green what the fuck did you do to look like this?* I was looking rough to say the least. Bloodshot eyes with dark marks beneath them. Unshaven, tired. *You look like shit buddy*. It must have been 12 midnight by the time I had got in.

It had been a formidable session. I got on with my morning routine, shower, shave, dress, smoke more, drink coffee, watch the news on TV. All of this followed by the grand opening of the curtains to see what kind of day lay ahead. With a smidgen of misguided optimism I drew the curtains to a familiar sight. *Well, fuck, fancy that*. The scene in front of me was one of wet grey misery. North London in mid February. The huge gas storage tanks in the distance. Brown and soaked high rise buildings obscuring any hope of a horizon, a few token trees devoid of any leaves or colour. Mothers huddled into thick coats with hoods dragging small children to the preschool nearby. The not so glamorous life of an insurance fraud investigator in London. *Did I really sign up for this? Surely not, surely not*. With a deep sigh I turned away from the window and headed to the small kitchen to make a breakfast.

Twenty minutes later and fuelled by the eggs, bacon, sausages and black pudding I turned on my mobile phone, opened my laptop and had a look at what the day had in store for me. There was an appointment with a certain Mrs Tracy Summerfield of Finsbury Park at 11am. She had contacted me through my website a few days prior and I knew that she suspected her husband of having an affair. I remembered her nervous, slightly shaky voice on the phone.

It would mean a week of following some unsuspecting middle aged bloke around, a few photos, perhaps a bugging device, some discreet questions, the preparing of a report more than likely followed by a tearful meeting. All of this culminating in an exchange of cash. I had seen it a thousand times. My freelance work with the insurance company allowed me the time to pursue private jobs of this kind. Not massively exciting but it paid the bills. I sat back and considered my transport options to get to the appointment. It would be a choice between a drive or the Tube. I opted for the drive. I couldn't face the gloom and filth of the Underground that day. The traffic wouldn't be a problem as the appointment was mid morning. *Plenty of time.*

At 10.30 I wrapped up warm, grabbed my bag and unlocked my door. Five floors up the air was so cold it was like walking into a blast freezer. I huddled into my jacket and walked as fast as I could along the open walkway to the lift. The interior of the lift smelt of urine and I tried to hold my breath as it trundled downwards. On the ground floor I headed out of the building quickly and unlocked the door of my 1968 Mercedes 280s. I was starting to feel human again. The day was improving.

I smoked and thought about my life as I drove. I was 49 years old. I had been born in the southern African country of Rhodesia. Now Zimbabwe. Despite war that was raging at the time it had been a very happy childhood. After high school I had joined the army as was required for all young men. I had joined the Rhodesian light infantry at the age of 18 to fight in the guerrilla war of the late 70s. Military life had come naturally to me and I had excelled in every aspect of war. I had thrived with both the physical and mental challenges of the army and subsequently, at the age of 19, I had been recruited into a shady group that was without a doubt the toughest and most efficient killing machine in Africa. The Selous Scouts. Its members consisted of some of the finest fighting men in the western world. Unconventional and unorthodox. A secretive and elite unit that was the envy of the rest of the Rhodesian forces. We had been involved in pseudo operations. Often spending weeks deep in the bush, slowly infiltrating terrorist bases and groups and gathering intelligence.

During that time I had killed thirteen people that I knew of. The fact had never bothered me. It had been a war and in war there are casualties. But all too soon and very much to my disappointment the war had ended and the transition from Rhodesia into Zimbabwe had begun.

Having come from such a controversial unit of the army and uncomfortable about watching my beloved Rhodesia descend into the inevitable chaos that would surely come, I had decided to make a clean break from the country of my birth. Having been born from English parents and holding a British passport, the United Kingdom was my only real option.

There were still so many memories, although distant, of my childhood. Of the many friends made over the years of youth. Of the boarding school on the dusty Rhodesia / Botswana border. Of the Msasa trees. Of playing in the huge lush garden in Salisbury with the family dogs on hazy warm afternoons. Of family fishing trips to the mountains of the Eastern Highlands and the hot Zambezi Valley. Of the old family cook who had taught me to speak the local Shona language. I had been fluent and this was one of the reasons I had been recruited into the Scouts. These memories of Africa were fading. Time seemed to race by in London. One week quickly turned into one year, one year even faster into five. That's London. Fast.

The transition into civilian and married life in London had been more difficult than anything I had faced in the bush war. I had been married for ten years to an English girl but the marriage had gradually fizzled out due to a mutual lack of interest. I had been working as an insurance fraud investigator for a large multi-national company at the time. It had been an incredibly boring and repetitive nine to five existence that inevitably ended as well. It ended with my immediate boss suffering a broken nose and my being charged with assault. I had serious difficulty with figures of authority since leaving Rhodesia and the Scouts. There was a constant deep-seated frustration and smouldering anger associated with the sudden forced departure from the continent I loved and the country of my birth, to the comparatively sterile and lawful United Kingdom. Fading memories of family and friendships forged and suddenly lost. Although they had mellowed with time they were still there. Hidden away but not forgotten.

At 49 years old I was still slim and fit, even with the increased alcohol consumption since the divorce. I kept my dark hair short and neat and was always clean shaven. The years of physical training at school and in the army had done me no harm at all and I was determined to keep it that way as long as possible. I visited the local gym at least three times a week. I was financially comfortable and owned three properties in London that brought in a good monthly rental. I had made some friends in London and surrounds - all of them convinced that my current life, the life of a freelance investigator was one of high excitement and danger. How wrong they were!

They had no idea what I had been through during the bush war and I didn't care to tell them much about it either. I spent my days sitting in the car waiting to catch an accident claim fraudster on camera or spending endless hours waiting for a cheating wife or husband to come in to the view of a hidden webcam. It was fine for them to think that my world was one of intrigue and danger, even though it was quite often very boring.

The rain started as I arrived in Finsbury Park and finally found parking. I made my way to the entrance of the ground floor flat and rang the bell. Mrs Summerfield was obviously waiting and opened the door quickly. She was very tall and statuesque. Long sandy hair, expensive perfume, Chanel no 5, well-dressed. She looked like a young Sophia Loren. I put her age at about 44. We exchanged greetings and a handshake and I was ushered through the hall to a sunken lounge.

The place was tastefully decorated; leather couches, expensive looking antiques and old books filled the room. There was a large brass telescope by a huge bay window leading out to a lush green garden. The place smelled of money, and I was relieved by this. *No problem getting paid on this one.* Mrs Summerfield offered me a chair and sat nervously in front of me, "Thanks very much for coming to see me Mr Green," she said in a well spoken voice. I could see the tears welling up as she reached for a box of tissues. I felt pity for her and immediately moved to reassure her, "That's no problem, I'm here to help, what can I do for you? What's the problem?"

She fixed herself and began. It was the usual story. "Well, I think my husband may be having an affair, Mr Green. I can't believe I am actually asking you to do this but I have to know. He's changed in the past few months, he keeps his mobile phone off when he's in the house. He hardly calls anymore. He has these long business meetings and weekend seminar. He comes home late. He's wearing a lot of after shave and he's become quite secretive....I just..." More waterworks, more tissues. It was time to take over and reel her in. "Alright, I understand, you have to know the truth. You might be wrong, and I hope you are, but if your husband is having an affair I can find out for you, that's what I do."

Putting her at ease I went on to explain the way I worked. £150 a day plus expenses. The usual time frame for such a job was about a week. I knew full well that if it was the case that her husband was straying from the marital bed, I would probably know within a day or so, and be able to prove it. But that was the game and it was standard procedure. I spent the next half hour taking notes and chatting to my client. She became more and more relaxed as time went on.

I was given a photograph, his work details, company address, habits, times, routines etc. Finally it came down to the money.

"Now," I said, "I hate to talk about this sort of thing but I have to ask for a deposit before I start." "Of course," she interrupted and jumped up, "no problem, I understand completely, please accept this as a deposit." She walked over to an antique tea caddy on a sideboard and drew out a wad of cash, I stood as she counted out £500 in £50 notes and handed it to me. "No need for a receipt Mr Green, and thank you very much for this. I really appreciate your help. Quite honestly I'm beside myself with worry." Her hand grabbed my left forearm and she looked at me with open, trusting, almost pathetic eyes. "I'll get the answers for you Mrs Summerfield, just leave it with me. I'll stay in contact and when I'm finished I'll have a report for you."

I made my way to the front door and she let me out into the dreary, frozen day. She said her goodbyes with an anxious look on her face. "Don't worry," I said reassuringly. Her expression lifted and I knew that I had her complete trust. I felt an unusual pang of sympathy for her. It was something that never usually happened to me. I had done so many of these types of jobs and never allowed any emotion to cloud the task at hand. She was gorgeous and obviously devastated. *What kind of fool fucks around on a stunner like that?*

I jogged through the freezing drizzle to the car. Regardless, the money was paid. The job was on.

CHAPTER TWO

- RODNEY SUMMERFIELD

Rodney Summerfield was a lawyer. He should have known better. I planned the afternoon as I drove back to my flat in Seven Sisters. The offices of Coughlan, Summerfield and Fraser were in Soho Square, right in the centre of London. There was no way of driving there in time and Rodney Summerfield used the Underground to get to and from work anyway. I figured I could be there by 2pm using the tube from Seven Sisters. It would be easy to blend in to such a busy place. I parked the car and took the fifteen minute walk to the Tube station. I paid for a one day travel card and descended into the filthy anonymity of the London Underground.

As I travelled down the escalator I watched the line of people travelling up on the other side. All of them reading papers or looking at the adverts on the walls. Anything possible to avoid eye contact with another human being, heaven forbid. Suddenly I caught the eye of a tall brunette wearing a thick black coat and a grey scarf. Tube etiquette dictated that I should look away immediately but I held her gaze. She smiled with genuine warmth as she held my eyes. This was quite unusual. I gave a half smile back but all too soon the moment was over as we passed each other.

Pleasantly surprised I stepped onto the Victoria Line Southbound for Oxford Circus. There was plenty of room to sit and I passed the time reading my paper. Oxford street was a hive of activity as usual. Thousands of tourists braving the cold, pounding the hard streets with a sense of purpose and spending lots of money. I bought another newspaper from a vendor and turned left down a short road that led into Soho Square. The offices of Coughlan, Summerfield and Fraser were discreetly marked on the large windows outside the reception. It looked like a successful firm. The interior was plush and warm looking. I walked past the window, glanced in and noticed a thirty something brunette on reception. She wore glasses and appeared busy and efficient, even bossy, like a librarian.

Across the road towards the middle of the square was a bench. It would have to do. I made my way over and sat on the damp cold wood. *£150 a day, £150 a day,* I kept telling myself. Wishing I had brought gloves, I removed the photograph of Rodney Summerfield. I opened the newspaper and held the picture on the inside. The photograph was obviously taken on a holiday in happier times. A beaming sunburnt Englishman, Rodney Summerfield was laid back on a sun lounger, shirt off, a book in hand resting on a huge bronzed stomach. *Barbados perhaps?* He was a thick set chap with a rotund face. Easy to remember.

At 47 years old he was just the right age for a midlife crisis, a sports car, and an affair. He didn't look like a typical womanizer, I thought, but then who does? I made a mental note of his face and replaced the photograph. I removed my mobile phone and made a call to the law offices in front of me. I watched out of the corner of my eye as the woman at reception answered quickly with a southern Irish accent, "Coughlan, Summerfield and Fraser, can I help you?"

"Is Mr Summerfield there please?" I asked. "He is sir, can I ask who's calling please?" "Hello, hello?" I said and then, satisfied, I hung up. He was there at work. The librarian lookalike behind the glass silently mouthed the words "Hello, hello, can you hear me?" then hung up and busied herself with other tasks.

Half an hour passed. I smoked, read the paper and then feeling bored and chilled to the bone, I glanced around the square. I noticed there was a branch of the local Hare Krishna group on the other side of the square. *Quite a prestigious address.* Just then a group of four Krishna devotees left their offices and made their way towards Oxford Street. *They must be fucking freezing in their orange robes.* I watched them walk, wondering what they were all about.

There was a small removals van on the corner with a fat, red-faced man in the driving seat. He opened his window and began singing loudly in a broad cockney accent, "Harry Secombe, Harry Harry Secombe, Harry Secombe, Harry Harry Secombe!" He sang in the Hare Krishna tune. The visibly embarrassed devotees ignored him and rushed on their way. I had to laugh out loud at the spectacle. *Fucking hell.* It wasn't such a bad day.

An hour passed, I lit a cigarette and checked my watch. It was 3.45pm. At that moment Rodney Summerfield walked out of his offices. He wore a long thick woollen coat over a dark suit and carried a vintage slimline Samsonite briefcase. He walked in the opposite direction of Oxford Street. I casually stood and started following from a distance. After 40 metres or so he made a left turn. The streets were getting darker now but were still noisy and busy with people and cars. A few minutes later I saw Summerfield duck quickly into a pub on a corner. I gauged the place from the exterior and hung around for a few minutes assuming he would be ordering a drink. Satisfied he would be seated by now, I entered the warmth of the pub.

It was a small place with old wooden floors decorated with posters of rock bands - The Doors, Jimi Hendrix, Iron Maiden, AC/DC. It smelt of stale beer, an unlikely spot for a city lawyer to drink.

I noticed Summerfield had sat facing the wall to my left. *Good.* His thick neck was bulging around a tight white collar. He was drinking something that looked like a gin and tonic and was engrossed in some papers from his stylish briefcase, with his back turned from the bar. A busty barmaid asked me if she could help me. I ordered a pint of Löwenbräu and sat with my newspaper. The beer was cold and strong and I downed a full half-pint. The feeling was painfully starting to come back into my fingers from the cold outside, and the alcohol started to warm my body from the inside.

I kept an eye on Summerfield, mentally toasting him for the beer he was unknowingly paying for, and ordered another. At 4.20pm Summerfield received a call on his mobile phone. He glanced towards the door as he spoke, it was a very short call. Immediately after hanging up he turned and made his way to the bar for another drink. I held the paper higher making no eye contact at all, but listened. "Same again and a John Powers whiskey and ice please," he said. His was the voice of an educated man. An educated man in a very unlikely place. Someone was coming to meet him. *Who?* Summerfield returned to his table with the drinks.

I discreetly removed the miniature camera from my bag and pocketed it. All feelings of the hangover were gone now thanks to the drink. A perk of the job. The pub was getting busier with all sorts of people, young and old, locals and tourists. It was a grubby, but lively place. The kind of place Rodney Summerfield could disappear and become nameless quite easily. Summerfield drank and glanced at the door often. *Anytime now,* I thought, *surely it's not going to be this easy?*

At 4.35pm, the door opened. In walked the woman from the reception at Coughlan, Summerfield and Fraser. Still wearing her glasses and a huge smile, she made a beeline for Summerfield and kissed him squarely on the lips. *Unbelievable.* She removed her coat, sat down and was immediately in animated conversation with Summerfield. They chatted like excited kids. I studied her. She was quite beautiful in a bookish sort of way. Straight, silky dark hair just over her shoulders, flawless Irish skin, stylish blue metal rimmed glasses on a noble nose, red lips without the aid of lipstick, slim and well-dressed. She drank the whiskey. I mentally noted the brand Summerfield had ordered. John Powers.

I removed the camera casually from my pocket. After deactivating the flash I pretended to be looking at pictures on the small screen. The couple were busy talking and were totally oblivious of anyone around them. Turning the camera to the left at waist level, I took five photographs at different angles. I checked the pictures on the small screen one by one.

The first two were taken from the wrong angle but the last three were absolutely perfect. Two smiling lovers locked in conversation. Hands on each other's legs. *A picture says a thousand words. You are so fucking busted, Summerfield.* I couldn't believe my luck. I could have wrapped up the job right then with those photographs but I knew I would have to drag it out for at least three or four days.

I felt an unusual pang of guilt about it, but that was the name of the game. Poor old Tracy Summerfield. Just before 5pm, the woman rose, kissed Summerfield again on the lips and made an exit. Summerfield stood up as she walked away and smiled at her. I saw that he too was about to leave and was finishing his gin. I made ready to follow and downed the last of my beer. Summerfield put on his coat and left the pub turning right back towards his offices. The woman from reception was long gone and again I followed from a safe distance.

He walked down the dark wet streets straight past his offices and into the bright lights of Oxford Street. It was still packed with people and I picked up the pace so I wouldn't lose him. Summerfield made his way towards the Tube station. I followed him through the crowds down the escalator to the Victoria Line Northbound. *Perhaps he's going home?* It was only four stops to Finsbury Park. Travelling in the tube system was like being in a smelly sardine tin at that time of day, but Summerfield was tall enough to stand above most people. I had no problem tailing him and took the next carriage. I was able to observe him through the two panes of grimy steamed up glass that separated the carriages.

Ten minutes later he got off the Tube at Finsbury Park and made his away up the escalator, out of the station and across the busy streets towards his house. *No funny business tonight then.* The mobile phone in my pocket rang as Summerfield approached the door of his ground floor flat. My local pub was no more than a mile up the road from Summerfield's flat, albeit through a slightly rougher area. Despite the freezing temperature I had had enough claustrophobia for the day and decided to walk it rather than catch a cab or a bus. Further up in the semi darkness, there were a few prostitutes on the other side of the road. They were hanging around in the car headlights as they passed. They were dressed in miniskirts despite the weather. A group of young men drove past them in a small red car. "You're fucking rough!" one of them shouted as they drove past. "Am I?!" one of the girls retorted loudly.

I shook my head and carried on up the street. I knew I would need to find something to eat before heading to my local. Fifteen minutes later, I ordered a quarter pounder with cheese at the takeaway opposite the pub.

Love your healthy diet, buddy. There was an arctic wind howling through the dark streets. It rattled the windows and signs on the shop fronts and travelled straight through my clothes into my bones. It was a blessed relief to walk through the doors into the familiar friendly warmth of the pub. Various greetings sounded from the locals as I sat. I ordered a John Powers Irish whiskey with ice from the barman, who pushed the pale spirit over to me. It was smooth and pale. Similar to J&B scotch but with a smoky, fruity aftertaste. It was very good and was the first of many that night.

At 11o'clock the barman shouted, "Time at the bar please, time at the bar." I ordered a taxi which arrived in minutes for the short drive home. I got out, paid the driver, and made my way to the security door outside the block. I entered using my key and pushed the button for the lift. There was a slimy, sticky feeling on the button. "Fucking cunts! Fuck's sake!" I cursed loudly. The local kids had wiped snot on the button for the lift as a joke. Still cursing, I scraped my finger on the raw brickwork and made my way into the waiting lift and up to the fifth floor. The Polish house cleaner who came three times a week had been in, and the flat was clean and tidy. I washed my hands, brushed my teeth and gratefully headed for my bed.

CHAPTER THREE

- GARETH LEWER-ALLEN

I awoke to the familiar sounds of my north London flat. I was feeling a whole lot better than I had the previous day. I reached for my cigarettes and glass of water and my mind went to my client, Tracy Summerfield. The proof of her husband's affair was in my hands. I needed no more. The routine of the morning began as usual and culminated as always with the grand opening of the lounge curtains. The sight was exactly the same as the previous day. Dark, grey, wet and miserable. *Fucking hell.* I cooked breakfast before turning on my mobile phone and opening my laptop to transfer the digital images from the previous evening. I decided I would contact Tracy Summerfield a bit later before travelling to Soho Square at lunch time. From there I would observe the movements of Rodney Summerfield once again. This time I would remember my fucking gloves. I turned on the television to watch the news. At that moment, the phone rang. The number was not recognized. Turning down the volume on the television I answered,

"Hello can I help you?"

A deep voice said, "Could I speak to Mr Jason Green please?"

"Speaking…"

"Mr Green, my name is Gareth Lewer-Allen. I have been given your number by an associate of mine. I would like to see you as soon as possible on an extremely urgent matter." The voice was clearly from a man who was used to being in charge of people and things. Defined, well spoken, and devoid of bullshit. This was slightly annoying to me at that time of the morning.

"May I ask who referred you Mr Lewer-Allen?" The man on the phone gave a name of a previous client of mine. It seemed kosher.

"Well I could see you this morning, I do have some commitments from lunchtime onwards."

"Mr Green, I assure you I will make it worth your while. As I said, it's an extremely urgent matter."

Intrigued I replied, "Sure, can I have your address please?"

Gareth Lewer-Allen was abrupt and quick with his answer. "I have been given your address Mr Green, and I have a car waiting for you downstairs at this moment. You will be driven to my offices and returned immediately after we have met. I trust this is alright with you?"

"Yes, that's fine, tell your driver I will be down in five minutes." "Thank you Mr Green."

The phone hung up. *Who is this cheeky fucker and what does he want?* I dressed quickly and glanced at my watch. Ten past nine. There would be plenty of time to get to Soho Square and Summerfield if the client was as quick as he had been on the phone. I left the flat and pushed the button for the lift using my key instead of my finger this time. The waiting vehicle was none other than a chauffeur-driven Rolls Royce. A modern and very expensive rolls Royce. Dark blue in colour, it was certainly out of place in the Seven Sisters area. The standing driver was obviously expecting me.

"Good morning sir," he said, as he opened the back door nearest to the building.

He was dressed in full chauffeur regalia including the cap. I smelt the leather upholstery and noticed the wooden panelling of the interior. *Very nice indeed.* The car pulled away smoothly and almost silently. I started on the driver.

"Do you have any idea why Mr Lewer-Allen wants to see me so urgently?"

"I'm sorry sir, I have no idea," he replied.

"Well can you tell me a bit about him? Where he works, what he does, he told me very little." I was still annoyed.

Why all this cloak and dagger shit? The driver sensed this and opened up a bit.

"Mr Lewer-Allen is an investment banker in the city sir. A very wealthy man. I have no idea why he wants to see you sir, I'm just the driver."

He glanced nervously at me in the rear view mirror as he spoke. I accepted his explanation and sat back in the seat. *Probably the usual cheating wife or similar.* I defiantly lit a cigarette and enjoyed the ride. *Better be worth my fucking while.* I was not a morning person.

The car drove for forty minutes or so before reaching the bank area of London. It pulled up in front of an imposing Gothic four-storey building, where the car was met by a doorman in uniform. I was ushered through a reception hall and past a sign which read Omega European Investment Bank. We walked on until we arrived at an elevator. The place reeked of money. Marble flooring, impressive art deco style lighting. There were large portraits of stern looking men on the walls. The hushed corridors of international finance.

The lift was summoned. *No chance of any snot on those buttons.* The reception to Gareth Lewer-Allen's office was modern and completely sound-proofed. A smart looking elderly woman behind the desk gave me a curt smile and offered me a sumptuous chair. She immediately picked up the phone and informed the person behind two ornate wooden doors that I had arrived. I was shown into a huge and extremely plush office. There were massive bookshelves with finely bound leather volumes surrounding the walls. Near the window on the right stood a large antique globe. I walked across a Persian carpet and straight up to the desk.

"Jason Green," I said, offering my hand.

Gareth Lewer-Allen stood up and responded with a very firm handshake. He was visibly gauging me from the start.

"Thank you for coming on such short notice Mr Green. Please take a seat."

The man was dressed in a dark pin stripe suit, crisp white shirt, and silk tie. The driver had been right. He was obviously an extremely wealthy man. He was balding and grey, but impeccably turned out. I put his age at about 65. My slightly more casual attire of black jeans, collared shirt, dark pullover and leather jacket were a bit out of place here, but it didn't bother me. The man's cold blue eyes were piercing and I imagined they would scare most people. The frown lines on his face told me that he was a deeply worried man. We both sat down.

"What can I do for you sir?" I asked.

"Mr Green, I am not going to waste your time. I have a serious problem. My 39 year old son lives here in London. He has a small surf shop close to Liverpool Street Station. They sell adrenaline sports equipment, snow boards, surfboards, kite boards. You know the kind of thing?"

I nodded.

"Well, Mr Green, I am a businessman, and I know when a business is making money. I also know when a business is not making money."

I nodded again in understanding.

"Now, I financed my son's little enterprise three years ago. It cost me £600k at the time."

He dismissed the amount with a casual wave of his hand as if to indicate this was basically small change. He lent back in his seat as he continued. He spoke slowly and clearly as if not wanting to have to repeat himself.

"For the first year and a half, my son would approach me for money at least once every three months. Finance for stock and advertising etc. The business wasn't performing very well at all. However, it was his dream, his baby, and I was quite happy to help out every now and then."

I listened and wondered where this was going.

"Frankly I was grateful that he had decided to try to do something with his life and I thought it would do him some good. Even if the whole venture failed, he would have at least had some experience in the world of business."

I sat and nodded.

"Well Mr Green, he hasn't approached me for money in the past year and a half. He has moved into an expensive flat in Sloane Square. I don't know whether he has bought it or not. He tells me he is renting. On top of that he has bought a brand new Aston Martin. Now that is a very expensive car, Mr Green. He travels extensively all over the world. Basically, he's living the high life and I don't know how the hell he is paying for it."

"Have you asked him how he's managing all of this?" I asked, stating the obvious.

"I have, and he has told me the shop is doing very well. Quite frankly Mr Green, that is bullshit. I pass that shop twice a day and I have never seen any change in the place. It's as dead as it has always been. He hardly spends any time there at all. Make no mistake, the place is well stocked and it looks good from the outside.

He has a website and a staff of two who seem to be doing a good job looking after the place. But I have been in business for too long Mr Green, and I know there is no way that little shop is making the kind of money he is spending. Not a chance."

Intrigued, I shifted in my seat. "And you would like me to do what?" I asked.

The man sat forward and leaned on his desk. He glared at me with his cold pale blue eyes. "I want you to watch my son, Mr Green. I want you find out where he's getting all this money from."

"You're worried he might be doing something illegal." I said.

"I am," he replied. "I am a very busy man and I don't need this in my life. If my son were to get into trouble of any kind it would have far-reaching consequences for my family and my business. I'm sure you understand?"

Suddenly I had the feeling this man thought he was talking to one of his employees. One of his 'yes' men. For me, this was the wrong approach. Annoyed, I decided to play along.

"I do understand Mr Lewer-Allen but I am also a very busy man and..."

Lewer-Allen raised his hand and interrupted, "Please Mr Green, just hear me out. I understand your fees are £150 per day plus expenses. Now, I have instructed my secretary to immediately transfer £10 000 into the account of your choice if you agree. I am offering you £1000 per day to get me the answers I need. My wife is starting to ask questions. I cannot afford to have anything go wrong with my family. I need to have some peace of mind."

A few tense seconds passed. The offer was simply too good to refuse. The job would be a refreshing change from the norm and it surely wouldn't be too difficult to ascertain the source of young Lewer-Allen's wealth. I held the man's gaze without changing my expression.

Leaning forward I offered him my hand. "I'll begin immediately."

Instantly his expression lifted. It was as if a huge weight had been taken from his shoulders.

"Thank you, thank you Mr Green," he said, shaking hands with the same vigour as before. "I'm very pleased you're on this for me."

He handed me a personal calling card. The print was raised and it had an address, phone numbers and personal email. We both stood up.

"I will contact you when I have some definite information. I don't play guessing games." I warned.

"That is perfectly fine," he said. "My secretary has a file with all the information I think you'll need. She will also take your bank details. The money will be in your account by the time my driver gets you back home. It's a huge relief for me to have you working on this matter. Thank you again."

"Thank you," I replied as I turned and headed for the two heavy wooden doors. I walked out without looking back and sat down with his secretary. She handed me a sealed red file. I gave her my bank details which she jotted down efficiently. She thanked me and nothing more was said as I headed to the lift. The doors opened immediately and I entered and pushed the button for the ground floor. Alone on the way down I shook my head in disbelief. *Fucking hell, what a score.*

The chauffeur was diligently waiting for me at the back door of the Rolls Royce.

"Home, Jeeves!" I said cheerfully.

"Yes sir," was the reply. I threw my bag onto the back seat and got into the car. I opened the red file and began to read in silence as the car purred away through the traffic and the freezing grey drizzle.

CHAPTER FOUR

- RICHARD LEWER-ALLEN

I browsed through the file on the way home. It was a breakdown of his entire life and made interesting reading. Richard Lewer-Allen was 39 years old. He had had a privileged upbringing, attending expensive private schools and was at one stage, 15 years before, on the brink of becoming a professional golfer. This hadn't worked out as planned and was obviously a cause of great disappointment to his father. It seemed Richard's relationship with his parents was a bit distant. Cordial, but detached, as if father and son had a mutual dislike for each other but would endure that to keep the peace within the family. By all accounts, Richard seemed to be a very sociable person. He had a large circle of friends and seemed to enjoy the good life, with constant parties and general merry-making being the order of the day. On arrival back in Seven Sisters I decided to prepare a report for Mrs Summerfield and get it done with. It was a bit of a relief. I never really felt comfortable about needlessly extending the time frame for jobs. Especially for such an undeserving and beautiful woman. It would be a simple task. The photos would basically say it all. No doubt there would be drama, wailing and a great gnashing of teeth. There would also have to be a refund. I opened my laptop and wrote a quick summary of what had happened the previous day. I then printed the photographs and the report and put £350 cash into an envelope and called her. She answered immediately and seemed surprised at how quickly I had moved. Her voice trembled as she agreed that we would meet at 1pm that day. I logged on to my internet bank account and sure enough the £10 000 was showing in credit, just as Lewer-Allen had promised. *Fucking hell, what a day.*

I decided to travel on the Tube to Finsbury Park and on to Liverpool Street Station from there. I looked out the window and saw with relief that it had stopped raining. I grabbed my bag and jacket and headed out and down towards the station. The events of the day had lifted my spirits. Although I told myself I had never suffered from seasonal affective disorder, I doubted I would ever get used to the English winter. It seemed to drag on forever. The sun never getting very high in the sky. The hours of daylight shortened, and of course the biting cold and wind. *Fucking miserable! Still, nothing like a cool ten grand to warm things up a bit.*

The Tube journey to Finsbury Park was uneventful. I read more of the file and studied the photograph of Richard Lewer-Allen. He was a tall chap, two inches taller than myself, six foot three, wore glasses and had a liking for trendy bespoke clothes. A dedicated follower of fashion.

The rain was still holding off as I walked out of Finsbury Park station. I lit a cigarette and decided I would make the short walk to Tracy Summerfield's house. As I made my way, I noticed a group of five black youngsters walking towards me. They were dressed in tracksuits and Nike trainers. They wore corn rows in their hair and were adorned with a plethora of gold or fake gold rings, chains and necklaces. The youngsters all seemed to have a similar swagger mixed in with a fake limp. *What's the story with the fake limp? Fucking dreamers.* I prepared myself for the inevitable drama as I approached the steps to Tracy Summerfield's house. Taking a deep breath I rang the bell. She was obviously waiting and opened the door quickly.

She was well dressed as usual and her face was expectant, anxious, and beautiful all at the same time.

"Hello Mr Green, please come in, it's freezing out there."

"Please call me Jason," I said as I wiped my boots on the doormat.

"In that case, please call me Tracy," she replied in a shaky voice.

We made our way to the lounge and sat as we had done the previous day. I removed the large brown envelope with the report and the photographs and held it to one side.

"It's not good news, Tracy. I believe your husband is having an affair with the receptionist from his firm." I had decided not to delay the inevitable. I felt a pang of genuine compassion for the clearly distraught lady sat in front of me. A true lady, tall and dignified. She didn't deserve this sort of nightmare. The tissues came out as I knew they would.

"Fucking bastard," she said under her breath. I removed the photographs and handed them over to her, she took them and spent a few seconds looking at each of them, all the time barely managing to maintain her composure.

"I'm so sorry to have to tell you this. Unfortunately I have to do it quite a lot in this job. I also have this for you, it's the balance from your deposit," I said handing her the small envelope with the £350.

"Thank you Jason," she said as she took it. And thank you for doing this so quickly for me. At least I can get on with my life now."

The tears and sobbing came now. I felt an unusual urge to get up, sit next to her and give her a comforting hug, but that would be wrong. Instead I sat grim faced and waited it out. After what seemed an eternity she regained her composure and looked up at me, forcing a smile.

"I don't know what I'm going to do," she said.

"Perhaps talk to a friend? Someone you can trust?" I said.

"Yes, yes I'll do that," she said. I stood up and made ready to leave. She stood and ushered me through the hall. I opened the door and took a step outside into the bleak afternoon. As I turned around to say good bye she suddenly lunged at me and held me in a hug around my neck. She smelled good. This was unusual and certainly unprofessional, but I reciprocated and held her also for what seemed a long time. Eventually she let go, straightened herself and smiled.

"Thank you again Jason," she said.

"No problem Tracy, you look after yourself."

I turned and walked away, feeling bad for her. *Rodney Summerfield you fucking asshole.* I shook my head as I started the walk back towards Finsbury Park tube station. *Anyway, job done, another happy customer.* I smoked. The walk back to the station was uneventful as was the trip to Liverpool Street Station. I bought a newspaper from the newsagent. It was a short distance from the massive station through the chill to the business premises of Richard Lewer-Allen.

The shop was called The Boardroom. It looked professional from the outside as I walked past. It was a mixture of old and new. The building was obviously ancient but it had four large bay windows all crammed with brightly coloured surf, snow, and skate boards. There were mannequins kitted out in the latest sports gear and accessories. There was a huge black canvas sign over the top of the windows with the company logo and name. Above each window hung a separate canvas with smaller signs reading 'hardware', 'clothing', 'accessories', 'free internet'.

As I walked past I noticed there were boards and branded posters hanging from the ceiling inside. Gareth Lewer-Allen was right, the place was well stocked and for anyone keen on extreme sports, it was a good looking and inviting shop.

There was a young man behind the sales counter, he had long blonde dreadlocks and was chatting on the telephone with a bored look on his face. I continued past the shop and on for another fifty metres or so. Turning around I noticed there was a pub directly opposite the shop. It was called The Mare and Melon. It would provide a warm place from which to observe the shop. I lit another cigarette before crossing the street. I needed to smoke before going in. The smoking ban had been in effect for years. Although I despised the fact I was an addict, it was a cause of great annoyance. I made my way back towards the pub, crushed the stub out on the wet pavement with my boot, and pushed the brass handled doors open.

The place was fairly decent. It had the comforting smell of stale beer, and was reassuringly dark and full of partitioned nooks for privacy. More importantly, it was warm. I approached the bar and was greeted by a fat bald man in his late sixties. He looked like a man who enjoyed his drink - big red nose, bright rosy cheeks and a terrible comb over. I ordered a pint of Löwenbräu and made my way to one of the tables at the windows. I took a seat and a deep draw of the beer, placed my newspaper on the table and relaxed. Fifteen or twenty minutes passed. I sat, drank, and watched the shop across the road. The rain and drizzle was holding off. Hundreds of people had walked past the shop, all of them rushing, huddled into their coats, a few of them glanced inside but not one person entered.

The pub started to fill a bit. There was occasional laughter and muffled conversations. I left my bag and newspaper on the table, ordered another beer and put it with the bag. I motioned to the barman to keep an eye on my table, he nodded his understanding and I headed out for a smoke. I leant against the wall of the pub, lit up, and looked around. I figured it wasn't really the time of year for this sort of business, it would be for the snowboarding I guessed, but the majority of sales for that sort of kit would have been before Christmas. Perhaps it was the wrong location? There certainly was a lot of passing trade but no customers. I could see through the glass door that the young dreadlocked salesman was still chatting away on the phone. I guessed that Richard Lewer-Allen was probably not in the shop and decided to cross the street to check it out. I pushed the doors open and stepped on to the pale wooden floors of The Boardroom.

The young salesman dropped his head, made his excuses to whoever he was talking to on the phone and hung up.

"Good afternoon sir, can I help you?" he said with a surprised look on his face.

"Yes please," I said "I wanted to have a look at some skateboards.

My son is having a birthday in a few weeks."

"Sure thing!" he replied pleasantly. "If you would like to step this way I'll show you some cool boards."

I followed the youngster to a corner dedicated to all things skateboard. The sales banter continued, I was shown all sorts of boards, wheels, and accessories by the enthusiastic salesman. We spoke for five minutes or so. I implied that for the moment I was just pricing the equipment and asked for a list of his chosen items. The salesman cheerily agreed to this and we returned to the sales counter. As he wrote I casually asked, "so have you been busy?"

"No sir," he replied, shaking his head with feigned concern. "It's been very quiet. Right, there you go sir." he said politely, handing the paper to me.

"Thanks very much," I said, "I'll be back closer to the birthday."

We said our goodbyes and I left the shop. I turned right and walked for thirty or forty metres before crossing the street and walking back to the pub. My bag and beer were on the table where I had left them, the landlord nodded at me as I returned to my seat and sat down. I glanced at my watch, it was 3pm and the grey sky was starting to darken. I wondered if Richard Lewer-Allen would show up at work today. I took out the red file and studied the photograph of him. It was obviously taken with some friends. He looked relaxed and happy. There were a couple of good looking girls in the background, drinks on the table, probably taken in the garden of a pub in Sloane Square in the summer. Richard was wearing expensive-looking prescription sunglasses. I removed my laptop and camera, snapped a few shots of the shop across the road and set about transferring the images to the computer. As I was moving the images across I noticed that the laptop was connected to the wireless network from The Boardroom across the road. I ordered another beer, returned to my seat and watched the shop through the window as I drank.

My mind wandered. From what I could gather from the file, Richard was a socialite with a large circle of friends, mostly quite well-to-do. He enjoyed his life to the full by all accounts, with a steady stream of girlfriends. I logged onto G mail and entered the email address of Richard Lewer-Allen. Next job would be to hack the password. I tried a few combinations based on his date of birth, his company name etc. but every attempt failed. I sighed and drank deep of the Löwenbräu. The shop lights had been put on now, showing the colourful kit on display.

Still no punters and the shop assistant was grinning into the telephone again. At that moment a car pulled in and parked right outside the window from which I was looking. It was a silver coloured Aston Martin DB9. A new one. I immediately closed the computer screen and watched attentively. It was surely Richard Lewer-Allen. An extremely tall and thin man got out of the car, he was wearing jeans, an expensive looking jacket and a scarf. He glanced across at the shop front as he locked the vehicle, he looked about the right age and he was wearing spectacles. I shuffled the papers in the file and looked at the photograph. The man outside was a winter version of Richard Lewer-Allen. There was no doubt. I gave a sigh of relief as I saw Richard cross the street and make his way into the shop.

The shop assistant quickly got off the phone and rose to meet his boss, shaking hands. They smiled at each other and seemed to chat like old friends. Richard pulled up a stool and sat in front of the sales counter. He appeared to be a very relaxed and cheerful person, both him and the salesman were now laughing. A very pleasant working environment for them both. Wondering what the two were talking about, I discreetly took a photograph of the car outside the window and again of the shopfront. I made a mental note of the time, 3.30pm and getting dark fast. It was a welcome change for me to be involved in a case which actually required some mental effort. Not the usual crap. This was going to be a challenge and an interesting one at that. Plus it was paying very well indeed. I had no qualms about relieving Gareth Lewer-Allen of some of his cash. Neither did I have any qualms about extending the time frame for this job. I felt sure, with the right surveillance, in a matter of days I would have ascertained the source of Richard's wealth.

The two people in the shop across the road laughed and chatted away, not a lot of work seemed to be happening, more like old friends catching up after a long time apart. I watched and my mind wandered. *Who was Richard Lewer-Allen? What sort of life did he lead? What did his house in Sloane Square look like inside? Would it be a modern minimalist space in keeping with his very flashy car? Did he have a girlfriend at the moment? If so what did she do? Where did she work? What did Richard do on Sunday afternoons? What channels did he watch on TV? What food did he enjoy? What countries did he like to travel to and what would he do on those holidays? What are your secrets Richard?* These were all questions to which I would have to find answers. *Yes, it will be interesting.*

I took another draw of the strong beer. It was starting to taste good. An hour passed without incident. At 4pm Richard Lewer-Allen stood up, shook hands with the salesman and left his place of business.

I held the newspaper up to block my face hoping that Richard wouldn't come into the bar. It wouldn't be a train smash if he did, but it was best to stay unrecognized. I glanced around the paper to see the tall figure unlocking and entering his car. He looked like a thoroughly likeable person. He had a kind, somewhat mischievous face. The car drew admiring glances from the people on the street as it pulled out and drove away down the road. I decided to call the shop across the road. The number was in the file and was also on the canvas on the shop front. I keyed the number into my mobile phone and watched the dread locked salesman lift the receiver across the road. "Boardroom, good afternoon," he said.

I changed my voice slightly so it wouldn't be recognized,

"Oh hi, can I speak to Richard please?" I said, "I'm sorry sir you've just missed him, he's gone for the day."

"Oh right," I said, "I'm actually a friend of his, do you know where he's gone?"

"I'm sure he's gone home sir, can I take a message or perhaps you'd like to call him on his mobile?"

"No problem, I'll do that, thanks a lot, bye," I said hanging up.

I knew it would take Richard at least an hour to get back to Sloane Square through the traffic. I would beat him easily by taking the Tube. I finished my pint, stood up, grabbed my bag, nodded in thanks to the barman and made my way out of the pub and down the busy road toward Liverpool Street Station. It was just before rush hour and the huge building was beginning to fill up. Thousands of people filed in like robot moles and made their way down their respective holes. I made my way down the escalator to the Circle Line Westbound. The train took two minutes to arrive. There were no seats so I held on to the railing as the train trundled off into the dark tunnel. As usual there was not a lot of human interaction going on. Everyone was reading, sleeping, pretending to sleep, or listening to music with headphones. *What a fucking nightmare.* I hated the Tube. After what seemed an eternity the train pulled up at Sloane Square. There was a pre-recorded voice that came over the speakers in the train,

"Mind the gap," it said.

Obediently I stepped well over the gap between the train and the platform and made my way up onto the street grateful to be out of the closed claustrophobia of the Tube system. It was totally dark now and all the street and shop lights were on. I had memorized Richard's address but I needed directions to his road. I got the information from a newspaper vendor who was shivering in his scarf and beanie. It was not far and I made off, lighting a smoke. Sloane Square was a far cry from Seven Sisters. There was no litter, and the road was lined with trees on either side. There were fashionable designer shops, trendy wine bars and restaurants filled with the well-to-do. The place felt a lot less threatening than the rest of London, a lot more relaxed. The cold night air was starting to bite now. I wished I could duck into one of the pubs and have a whiskey but I needed be around when Richard Lewer-Allen got home. If indeed he was on his way home. My hands were aching now. I removed my gloves, put them on and pulled my jacket tighter around me as I walked. I arrived at Southwall Road. It was impressive. Lined with trees and four storey Georgian mansions on either side. There were service lanes on each side of the busy street to enable the wealthy residents to park their cars. I made my way up a small hill into the lane on the right. I was looking for Grimsby Mansions, which was number 48. There was a polished brass sign on the first building I passed which read 34 Southwall Road. I had picked the right side. I pressed on past the ornate wrought iron balustrades that lined the grand old buildings. There were some pretty good looking cars parked on either side of the lane. Porsche, Mercedes, BMW. Eventually I came to Grimsby Mansions on my right. It was much like the rest of the buildings on the street. I knew Richard lived on the top floor so I crossed the street to have a look up at his flat. There were a few empty parking places under the trees, I guessed one of them would be for the silver Aston Martin. I looked up at the building, every floor had lights on except the top. *Good.* He hadn't got home yet, I had beaten him. I couldn't stand around in the dark waiting for him to arrive, it would appear suspicious and I didn't want him to pull in and see me in his headlights. Just down on the main road there was a bus stop under a street light. I would not seem out of place down there and I could easily keep an eye on Grimsby Mansions. I stepped over a small railing and down some slippery grass onto the pavement of Southwall Road. There were four or five people huddled in the shelter waiting for a bus. I leant against the outside of the shelter, lit a smoke and waited. A double decker bus arrived after five minutes and the waiting people rushed to get in to the warmth. *Lucky fuckers.* I figured I would give him an hour to get back, or I would move on and call it a day. *What the hell, I had made £1000 already.*

I stood, gloved hands in my pockets, stamping my feet on the damp concrete pavement in an effort to keep moving and keep the chill out.

Fifteen minutes passed, I was beginning to think he must have gone somewhere else when I noticed headlights coming up the service lane where I had walked. The car pulled in under the tree where I had been standing. Sure enough, it was the Aston. The tall figure I had seen at Liverpool Street got out of the car, locked it and crossed the road towards Grimsby Mansions. *You really did have a very easy working day Richard, an hour or so chatting to your manager and that's it. Very nice.* I saw Richard enter the building and watched for the top floor lights to come on. A minute later they did. One by one as Richard moved around his flat. I saw a blue tinge change the light in what I imagined would be the lounge, he had just turned on a large television screen. *So, no girlfriend waiting indoors for you Richard? Single at the moment maybe?* I decided I would give it an hour. If he didn't move or no one arrived, I would call it a day. I had to keep moving or I would become an ice sculpture, so I decided to walk up and down the main road close to the traffic for a hundred metres either side of Grimsby Mansions. That way I wouldn't seem suspicious to any residents on the service lane, and I could keep an eye on the top floor flat and the car.

The traffic was constant on both sides. There were only a few pedestrians and most of them were heading to the bus stop. They were all far too cold and in a hurry to worry about me. Forty minutes passed. I thought I would take a walk up to Richard's car and have a look at it. It was parked in a dark area under a tree, I didn't want to hang around too long in case someone thought I was a thief. As I walked up the service lane I removed a pencil light torch from my bag. I made my way in the space between the parked cars and the ridge going down to the main road until I came up to the Aston. The lights were still on in the upstairs flat. I glanced around to check I was alone as I flicked the switch on the torch. I scanned the interior. There was nothing in the back seat, no papers, no personal belongings at all. I moved to the front passenger window and took a look inside. Still nothing. I took another step forward to have a quick look through the windscreen at the dash board. As I looked, I noticed what looked like a white dinner plate under the passenger seat. At that moment one of the front doors on the next door building opened and two young girls stepped out, both in excited conversation. They made off in the opposite direction giggling. This was my cue. I flicked the switch on the torch and jumped over the rail over the wet grass down to the main road and the bus shelter. There was no way I was going to take the Tube back to my area so I waited on the side of the busy road for a cab. £1000 a day plus expenses and that includes taxis. Lewer–Allen could certainly afford it. After a few minutes a black cab came along, I hailed it and gratefully jumped into the warm interior. The driver was a pleasant Rastafarian.

"Where you wanna go mate?" he said over the reggae music.

"I need to get half way between Finsbury Park and Highbury Islington station."

"No problem."

"Do you mind if I smoke in your cab?" I asked.

"No problem!" came the reply again.

There was the residual sweet smell of weed in the cab.

"I didn't think there would be." I said with a half smile and I caught his uncertain bloodshot eyes looking at me in the mirror.

As the cab made its way through the traffic and the yellow glow of the street lights I thought about the day. *Interesting. This was going to be a welcome change, something different for once, thank fuck.* I wondered about how I would tackle the next day, I needed to get into this Richard's life, into his email account, into his plans. He seemed pretty normal to me so far. A spoiled kid with a flash car and a surf shop. But there was something niggling in the back of my mind. *Why the fuck would someone keep a dinner plate under the passenger seat of an Aston Martin?* I tried to put it all out of my mind as the lyrics of a Bob Marley song came over the speakers.

"Don't worry, about a thing, coz every little thing, is gonna be alright."

After half an hour, the cab pulled in to a parking spot near my local pub. I collected a receipt from the cab driver and headed to the same take away I had visited the previous evening. *Love your diet Green. Health food all the way.* It had been like this a lot of the time since the divorce. I decided I would try to eat a bit better. Tomorrow. I devoured the takeaway and crossed the road into the pub. The evening continued till 11pm when the barman shouted his usual warning,

"Time at the bar please, time at the bar."

I made my way home in a cab as I had done the previous evening. The driver complained about black ice on the roads. He told me he had been listening to the radio and had heard the UK was expecting an arctic front to come in with gale force winds. *Sweet.*

I made my way up to my flat carefully avoiding the lift buttons. The windows in the lounge were shuddering as the wind howled outside. I quickly switched on the central heating, jumped in the shower and headed for bed. As I drifted off to sleep, my mind was rolling images of the day gone by. In my last semi dream-like thoughts I saw an image of Richard Lewer-Allen approaching me, smiling, holding a white dinner plate with a pile of cash on it. He was offering it to me. Then there was darkness.

CHAPTER FIVE

- A NERVOUS EXCHANGE

I woke to the sound of the wind roaring like a giant white ghost trying to smash into my flat. The windows were shuddering violently. The taxi driver from the previous evening had been right. There was a gale blowing outside. I went through my usual morning routine with a bit more enthusiasm than usual. The thought of the job as something new and a bit more interesting than the norm had put a spring in my step. That, and the money of course. I decided to eat breakfast at the cafe nearby instead of cooking for myself. I would plan the day from there and move straight after. I didn't even bother opening the lounge curtains. There was no point. I decided at some point during the day I would plant a tracking device in the Aston Martin. I packed one of the tiny Japanese devices with fresh batteries into my bag. I grabbed all my warmest kit, braced myself and opened the front door.

It was a white out. I had never seen so much snow in London in February. It actually was quite a pretty sight for once, but I knew this would be short lived. Soon it would all become brown, dirty, icy and slippery. I smoked as I took the lift down and made the short walk to the cafe. I had to wrap my scarf tightly and tuck it in to my jacket. There was hardly anyone on the street today. I guessed the preschool was closed for the day because of the weather. The windows of the cafe were steamed up from the inside. The place was full of the good smells of bacon, eggs and black pudding. I ordered a full English with tea. There was a local morning newspaper on my usual table. I started reading the front page as the tea was delivered. The front page carried a sad story. A young nurse had been killed by a falling shop sign just up the road at Wood Green. She had been on her way home after the night shift at a nearby hospital the previous evening. The arctic front had claimed its first victim.

I ate the hearty breakfast and started planning the day ahead. I needed to hire a car. I would follow Richard Lewer-Allen's movements today. My old Mercedes wouldn't look out of place in Sloane Square but it would be better to have a totally nondescript vehicle for the task. I called the local minicab company and ordered a cab to Wood Green. There was a branch of Budget Rent-a-car that I had used many times in the past. I would hire something small and quick for a week or so.

The cab arrived as I finished my second cup of tea. I paid the waiter, thanked him and made my way out to the car. The snow on the pavement and the road was starting to turn into a filthy brown mess.

"Wood Green please mate," I said to the driver.

He grunted in acknowledgment as he drove off down the main road looking for somewhere to turn off and make a U turn. *Miserable fucker.* It took ten minutes to get to Wood Green and to the car hire place. I paid for the cab and headed in to the shop. A bubbly blonde woman was there to greet me. She was in her late twenties and wore the company uniform well. We made small talk as she processed my rental on her computer.

Inevitably the conversation was about the British people's favorite subject: the weather. I swiped a card and after ten minutes we made our way through the back door and into the yard. I had chosen a Ford Fiesta for the job.

"Are you sure the heater's working?" I asked suspiciously as we walked towards the car.

"Yes sir, Mr Green, I'm sure it is. Any problems, call me." She handed me the keys and gave me a huge sunny smile.

"Thanks very much" I replied.

I jumped in the car and started it up. I let it idle for a minute and waited for the heater to start working properly. The car was a typical rental. Everything felt a bit loose and over used but it would do the job. The sun was just clearing the buildings as I drove out of the yard and into Wood Green. It was a pale and insignificant glow behind the clouds. The traffic was heavy in central London and I listened to the radio as I drove. It took almost an hour to get to Sloane Square and it was 10.30am by the time I turned into Southwall Road. I took the service lane on the right and was relieved to see the Aston Martin parked in the same position it had been the previous evening. A number of the cars that were parked nearby had moved, their drivers obviously off on their way to work.

I parked the small Ford four spaces back from the Aston with one car in-between us and waited. *A late start for you today Richard?* I needed access to his flat. I could place a bugging device in his living area and perhaps install some spyware on his computer at the same time. I decided to call an estate agent friend of mine. He would be able to tell me if Richard had bought his place or was renting. If he had bought the place it would certainly prove his father's suspicions that he was on to something extremely lucrative. I decided I would follow him for today and if nothing major took place I would attempt to gain access to his flat the next day.

I removed my mobile phone and called my estate agent friend. I gave him the necessary information and he told me he could easily find out from the deeds office. The information was open to the public. It was a start. I sat listening to the radio as the traffic passed endlessly on the main road. The sun desperately trying to burn through the cloak of grey clouds. The DJ was obviously trying to cheer up his listeners by playing happy tunes. La Isla Bonita by Madonna, Proud Mary by Creedence Clearwater Revival, Our House by Madness. If the people driving down the main road to my left were listening to the same station, it clearly wasn't working. They resembled a steady stream of grim faced auto zombies all staring blankly into the road ahead. *Miserable fuckers.* It occurred to me that I probably looked the same. An hour and a half passed.

A few people who lived in the same building came and went, but no Richard. A leisurely start to the day for him. I noticed there was a buzzer unit near the front door with six buttons. This would be easy to pass if I wanted to get inside. Another plus was Richard's flat was on the top floor so there would be no passing traffic if I needed to pick a lock. *Good.* I glanced at my watch. It was now 12.30pm. Suddenly the door opened and out stepped Richard Lewer-Allen. He wore black jeans, good quality leather boots, multiple layers of clothing and a brown suede jacket. He stood briefly at the door and wrapped a scarf around his neck. He then pulled out his mobile phone and started walking towards me on the opposite side of the road, obviously texting someone. He carried no luggage and seemed to be in no hurry at all. But he was on the move.

I waited till he had passed and walked at least twenty metres behind my car then got out and followed. He turned left at the main road towards the Underground station and made his way slowly up the street pausing occasionally to look into shop windows. He continued at his relaxed pace for a couple of hundred metres, then turned and went into a newsagent's. Worried that he might come out of the shop and head back to the flat, I crossed the busy street and had a look into a shop that sold Bang and Olufsen stereo equipment. A few minutes later Richard came out of the newsagents carrying a plastic bag. It looked like he had bought a loaf of bread, milk and a newspaper. I had been right. He was heading back towards his flat.

He walked quicker now, the cold was obviously getting to him. He tightened his scarf and clothing as he walked. He turned into the service lane as I crossed the road following. I got into the small Ford as he unlocked the front door of Grimsby Mansions. He had been totally oblivious to me following him. I decided to plant the GPS tracking device on the Aston now.

I took the small unit out of my bag, tore open the plastic on the pack of new batteries and inserted one of them into the device. A tiny green light showed the device was now fully charged and active. Surveillance technology had improved no end in the past ten years. The Japanese had certainly cornered the market for discreet webcams, bugging devices, and tracking units. They were expensive but small and very reliable. Once planted in the car, I could track Richard Lewer-Allen on my laptop to within a metre anywhere in the world. The magnetic unit would be good for three weeks, was totally waterproof and pretty much indestructible. It would attach well into one of the wheel arches and would send signal from then on. He would never know it was there. I just hoped he hadn't booked the car in for a service in the near future.

I sat wondering how best to install the device. I decided I would pocket the device, head back towards the entrance to the service lane, cross the road and walk to the other side of the service lane and come back towards the Ford. I would pause to admire the Aston on my way back and slip it into a wheel arch then. The car was a real beauty and I felt it wouldn't be unusual for someone to stop briefly to have a look at it. In any case there were not a lot of pedestrians on the service lane at this time of day. I made my way back down the lane, crossed the busy street and walked up the other side of Southwall Road. It was a wealthy suburb. The streets and buildings were immaculate. This was definitely a low crime area. If Richard had indeed bought the flat, the price surely would have been approaching six figures.

I crossed the road again and entered the top end of the service lane walking on the side closest to the parked cars. As I approached the Aston I grabbed the tracking device in my pocket and positioned it so the magnetic side faced up ready to go into a wheel arch. After a last brief look around and satisfied the coast was clear, I paused as if to admire the silver car. I stood in front of it then moved around to far side away from the building to my left. I lent over as if to look into the cab and with my left hand I slipped the device into the front left wheel arch. The magnet clunked loudly onto the metal. Satisfied it was secure I continued admiring the car from the side and then the back. Satisfied, I walked back to the Ford and got in. *Success.* It had gone smoothly and I hadn't aroused anyone's suspicion. *Good.*

I opened my laptop, attached my modem and connected to the internet. I opened the GPS tracking programme and within a few seconds it had found the device. The car showed clearly on the map on the screen exactly where it was parked in front of me. The signal was showing full power. The day was going well. As I sat, I logged onto G mail and attempted to crack Richard's email address once again.

I tried all sorts of combinations I thought he might have chosen as a password given what I had read in the red file. All to no avail. At 1.30pm my cellphone rang, it was my estate agent friend. He told me that Richard had indeed bought the flat a year previously. The sale had been outright with no mortgage. The price must have been enormous. My mind went back to Richard Lewer-Allen. He was certainly living the high life and his father had been right. *What was he up to?* I started to feel hunger pangs and noticed there was a deli on the other side of Southwall Road. I decided I would go across and try to eat something a little more healthy than I had eaten the previous days. There would be a view of Grimsby Mansions and the service lane from there. I put the laptop in my bag, locked the car and made my way down the service lane. I crossed the road and walked back up towards the deli. It was almost directly opposite Grimsby Mansions. The shop was warm and trendy-looking with pale pine floors and chrome fittings. There was a smell of freshly baked bread, coffee, and expensive cheeses. I approached the counter and ordered a chicken salad and a coffee. The friendly assistant offered me a seat at a table and said she would bring my order to me. As I sat I noticed I could just see the front of the Aston from behind the bus shelter I had stood at the previous evening. A good vantage point.

I opened my laptop while I waited for my order. I decided I would sit a while and try to crack Richard's email again. The window on the tracking system was still open and active, so I was in a good position for now. My order arrived as I opened the window for G mail and entered Richard's email address once again. As I ate and drank the coffee I read from the red file once again. Gareth Lewer-Allen had prepared a list of places he knew Richard had visited in the past five years. Prague, New York, Moscow, Thailand, Laos, Cape Town, Paris, Nairobi, Dar Es Salaam. The list was endless. He certainly liked to travel a lot. I started trying the various cities and countries in the password box. All of them failed.

'Password incorrect'. I wondered if there was a password search tool I could use to hack the email address. I googled it and found a few options. As I was logging into one of these hacking tools I saw the front door of Grimsby Mansions open. A tall figure locked the door behind him. Richard Lewer-Allen was carrying a black shoulder bag. He was on the move again. Hurriedly I packed the red file and the laptop in my bag, rushed to pay the assistant and made my way out of the deli and back down Southwall Road. *Was he walking or was he driving?* If he was walking, I needed to be close so I didn't lose him. There was traffic on both sides of the street. I crossed regardless putting my hand up to warn the motorists I was in a hurry and not stopping. The traffic was moving slow enough for me to cross safely and I only got one hoot from some grumpy bastard.

As I approached the service lane I saw that Richard had got into the Aston and was moving away slowly in the opposite direction to me. This was a relief. No need to hurry any more. The tracking device would enable me to follow him at my own pace and there was nowhere to hide. I jogged up the service lane, unlocked the small Ford and got in. Immediately I opened the laptop and clicked on the tracking device tab. The unit was working perfectly. As I got to the end of the service lane I noticed that the Aston was stopped at the traffic lights indicating that it was turning right up Southwall Road. I slipped in and ended up four or five cars behind it.

As the lights changed, we all moved off at a sedate pace up Southwall Road. I could see him easily and occasionally glanced at the dot on the screen of the laptop to my left to confirm this. There was no way he could speed off in central London traffic. We travelled up Southwall Road for three kilometres when Richard took a right towards Notting Hill Underground Station. Craning my neck I noticed the Aston take a left into a side road not 500m from the station. I needed to follow but a London double decker bus had come up the lane to my left and was blocking my turning. *Fuck.* A look to the screen on my left confirmed it. The blue flashing dot was moving slowly down the side road and I was stuck. The DJ on the radio was still trying to cheer up his listeners and was playing Walking on Sunshine by Katrina and the Waves. This angered me, and in my frustration I turned it off roughly.

Eventually the bus moved on and I was able to turn left. I glanced at the screen and saw that the Aston was stationary a few hundred yards ahead. I needed to pass it to see if Richard was still in the car or had moved off in the same direction on foot. He was sitting in the driver's seat talking on his mobile phone as I passed him. 40 metres ahead, on the opposite side of the road, was a free parking. I took it, stopped the motor and immediately adjusted the rear view mirror to see what he was doing. He was still on the phone. Feeling pleased about the tracking device and my success at following him, I sat back and watched. After two minutes he finished his conversation, got out of the car with his bag, and started walking up the pavement towards the main road from where we had come. *Time to move.*

I closed the laptop, bagged it quickly, got out, locked up and followed on the opposite side of the road. He was walking with a sense of purpose now. A lot faster than he had been earlier in the day. At the main road, he took a left and carried on up towards Notting Hill station. Fifty metres before the station he turned left into what looked like a shop but turned out to be a restaurant wine bar called Da Vinci's. I imagined he was probably off to meet some friends for lunch.

I gave him time to settle into his environment before I made my entrance. Notting Hill was bustling as usual. There were even tourists braving the weather. They stuck out a mile with their curious excited faces. I took a deep breath and pushed the doors open into the wine bar. The doors needed some oil and squeaked as they opened.

The warm air smelled of good food. It was Italian themed with chequered table cloths and there was acoustic guitar music playing through hidden speakers. There were murals of Leonardo's paintings on the walls. I made a beeline for the bar. A plump Australian girl smiled from behind the counter and asked me what I would have. I ordered a Löwenbräu. I took a seat by the bar and looked around the establishment. Richard was sitting ten metres from me on my right at a table near the window. He was alone and was on his cell phone again. His face looked strained, he appeared stressed, nervous. The bag he had been carrying was at his feet. His right leg was vibrating and the fingers on his left hand were drumming on the table top. A waitress approached him with what looked like a scotch and ice. He looked up briefly at her and smiled as she put the drink on the table. Seeing he was busy she motioned that she would come back later and left him to his conversation. This was not the Richard I had seen the previous day, relaxed, cheerful, and going about his leisurely business with a smile. *Girlfriend trouble perhaps?*

After he had finished his conversation he pocketed his phone, crossed his left leg over the right, stretched his arms and looked around. I quickly looked at the bar. When I felt his eyes were no longer in my direction I turned to watch him again. He had made an effort to relax but was still stressing about something. The right leg was still vibrating and he was attacking the scotch with a vengeance. In what must have been two minutes, he had finished his drink. He turned and motioned with the empty glass towards the bar that he was ready for another. Presently the new drink arrived and I sat and watched again. In the bush war I had been trained to spot certain characteristics of people who are acting suspiciously, nervously, or erratically. He was definitely uncomfortable. The vibrating leg had stopped but the drumming of his fingers continued and he was glancing out of the large window onto the street expectantly. If it was going to be a lunch with friends it would be an uncomfortable one for sure.

I drank deep of the Löwenbräu savouring the cold bitterness in my throat. I was relaxed and enjoying myself today. For some reason this particular job had fired up my enthusiasm again. *Probably the ten grand.* I opened my bag, removed a writing pad and started making some simple notes.

Time, location, behaviour etc. Then Richard received another call on his cell phone. This time he glanced out the window to the left and right as he spoke and I could just hear him saying,

"Ok, ok, bye."

He hung up, took a deep draw of his whiskey and looked towards the door. I carried on with my notes, feeling his eyes, sensing his apprehension. After a few seconds I heard the doors squeak behind me. Two tall dark haired men had passed behind me and were making their way towards Richard's table. Out of the corner of my eye I saw Richard stand up and shake their hands while offering them a seat. The three men sat down now. I turned slightly to my right, doodling on the pad all the while and had a look. The two men who had come to meet him were of Asian origin. They both wore black leather jackets, had fairly long, but well-cut, jet black hair which appeared to be full of wet look gel. Both the men were chewing gum vigorously. Their eyes were wide and were darting around the room. They too were extremely nervous. *Something is going down here for sure,* I thought, *this is no social occasion.* I had to be careful not to catch one of their looks, but I was good at that. I had had ten years of marriage.

The waitress made her way to the table to offer drinks. The Indian man closest to me raised his hand as if to refuse for both of them. He seemed to be the one in charge. Richard too declined another drink. It was then I noticed the other Asian man hand a shoulder bag to his boss. It was identical to Richard's bag. The man closest to me nodded at his sidekick who then stood up and made his way behind me towards the door. I heard it squeak as he left and felt a brief rush of freezing air on my back. Now there were two. Quickly I removed my cellphone, turned it off, and pretended to make a call. I held the phone in my right hand and turned slightly towards them, making animated conversation with no one. Both of the bags were now on the floor and within seconds I saw the switch take place. The Asian man pushed his bag towards Richard using his right foot under the table, and at exactly the same time Richard did the same. If I had been much closer I might have missed it because the chequered table cloth hung quite low around the table and would have obscured my vision. I was lucky. Within a minute, both men stood up and shook hands. The Asian man quickly grabbed the bag, slung it around his shoulder and left the premises. Richard was seated again. He appeared to be deep in thought for a minute before picking up the switched bag, standing up and approaching the bar. I could not see him as there was a fake marble pillar between us, but I did see a large thin hand handing a £20 note to the waitress behind the bar.

She looked at the note with wide smiling eyes then looked up at Richard, obviously thanking him for the large tip. I saw the long bony forefinger of Richard's right hand tap the watch on his left wrist. He was making his excuses and was planning to leave, I was certain of this. He then walked directly behind me and out of the squeaking doors onto the busy street. I felt the hairs stand up on the back of my neck. The two men had been decidedly sleazy-looking characters. *What are you up to Richie boy?* I thought as I killed the last of the beer. I had to make a quick decision. Was I to follow him or was I to track him on the laptop. I chose to sit a while and take in what I had just seen. I would open the computer and pretend to do some work and see where he was going using the tracking program. The smiley Australian girl came up to me.

"Would you like another one sir?"

"Yes thanks, I'll have another." I replied. The beer arrived as I opened the laptop. There was no one behind me so I watched the flashing blue light on the map. It was still in exactly the same place it had been when we parked. *What was it that just happened here?* I thought, as I sipped my drink. *Drugs? Diamonds? Gold? Cash? Guns?* The bags had appeared to both have been fairly heavy and full. Gareth Lewer-Allen was right. His son was indeed up to something. Something very likely illegal and possibly dangerous. I savoured the moment. *Why couldn't all my jobs be like this one?* All thoughts of cheating husbands and insurance scams were gone from my mind now. I was totally engrossed in this new job and I was enjoying every minute of it. After three or four minutes the flashing blue light on the screen of the laptop started moving back up the side road we had both driven down. He had done a U turn. At the crossroads he turned right, tracing the route we had both taken earlier. It looked like he was on his way home. Fifteen minutes later Richard pulled into his usual parking spot outside Grimsby Mansions. Still watching the screen I nodded as I realised that he probably could do with a lie down after that tense little meeting. Now I had to decide what to do with the rest of the day. I finished my drink, packed my computer, paid and left the wine bar.

Having been so engrossed in thought and watching the tracking programme, I hadn't noticed the weather had changed. The snow that had fallen had turned into brown slush, and there was a light steady rain falling. As I walked, I tried to remember the last time I had seen sunshine. It had been so long now I had forgotten. Finally I made it to the rental car and gratefully threw my bag inside. My hands were aching with cold so the first job was to fire up the heater and then check the tracking program to see if Richard had moved.

His car was still parked outside his flat. *Good.* My plan was to go back there to sit and watch. I did a quick U turn and made my way back the way I had come. The traffic had become heavier since I had arrived, and being deep in thought I had forgotten to switch on the radio. The little Ford was now five cars behind the traffic lights that turned left into Southwall Road. Idly, I watched a group of people that had just made the pedestrian crossing and were walking on the pavement towards me on the left. All were huddled into warm coats and walking swiftly except for one.

He looked about 30 years old. He wore a loose fitting army surplus jacket that was far too big for him, and dirty, faded jeans. He had long blonde straggly hair and an untidy beard. More importantly he seemed to be looking straight at me, as if he had singled me out from the hundreds of motorists in the immediate vicinity. I glanced away for a second, but then looked back. There was no doubting it. His eyes were wide with intent and seemed to be locked into mine like a laser beam. He was now ten metres away and started walking faster than the rest of the group. I quickly glanced into my rear view mirror to see if there was something behind me which might have alarmed or incensed him. There was nothing except a queue of nondescript cars like mine. Now he was five metres away, and starting to run. I could see his bright blue bloodshot eyes staring madly into mine.

This bloke is a fucking psycho. He started reaching into his inner jacket pocket to get something. My mind immediately went back to my army training, thinking he might be reaching for a weapon. Time seemed to slow down, every second felt like an hour as my body tensed up and my fists clenched around the steering wheel. It was a case of fight or flight, which for me had always ended in fight. I had to sit and watch him, there was not a lot else I could do. In the last two seconds of his berserk approach, I noticed that it wasn't a weapon he had pulled from the jacket but a small green book. A metre away from my car he lunged forward and dived onto my bonnet. I heard the brass buttons of his jacket squeak on the paintwork as his dirty left hand slammed the book to the windscreen, inches from my face. For a split second, I looked at the book. The front had a gilt cross and clearly beneath that were the words Holy Bible. My body was like a coiled spring now, and a red mist of rage clouded my vision. My teeth clenched as I glanced at him once more. I saw his right hand come to his mouth. He sucked on a rancid stained forefinger briefly, removed it, and made the sign of the cross on the centre of the windscreen, the saliva leaving its mark. All the while, his terrified, insane eyes, never blinking or leaving mine. That was it. Within half a second I had ripped the seatbelt from around me.

I threw open the door, and as I stood, I slammed my open right hand onto the frosty top of the Ford. It landed with a thunderous metallic bang which obviously scared him. He jumped back off the bonnet and onto the pavement.

"What the fuck do you think you're doing, you fucking freak?"

I snarled at him viciously. The spectacle had obviously scared the people around us and they stared wide-eyed at us both. Some rushed past trying to keep as far away as they could. Others turned around and walked swiftly in the other direction.

"Get the fuck out of here!" I shouted as he scrambled away.

The light had gone green now and I was still standing, watching him retreat. Some cars behind me whose drivers hadn't seen the incident started hooting impatiently.

"Fuck off!" I shouted at them as well, and got back into the car.

Without putting on the seat belt, I sped off round the bend and into Southwall Road. *Why me?* I thought. *What the fuck was all that about?* I reached for my cigarettes and lit one as I drove. The nicotine had a calming effect. I realised that I might have over-reacted. London is full of disturbed people and I just happened to be on the receiving end of one today. I hadn't seen the red mist of rage for years now. I had seen it many, many times during the war in Africa and acted on it. I shook my head as I drew on the cigarette. *Jason Green, you have to learn to control yourself, your anger problem will only get you into trouble.*

As I made my way down Southwall Road I reflected that with so many millions of people living in London in such close quarters it only made sense that a certain percentage would be a bit loopy. The old rats in the cage experiment. *Fuck, how true.* I arrived fifteen minutes later and pulled into the service lane outside Grimsby Mansions. The Aston Martin was still parked in its usual place. The afternoon was getting darker by the minute now and all seemed quiet on the lane. I switched on the radio and relaxed. My mind went through the earlier events at the wine bar in Notting Hill. I was almost glad I didn't try to take a photograph. The two men who had come to meet Richard were extremely skittish and jumpy. I knew that Richard hadn't noticed me in the small crowd that was there, so that was a good thing. I had to sit it out for now and do my job. If he moved I would follow and watch.

A full hour passed by, I relaxed and surfed the web a bit. I was trying to find a hacking tool to get into Richard's email account. There were loads available but most were just amateur sites for kids. I persevered with the tools and the email address and came up with nothing. My phone vibrated in my pocket, it was a text message. It turned out to be from Tracy Summerfield.

"Hello Jason, this is Tracy Summerfield, I just wanted to thank you again for helping me out so quickly and efficiently, and also for being so kind and understanding, it meant a lot to me, so thank you!"

This was interesting. Interesting and unusual to hear from a client once the job was done. I typed in a reply to her.

"Hi Tracy, only doing my job, and sorry it wasn't better news. Look after yourself."

My mind went back to her sitting on her couch in tears. For the first time in my career, I had felt genuine compassion for a client. Her feeble sobs, her surprising use of contemporary swear words, and her embrace as I left her flat. I was suddenly jerked from my sentimental daydream by the sight of Richard Lewer-Allen leaving the front door of his building. My body tensed up as I realised he might walk in my direction, but I was instantly relieved to see him head once again for the silver Aston. Decision time was now. *Should I follow him or should I wait and track him?* I decided on the latter. As usual he made his way up the service lane in the opposite direction. I flicked the tracking program window up on the screen and watched. Briefly to my left I saw the sleek car pass me on Southwall Road. He then took a left and headed back toward Sloane

Street station. *Right Richard, let's see what your next move is then.* The streets were getting dark now. The lights in the shops on Southwall Road and some in Grimsby Mansions were being turned on. I glanced up at Richard's flat. There were no lights and no bluish tinge of a television to suggest anyone was there. *This might be an opportunity to get inside the flat. Wait and see where he goes.*

I glanced at the computer screen. Richard was steadily making his way towards Liverpool Street. If he was going to his shop, it would give me a plenty of time to get into his flat and have a look around. I glanced at my watch, I figured if that was where he was going he would arrive in five or ten minutes. I would wait and see. I lit a cigarette and waited hopefully as the radio played some dreadful 80s tune - I won't let the sun go down on me, by Nik Kershaw. I shook my head in disgust.

CHAPTER SIX

- HOME INVASION

As expected, the screen showed Richard had parked right outside his shop near Liverpool Street Station. I had at least an hour to get into his flat and have a look around. I quickly planned how I would do it. I turned my phone off, packed my computer, locked the car and made my way to the front door. I always felt a bit jumpy entering a house on a job. This wasn't helped by the strange events of the afternoon. There were five flats in the building, one to each floor. I decided to start with flat number three. I pressed the button on the intercom and waited for an answer. Fifteen seconds passed. Nothing. I then pressed the button for flat number two. Result. The voice was of an elderly lady on the other side.

"Hello?"

"Oh hello, I'm so sorry to bother you, I'm afraid I've been locked out, would you mind buzzing me in?"

There was no reply, only the clatter of the receiver being hung up in frustration and a loud buzzing sound as the door was opened. I was in.

The interior was as grand as the exterior. Fully carpeted with a wide staircase. The old wooden bannister was chunky and shiny, and there was a large chandelier in the centre of the ceiling. I had to be quick, I didn't need a nosy neighbour to see me. Thankfully, the stairs were also fully carpeted and I darted silently upwards. I was already fishing in my bag for my lock picking set as I reached the top floor and the door for flat number five. I would have to be careful. It wouldn't be unusual for an address like this to have an alarm system installed. Panting slightly from the run up, I went down on one knee, opened the green canvas lock picking set and went to work.

It was a standard Yale lock setup from the early eighties, probably installed when the grand old house was converted into flats. I suspected that Richard wouldn't have bothered to lock both the door and the latch so I concentrated on the brass latch. After two minutes with some fine tools, I heard the hammers in the lock click. I took a deep breath and tried it. Success. The door opened silently and slowly. I packed away my tools, stood up and peered inside, looking for an alarm or motion detector. There was nothing. The stairway behind me was silent. The coast was clear.

I walked into the flat closing the door behind me. It was huge compared to my small place.

There was a hallway leading to various rooms, all with the doors open. It had pale wooden flooring and, as I had suspected, a minimalist theme to the decor. The first room on my right was the kitchen. In keeping with the area there was an Aga cooker, a Smeg fridge, and a hanging metal central unit for utensils positioned over a central granite work surface. There was a pile of pizza boxes and takeaway cartons near the sink. Moving back into the hall, I got a bit of a shock when I saw a dark silent figure standing in front of me. It turned out to be my own reflection in a large mirror. Quietly cursing, I moved on.

Next was a dining room that was furnished with a black table and chairs for eight people. It looked like it hadn't been used in a while. I touched the back of one chair, my finger came back with dust on it. Blowing it off, I moved on. The next room was the lounge. It was huge with high ceilings and decorated in an oriental theme. There were large, low throw sofas and beanbags surrounding an equally low and very ornate antique table. All this on a Persian carpet. To the right of the room was a huge flat screen television. I had been right about the bluish light I had seen from the street. On the centre of the table was an oriental box in dark wood. I leant over to open it. Inside were several packets of rizlas, tobacco scraps, and a bag of weed. *You're a smoker then Richard.* I needed to find a computer so I moved back to the hallway, looking for the main bedroom.

I found it in the door to my immediate right. It was a stark, almost bare room, again with wooden floors. There was a king size Swedish bed with an unmade dark grey duvet to the centre and two bedside units to either side. Directly below the window, facing Southwall Road was what I had come for. The desk was untidy and covered with papers. Richard had left his computer on and as I sat down I noticed the screen saver. There were action pictures of bikini clad women riding surfboards. The pictures changed every ten seconds. I glanced around at the papers that were strewn about the desk. I didn't want to disturb anything. They were a mixture of invoices for the shop, utility bills, parking fines, and scraps. There was also a landline telephone. Nothing of great interest to me. I opened my bag and removed my laptop to see what was going on with the Aston. Placing it on the bed behind me I saw that it was still parked at Liverpool Street outside the shop. *Good. I had some time.*

I wanted to have a look at his private emails so I moved the mouse to clear the screen saver. Instantly the surfing pics disappeared and the icons of the desktop showed. I clicked on Gmail but much to my disappointment the programme was password protected. I was faced with the same problem I had been having since I started. Next, I decided to have a look at his internet history.

There were literally thousands of sites visited. I pulled the cursor slowly down through them, looking for anything that cropped up frequently. There was a well-known porn site and various social networking sites. Then I noticed a few extreme sports equipment manufacturing outfits cropping up here and there. One was called Lenny's Surf Works. I noticed the domain name showed the company to be in South Africa. This one cropped up quite a few times. Various airlines and travel agents were present. Nothing seemed to be of massive importance. I glanced at my laptop to check on the position of the Aston. To my alarm, the flashing blue light was on the move already and was travelling back in my direction. *Shit.* He was more than likely on his way home. I knew I had about forty minutes to finish up and get out, so I decided to quickly have a look at his internet bookmarks.

I opened the browser and quickly grabbed my digital voice recorder from my bag. As I scrolled down through the sites I read the names out loud into the hand held recorder. There was no time for browsing them. I would do that later on my own time. BBC News, South African Airways, Lenny's Surf Works, Tropic-air, live currency converter, British Airways - the list went on and on. There were at least fifty of them and it took a full minute to record them all. I turned the recorder off, threw it in my bag and made a quick check of the desk to see if everything was as I had found it. It all looked fine. I closed the windows I had opened on Richard's machine and checked the screen of my laptop again. The Aston was making steady progress through central London, still in my direction. There was no need to panic but I realised that I had less than half an hour to finish up and get out. Bagging my laptop, I decided to have a quick look around the bedroom and the rest of the flat. I made a beeline for the set of cupboards to the back of the room. As I opened them, the first thing I saw was a huge amount of clothing and shoes. Richard was indeed a dedicated follower of fashion. The next thing I saw was a strong box. It was a medium-sized office safe with an electronic access system. I crouched down to have a look at it. There was no way I could ever crack such an item. The bag I had seen Richard carrying and exchanging earlier was lying to the left of it on the floor. It killed me that the answers to all of Gareth Lewer-Allen's questions were now probably less than ten inches from my face. I opened the bag to find it empty. Whatever it had been that he was moving had been removed. I carefully closed the cupboards, made a quick check that everything in the room was as I had found it and moved on.

The rest of the flat was just spare bedrooms, bathrooms, showers and toilets. Nothing grabbed my attention. Now acutely aware that the Aston was fast approaching, I walked back to the lounge windows. I quickly looked out onto the service lane below. It was all quiet.

I knew I still had time but I didn't want to run into any of the other tenants either. It was time to go. I crossed the room and entered the hall. As I opened the front door, I stopped to listen for any activity on the floors below. There was no sound. I made my move and descended the stairs at speed. With relief I reached the ground floor and the front door of Grimsby Mansions. One more obstacle and I would be out. I took a deep breath, casually opened the door and waked out onto the street. I gasped as the freezing air rushed into my lungs. It was like suddenly sucking on a mouthful of extra strong mints. The temperature outside had dropped drastically. My periphery vision told me that no cars had arrived in the service lane since I had looked out from the window. This was all good. Although I hadn't found anything of earth shattering importance, it had been a successful foray into Richard's home. There was no doubt he was doing very well for himself. His father most certainly had been right.

The day was darkening rapidly and I was feeling famished. I decided to cross Southwall Road and grab some food at the cafe I had been to earlier. I had been living on a diet of junk for the past few days and I was feeling it. I hunched into my jacket in an effort to fight the chill and took the short walk across the street to the shop. The lights were on and luckily my old table was free. I sat, opened my laptop, and looked at the menu. Presently a waitress arrived. I ordered a fillet steak with blue cheese sauce and a side salad. To drink, I ordered a large fresh orange. As I had expected, the flashing blue light on the laptop's tracking page showed the Aston was still heading in my direction. Probably five or ten minutes away. Richard was heading home after an interesting day at the office. I spent the next ten minutes idly flicking between the tracking page and the internet on the laptop. I was still toying with the idea of using a password cracking program to hack Richard's email address. Eventually I decided that they were mostly a waste of time and I would have to persist with good old fashioned guesswork.

The steak arrived at the same time as the Aston. It came as ordered. Rare and cooked to perfection. As I ate, I saw the front lights as the car parked in the usual place on the service lane across the busy road. I counted down a minute in my mind and right on cue, the lights on the fifth floor were turned on. I felt a light sweat and a wave of nausea come over me. I was feeling decidedly unhealthy. Physical exercise was something I couldn't live without. It had been that way since my school days back in

Africa. I kept a membership at the local gym and visited at least three times a week. I needed to get my head straightened out and try and make some sense of what I had seen that day. An hour in the gym would take care of that. I felt more relaxed and my thoughts had more clarity after a good workout. I decided to drive straight there after the meal.

The waitress walked up to me to ask how the steak was.

"Very good, excellent, thanks very much," I said as I finished it.

I ordered a mineral water along with the bill and she made her way back to her station to prepare it. I opened the Gmail window on the laptop. Richard's address was still in the address box and the scolding red words 'password incorrect' were also there. Idly I started guessing passwords once again: snowboard - incorrect, skateboard - incorrect, Grimsby incorrect, astonmartin - incorrect, dinnerplate - incorrect. The waitress arrived with the bill. I thanked her as she put it on the table and she left. I continued with the passwords. All my guesses were incorrect. Having had enough of this, I picked up the bill for the food. It was £14. I opened my wallet, took out a £20 note and put it on the plate. My mind was swimming with the events of the day. I stared out at the lights of the fifth floor flat across the road. I snapped out of my daydream and prepared to leave. I put my scarf around my neck and reached over to close my laptop. The same red words 'password incorrect' were staring me in the face, taunting me. As I was closing the screen of the laptop my mind flicked back to Richard's bedroom. His computer. His screen saver. Surfboard. I had to give it a go. Slowly and with one hand only I typed in the letters and clicked on the log in button. Instantly the screen changed in front of my eyes. The background was suddenly replaced and the words 'Welcome Richard' appeared to the left of the screen. I was in. I had hacked it. *Yes!* I clenched my right fist in victory.

I realised that there was a chance that Richard might be accessing his email from the fifth floor across the road at exactly the same time as me. With a feeling of smug triumph I quickly logged out and closed the laptop. I bagged it, stood up, put my jacket on and left the restaurant. *Surfboard, why hadn't I thought of that before?* I had a spring in my step now. The job was moving along, keeping me interested, and paying very well. I couldn't complain. It was now totally dark outside and the yellow glow of the street lights gave an illusion of warmth. The frigid air stung my face with a slap. The traffic was thick as I drove back towards Seven Sisters but this didn't worry me. The radio played away and I tapped my fingers to the tunes for a good forty minutes until I reached Haringey and the car park for the gym. I made my way inside, put my bag into my locker and changed into some gym clothes. The place was empty save for maybe seven or eight people. I guessed the weather had broken their spirits and they had succumbed to their warm lounges. A lot of the punters at the gym treated the place like a social venue. I had never subscribed to this and preferred to get in, hit it hard for an hour and get out. I kept an mp3 player in my locker.

I put the earphones in and chose some music as I walked towards the weights circuit. The hard rock sounds of Motorhead blasted into my brain as I attacked the circuit. After one and a half albums I was done and headed for the shower. I had sweated out all the junk food and booze of the past few days and I was feeling good and tired. The steaming hot water blasted my face and shoulders. I stood, motionless, facing up into the water for a good two minutes. After washing vigorously I rinsed off and headed for my locker where I kept a change of clothes. Quickly I dried myself off and got dressed. I bagged my used clothes and headed out to the car park. I felt like a new man. My muscles were warm and my brain was crystal clear and focused. Ten minutes later, I arrived at the entrance to my building. I unlocked the heavy front door and headed to the lift using my keys to press the buttons. My flat was looking spick and span. The Polish cleaning lady had been in again. I spent the evening in deep thought. My mind going through the events of the day. There was no doubt the exchange of bags that Richard had made with the Asian men in Notting Hill was important. They had all been extremely nervous and tense at the time. I was certain that what had transpired was illegal, although I had no idea what it was. I knew part of the answer lay in the safe in Richard's cupboard. It was frustrating but compelling at the same time. The case had fired my enthusiasm. Renewed my interest. The list of insurance fraud cases in my inbox would certainly be put off until I had cracked this one. I felt drained and exhausted and decided to sleep. As I lay down I turned on the television in my bedroom in an effort to take my mind off the events of the day. That was hopeless and I ended up blindly staring at the screen as my mind raced. I was now totally absorbed in the case of Richard Lewer-Allen. There was nothing that was going to stop me from cracking this one. I decided I would track Richard's car in the morning and once I saw he was on the move I would take a look at his email. They would surely shed some light on his dubious activities. *But were they dubious? Were they illegal? It could be anything. It might be totally innocent, it could be he was dealing in rare stamps.* I put a sleep-timer on the television as I felt myself drifting off. In my last dream-like random thoughts before sleep, I saw the same image I had seen the previous night - Richard Lewer-Allen was walking towards me in a dark hallway. In his hands, he carried a white dinner plate. On the plate was a pile of money and on his face was a warm smile. He offered it to me and I accepted it. Then there was darkness.

CHAPTER SEVEN

- AN UNEXPECTED JOURNEY

I awoke to the usual sound of children screaming on the street below. Obviously the shocking weather of the previous day had calmed and the kids were able to go to school. The noise didn't bother me as much as usual. I reached for my glass of water and took a long drink from it. As I lay back and stretched, I could feel the effects of the previous evening's workout. A slight stiffness in my muscles told me it had been a good one and I decided that I would wait a while before succumbing to my first cigarette. My brain was still clear and I felt rejuvenated. I got up and took a hot shower. I opened my laptop, and as it booted up, I turned the television on and flicked to Sky News. Immediately, a cheery Irish girl was presenting the weather report. It was total doom and gloom as usual. Rain, rain and more rain topped with a maximum of three degrees Celsius and a minimum of minus six. Warnings of ice on the roads and no change in forecast for the next few days. *How super.* I made some coffee and headed to the curtains for the habitual grand opening. There were no surprises. I sipped the coffee as I stared out at the dark shiny greyness in front of me. That morning at least, I wasn't treating it with my usual abject hatred and disgust. I opened the window a section, lit a cigarette, and stood feeling the frigid air rushing in to the warmth of the central heating behind me. Even the annoying music of the news channel that hadn't been changed in ages wasn't bothering me. With the computer booted up I walked back to my desk to start work. First I opened the tracking programme. It took a few seconds to start up and revealed what I was expecting. Richard was still holed up at home on Southwall Road and the Aston was parked outside as usual. I was sorely tempted to log into his email account, but had to force myself not to. It was too much of a risk. There might be some conflict of interest that would make itself obvious if he was logged in at the same time. I had no idea what kind of computer knowledge Richard had. It wasn't worth the risk. I would wait until I knew he was out before logging in. It was frustrating, especially knowing the relaxed and casual way Richard went about his average day. I glanced at my watch, it was 8.30am. I decided I would take a walk down to the newsagent and buy a paper. It would kill some time and give me some fresh air, plus the rain was holding off for now. I put on my jacket and scarf and headed downstairs.

The walk to the newsagent's and back only took 15 minutes. As I walked into the flat, I saw to my surprise that the Aston was on the move. I made another cup of coffee and sat watching the flashing blue dot move slowly across London as I read my paper. Richard was heading north. He certainly wasn't going to the shop. Eventually the car stopped moving at what I knew was a large shopping mall five miles north of his flat. It was time to have a look at his email account. I opened Gmail, entered his address and password and I was in. I still had a feeling of smug accomplishment from the hacking job the previous evening. As I sipped my coffee, I opened the most recent email. It was from a woman by the name of Angelique. The email address was web-based so I had no way of telling where she was from, but I could clearly see that she struggled with typing in English.

"Dear Richard, I was so happy to know that you will once again be coming here. I have been thinking about you and your busy life in London and wondering what is it you have been doing. Life here is good as always but sometimes a little boring? I hope I write correct English! I do look forward to meeting you again soon, Angelique x."

It didn't read like a love letter to me, but Richard had clearly cultivated some mild interest from her. The next email was from a supplier of skiing equipment. It was a reminder to settle an outstanding account of £16000. I imagined that it would have been part of his Christmas stock.

It wasn't what I was looking for, so I carried on down to the next email. It was from Facebook. A friend had tagged Richard in a photograph. I made a mental note to attempt to hack into that site later on to see if I could find anything there. The email below was obviously from a friend of his.

"Looking forward to seeing you mate, drinks at The Bell Saturday night it is then!" it read.

The next email really did get my attention. It was from a company called Premier Travel based in Sloane Square. Immediately I put the mug of coffee down on the table, sat up straight and slowly read through it.

"Dear Mr Lewer-Allen. As requested herewith your itinerary and e-tickets for your trip. Please be sure to print this page out and take it with you to the airport. Please note, check in time is latest two hours before your flights, barring the transfer from Stone Town to Dar Es Salaam which will be one hour before departure.

British Airways, London Heathrow to OR Tambo International, Johannesburg, Friday 15th February, 10pm departure, arrive OR Tambo International, Johannesburg, Saturday 16th February, 9.40am.

South African Airways, Johannesburg to Cape Town International, Saturday 16th February, 10.45am departure, arrive Cape Town International 12.45pm.

South African Airways, Cape Town to Zanzibar, Monday 18th February, depart 7.30am, arrive Stone Town International, Zanzibar, 1.30pm.

Tropic-air, Stone Town International Zanzibar to Dar Es Salaam International, Tanzania, Monday 25th February, depart 4.30pm, arrive Dar Es Salaam International, 4.50pm.

British Airways, Dar Es Salaam International to London Heathrow, Monday 25th February. Depart 9pm, arrive London Heathrow, Tuesday 26th February 6am.

We would like to thank you for booking through Premier Travel and wish you a pleasant trip.

Jackie Strong

Booking Agent

I glanced at my watch. The date was Friday 15th February. Richard was going on holiday again, and he was leaving that very night. *Lucky for some.* Cape Town, Zanzibar. I had never been to either place, even having lived in Africa all those years ago. I would have to inform Gareth Lewer-Allen of his son's holiday plans. At least I would have ten days or so to sniff around Richard's private life while he was away. Maybe do a more thorough search of his flat and see if I could find anything else of interest. The time was 9.20am. Gareth Lewer-Allen would be at his offices by now. It was as good a time as any to give him an update. I decided that I would tell him that I suspected that he had been right all along. That Richard was indeed involved in some lucrative and possibly shady activity apart from the surf shop, but that I would need more time to find out exactly what. It was completely true after all.

I had nothing to hide and it would extend the time frame for the job nicely. I might be able to stretch it to three weeks, and at £1000 per day, that would be very sweet indeed. I opened my bag and found the personal calling card of Gareth Lewer-Allen. I quickly ran through what I was going to say and dialled. The phone rang three times and was picked up.

"Lewer-Allen," the deep voice said.

"Mr Lewer-Allen, this is Jason Green."

"Good morning Mr Green, I was wondering when I would hear from you. Do you have any information on my son yet?" True to form, all pleasantries were abandoned and he had cut straight to the chase.

"I have. Firstly, the flat your son is living in was bought outright. He is not renting. And I'm sure you're aware of property prices in that area."

He paused, "I knew it, I knew it! I knew he was up to something. What is he doing Mr Green? How the hell is he getting all this money?"

He sounded irritated and desperate.

"I'm afraid it's too early to say," I said slowly. "I did witness something irregular yesterday, an exchange of sorts. And with some very unsavoury characters. I don't want you to panic though. It could be anything and it might well be totally innocent. I am going to need some more time to find out exactly what he's doing."

"If my son is doing something illegal, Mr Green, my standing in the world of investment banking would be ruined, a lifetime's work would be lost."

"Another thing Mr Lewer-Allen," I interrupted. "Your son is booked on a flight to Cape Town, South Africa tonight. From there, he flies to Zanzibar, Tanzania on Monday and only returns to London on the 26th of February. I will use the time he is away to do some more research into his private affairs and his circle of friends. I hope to have something concrete for you before he gets back."

There was a long pause.

"No," came his reply, "no, I would prefer if you were to follow him on this trip. Watch him like a hawk, and report to me whenever necessary."

I was instantly taken aback, this was totally unexpected.

"You want me to follow Richard to Cape Town and then on to Tanzania?" I said, incredulous. There was another pause.

"Yes Mr Green, I would like you to do exactly that. You have no idea of the pressure I am under. This uncertainty of what Richard is doing is affecting my personal life and could quite possibly affect my business in a very negative way. I would like you to follow him please Mr Green."

Once again, I realised I was dealing with a desperately worried man.

"If you are in need of some more money, let me know and I will arrange it immediately."

My mind was spinning.

"No, there's no need for that," I paused in thought.

"Very well," I said. "I will follow him to Cape Town and I will see what I can find out for you."

"Thank you, Mr Green, thank you. I'll leave it to you and you will call me when you have something yes?" he said.

"Yes, I'll do that, thank you, goodbye." I hung up feeling totally stunned.

This was turning into a roller-coaster ride. *Johannesburg, Cape Town, Zanzibar. Tonight. Fucking hell.* I lit a cigarette and started pacing up and down the lounge. My mind racing. I would need to try to get on the same flights as him, all the while not being seen. I would need to book the flights, pack for the trip and organise car hire at the other side. *Green, you had better start jumping around, old boy.*

I crushed out the cigarette and went back to the laptop. The Aston was still parked at the mall in north London. *Shopping for your holiday are you Richard?* His Gmail was still open, so I started looking for any other correspondence pertaining to his trip. One was from Hertz car rental at Cape Town International Airport.

Dear Mr Lewer-Allen. We are pleased to advise that the 4x4 Land Cruiser vehicle you requested is available and will be ready for you on your arrival on Saturday 16th February. Please proceed straight to the Hertz desk in the arrivals hall where you will be met by our representative, who will arrange everything for you.

It went on to give names, times etc. I printed off his flight schedule and the car hire details. I realised I needed a lot more than this. *What if I lost him in Cape Town?* The only contact would be his cell phone. This was another unknown. I didn't like unknowns. I searched his inbox for more information. It came in the form of an email from The Blueberry Guest House, 45 Walker Road, Kalk Bay, Cape Town.

Dear Richard, yes we have your usual rooms available for you for the nights of the 16th and 17th February. We are looking forward to seeing you again. Please let us know if there is anything you need us to do for you prior to your arrival. Kind regards, Jerry and Kate Grobelaar.

That was a real result. I was pleased. At least there would be an address to watch and I wouldn't be stuck in Cape Town, looking for a needle in a haystack. I quickly did a search for accommodation in Kalk Bay, Cape Town. There were about ten results. All of them hotels and guest houses. The Blueberry Guest House was one of them. I went to the website to have a look at where Richard would be staying. It was an old colonial-style house, boasting rooms with expansive sea views. It would make a lot of sense to try to find something close by. I quickly searched for a map of the Kalk Bay area of Cape Town. Walker Road was easy to find and close to the main road to Simons Town. I found a decent looking place that was only three blocks from the Blueberry - Binkie's Bed and Breakfast. From the website it seemed that although it wasn't as smart as the Blueberry, it would do fine for me for two nights. There was a phone number at the bottom of the site. I called the number. It rang for an eternity, then was answered by a man who sounded like he had a dreadful hangover.

"Binkie's Bed and Breakfast, can I help you?"

"Oh hello, I'm calling from the UK, I was wondering if you have a room for Saturday and Sunday night?"

"Umm, ahh, hang on just a moment please," said the groggy voice.

The receiver was put down and whoever had answered was coughing and rummaging through papers. After a while, the receiver was picked up again. Clearing his throat, the man spoke,

"Ah yes, we do have a room for those nights. Have you been here before?"

"No I haven't, but it seems pretty clear from the map on your website. I should have no problem finding you."

"Ahh ok, can I get your name please?"

"Jason Green."

"Ahh ok Mr Green, do have any idea when you'll be arriving?"

"I'm not sure but I would say some time in the late afternoon."

"OK, that's fine, I've got you in room number five. I'll expect you tomorrow afternoon then."

"Thanks very much, see you then." I hung up feeling relieved.

I made a list of what I would need to do. There were still too many unknowns. I took another look at Richard's email account again. I needed to find out his plans once he got to the island of Zanzibar. After a few minutes browsing the mails I found one from a place called Eden Beach Lodge' in Paje, (pronounced pah-jay) Zanzibar.

Dear Mr Lewer–Allen. We can confirm your booking from Monday 18th Feb to Monday 25th February. The staff and I are looking forward to seeing you again. Thanks for choosing Eden Beach Lodge.

Kind regards, Jose Santiago, General Manager. Eden Beach Lodge, Paje, Zanzibar.

There was a link to a website for the resort at the bottom of the email. I clicked on it to see what sort of place I was looking at. It seemed Richard would be staying in what I could only describe as a tropical paradise. There was a gallery crammed with pictures of the resort. It had three hundred metres of beach front with various bars, and an award winning restaurant. There were twenty separate bungalows with air conditioning, cable TV, and sea views. There were swaying palm trees on pure white sands that stretched out to turquoise waters beyond. I shook my head, incredulous. It was unbelievable that I too would be there in a few days. I had done my fair share of travelling during my marriage. Europe, the US, India, South East Asia. But I hadn't stepped a foot in Africa for more than twenty five years.

My list of things to do was getting longer by the minute. Car hire for Cape Town and Zanzibar, accommodation for Zanzibar, preferably in the same resort as Richard, flight bookings, passport and visa requirements for Zanzibar, packing.

I glanced at the tracking page on the laptop. Richard was still parked at the shopping mall in north London. I then went to the websites of the airlines on Richard's flight schedule. It was a complex procedure to try to book and pay online.

I decided I would drive up to Wood Green to my travel agent with Richard's schedule and book from there. I dressed warmly, packed my bag, and left the flat. All thoughts of the cold were far from my racing mind as I opened the little hire car and started it. I figured if I could organise the flights, I would be OK. I would have the rest of the day to arrange car hire and hotels for the rest of the trip.

The rain had started by the time I reached Wood Green. As usual, parking was a problem so I headed for a pay parking arcade with four floors of space. I took the ticket from the automated boom and drove to the third floor where I found space. I parked and headed into the shopping area. The travel agents were on the ground floor of the mall so I took the escalator down, all the while my mind racing with thoughts of the trip. *You will get on the same flights and you will find accommodation in Zanzibar, just relax,* I told myself.

The windows of the travel agent were plastered with posters of exotic, sunny locations. A chubby, surprised looking woman with spectacles stood up, smiled, and invited me to sit down at her desk. I pulled Richard's printed flight schedule from my jacket pocket and started.

"I'm afraid I've got a bit of a rushed trip to organise. I have a friend travelling to South Africa tonight and I would like to get on the same flights." I said apologetically.

"No problem sir, if you can give me the flight details, I'll try to organise that for you." I handed her the schedules.

She pushed her glasses up her nose and immediately went to work on the desk top computer. My heart sank when she came back with bad news.

"I'm afraid that the British Airways flight to Johannesburg tonight is fully booked, and the South African Airways to Cape Town is also fully booked. Would you like me to try some other options for you?"

"Yes please," I said, "it's really important that I get there around a similar time."

"Ok, just a minute," she said and busied herself once again. After what seemed an eternity, she came back with an alternative.

"I can get you on a Virgin Airways flight to Joburg tonight at 9pm, arriving 8.40am, and then on a local South African carrier to Cape Town, leaving 10.15am, arriving 12.15am. The Virgin flight is full and I can only get a ticket for first class. Will that be OK sir?"

"Yes that's fine," I said. "Could you go ahead and book those for me please?"

"Ok, I'll do that right now, and what other flights would you like me to look at for you?"

I went on to tell her about the flight from Cape Town to Zanzibar on Monday the 18th. To my disappointment, this flight was also fully booked.

"I can get you on a South African Airways flight to Dar Es Salaam, Tanzania on Monday, leaving Cape Town International at 6am, arriving Dar Es Salaam at 11am? Would that be OK for you?" she asked.

"How will I get across to Zanzibar?" I asked.

"I'm afraid the carriers are small operators across to Zanzibar, I don't think I can issue tickets for that from here. Especially as you're in such a rush. I'm sorry sir."

"Ok, no problem, I'll take care of that myself when I get to Dar Es Salaam. Can you go ahead and book those flight for me then?"

"I've done that already sir, now what about your return flights, when are those?"

I gave her the dates and times for the flight from Dar Es Salaam back to London. Again the flight was fully booked. I opted for an Ethiopian Airlines flight to London via Addis Ababa later that night.

The trip was expensive. I handed over my credit card and paid. *Gareth Lewer-Allen will be footing the bill for this*, I thought, *and I have no problem flying first class on his tab*. Ten minutes later all the tickets and boarding passes were issued and handed to me.

"There is no visa requirement for Tanzania and Zanzibar if you're travelling on a British passport sir, so I think we are done."

"Yes, looks good," I said as I paged through the various tickets. "Thanks very much."

"Have a good trip sir!" she said smiling at me as I stood and made my way to the door.

I was relieved. It wasn't perfect but all my flight times were around the same time as Richard's. I packed the tickets into my jacket pocket and headed back into the mall. *What else have I got to do here,* I thought. Suddenly I realised that I was starving. I knew there was a good coffee shop on the first floor so I headed up the escalator to get something to eat and sit down for a while to gather my thoughts.

I ordered a full English breakfast, sat down, and opened my laptop. The Aston was on the move again, heading back towards Sloane Square. I watched the flashing blue dot moving slowly through the maze of streets on the screen. *We've only known each other a few days Richard, and now were off on holiday together,* I thought, with a half smile on my face. My stomach rumbled as I smelled the breakfast cooking. I opened a search page for Zanzibar accommodation. I had forgotten the name of the place Richard was staying at in Zanzibar so I opened up his email again to find the name. After a few minutes I had found the email. The place was called Paje. I Googled it and it came back with a lot of information.

Paje was a small town on the east coast of Zanzibar. There were many choices of places to stay, from budget accommodation right up to the sort of place Richard was booked into. I decided to call Eden Beach Lodge to see if I could get into the same place. The international dialling codes were at the bottom of the web page. Eventually the call went through and started ringing. "Eden Beach Lodge, can I help you?" was the answer.

"Yes please, I'm phoning to ask if you have any accommodation for next week. I'm arriving in Zanzibar on Monday afternoon, I'm hoping to stay for seven nights."

"Just a moment please sir."

There was a long pause as the receptionist thousands of miles away looked at the register.

"I'm sorry sir, we are fully booked for the next two weeks. Have you tried Paje Village Hotel?"

"No I haven't," I said, "where is that? Is it nearby?"

"It's less than a kilometre down the beach from us, sir. Can I give you their phone number?"

I jotted the name and phone number on my list of things to do, thanked the lady and hung up. I Googled Paje Village Hotel. It immediately came back with a website. It seemed that the hotel was a lot smaller than Richard's, it had only 10 beach bungalows, no air-conditioning or cable TV, but from the pictures I decided it would be fine for what I needed. There was also some information on Paje itself. I read through it for a while.

'Paje is a small village on the south east coast of Zanzibar, 50 km from Stone Town and the International Airport. The villagers make their living mostly from fishing and seaweed farming.'

I carried on browsing the site and had a look at the rooms. They looked good and given the proximity to Eden Beach Lodge where Richard was booked, I decided to call to see if I could get in. The number rang a few times and was answered by a German sounding man. To my relief there was accommodation available and I booked myself into a beach bungalow for the duration of my stay in Zanzibar. I sat back, satisfied that in a matter of hours I had been able to organise pretty much everything I thought I would need. I felt sure that I would be able to watch Richard at both locations. If he hired a car in Zanzibar, I had tracking devices I could use to follow him. I tapped my fingers on the Formica table, racking my brain for any last minute things I should take with me. *Cash*. I would go to the bank and draw £2000 which I would then change into Rand and US Dollars. After the bank, I was pretty sure I had everything I would need for the trip. I glanced at my watch as I rode the escalator up to the car park. The time was 12.30pm.

I made my way out into the open air of the parkade and felt the blast of chilled air on my face. *In less than twenty fours you'll be out of this,* I told myself. As I stood in the queue for the automated ticket machine, I lit a cigarette. There was a young couple standing in front of me. The woman turned having smelled the smoke.

"Disgusting fags!" she said with venom.

"Terrible habit isn't it?" I replied sarcastically and carried on smoking.

Having paid, I made my way back to the Ford, got in and immediately switched the heater on to full. There was still enough heat in the engine to warm the interior quickly. I started it up and headed down the wet concrete spiral to the road below. I spent the ten minutes it took to get back to my flat racking my brain for anything I might have overlooked. One thing I hated was being caught unprepared for a job and Gareth Lewer–Allen had certainly sprung this one on me. In between packing, I set up the laptop so I could monitor what Richard was doing.

The Aston was now parked outside his flat at Grimsby Mansions. I imagined he would be doing pretty much what I was doing. I packed the tools of my trade in the main bag that would travel in the hold of the aircraft. The rest would travel with me as hand luggage. When I was finally finished it had gone 1.30pm. I was done. I was ready to go. I still couldn't believe that this was actually happening.

Gareth Lewer-Allen, if you want me to go off half way around the world, spying on your son, on holiday, travelling first class, and you want to pay me £1000 a day to do it, that is perfectly fine with me. Anytime old boy, anytime.

I went to the laptop, the Aston was still parked on Southwall Road. I did an online search for a traffic report for the drive to Heathrow Airport. It wasn't looking very good. There was a real chance of getting stuck in traffic on the way there and I couldn't risk missing my flight. I decided I would have to travel to Heathrow on the Underground. Certainly not my favourite mode of transport but at least I knew I would get there on time. Heathrow was exactly one hour from Seven Sisters station. I would call for a minicab at 4.30pm to make the airport by 6pm. I spent the rest of the afternoon watching for any movement from the Aston and researching Cape Town, the area of Kalk Bay especially. Having never been I thought it would be a good idea to kill some time reading up on the place. It turned out that Kalk Bay was originally a fishing village on the coast of False Bay. From the pictures, I saw that it was set in a truly spectacular location wedged between the ocean and sharply rising mountainous peaks. It had now become a suburb of greater Cape Town. I was also pleasantly surprised that the climate in Cape Town was particularly good in mid-February. I wondered about Richard's trip. It struck me as a bit odd that he would travel all the way to Cape Town for two nights only to travel back to Zanzibar for the rest of his trip. I guessed he was simply living up to his reputation as a globe trotter and in any case, I wasn't complaining. After an hour, and satisfied I knew enough about Cape Town and Kalk Bay, I had a look at Zanzibar. An island in the Indian Ocean off the coast of the Republic of Tanzania. A long history of trade with the Arab nations and this was reflected in the architecture of the capital, Stone Town.

A maze of narrow streets, ancient buildings, and sultan's palaces. The island was originally noted for the growing of spices, cloves, nutmeg, cinnamon, and pepper. For this reason, Zanzibar, and the surrounding islands were sometimes known as the Spice Islands. It was a place I had never given any thought to in the past and certainly never imagined I would visit.

I drank coffee and smoked as I browsed, taking in as much information as I could. Eventually at 4pm the waiting finally got to me. Frustrated, I called the Polish house cleaner to tell her I would be away for ten days and to carry on as usual in my absence. Then, after leaving her wages on the table, I packed my laptop away and called the minicab company. It was time to go. The prospect of the one hour tube journey to Heathrow followed by many, many hours stuck on an airplane to Cape Town was daunting. I decided I would wait downstairs for the cab and have a final smoke. I checked all the appliances were turned off, picked up my bags, locked the flat and made my way down.

As I stepped out onto the concrete pavement, there was a shrill wind racing up the street. It carried with it light stinging droplets of rain that appeared to be travelling sideways. The grey afternoon was darkening fast. *A couple of hours and you'll be out of here, Green, thank fuck for that.* I thought as I lit my cigarette. The minicab arrived after two minutes. I crushed out my cigarette and loaded my bags into the car.

"Seven Sisters station please," I said to the driver as I got in. The drive only took a few minutes but I was glad that I had ordered the cab. The driving rain was starting to come down hard. I paid as we arrived, got everything out and bought a newspaper at the entrance to the station. I got a one way ticket to Heathrow from the automated machine and headed through the ticket barrier and down into the gloomy bowels of London. As I travelled downwards on the escalator, the air became warmer and more humid. As I reached the platform, a train arrived. I quickly got my bags in and found a seat. It was just before rush hour so there were plenty.

I spent the next hour totally engrossed in my newspaper reading anything I could. Anything to avoid the nervous glances of the other passengers. Eventually, the train stopped at Heathrow. Gratefully, I disembarked with my bags and made my way up to ground level. The prospect of not having a cigarette until the following morning was worrying me. I found an area designated for smoking near a bus stop. It had some overhanging roof for protection so I joined my fellow addicts for an absolute final. Heathrow was busy and hectic as usual. I made my way to the Virgin desk, checked my bag in and was given my boarding pass.

It made a refreshing change being in first class as there was no queueing in line. I cleared security and made my way into the departure lounges. There was nothing of interest for me in the shops so I looked around for the first class lounge for Virgin Airlines.

As I walked in I produced my ticket and boarding pass to a lady at the door. She inspected them, thanked me and ushered me in. It was a pleasant enough room with huge windows that looked out onto the runways and parked planes beyond. The whole area was lit with floodlights as it was totally dark outside. Men in reflective jackets were busy unloading baggage from planes and driving around in catering vans servicing the aircraft. I could see planes taking off and landing in the distance. I made my way to the bar and ordered a double Powers whiskey on the rocks. There were magazines of all kinds to choose from, so I picked up a few and made my way to a window seat to relax with my drink. I passed the time, flicking through the magazines and people watching. There were smart business travellers in suits busily talking on their cellphones and tapping away on computers, a few elderly passengers here and there for whom economy class was no longer an option, and a fair smattering of good looking women jealously guarding their privacy reading books and drinking mineral water.

I opened my laptop to have a look at what Richard was up to. The tracking page loaded up and I was surprised to see the Aston moving through the streets. He was obviously braving the Friday night traffic and driving to the airport. I figured he planned to use the long stay car park at Heathrow. That would be expensive but then I knew Richard wasn't too concerned about money. I left the laptop open and made my way back to the bar for another drink. They were going down well. I was developing a taste for the fruity, smoky Irish tipple. When I got back to my computer the Aston was approaching Heathrow. I watched it enter the airport grounds and park as I sipped my drink. The stationary flashing light told me that he was now in the airport and more than likely checking in at the British Airways desk.

I could have gone back into the departure hall and waited for him to come through but I felt sure he would do the same as I had and go straight into the airline lounge. There was no point in watching him now. I would leave that for the next day in Cape Town. An hour later and with another double under my belt I packed away my computer and made my way to my gate. After a few more formalities with my passport and boarding pass I was ready to board. Outside the window was the huge glistening bulk of the jet aircraft in the night. I sat for a few minutes until the call for first class passengers came over the speaker.

As we walked down the boarding platform I heard the wind howl outside and felt the cold coming in through the gaps. I was grateful to be getting out of it. The stewardess greeted me with a well practised smile as I entered the aircraft. The first class cabin was upstairs from the rest and was modern and spacious. The huge comfortable seats each had large flat screens and work stations. I took my laptop computer and mp3 player out of my bag before packing it away in the storage unit above. *I could get used to this* I thought as I sank into the seat.

Soon after, a stewardess arrived with a glass of champagne. The glass was real and the champagne tasted real as well. The passenger next to me arrived. He was a massively overweight businessman in a suit. He packed his bag away in the compartment above, sat down, put his seatbelt on, and immediately went to sleep. *At least he won't be bothering me all night,* I thought.

After half an hour the plane was fully loaded and the captain came on the intercom.

"Good evening ladies and gentlemen, and welcome on board this Virgin Airlines flight to Johannesburg, South Africa."

He went on about the flight time and altitude etc. The stewardess started her emergency evacuation routine as the massive plane taxied towards the runway. Eventually we had the all clear for take off and I felt a twinge of excitement as the thrust pushed me back into the seat. I was pleased at how quiet the first class cabin was. I hated long haul flights. My fellow traveller next to me was out cold. After a while, drinks and an excellent dinner were served. The movie selection was standard airplane fare designed to relax and not offend in any way. I decided I would rather listen to music. I ordered one final drink and popped a sleeping tablet. It would take effect in half an hour. I only used sleeping tablets for long haul flights. I didn't like the way they left me feeling groggy the next day but it was a necessary evil for an eleven and a half hour flight. I fitted the earphones, adjusted the seat to the sleeping position, and within half an hour I had drifted off to the sombre sounds of Leonard Cohen.

I awoke feeling someone gently shaking my shoulder. It was the stewardess from the previous evening.

"Wake up sir. We're about to land in Johannesburg. You've missed breakfast. You were fast asleep. I hope that's ok?"

"Yes that's fine," I said, still dazed. I asked for some water. I felt a little dehydrated as was always the case with long haul flights.

"Sure, I'll get you one right away," she replied. As she went to get the water I lifted the window cover to one of the most beautiful sights on earth. Sunrise over Africa. Great swathes of orange and red were washing over the sleeping continent. It brought back a wave of memories as I realised that this was a sight I hadn't seen in over twenty five years. Staring out at the spectacle with groggy nostalgia, all thoughts of Richard Lewer-Allen were far from my mind. My fellow passenger in the seat next to mine was awake too. He looked as tired as he had been the previous evening.

"Good morning, sleep well?" he asked.

"Morning, I did actually, didn't wake up once the whole night, amazing," I replied.

"That's first class for you," he said.

I returned my seat to the upright position as the giant aircraft made its descent. The huge gold mine dumps of Johannesburg glowed yellow below in the morning light. The sky above was completely blue, with not a cloud in sight. *What a pleasure,* I thought. Ten minutes later we landed and the huge OR Tambo airport lay to the left as we taxied towards the gate. It was a completely different airport to the one I had travelled through all those years ago. Back then it was called Jan Smuts International and was a pokey little place. This was now a major international hub with all the trappings of Heathrow or Schipol. Being in first class, we were the first to leave the airplane and make our way down the moveable stairway to the concrete below. My eyes were unaccustomed to the brightness and I had to fish my sunglasses from my hand luggage. Even at 9 in the morning, the temperature was around 23 degrees, I removed my jacket as I boarded the waiting bus. The packet of cigarettes in my chest pocket were starting to burn a hole. I wondered if there would be a smoking area between the international and the domestic terminal. The first class and business class bus made its way to the huge airport building as the rest of the passengers were made to wait.

We exited the bus and made our way into the building and up an escalator towards the immigration area. There were twenty separate lines bordered off with groups of people queuing. The passengers with South African passports were moving through quickly while the rest of us were made to wait. Eventually, after an infuriating twenty minute wait I made it to the immigration official.

It took her two minutes to process my passport and stick the holiday visa into it. Then I was through and on my way to the baggage reclaim. I quickly ducked into the gents restroom to wash up and brush my teeth while I waited for the luggage to appear. When I got out I was pleased to see that the circling baggage claim was already turning with bags. Presently my bag appeared. The small padlock was still in place on the zipper.

I grabbed it and made my way to the exit into the arrivals hall. There were two choices, the red route and the green route for those who had nothing to declare. I was worried about the surveillance equipment I was carrying but decided to go straight through the green route. There were a mixture of white and coloured, male and female customs officials strategically positioned in the green route. I felt their eyes on me as I walked. I made an effort to look bored and tired as I moved. A young lady in front of me was politely asked to stop and place her bags on a metal table. I carried on moving and in a few seconds I was through into the arrivals hall. There were hundreds of people with expectant faces, waiting for friends and relatives on either side of rope barriers. I walked quickly through them, my eyes darting around the massive bright advertising boards looking for an exit sign. To my left I saw a sign which read, Taxi rank, Exit, Domestic Terminal. I made a beeline to this and, as I walked out, I saw groups of fellow smokers gratefully puffing away on the pavement. The place was bustling with buses, taxis, cars. I lit a cigarette and took a deep draw with relief. It felt good to see the colourful people of Africa again. There was a strip roof high above us, but I could see the blue sky above. It was liberating to feel the cool breeze on my arms. I felt free and relieved not to have layer upon layer of clothes constricting my movements. I was acutely aware that time was short and I would have to rush to the domestic terminal to make the connecting flight to Cape Town.

I started moving down the concrete pavement as I smoked. I crushed out my cigarette as I arrived at the smaller domestic terminal. I fished out the ticket for the connecting flight. It was a local airline called Air-link. I made my way to the desk. I was greeted by a dark-haired Afrikaans woman with a heavy accent.

"Good morning sir, ticket and ID please." I gave a half smile as I handed over the documents.

The unforgettably thick accent brought back all manner of memories from my youth.

"Right sir you must proceed straight to gate 12 upstairs. Your flight is about to board."

"Thanks," I said as I packed away my ticket and passport.

Johannesburg Airport was a far cry from the sleepy place I remembered from twenty five years previous. When I got upstairs to my gate, the crowd was already moving through towards the lounge. The small jet was parked on the runway outside. I marvelled at the huge expanse of blue sky as I gazed out at the activity outside. Eventually we were ushered into the gangway to the waiting aircraft. The interior of the plane was narrow and cramped compared to the luxury of the first class cabin I had just been in. Still, it was only a two hour flight and then I would be free.

I found my seat, packed my bag away and sat down. I was hungry having missed breakfast on the previous flight. After fifteen minutes the plane started taxiing down the runway. I retrieved the file on Richard from my bag in the overhead compartment and busied myself reading it. It was a useful one and a half hours as there was a lot of the file I hadn't read. Richard's father had been methodical and ruthless in compiling it. It was obvious he was extremely concerned by his son's activity. I still couldn't quite believe I was flying over Southern Africa on my way to Cape Town. It was bright in the packed cabin. I wore my sunglasses as I read. Gareth Lewer-Allen surely had more money than sense sending me on holiday following his son but, as I had decided the previous day, it was fine by me. As we began our descent, the massive orchards of Stellenbosch were spread out below me. It was a glorious sight. Endless rows of vineyards and fruit surrounded by majestic mountains bathed in warm sunshine. On the final leg of the descent I caught my first glimpse of Table Mountain. It was as stunning as it had been in the pictures I had seen all my life. The city nestled below, between the foot of the great flat behemoth and the sea. It was breathtaking. As the plane came down to land, I had to force myself to concentrate on the task at hand. I would need to hire a car and find a place from which I could follow Richard once he arrived. This was another unknown. I knew where he was staying, but it would be unprofessional to proceed straight to his address. I might miss something and I would kick myself if I did.

The plane landed and taxied towards the airport building. I made myself ready for a rushed hour or so ahead. There was a queue of people in front of me by the time the doors opened and we slowly made our way out into the sunshine.

There was a waiting bus and I chose a seat which would ensure I got out quickly into the airport building. Being a domestic flight, there were no immigration procedures. I would have to wait for my bag but being one of the last to check in I hoped that my bag would be one of the first out. I made my way into the airport building. It was full of advertising boasting Cape Town's attractions. I made my way to the baggage reclaim and waited impatiently for my bag to appear through the rubber flaps. As expected it was one of the first to appear. I had made good time. The south African airways flight that Richard was on had not arrived yet.

The arrivals hall was full of the sun-tanned and beautiful people of Cape Town. I made my way quickly to the Hertz counter to arrange a vehicle. The procedure was quick and efficient. I hired a Mercedes 280. After ten minutes, I was escorted to the parking bay. Although a lot smaller than the airport in Johannesburg, Cape Town airport was busy with traffic and taxis. The parking bay was away from the main building to the left in a fenced off area. There was an armed security guard. The Hertz lady led me to the Mercedes. It was a new model, sleek, cream in colour with a sunroof. She handed me the keys and wished me a pleasant stay in Cape Town. I slung my bags into the back and sat down in the driver's seat. A map of Cape Town appeared on the sat-nav showing my location at the airport. *Good.* I lit a cigarette as I checked my phone. It showed Vodacom with full signal. I was ready for Cape Town. It was then I noticed the guard at the gate watching me. There was only one Land Cruiser in the yard so I had to assume it would be the one Richard was booked to hire. I pulled a pen out of my bag and made a note of the licence plate number. I decided I would pull out of the Hertz bay, try to find a parking close by and wait for Richard. There was a lot of free space as we were fairly far from the main building. I couldn't see any problem.

The automatic Mercedes started first time and I glided out of the bay past the waving guard. I found a parking spot a hundred metres from the bay. It was right on the path I had taken. I assumed Richard would take the same walk as I had. I reversed into the parking space to give me a clear view of anyone walking past. It would be easy to follow any car coming and was a perfect vantage point. I sat back feeling pleased with myself and took a deep drag of the cigarette. My back was sweating lightly on the leather seat. It dawned on me that I was parked in a Mercedes in Cape Town in full sunshine and warmth. The freezing wet misery of London in February was thousands of miles away.

A large South African Airways plane was landing on the runway to my right. I glanced at my watch. It was definitely Richard's flight. I could expect him to walk right past me in half an hour or so. I opened the sunroof and leant my head back on the headrest. I felt the warm glow of the African sun on my face. I closed my eyes and let it sink in.

It had been too long. Way too long.

CHAPTER EIGHT

- CAPE TOWN

I spent the next half an hour waiting for Richard to appear. On my second cigarette he did. He walked past, completely oblivious to my presence. My heart was beating faster. He wore designer jeans and a bright cotton shirt. A picture of wealth and easy-going freedom as he casually pulled his luggage behind him and chatted to the Hertz lady. He would be out in a matter of minutes. The Land Cruiser pulled out of the parking area and drove past me. Richard's eyes were straight ahead. He was talking on his cell phone. The Mercedes pulled out smoothly and we entered the traffic heading towards the airport exit. Eventually we entered onto what I imagined was the main highway to the city. There were billboards to the left and the right. The Land Cruiser sped ahead and entered the fast lane. I was pleased I had chosen the Mercedes for its power and speed. I would have no problem keeping up with Richard. I was feeling tense. It was obvious Richard knew exactly where he was going and I didn't have a fucking clue. I was desperate not to lose him. There was a Volvo in between us, but the Land Cruiser was high enough for me not to lose sight of him. We drove through a low income township area. It stretched for miles on either side of the highway. I remembered the previous day I had been reading online about Cape Town. It was the Khayelitsha township and a notorious piece of road called 'the hell run' by locals. I knew Cape Town and South Africa were notorious for violent crime. I wasn't worried about it but I reminded myself to be on guard all the same. Eventually we entered the outskirts of Cape Town city. I caught a glimpse of the sea and the port through the high-rise buildings. Everything appeared bright and clean. Richard kept to the right hand lane and powered on past the city to the left. The magnificent Table Mountain rose above me to the right. I couldn't help the occasional glance as we drove but I forced myself to keep my eyes locked onto the grey Land Cruiser.

Up ahead of us was a traffic light. Richard was approaching when the light went amber. My heart jumped as I realised that he might drive through it. The Volvo man in between us, being a Volvo man, would definitely stop and I would lose Richard. Thankfully the Land Cruiser stopped at the light and I breathed a sigh of relief. As we waited for the lights to change, I glanced at the sat-nav. To my right was the Cape Town University with its grand staircase in the sun. To my left was a built up area. The sat-nav told me that we were travelling down the main road to Simon's Town. Richard was heading to his guest house after all and I needn't have worried about going through the stress of following him through this unfamiliar city. Still, it was the job and I wasn't complaining. We carried on after the lights changed and I noticed the areas to the left and right were more affluent. The gardens were bigger and the shops seemed cleaner.

We drove through an area called Constantia. I had read about it the previous day and had learned that it was one of the best residential areas of Cape Town. The rolling green lawns of the massive estates were testimony to that. Eventually the road became narrower and drew closer to the sea which was rough and crashing into the rocks to the left. It was clear why Richard liked Cape Town. After ten minutes the Volvo disappeared and I was behind the Land Cruiser. Richard was obviously listening to music. I could see his fingers tapping on the thick steering wheel. The traffic started building up again and three cars came in between us through a filter lane. This was a situation I was hoping to avoid. The sat-nav told me we were now in Muizenberg. There was a huge golden beach stretching out to my left. As we reached the the centre of Muizenberg, I lost sight of the Land Cruiser. To add insult to injury a large tipper truck pulled out in front of me from the left. I was certain I had now lost him. Cursing loudly I pulled the Mercedes into a service station to the left. The traffic was so heavy now and the road so narrow it would be impossible to follow anyone who had got ahead.

Frustrated, I lit a cigarette and entered the address of Richard's accommodation to the sat-nav. The Blueberry Guest House, 45 Walker Road, Kalk Bay.

"Go straight for three kilometres, then turn right," the automated voice said.

Obediently I pulled out of the service station and continued down the main road through the traffic. Eventually as we cleared Muizenberg the traffic calmed and once again I marvelled at the beauty of Cape Town. I approached the quaint and picturesque fishing village of Kalk Bay. There were numerous antique and book shops on either side of the road. On my left a train passed me not twenty metres from the sea. All around were relaxed-looking people ambling, eating ice cream and browsing craft stalls.

"Turn right in one hundred metres," said the voice from the sat-nav.

As instructed I turned and made my way up a steep hill past multi coloured houses on either side, the massive Table Mountain towered above me.

"After two hundred metres, turn left," came the voice again.

After winding steeply up the narrow street I turned left at a stop street. There was a sign on my left which said Walker Street. I knew I was close to Richard's guest house. I prayed that he would be there. If not, there would be an anxious wait until he arrived and there would be more unknowns.

My instructions were to watch him like a hawk and I fully intended to do that to the best of my abilities. Above me to my right was a high mountain road. Already from where I was I could see the most incredible views of Kalk Bay between the houses to my left. Anxiously I drove on until I heard the words,

"You have reached your destination."

My eyes darted around the street for the Land Cruiser. To my relief I saw it parked under a tree to my left and recognised the number plate. I pulled the Mercedes over into a parking space fifty metres ahead of it and sat watching through the rear view mirror. Richard was nowhere in sight and had obviously gone into the guest house to check in. I now had to make some decisions as to what to do. I could quite easily wait it out until he left and follow, or I could place a tracking device in the Land Cruiser and move off to my digs. I decided to relax for a while, have a cigarette and think it through. I was relieved that I had found him after losing him, so half an hour or so wouldn't kill me.

I noticed a young white couple walking towards me in the distance. They were obviously tourists, taking photographs and talking. Very few cars were travelling on the street. The majority of the traffic was on the more scenic road above me to my right. I pulled out the red file on Richard to use as a diversion for when they got to the car. I didn't want to look suspicious in any way. A man sitting in a car supposedly catching up with some work wouldn't ring any alarm bells. After ten minutes the couple had passed me and were ambling back towards the Land Cruiser. I decided I would do the same. I pulled out my camera, slung it around my neck and checked in the rear view mirror. All was quiet outside the Blueberry Guest House. No sign of Richard. It was an opportunity I couldn't miss. I dug in my bag and retrieved one of the tiny Japanese tracking devices. I inserted a fresh battery and the red light flashed indicating it was good to go. I closed the sunroof of the car, placed my bags in the boot for security, locked up and started down the street towards Richard's car. Every now and then I stopped and pretended to take photographs of the views to my left and right. Thirty metres before I reached the car I noticed a domestic worker in a tiny garden to the left. He was clipping a hedge.

"How are you sir?" he asked.

"I'm fine thanks how are you?"

It was a typical exchange of greetings in Africa which brought back memories for me. He appeared totally at ease and carried on with his work as I walked. I decided that I would place the tracking device on my return journey back down the street. It would be a good idea to have a look at the entrance to The Blueberry first and get some distance between myself and the worker. As I reached the Land Cruiser I caught my first glimpse of Richard's guest house. There was a white picket fence with a small brick driveway. The garden was obviously a source of pride to the owners and was full of exotic palms, tree ferns and bright orange bird of paradise flowers. On the gate was a small sign with the words The

Blueberry Guest House, welcome. It was painted bright blue like the sky above me. There was no one in sight. I walked past and continued towards the crossroads.

On arrival at the stop street, I took a moment to marvel at the spectacular sight far below me. The harbour was full of multi-coloured fishing boats bobbing and rocking in the rough sea and a long pier stretched out into the ocean. Kalk Bay had a relaxed and bohemian feel to it. I understood why Richard favoured it. I lit another cigarette, and started back towards the Land Cruiser. My plan was to place the tracking device in the front left wheel arch as I had in the Aston Martin. I would have to be quick. It would be a disaster if someone was to suddenly walk out of the front door of the guest house and see me. All was quiet as I approached except for the noise of the traffic on the scenic road above. My right hand was in my pocket clutching the magnetised device as I passed the white wooden gate to Richard's digs. It was now or never and I decided to go for it. My hand came out holding the device. The wheel arch was particularly high on the 4x4 vehicle. This made it easy. Quickly and without stopping I slipped it under and heard the reassuring clunk of the magnet land on the metal of the wheel arch. I carried on un-noticed and smiled to myself as I walked towards the Mercedes. It had been another success. Once again, there was nowhere for Richard to hide.

As I got into the hire car, I opened the sun-roof and pulled my laptop from my smaller bag. The battery was low, so I attached it to the car lighter to charge it. It took some minutes to load the settings for the tracking page but eventually I got it all working. I was online and the tracker was showing Richard's car with the usual flashing blue light not fifty metres from where I was parked. Success. I glanced at my watch. It was 3pm and the sun still shone bright above me.

What a fucking pleasure, I thought as I gazed into the rear view mirror. I was pretty much sorted for the day. I decided I would drive to my guest house and check in. I needed to have a shower and get a change of clothes. I typed the address of Binkie's Guest House into the sat-nav.

"Go straight for three hundred metres and turn left," was the instruction. I started the car and moved down the street away from The Blueberry. There was another stop street similar to the one I had come up on. It led back down to the main road of Kalk Bay.

"Go straight for fifty metres and turn left," came the voice. As I turned left into the narrow street the voice announced,

"You have reached your destination." I stopped the car and found the sign on my immediate right. Binkie's Guest House, parking inside. I drove onto the stone driveway. The old building was a bit ramshackle. It was obviously in need of a paint job and the tiny garden was overgrown. I got out the car, locked up and knocked on a red wooden door with peeling paint. There was a shuffling noise from inside and after a few seconds the door was opened by a tall man dressed in long blue shorts, slops and a faded orange tee-shirt. He had a deep suntan, long curly hair and slightly bloodshot eyes.

"Hi there, are you Mr Green?" he said with a smile.

"Yup, that's me," I said.

He immediately offered his hand, which I shook.

"My name is Binks, welcome. Did you find the place ok?"

"Yup no problem at all."

"Well come in please, let me show you your room," he said.

It was an old colonial building with wooden floors and pressed lead ceilings. There were threadbare armchairs and old oil paintings, but the place looked spotlessly clean. He led me onto a verandah under an old tin roof which led around the left hand side of the house to the front. There were easy chairs placed randomly about for guests to relax on. We paused and took in the view. Overhead there were seagulls squalling in the breeze. Below was more overgrown garden with a pathway that led down to the main road and the harbour below.

"Great view," I said.

"Yup, it's not bad at all," he replied with a smile.

I was warming to the place.

"I've put you in room number two, here's the door," he said grappling with a bunch of ancient looking keys.

The room had the same wooden floors and high ceilings. It was painted white and had a large double bed, two armchairs, a dressing table, and two huge bay windows looking out onto the ocean.

"This will do just fine, thanks very much," I said approvingly.

The place had an old world colonial charm and was obviously well looked after.

"Excellent, can I help you with your bags?" He asked handing me the key.

"No that's fine, I'll sort that out."

I wandered back through the house to the car and retrieved my luggage. When I got back into the room I plugged my laptop in to the wall socket immediately. The Land Cruiser was still parked where I had found it. I turned the taps on an old cast iron bath with clawed feet. As it ran I went outside and lit a cigarette. It had been a hectic few days. I was feeling a mixture of elation and mild exhaustion. The owner, Binks had seen me standing there and came to join me. We chatted about London briefly and the flight to South Africa.

"I have some cold beers, would you like one?" He asked.

"Absolutely!" was my reply.

He disappeared into the private section of the house and returned with two bottles of ice cold Castle Lager. It was a beer I hadn't tasted in many, many years and I savoured the cold bitterness as we drank. We spoke about Kalk Bay in general, where to eat and drink etc. He suggested a pub directly below the house near the harbour called The Brass Bell. It was known for excellent food. He invited me to accompany him later on for a few drinks and suggested we could both take a walk down. I told him I had a lot of work to do and some people to see but I may meet him later. He was a pleasant soft spoken Capetonian. A true beach bum. I felt welcome and was almost disappointed that I would only be staying for two nights.

As I went to my room for my bath I had to remind myself that this was a paying job and not a holiday. Before I jumped in the bath I checked my laptop and saw with relief that Richard was still parked a few blocks away at The Blueberry. It was 5.30pm by the time I was shaved and dressed. Richard's car was still parked. Again it was decision time as to whether I should drive up to Walker Road and watch the car or wait for it to move first. I decided on the latter and went out onto the verandah to enjoy the early evening. Right on cue, Binks appeared with another two ice cold beers. We smoked and talked for the next hour with me making regular trips into the room to check the laptop.

At 6.30pm exactly I noticed with brief panic that the Land Cruiser was on the move again. I sat and watched it travel slowly up Walker Street and down towards the main road. It stopped after only five minutes and appeared to be parked directly below near the harbour. I made my apologies to Binks who was still on the verandah, packed my bag and went to the car. I made my way down the steep street towards the main road, the laptop sitting on the passenger seat to my left. Finding the Land Cruiser was my priority. I could wander around a bit once I had done that. As I got to the T junction at the main road I glanced at the screen again. The traffic on the main road was heavy. The Land Cruiser was right in front of me. I noticed an entrance to a car park on the opposite side of the road to my right. *He must be parked in there*. I waited for a gap in traffic, crossed the street and turned into the car park. There was a railway line not three metres away from me behind a balustrade wall. Beyond the tracks were glistening black boulders with waves pounding into them continuously. I put the laptop into the bag, locked the car and took a look around. Richard's car was parked thirty metres from me. I noticed a sign which read The Brass Bell mounted on the top of a pedestrian subway that went under the train tracks. On the other side was a raised building which hung over the waves. I looked around at my surroundings. There was a number of book shops on the other side of the street. In between these was what looked like a cafe restaurant. I decided to cross and check it out. It was a slightly scruffy but obviously popular establishment by the name of Guido's. It had huge glass fronted windows that looked directly out onto the street and the car park beyond. Feeling some serious hunger pangs I decided to go inside and eat. I sat at a tiny table and was approached by a lady with dreadlocks and a head scarf. The place was buzzing with conversation and she was obviously busy.

She pointed at a huge blackboard on the far wall.

"Everything on the board is available sir, I can recommend the lasagne."

"In that case, that's exactly what I'll have."

"And to drink?"

"I'll have a Castle please."

"Sure thing," she said as she went off hurriedly.

I sat back and took in the hectic but enjoyable atmosphere. There was a lady on the next table with two young children. They were eating fresh mussels in cream sauce with bread and making a hell of a mess. No one seemed to mind. The music and conversation blared away as I sat. There was no point in opening the laptop as I could clearly see the entrance to the car park across the road. My food arrived. A huge portion with a salad which was excellent washed down with the cold beer. It was 8pm by the time I paid and made my way out into the now dark street. I decided to make a foray into The Brass Bell to have a look at what Richard was doing. I crossed the street and walked into the parking area. As I passed the Land Cruiser I could hear the waves crashing on the rocks to my right. I descended into the walkway that ran under the railway tracks. I came up onto the Kalk Bay station platform and saw the entrance to The Brass Bell pub to my right. It was a big place and there were a lot of people inside. This was good. I needed cover. There was a lively humdrum of noise as I walked into the pub. On the right, looking over the railway line towards the mountain was the bar while on the left the building stretched out over the sea. There were huge, mist-sprayed windows on all sides giving a 360 degree view of the lights of the moored fishing boats and the shops and houses that surrounded the bay. My eyes darted around the area looking for the tall figure of Richard. I found him sitting facing the bar, his back toward me. He was in conversation with a tall suntanned man with shaggy blonde hair. Directly behind the bar in front of them was a large brass bell which shone in the mellow lighting. I glanced to my right and saw an area near the far window which had some free space. It would afford me a great spot to sit and look out over the ocean while keeping an eye on Richard.

I sat down at a small table near the open window and I could feel the salt spray lightly on my face every now and then as the sea crashed on the rocks below. I ordered a beer from a waiter and settled in. Richard remained in his seat for the next half hour talking to his companion. They laughed and joked, smoked cigarettes, and ordered drinks including what looked like shots with whiskey chasers. It was a party night for young Richard.

The drive from the pub to his guest house was pretty much straight up the steep, quiet road across the street. There would be very little chance of being stopped by police for drink driving if he intended to go back there. Every now and then Richard would get up and head for the toilets. When he returned, his companion would do the same. It was as if they were two old friends catching up after some time apart, having a good time. Nothing unusual. Nothing exciting. Nothing to write home about. And so the game of cat and mouse continued into the night.

At 9.30pm, I noticed a man waving to me from the other side of the bar. It was Binks, the owner of the bed and breakfast where I was staying. I smiled and raised my hand in recognition. He motioned to me asking if I would like a beer. I gave him the thumbs up and he went about ordering before ambling towards me carrying two pints of beer.

"How are you doing?" he asked as he sat down.

"Well thanks, nice place," I said as he passed me the glass.

"Yup, it's a famous pub. Been here a long long time."

"Is it always this busy?" I asked.

"On the weekends it is, during the week it's more of a local crowd and a bit more chilled out. The locals love this place, bit of an institution."

"I can see why. It's quite something," I said. We chatted and drank for the hour with me keeping an eye on Richard and his drinking buddy. I could see the shots were coming thick and fast. Apart from the occasional trip to the toilet they were firmly ensconced in their increasingly animated conversation. At 11.30pm the barman called time by ringing the huge brass bell behind the bar. There was a groan from the crowd as they realised their time was up, and last rounds were called. It was at this point that I noticed Richard and his companion stand up.

They shook hands and clapped each other on the back, smiling and laughing. I could see that Richard was about to leave. I needed an excuse to do the same. I glanced at my watch and made as if I was late for an appointment.

"I have an important call coming through anytime now and I really need to catch up on some work. I'm gonna have to go Binks. Thanks for the beers. I'll see you tomorrow."

"No problem Jason, see you later," he said. Richard was already well out of the door and probably in the subway under the railway tracks when I picked up my bag and left the pub. I walked slowly not wanting to run into him. As I came out of the subway and into the car park I noticed that the Land Cruiser had gone from its space. I was acutely aware that both Richard and I were well over the limit for driving as I got into the Mercedes. I opened my laptop. To my relief the flashing blue light showed that Richard was indeed driving up the steep hill opposite me towards his guest house. I sat for five minutes watching the screen until I saw the light stop outside The Blueberry on Walker Road. I started the car and made my way out of the car park and across the now quiet street. Slowly I drove up the steep hill glancing every now and then at the screen. There was no movement. I was feeling pleasantly tired and I was sure Richard would be feeling the same way. With any luck he would be in for the night and I could do the same. I turned right and drove slowly down walker street. The Land Cruiser was parked where it had been in the afternoon. There was no movement and all was quiet. Slowly I made my way back to Binkie's Guest House, parked the car and walked to my room.

I pulled the table close to the bed, plugged in my computer and lay down on the duvet with my hands behind my head. I reflected on the hectic events of the last 24 hours as I lay watching the screen. It had been a success as far as doing my job went. I had followed my brief. I had flown half way around the world and watched him like a hawk. In a matter of minutes, I fell into a deep dreamless sleep.

At 6am exactly on Sunday morning my body clock clicked in as usual. *Where the fuck am I?* I thought as I opened my eyes and saw the unfamiliar room. In a split second it all came back to me. Heathrow. The flights. The car hire. The chase to Kalk Bay. The guest house. The Brass Bell. I had slept the entire night in the same position without moving or getting under the duvet. I could hear seagulls squalling overhead. Immediately I looked at my computer screen. It had gone black due to inactivity. I ran my finger across the mouse pad to revive it. A second later the screen showed and the reassuring flashing light of the tracking device in the Land Cruiser showed Richard was still at The Blueberry.

I stretched, got up, grabbed my cigarettes and walked out onto the balcony. In front of me Kalk Bay stretched out on either side. A feast of colour. Down in the harbour there was a hive of activity as the fishing boats made their way out to sea for the day. They bobbed up and down on the white crested waves as puffs of smoke bellowed from their engines.

To my left in the distance were the golden sands of Muizenberg beach. Below me, the pastel coloured houses showed pale in the morning light. There was a passenger train pulling out of Kalk Bay station going towards Cape Town. Above was a huge expanse of blue sky without a single cloud and a cool breeze blew in my face. I lit a smoke and lent on the railing gazing out at the spectacle. *I could get used to this.* There was a kettle and some coffee in my room, I boiled it and made a cup which I brought back out onto the verandah. My mind went to the task at hand. As I drank the coffee I wondered what the day would hold for Richard and myself. He only had 24 hours left in Cape Town and it still puzzled me why he would come all this way for such a short time. After my coffee, I ran a hot bath and lay in it for half an hour thinking about Richard and his globe trotting. I could see the screen of the computer through the open door to the bedroom. There was no movement. At around seven after I had dressed there was a knock on my door. A very bleary eyed Binks asking me what I would like for breakfast. I ordered a full English which he said he would serve on the verandah.

Half an hour later as promised a maid produced a huge spread on an old wooden table overlooking Kalk Bay. Binks and myself ate together. Drank coffee and smoked. He asked me what my plans were for the day to which I gave a vague explanation that I was waiting for a business associate to email or call me with instructions. Occasionally, as we sat I put my head round my door to have a look at the screen. There was still no movement. Richard was sleeping off a heavy night. I recalled him and his companion downing numerous shots. At around 9am I made my excuses to the affable Binkie and collected my computer and bag from the room. It was time to do my job and my job was to watch Richard. I could have quite happily taken a walk down to the main road and wander around the shops and the harbour but I had to do what I was being paid to do.

The Mercedes started first time and I took the short drive to Walker Road and the Blueberry Guest House. My laptop by my side. The Land Cruiser was in its usual parking and I found a spot fifty metres away from where I could see it clearly ahead of me. It was time to hurry up and wait again. There was a fair amount of traffic on the road. Cars and pedestrians. All of them seemed to take no notice of me sitting there with the sun-roof open. I browsed the internet as I sat checking news sites, sending a few emails and researching the island of Zanzibar. It helped to pass the time a bit although I was more than happy sitting in the sun. I saw in the rear view mirror that I was getting a bit of colour back in my face.

It was 10.30am when Richard came out of the guest house and onto the road. He was wearing Bermuda shorts and a tee shirt and looked a bit pale and slow.

I knew he was nursing a hangover behind his dark glasses. It made me smile. He walked around the Land Cruiser and tugged at the roof rack as if to check it was attached securely. He was carrying a small bag similar to the one I had seen him exchanging in London at the restaurant. He stood for a moment looking at the roof rack and running his hand through his hair. He unlocked the car and got in. I followed him up Walker Road to the stop street where he turned left and drove down the steep hill to the main road. I felt a pang of anxiety at the thought of losing him in the traffic like I had the previous day but I put it out of my mind when we got to the main road. Being a Sunday the traffic was lighter. At the main road he turned left and drove towards Cape Town. *What's the agenda today Richard?*

I followed him up the beautiful coastal road. I kept an eye on the sat-nav as we drove, my vehicle a safe fifty metres or so behind his. I marvelled at the contrast of colours around me. The brown boulders of the huge mountain to my left against the pure blue sky. The golden sands of Muizenberg beach stretching out into the breaking waves of the ocean. After ten minutes or so Richard indicated right. I glanced at my sat-nav which told me we were in Muizenberg. I felt a bit exposed at the traffic lights as my car was right behind his but he paid no attention to his rear view mirror and made the turn when the lights turned green. We drove past a post office and various hotels and restaurants until we reached a large building on the left. It was opposite a water park which was busy with families and kids having fun on the slides in the sun. Beyond the water park was Muizenberg beach. There were a lot of people on the beach that Sunday. Sunbathing, fishing, surfing, and walking dogs. Richard parked his car outside the building near a real estate company and a shop by the name of Lenny's Surf Works. I remembered that Richard had visited the shop's website, I had seen it when I looked at his internet history while I was in his flat. All of the shops were closed being a Sunday and I wondered what he was up to. I parked the Mercedes on the far side of the parking area facing the water slides and turned in my seat to watch what his next move would be. He was making a call on his phone while sitting in the parked car. I watched and waited as he got out of the car and walked up and down the various shop fronts looking in at what was on offer. Two minutes later, a blue pick up truck sped into the car park and parked directly next to Richard's vehicle.

The man who got out was Richard's drinking buddy from the previous night. They smiled and shook hands. He was dressed pretty much as he was the previous evening in shorts and a tee shirt with slops. Standard Cape Town attire. He was fishing in his pockets for keys as they walked towards the surf shop.

They both paused at the door while the right key was selected then unlocked the door and walked in. At that moment two coloured men staggered up the pavement towards my car. They were both obviously paralytic drunk and appeared to be having an argument over a large plastic bottle of cheap sherry. The two were obviously tramps. Scruffy clothes and missing teeth. I was struggling to see into the darkness of the surf shop while my attention was being disturbed by the two drunks. The one who was carrying the bottle was now clinging to a street lamp trying to avoid the other who was desperately trying to get hold of the booze.

"It's mine, it's mine!" He shouted as he spun around the pole evading the flailing arms of his assailant.

"No, no china, it's ours. We sharing! We sharing the dop! Pass it to me man."

Their accents brought back memories of my childhood. My eyes flicked back to the front of the surf shop, there was no movement and both men were still inside. I wished I had found a closer parking so I could have taken a walk past and looked in. It was too late now. The coloured man who was trying to get the bottle was sensing he was fighting a losing battle and started swearing at the other who was still hanging onto the pole of the street light. He staggered two metres away, turned to his companion and started a tirade of comical abuse.

"Fuck you man, fuck you man, it's our dop ekse!" He spat while swaying on his feet.

"It's mine! It's my dop!" The other replied.

All of this was happening metres from my car. They paid no attention to my presence and I wondered if they even knew I was there. Then the one without the bottle turned his back to his companion, dropped his filthy trousers to his ankles and bent over exposing his bare buttocks to his friend who was swigging away happily. I noticed a few families across the street at the water park hurry their children away from the spectacle.

"Nigh me china! Nigh me ekse!" Shouted the naked man as he pointed at his rear end.

I couldn't help but laugh at this bizarre bit of street theatre that was playing out in front of me.

"Nigh me ekse! Nigh me china!" He repeated. I recalled the meaning of the slang from my youth, nigh meant 'fuck' and dop meant 'drink'. 'Ekse' was slang for 'I say' from the Afrikaans. Still laughing I glanced back at the shop front. The door was open and Richard was still inside.

"Nigh me china! It's our dop!" The naked man repeated before he staggered forward, tripped on his trousers and crashed into the pavement in a heap.

All this in full view in bright sunshine. As he tried to pull his trousers up, the man with the bottle let go of the pole and stumbled past mumbling to himself. Eventually the man on the pavement managed to get his trousers up and followed his companion up the pavement and away.

"Never a dull moment Green," I said smiling to myself, "never a dull moment".

I pulled my camera from my bag and took a few shots of the surf shop front and the two vehicles making a mental note of the time and address. After five minutes the two men walked out of the shop both carrying surfboards under their arms. They both checked their respective vehicles were locked and started walking towards my Mercedes. I quickly turned and faced forward watching them in my rear view mirror. They were steadily walking towards my car talking to each other. They were hitting the beach for a morning of surfing. They were now only three metres from my car and approaching rapidly. I pretended to be working on my laptop as the two passed within a metre of me. I was relieved that neither of them paid any attention to my presence as they passed. I quickly packed the computer and camera into my bag, locked the car, and followed them. They walked up a grassy mound of sand and down onto the beach before veering off to the left towards a family who were sunbathing on the sand. I couldn't hear anything that was said but it appeared they had asked the father if he would look after their belongings while they surfed.

Both men removed their sunglasses and shirts and dumped their bags near the family before jogging off towards the breakers. Richard's ultra thin body was shockingly white compared to his companion. I sat at a safe distance and removed my shirt as well.

"What a pleasure," I said to myself, as I lay back on my elbows and soaked up the warm sun. For the next hour and a half I watched the two men ride the huge waves. Richard was obviously a beginner and constantly fell off his board while his companion surfed like a pro.

My camera was by no means out of place and I took numerous photographs of the two. At around 12pm the two made their way back to the sunbathing family and sat down. Richard was obviously exhausted and lay flat on his back on a towel, his white chest rapidly rising and falling as he caught his breath. The two men then sat talking and staring out at the ocean for the next half hour before picking up their boards and belongings and making their way back up the beach towards the car park. Dutifully I did the same and followed from a distance. After crossing the road and reaching their vehicles, the two men placed the surfboards on the roof rack of Richard's Land Cruiser. Richard dug in his bag and brought out a bunch of stretch ropes with hooks and proceeded to secure the boards. Once this was done the two men shook hands and both got into their respective vehicles. I started the Mercedes and waited for Richard to reverse his car and exit the car park before I did the same. We made our way back through Muizenberg and up to the main road where Richard made a left and drove towards Kalk Bay. His companion was nowhere to be seen and must have turned off somewhere. This was of no concern to me. The grey Land Cruiser was three cars in front as we drove and as instructed, I only had eyes for that car and its driver.

"Where to next Richard?" I said to myself. He was obviously enjoying his holiday. As was I. Richard continued down the main road towards Kalk Bay. Just before the village he pulled into a small shopping complex to the left. It comprised of about ten small souvenir shops mainly geared for tourists and a well known take away franchise. I parked my car at the far end of the block and waited. Immediately he got out of the Land Cruiser and walked directly into the take away. He was obviously hungry from the exercise and so was I. Three minutes later he walked out carrying a bright red carton of takeaway food. He then got back into his vehicle, reversed and was off again. I paused wondering what to do. I was ravenous and decided to take a risk by getting a takeaway as well. Being aware of the high crime statistics I folded my laptop up, put it in my bag, locked the car and took the short walk to the takeaway. The place smelled of fried chips and greasy chicken. Perfect. I ordered a burger and a soft drink and headed back to the car to eat. As I sat I opened the laptop again to follow Richard's movements. As expected he was on Walker Road and about to park the car outside The Blueberry. As I ate, I watched the screen and wondered what Richard was actually doing in Cape Town. *Surely no one flies all this way to get drunk in a pub and go surfing?*

"What the fuck are you doing here, Richard?" I said under my breath as I wiped my mouth with a paper serviette. I turned on the radio as I took a slow drive into Kalk Bay and up the hill to Walker Road.

The music lifted my spirits and imparted a holiday feel to the afternoon. My mind drifted as the car made its way up the hill in second gear. The warm sunshine glaring through the windscreen caused me to squint slightly behind my sunglasses. *Stop worrying and enjoy yourself Green. After all you're doing what was asked of you are you not? Would you prefer to be in London right now? I think not. No, you just carry on doing what you're doing and you can finish with a clear conscience.* But what *was* in the bags that were exchanged in London? It had been a tense meeting with some dangerous looking people. There was no doubt Richard was up to something. How *did* he afford the Aston Martin? The flat? *Don't get over involved Green. Stay impartial.* I parked the Mercedes in the same spot I had in the morning and lit a cigarette. The surfboards were still attached to the roof rack of the Land Cruiser.

They glinted in the sun as did a billion specs of granite in the rocks of the mountain to my right. A group of black women walked past me from behind. They wore spotless white dresses with head scarves and were singing in perfect harmony. Being a Sunday, I knew that they had been to church. The rich voices brought back distant memories from my childhood. I turned the radio off and closed my eyes to listen as they passed. When the voices had finally faded into the distance I opened my eyes. I got a shock to see Richard Lewer-Allen standing behind the Land Cruiser. He was busy removing the stretch ropes from the roof rack. After he had finished he grabbed both surfboards and made his way back into the leafy, shaded garden of The Blueberry Guest House. I half expected Richard to come out pretty much immediately but there was no movement from the building except the trees swaying in the breeze.

I sat there for a full hour, smoking the occasional cigarette and watching. Eventually I decided Richard was probably resting after his exertion in the morning. I decided I would go back to my digs to do a bit of the same. The drive took less than three minutes and I was back on the verandah of Binkie's bed and breakfast, unlocking the door to my room. I plugged the laptop in and opened it to the tracking page. I lay down on the bed staring up at the white pressed lead ceilings. There was a knock on the door. I jumped up and opened it. A smiling Binks was clutching two ice cold cans of beer.

"Hope it's not too early for you?" He asked with an uncertain look on his face.

"Not at all. Cheers!" I replied as I pulled the tab off the top of the can.

We sat down on the verandah on the ancient easy chairs and stared out at the view.

"It's a pity you're leaving so soon, why such a rushed trip?" He asked between sips.

"You know, there would be nothing better for me than to stay here for another two weeks, but I'm on a business trip and I don't have any say in it."

"What do you do?" He asked. I paused for a moment thinking about my response.

"I'm an insurance claims investigator. I've come down here to check up on something and I'm off to Zanzibar in Tanzania tomorrow morning. It's a pity I have to go, you've got an amazing place here."

He sensed that it was wrong to ask any more questions about the job.

"How long have you been here? In this house." I asked, changing the subject.

"Oh this house has been in my family for forty or fifty years," he replied.

"Ok, so you decided to make it into a bed and breakfast?" I asked.

"Ya, I used to live in Zimbabwe but I had had enough up there so I came down here. I had nothing to do so I decided on the tourism idea."

"Oh right," I said, "I used to live in Zimbabwe too, a long long time ago"

"Really? I thought I could hear something in your accent. When did you leave?" He asked.

"In 1980," I said.

"Were you in the war?" he said, glancing at me as I sipped my beer.

"I was. I was actually in the Scouts." I said quietly.

There was a long pause as he looked at me, thinking of what to say.

"Phew, that must have been pretty hectic." It was more of a statement than a question.

"Yup." I said, "it was."

He sensed my reluctance to talk about my time in the army and changed the subject immediately.

"So are you going down to The Bell tonight?" he asked.

"I'm not sure buddy, I'm waiting for either a call or an email but I will if I can. Are you going down there?"

"Ya I'm down there most nights."

"Ok, well might see you there, will see what happens later."

We sat for the next two hours chatting about London and Cape Town and Zimbabwe. I made my usual frequent trips to the room to check up on the Land Cruiser. It was good to talk to someone who understood my roots. We had a lot of common ground and I enjoyed his laid back attitude to life. At 5pm after three beers I told him I needed to bath and change. I had a feeling that Richard would be doing something on his last night in Cape Town. Binks suggested we should meet in half an hour on the verandah for a sundowner. I agreed wholeheartedly and headed into the room. I bathed, shaved and dressed for the evening. There was still no movement from the Land Cruiser and as promised Binks was waiting when I made my way out into the early evening. The fishing boats were making their way into the harbour for the night.

I could hear a faint repetitive drumming sound in the distance.

"What's that noise Binks?" I asked as I sat down.

"Ah that's the locals. Every Sunday night they have this impromptu party down at the harbour. They bring drums and horns and make a racket. It's quite a spectacle. If you can get down there it's worth going to have a look at. There's also a great restaurant and club down there. They have an excellent band down there on Sunday nights. I might walk down there later too." He said.

"Oh right," I said thoughtfully. "I might see you later."

We sipped our beers slowly, watching the sun go down for the next hour. There was a cool sea breeze coming off the ocean.

I got up to use the toilet in my room and saw immediately that the Land Cruiser was well on its way down the hill towards the main road. Instantly I folded up the computer, bagged it and headed out.

"Sorry buddy, I've just received that email I was telling you about. I have to go. Hopefully I'll see you later. Thanks for the beers."

I made my way around the wooden verandah to the parked Mercedes. I hated being left behind and I revved the car as I reversed out onto the street. As I turned left to make my way down the hill I saw on the screen to my left that Richard had made a right turn at the main road. He was going somewhere new. The anxiety of possibly losing him came back to me as I drove at speed down the mountain road. At least I had bathed and changed when I had. There was more than the usual traffic on the main road when I got there. Enough to delay my right turn for a good forty seconds. I tapped the steering wheel impatiently craning my neck looking for a gap in the traffic. It was almost totally dark now and the street lights were on. It was then I noticed that the Land Cruiser had stopped to the left of the main road. The map on the screen showed Richard was parking directly outside Kalk Bay harbour. This was no more than half a kilometre down the road. With a sigh of relief I eventually made the turn and followed. Binks had not been wrong when he had described the party atmosphere at the harbour. It took me a few minutes to find a parking in amongst the hundred or so cars.

I was greeted by the raucous sound of the drumming and horns I had heard from above. There were hundreds of coloured people dancing around the concrete fish tables of the harbour. A long concrete pier stretched out for 300m into the ocean. Along the left were the fishing boats moored for the night. Some of them still had crew who were cleaning and polishing. All around were lights and activity. On the other side of the pier the waves were crashing violently into the rocks and concrete wall sending huge plumes of spray into the air. There was a carnival atmosphere. I looked around for the tall figure of Richard. He was nowhere to be seen. To my right was a large building with a sign that read The Harbour Grill. Like the Brass Bell, it was raised and hung over the waves to the right of the pier. It was busy with a queue of people at the door. I had seen the parked Land Cruiser on the way in so I knew Richard was in the area, I just didn't know where. I decided to take a walk down the pier. Every twenty metres, there was a lamp post. As I walked onto the pier, I noticed a group of children clamouring around the wall to my left. They were shouting excitedly and pointing to the swelling sea below. All I could see was a moored fishing vessel so I moved closer to the wall to see what all the fuss was about. It was then I saw the seal in the water below.

It cavorted through the water swimming under the boat and back to look up at the shouting children. It barked for scraps of food as it twisted and dived through the water. All the while the drums and the horns played their tuneless but hypnotic rhythm.

I carried on down the pier. There was no sign of Richard. Further down there was a group of young men with huge fishing rods. They were cast out to the right in the heavy seas. One of them had a fish on at the time and was shouting furiously at the others to reel in their lines so as not to get tangled with his. I felt the urge to stay and watch him bring in his catch but had to force myself to carry on walking past. I had to assume Richard was either in the restaurant or in the club below that Binks had told me about. I made an about turn and walked back through the crowds.

I passed the young fishermen as I walked and saw that they had caught a young shark. It was about two feet long and thrashed about on the floor of the pier. Its black skin shone in the light of the lamp above. Eventually I made it back onto dry land and decided to have a look in the restaurant. I walked up the stairs to the entrance and paused at the door to have a look inside. Through the huge windows I saw the expanse of the place, it was very plush. In the centre was a large table covered in a great mound of ice and sea food of all descriptions. On all sides of that were Roman style loungers and sumptuous chairs for the waiting diners. The floor stretched out over the rocks and waves to my left. My eyes darted from table to table until I saw him.

He was sitting on the far side of the sea food table sipping a glass of wine. As far as I could see he was alone but my vision was obscured by the doorway and the many people walking around. I had to get in. I walked through the door to the reception area where I was met by a young white man in uniform. He was in his twenties. His hair was full of gel and he wore a goatee beard.

"Good evening sir, do you have a booking?" He said politely.

"Actually I don't. I was hoping to get a table for two. Can you manage that?" I asked hopefully.

"I'm very sorry sir, as you can see we are fully booked tonight" he said, motioning with his hand to the bustling scene to his right. "I'm really sorry."

"Ok, no problem, thanks." I said and walked back out onto the landing above the stairs. I paused and glanced back in at Richard who was still seated where he had been before. He was dressed smartly in blue jeans, boots and a summery cotton shirt with long sleeves. He was clean shaven and his wavy hair was gelled back to make it tidier. I paused wondering what to do. The words 'watch him like a hawk' came to my mind and I realised I *had* to get into the establishment. I pulled my wallet out of my bag and withdrew R1000 in cash. I folded it neatly and hid it in my right fist as I walked back into the restaurant. The youngster who I had met at reception saw me coming back and raised his eyebrows with a worried look on his face. I smiled at him and leant forward over the reception table.

"Listen buddy. In my right hand down here is a thousand Rand. I really need to get a table for two. Can you help?"

His eyes looked down and saw my fist below the table. Then they came up and glanced around the room briefly. I felt his hand touch mine and I handed over the cash. It disappeared immediately into his pocket and he stood up.

"I'm sure I can find something for you, sir" he said.

He pointed towards the area to the centre of the room with the mound of ice and seafood.

"Please make your way to the lounge area, have a drink and wait to be seated. I can have you a table within half an hour?"

"That will be great. Thank you very much," I said.

"Thank *you* sir," came his grateful reply.

It was the equivalent of a hundred US Dollars and probably what he earned in a week. I walked slowly through the crowds and tables towards the massive centre piece knowing that Richard was sitting opposite. I was happy that I had been able to get in and I was feeling hungry as well. I would kill two birds with one stone tonight. I chose a table with two small chairs which was positioned about seven metres from where Richard was sitting. There were four parties of waiting diners between us. They leant towards each other, drank wine, and talked. It seemed Richard and myself were the only people who were sitting alone. A waiter came and I ordered a beer. It arrived within a minute and I sat back, relaxed, and did my job. Richard was a picture of relaxed cool.

He was drinking a large scotch as usual. Between sips he tapped his fingers lightly on the ice filled glass which was sweating on its coaster. He had an expectant, almost excited look on his face. For the first time I noticed what looked like a Rolex Oyster Perpetual watch on his thin wrist. He glanced at it often. My mind went back to the restaurant in Notting Hill in London where I had seen the dubious exchange of bags. This was different. He looked relaxed. After a few minutes a waiter walked up to him carrying a cloth covered tray. He glanced once more at the door then got up and followed the waiter to a table at the far side of the room that overlooked the ocean.

I shifted my chair to the right so I could keep watching him. He was in conversation with the waiter. As he spoke, his right hand dropped some cash into the young waiter's top pocket. *Birds of a feather,* I thought as I took a sip of the beer. Richard sat. The waiter appeared carrying a silver ice bucket with what looked a bottle of champagne. He placed it at the side of the table and surrounded the neck of the bottle with a white cloth. *It's got to be a date,* I thought. *There was none of this pomp and ceremony last night. No flash new clothes. No Rolex watch. No tidy hair or champagne. Last night was a piss-up with a friend. Tonight is different for sure.* Thirty seconds later I saw Richard move faster than I had ever seen him move. He almost jumped out of his seat and immediately started walking towards me beaming from ear to ear. Thankfully he chose a path through the tables to my left as the quickest route to the front or he might have looked me straight in the face. I put my beer down on the table and slowly turned around to see what all the fuss was about. It was then that I saw her.

She was, without a doubt, one of the most beautiful woman I had ever seen. It was as if all time instantly stopped and the hum of the restaurant fell silent at the sight of her. It was as if she walked in slow motion. She was at least six foot tall. Outrageously slim with long cascading brown hair that was tossed over to one side. Her face was a picture of classic European beauty. Radiant and glowing with thick, dark, perfectly sculpted eyebrows. Her face was impossibly symmetrical and her skin was the colour of milky coffee. Her lips were a pale pink colour. Her large, smiling eyes were a dark and dreamy hazel surrounded by perfect white. Above her long eyelashes was a delicate but noticeable amount of gold make up which more than added to her almost impossible beauty. Around her long slender neck she wore a diamond necklace. Again, it was understated but obvious. The tendons in her neck showed slightly as did her collar bones above her top which hung low on ultra thin strips of shiny silver material. Her skin was tanned to a golden brown in stark contrast to the loose silvery top under which the small youthful breasts bulged. I put her age at about twenty seven.

She wore tight fitting designer jeans on her long legs and around her waist was a thick, loose fitting leather belt with tassels on the front. On her feet she wore elegant high heels, again in silver. She tilted her head to the left, exposing a diamond earring as she walked, and smiled with genuine affection at the approaching figure of Richard. I was so absorbed I could only see him out of the corner of my eye. Her teeth were pure white. I forced myself to look away briefly and glanced around the surrounding tables. Her entrance had the same effect on the nearby diners as it had on me. Both men and women were stopped in their tracks by her presence. There was a table with two couples sitting close by. I saw the woman sitting furthest from me kick her husband or boyfriend sharply in the shins under the table as punishment for his window shopping. The whole surreal episode ended as Richard and the woman finally reached each other. With a huge smile on her face she paused and held out her right hand. Around her wrist was a diamond bracelet. Richard held her hand lightly, leant forward and kissed her once on each cheek. He then motioned towards the table he had been sitting at and they both made their way to sit down. I looked around again at the people at the tables who had witnessed her entrance. Clearly she had caused a stir. The men acknowledged her arrival to each other as they ate with raised eyebrows while the women did the same with scowls. It had been quite an entrance. Richard and the woman made their way back to the table and sat down. At the same time I was approached by a waiter who asked me if I was ready to be seated. I asked him where the table was and he pointed towards the centre of the room. I gauged that I would have a view of Richard's table from there so accepted and walked with the waiter to my seat. I explained the person I was waiting for hadn't arrived and ordered a beer in the mean time. As I waited for my order I positioned my chair so I could watch Richard and the woman as I sat.

They smiled as they spoke. Although they were deep in conversation I sensed an excited nervousness about them. It was as if he was trying to impress her with his wit or his stories. There was no physical contact between the two of them as they spoke. This gave me the impression that they were not yet lovers. Richard called a waiter who promptly opened the bottle of champagne he had cooling and they both toasted each other. The waiter handed them menus and they began making their selections for dinner. The waiter arrived with my beer. I explained that my dinner date was late and that I would like to see a menu in the mean time. He pulled one out from under his arm and I began browsing it. The selection was sumptuous. I could see why this particular establishment was so popular. I decided on a starter of melon wrapped in parma ham followed by a main course of fillet steak with a blue cheese sauce. The waiter appeared concerned that my dinner date hadn't arrived when I made the order.

I told him not to worry and go ahead and take it. As I waited, I continued watching Richard and his lady friend. He had certainly made an effort with the table, the champagne, and his appearance. But it had been a worthwhile effort, and I fully understood why. She was dazzling. There was no other word to describe her. Eventually my starter arrived and the waiter enquired if I would be wanting any wine with my meal. I told him the beer was fine for now and, feeling ravenous, got stuck in. I watched Richard's table out of the corner of my eye as I ate. Presently their starters arrived as well. She had an incredible ladylike daintiness in the way she ate. It was as if she hardly held any food at all on her fork. *With a figure like that I'm surprised she eats anything,* I thought as I finished the last of my starter. I sipped my beer as I waited for my main course to arrive and as I watched, I decided that if there was any reason to travel half way around the world for two nights, she was it. I fully understood why he would do such a thing. I would have done the same. Their main course arrived at the same as mine. They had both ordered the lobster. My steak was absolutely huge and took up most of the plate. It was cooked to perfection with rivers of the pungent blue cheese running off it. I made an effort not to be seen to be staring at the couple and instead watched them out of the corner of my eye. She was still getting admiring glances from men in the room. I wondered if she was a celebrity or perhaps a famous fashion model. She certainly had all the attributes.

The evening went on like this for a good two hours. The two of them chatted and laughed. They drank white wine with their meal. She held the stem of the huge glass delicately as she drank. Taking tiny sips. I noticed Richard was getting through at least two glasses to her one and on more than one occasion she raised her hand with a smile to refuse a top up. *Shame on you Richard,* I thought, *trying to ply a nice girl like that with drink. Don't blame you though.* I asked for my bill from the waiter as they finished their desserts. I needed to get it out of the way and pay in case they left suddenly. I paid cash and left a generous tip for the waiter. By now the two of them had removed the white serviettes from their laps. Richard was leaning slightly forward on his elbows as he spoke to her, as if in an effort to get closer to her. She was unmoved and kept her perfectly straight posture as she laughed at his jokes. Eventually Richard motioned to the waiter to bring his bill. It arrived as mine had in a folder and dutifully he paid using a credit card. After the waiter had left I noticed Richard making what appeared to be some dance moves with his arms as he sat. She laughed gaily at this and then took a look at her watch. She smiled and said, "ok!".

Richard, looking pleased, got up, walked around the table and pulled her chair out for her. Again, a perfect gentleman.

The two of them walked out towards the door with her in front once again getting admiring glances from the patrons. It was my cue and I after a few seconds I did the same. I allowed them both to exit the door of the restaurant and then, pulling my car keys from my pocket I followed them out and down the stairs. Instead of heading towards the car park, I saw the couple make a sharp left and walk down another set of stairs below the building we had been in.

I remembered Binks mentioning the club that was situated below the restaurant and the fact that he may well be there that evening. Sure enough the couple carried on down a corridor and towards a reception area. There was a large man at the door to the club. He looked like a bouncer. Not your typical London club goon in a tuxedo but a more relaxed, long haired and cool, Capetonian bouncer in shorts and tee shirt. Richard and the woman made their way towards the big man and stopped briefly to have a word. There was still no physical contact between them at all. The bouncer gave a surprised smile to them both and motioned them to enter the club which from the outside looked as if it was pumping with people. Once Richard and his date had entered and gone out of sight I made my way to the door.

"Hi good evening," said the big man.

"How are you doing?" I said. "What's going on tonight?"

"Tonight we've got Leo and the Juggernauts, they're a mixture of Congolese dance and lounge music." He said with a smile.

"Sounds interesting," I said raising my eyebrows, "any cover charge?"

"No cover charge, carry on, enjoy!" he said, ushering me in.

"Thanks very much," I said, and walked in slowly.

The place was packed with people of all kinds. There were dread-locked beach bums in saggy clothes mixing with sharp dressed sophisticates sipping wine. There appeared to be a mix of tourists and locals. A large percentage of which were dancing to the band which was playing a repetitive but appealing song with a pounding beat and steel drums. I stood for a moment to take it all in. There were a series of darkened rooms at sea level. To my right I saw there was a veranda area with a low retaining wall which stretched out in the open air towards the rocks and the crashing waves. There were comfortable looking chairs and couches all along it with groups of people sitting drinking and talking.

On the inside where I was standing there was a long bar to my left with flustered looking staff trying to keep up with the demands of the thirsty punters. In front of me was a series of levels with chairs and tables gradually going down to the dance floor which was heaving. On the far right of the interior was the band. They were all seated and busy thrashing out the strangely addictive tune on their respective instruments. I had walked into a hell of a party.

Suddenly I remembered what I was there for and quickly looked around for Richard and the woman. They were at the far end of the bar attempting to order drinks. Richard's tall frame was leaning over the bar, a banknote in his hand trying desperately to get the attention of the staff while his companion stood with her back to him, smiling and nodding her head to the rhythm of the music as she watched the band and the dance floor. I made my way slowly through the crowd to the bar. There were at least sixty people between us trying to get drinks so there was little risk of being singled out. I arrived at the bar and stood between a short sun-tanned girl with untidy hair and a smartly dressed man who was clearly drunk and frustrated. The girl to my right swung her hips constantly to the pounding music. The sound system must have been of good quality because although the band was loud, I could still hear the calls of the thirsty punters as they vied for the attention of the bar staff. I looked at the man to my left. He had a pinched face which reminded me of a rat. I put his age at about forty. He was suntanned and had long straight blonde hair.

"You been here a while?" I asked, trying to strike up a conversation.

"This place is fucked! This is a fucking joke! Been here for ten fucking minutes!" He shouted with speckles of saliva flying from his mouth, "and I'm before you!" He shouted raising his eyebrows at me.

"Hey, no problem, no problem at all," I said, "I'll help you get their attention".

Wish I had never spoken to the prick, I thought as I drew a hundred rand note from my wallet and waited. Out of the corner of my eye I saw that Richard had succeeded with his order and was taking delivery of a bottle of white wine and two glasses. I stood my ground and waited. It would be easy enough to spot him wherever he sat in the club.

After two or three minutes the patience of the man to my left ran out and he started shouting again.

"Can you hear me?" He screamed, "Can you fucking hear me? I've been standing here for fifteen fucking minutes with no service! What the fuck is going on?!"

It was becoming uncomfortable and he was starting to make a spectacle of himself. There were looks coming from the people surrounding us. This was the last thing I needed. Some asshole causing a fight or a disturbance and the attention of the whole club focusing on me by accident. Just then he flicked an empty glass off the bar and onto the floor behind, it landed and smashed.

"Will you wake up and serve me now?!" He shouted slamming a clenched fist onto the wooden surface. He had now got the attention of the bar staff who looked at him with tired expressions on their faces. I decided to attend to him myself. I smiled and nodded at the bar staff. I quickly put my left arm around his neck as if we were old friends. I brought him close to me and squeezed hard. His fingers came up to try to free himself but it was too late and by then I was causing him some serious discomfort. Still smiling, I held my head close to his and heard him give a quiet groan.

"Nnnnggg you're hurting me." His face was now going red and his bloodshot eyes bulged a little.

"I haven't even started hurting you buddy. If you don't walk out of here quietly, right now, I'm going to take you outside and put you to sleep for a while. Do you understand?" I whispered in his ear.

"Nnnnggg, yes, sorry, I'll go, I'm sorry," he grunted.

"Don't make me come after you because you will regret it." I said.

"No, I'm going, I'm sorry."

I let go of him and watched him as he made a hasty, staggering retreat up the levels and out towards the door. A tall young barman with slicked back hair came up to me immediately from behind the bar.

"Thanks for that. My staff were refusing to serve him. What can I get you? Oh, and this one's on the house."

"I'll just have a beer please, Castle is good," I said glancing around.

The situation had been normalised and the beautiful people of Cape Town had got back to the serious business of partying. I poured my beer and turned around resting my elbows on the bar. I could see through the window behind the band that Richard and the woman had made their way outside to the open air section of the club. They were seated on a couch at the far side nearest the ocean with their backs to the low retaining wall. The woman was obviously enjoying the music and was clapping her hands to the beat as Richard poured the wine. In an effort to exclude themselves from the crowd in the club Richard had chosen an ideal spot for me to keep an eye on them. I made my way out of the nearest exit to the outside area and found a small table with a few armchairs around it and sat down. They were about twenty metres from me now and there were various groups of party goers between us. Some sitting on the wall, others on the chairs and tables. It was a festive and busy scene and I had some great cover. I sat back, relaxed, and took in the atmosphere.

There was a cool, salty breeze coming in off the sea to my right and the hypnotic rhythm of the song pounded away as the crowd swayed and bobbed to its tune. I realised I was thoroughly enjoying myself. The incident with the man inside earlier was forgotten now and all was well in my world. The prospect of flying off to another exotic location in the morning was all fine by me. I glanced again to my right to have a look at how Richard's evening was going. They were both still sat on the sofa at the far end. Although there was still no physical contact between the two I noticed that Richard was leaning ever closer towards her. She was certainly playing it very cool, maintaining her posture and her smile all along as she clapped and moved about to the music. Eventually the song ended and another one began. Richard and the girl stood up and, leaving their glasses and bag on the table, made their way to the dance floor. It was clear that wherever this woman went she caused a bit of a stir. As they started dancing it seemed that people made a bit of extra room for her just so they could admire her. She was a great dancer.

Richard on the other hand was a bit too tall and gangly to move with her sort of style and resorted to outlandish jerky movements which seemed to delight her and she giggled continuously. I felt like I knew him now and I was almost proud of his efforts to win her over. At that moment I heard a voice behind me to my left.

"Jason, Jason, how are you doing man?" I turned to see a scruffy man in shorts and a tee shirt making his way over the rocks and sand dunes towards me. It was Binks from the guest house.

"Glad you could make it!" He said as he swung himself over the low wall,

"Can I join you?" He asked with a smile.

"Sure you can. How are you doing?" I replied.

"Ya great. What do you think of the band?" He asked.

"It's actually quite good."

And so the evening continued like this. Richard and the woman finished dancing and returned to their seats. Binks and myself made small talk and drank beer while the music continued and the people danced. At 11pm I noticed the woman with Richard begin looking at her watch as if to indicate that it was time to go. Binks was talking away about life in Cape Town and I realised that I would have to make my excuses and leave at any time. Then I saw her reach into her bag and pull out a cell phone. She answered, spoke briefly with a serious look on her face and hung up. She gave a resigned smile to Richard and I knew that they were both getting ready to leave. As they stood I reached for my phone and pretended to Binks that I had received a message and would have to leave. He looked slightly disappointed but understood as I grabbed my bag and prepared to leave. I allowed the couple to walk through the main area of the club and towards the door before I followed.

The club was fuller now and I just caught them walking out past the bouncer as I followed. I nodded to the bouncer as I walked out of the club and cautiously made my way into the wide corridor that led to the parking area. As I reached the open air, I looked around for the two of them. They were standing to my left in amongst the cars and for the first time I noticed some physical contact between the two. Richard was holding her left hand and they seemed to be deep in conversation. I couldn't hear a word they were saying so instead I lent against the wall and lit a cigarette. There were people still coming out of the restaurant above me and a few making their way out of the club so it wasn't as if I stood out. I was just another face in the crowd. It looked like he was desperately trying to convince her to stay with him. For the first time I saw what looked like sadness in her expression. It was obvious that she had a prior appointment, some arrangement to be somewhere else, a deadline of some sort. Suddenly and without warning she lunged forward, and wrapping her long arms around Richard's neck, they kissed. *Well done old boy*, I thought to myself as if he was a friend of mine. *Your perseverance has paid off.* Then I noticed a black Hummer pull into the car park. It shone in the pale light of the overhead lamps. She immediately pulled away from Richard and turned to look at it. She held his arm briefly and said something to him.

I wished I could have heard what she said but there was no chance. She quickly walked away leaving Richard awkwardly standing where she left him. She walked around to the driver's side of the Hummer and was briefly out of sight as she spoke to the driver. Richard held his ground and continued to stare at the vehicle. *She's gone,* I thought, *she's got in the car and she's out of here.* To my surprise the car drove out of my line of vision and there she was. She stood with a nervous but excited look on her face which burst into a smile which lit up the world. Richard walked towards her and they embraced each other again and kissed. They both started walking hand in hand towards Richard's Land Cruiser. It was time to move. I wondered where they would be going, another club perhaps? Maybe to Richard's digs? He had certainly won her over and it looked like that may well be on the cards. They both got into the big car and pulled out of the car park. I made my way to the Mercedes and immediately opened my laptop. The tracking page flashed into life and I saw the blue light of the Land Cruiser making its way up the familiar hill towards The Blueberry Guest House.

"Well *done* old boy," I said under my breath. I gave them a few minutes to get back and park the car before I made my move. As expected he had made a bee line for his digs and wasn't stopping for anything. I watched as the car parked in its usual spot before I started my car and drove out onto the main road. I was aware of the fact that I had had a few too many beers to be driving but consoled myself that it was a short drive up a very quiet street to Walker Road and The Blueberry.

When I finally got up there everything was as I expected it to be. All quiet. I decided I would give it fifteen minutes or so before heading back to Binkie's. There was no point in hanging around as I was sure they would be busy for a while. I lit a cigarette and opened the sun roof. I lay my head back on the headrest and gazed up at the canopy of stars above. It was a cool and beautiful night and I had a warm, contented feeling as I smoked. I finished my cigarette and decided to call it a night. It would be a busy day to come and I needed to be up and on the ball long before my good friend Richard. I made the short drive back to Binkie's, locked the car and went to my room. I plugged the laptop in and set it up where I could see it from the bed. As expected, there was no movement from the Land Cruiser and as I lay there with my hands behind my head my thought went to the gorgeous woman. She had to be some sort of celebrity or a model. I lay there for the next hour and a half preparing myself mentally for the next morning. I decided it would be best to get up early, pay Binks, and stop off briefly at The Blueberry before heading back to the airport. It would be a long day. I looked at my flight schedule and saw that it would be a four and a half hour flight to Dar Es Salaam. I still had to make a plan to get across to the island of Zanzibar.

The idea of a ferry didn't really appeal to me. It would waste precious hours and I would be late if I had to use it. I was just drifting off to sleep when I saw the blue light on the tracking page of the laptop start moving. I jumped up suddenly, wondering what to do. I gave it a few minutes as I watched it move slowly down the hill towards the main street. It appeared to park at exactly the same spot it had outside the restaurant earlier that evening. Feeling tired and slightly annoyed, I got up, grabbed the computer and headed out to the car. *Where the fuck are you going now Richard?* I thought to myself.

As I reached the T junction that led down the hill to the main road I saw that the Land Cruiser was moving again. It was heading back up the hill towards me. I made a split second decision and headed back up towards

The Blueberry. I only had a few minutes to park if indeed he was making his way back there. Fifty metres before The Blueberry, I pulled over to the right and lay flat over the passenger seat with the laptop in the floor well. I could hear my breathing as the blue light slowly moved closer and closer to me on the screen. Right on cue I heard the low hum of its engine and crackle of its tyres on the road as it passed me slowly. Then the engine stopped and I heard one door slam shut. I sat up slowly and peered over the dashboard. Under the street light I saw the figure of Richard, still wearing the same clothes, but with his shirt untucked and wearing slops. As he activated the alarm on the vehicle and made his way back into his guest house, he was alone. He had obviously dropped the woman at the car park of the club so she could get her lift back to wherever she was going. Albeit a bit late.

"Bed time now Richard," I said under my breath, "you've got a long day tomorrow." He disappeared through the gate and into the leafy garden and all was quiet again. It was late and I was tired. I drove back to Binkie's and fell asleep within minutes. I awoke at 3am to the alarm I had set on my phone. I was tired and battled to get motivated as I ran a bath. My flight to Dar Es Salaam was booked to leave at 6am so I only had an hour to get to the airport. I bathed and changed quickly while drinking a cup of instant coffee. I very much doubted that I would meet Binks so early in the morning, so I left an envelope with the money for my stay and a short note. Richard's flight was booked to leave at 7.30am and was going directly to Zanzibar.

There would be no chance of seeing him until I arrived on the east coast of the island. It wasn't an ideal situation but there had been no option at the travel agent in London, so it would have to do. I made my way out quietly and took one last look out onto the silent moonlit vista of Kalk

Bay. The Mercedes started immediately and I drove quietly out onto the street.

I decided to drive once more past The Blueberry Guest House to see if I could recover the tracking device from the car. As I drove up Walker Road towards the Land Cruiser, it was all quiet and I retrieved the tracking device with no problems. I entered the words Cape Town International Airport' into the sat-nav and waited for the instructions on where to go. It was an easy route and I could have driven it without the sat-nav but time was short and I didn't need any trouble or delays. The roads were quiet and I was able to drive a lot faster than I had during the day. The sight of the mammoth Table Mountain looked eerily overbearing in the moonlight to my left. The drive took twenty minutes and I drove in and followed the car rental signs for the drop off point. There was a sleepy looking security guard at the gate who took my details and the registration of the vehicle. I parked, grabbed my bags and started the walk to the main terminal. The airport was empty compared to when I had arrived. There were cleaners everywhere with mops and dustbins preparing for the day's onslaught of travellers. I dropped the keys, completed the formalities at the car hire desk and proceeded straight to check in. Immediately I saw a message on the screen above that my flight had been delayed until 7am. There were two people in the queue in front of me and I quietly cursed the delay under my breath. After check in I made my way to the information desk to enquire about Richard's flight. I was greeted by a fat coloured lady who wore too much make up.

"Good morning," I said, "I know the 6am flight to Dar Es Salaam has been delayed for an hour, is the 7.30am flight to Zanzibar also delayed?"

"Just one moment please sir," she replied

"No sir, that flight is scheduled to leave on time at 7.30am."

"Thanks very much." I walked off to find a cup of coffee and a newspaper. I found an open cafe near the departure gates and bought three newspapers and a pot of coffee. As I sat down to read I realised that Richard would be due to walk in at roughly 5.30am to make his flight. I would only be boarding my flight at around 6am now so there was a very good chance that I would catch him. That's if he was even going to make his flight. The memory of the woman from the previous evening was still fresh in my mind and if I was him I would rather stay in Cape Town for a while. She would certainly be worth extending for, but I was resigned to my bookings and would go through with it either way.

One of the newspapers I read had a pull-out feature of a fashion event that had been held at the Waterfront in Cape Town over the weekend.

There were various pictures of models walking down the catwalk in outlandish costumes. I looked with interest at the pictures to see if could see the girl Richard had been with. She wasn't there. I was certain of that. Hers was a face I would not forget for a while. I passed the time reading and drinking coffee, whilst keeping an eye on the sliding doors of the entrance to the terminal. The pale glow of daylight began to creep through the massive windows above. There were more and more people arriving now so I decided to step outside for a last cigarette before heading into the departure lounge. I folded the newspapers under my arm and made my way to the front doors. I was aware that Richard might walk in at any time. I noticed a few fellow smokers to my left so I joined them and lit up. The daylight was growing and I was halfway through my smoke when I noticed the unmistakeable figure of Richard Lewer-Allen pushing a trolley towards the terminal. He was sixty metres away from where I stood but I knew it was him. It was time for me to go. I crushed out the cigarette and walked swiftly back into the terminal. Once inside I made a bee line for the departure gate but at the entrance my curiosity got the better of me and I stopped to watch him come in.

Looking slightly dishevelled, he made his way to the check in desks. This was my cue and I proceeded through the departure gates to passport control. I knew exactly where he was going and there was no reason to get any closer than I had been or was right then. It was a quick formality to get the exit stamp in my passport and I walked through to the departure gates and duty free area. There was a screen with flight and gate details. My flight was leaving from gate number 4 and Richard's was from gate number ten. I decided to get to my gate as soon as possible and wait out the remaining time until my flight. At the duty free shop I noticed a rack of travel books. On the shelf was the Lonely Planet guide to Tanzania and Zanzibar. I decided I would buy it as it would make interesting reading on the flight and might come in handy in Zanzibar. I quickly purchased the book and made my way to my gate. I spent the next hour reading my newspapers as my fellow passengers filed into the lounge and took their seats. A voice came over the speaker and announced that the first class passengers were now required to board. I joined a small group of passengers at the gate and we made our way outside to a waiting bus. It was a short ride to the waiting aircraft and on arrival we made our way up the stairway and in.

The first class cabin was spacious and bright. My window seat was at the front of the aircraft on the right. I packed my bag into the overhead storage and sat down with my newspapers and travel book. There was only one seat next to mine and this was taken by a huge black man dressed in a long white gown and sandals. On his giant bald head he wore a matching skull cap.

"Good morning," he said in a deep voice as he sat down in a heap. A man of few words. That suited me fine. The rear of the plane was a hive of activity as the other passengers boarded. We were given orange juice as we waited and I sipped it as I watched the ground crew outside preparing the plane for take-off. I was tired and hungry. It would be a four and a half hour flight to Dar Es Salaam. I decided I would catch up on some well-deserved sleep after breakfast. Eventually the pilot's voice came over the intercom and announced that we were about to take off for Dar Es Salaam. The engines rumbled and the plane started taxiing towards the runway. Ten minutes later the plane stopped and the pilot's voice instructed the flight crew to take their seats for take-off. The engines roared into life behind me as the acceleration pushed me into the seat. We were off. I wondered what was in store for Richard and myself as I gazed out over the vineyards of Stellenbosch below. It had been an interesting and enjoyable job so far but I still hadn't come up with any answers. This bothered me a little but I decided to put it out of my mind and just get on with it.

Fifteen minutes later a fine English breakfast was served, followed by coffee. Feeling warm and tired I read through the guide book to Zanzibar for a while before drifting off to sleep with the sun shining through the window onto my clothes. I woke up briefly at some stage during the flight to close the sun visor on the window. The brightness had woken me but only for a few seconds. Once closed I was immediately back in a deep, dreamless sleep. I was awoken by the pilot's voice announcing that we were beginning our descent to Dar Es Salaam International. I rubbed my eyes, lifted the sun visor and took a look out the window. Beneath me to the right was the Indian Ocean in full blue splendour. It stretched out to the horizon in a cloudless sky. I could just see the beginnings of a sprawling city ahead of us in the distance. I straightened my seat and buckled my seat belt in preparation to land. The jet flew in fast over the city and descended rapidly towards the airport. From what I could see Dar Es Salaam resembled a huge dusty shanty town. But then airports were usually situated in poorer areas of cities. The plane cruised in and made a smooth landing on the runway. As we slowed down and taxied towards the airport, the pilot thanked us for choosing the airline and reminded everyone to stay seated until the airplane had come to a halt. I gazed out at the sun-baked concrete of the airport and immediately started to worry about how I would get across to the island of Zanzibar.

Eventually the plane came to a halt and the doors were opened. The man who had been sitting next to me took his time getting his hand luggage from the overhead storage. I was anxious to get out.

The sleep on the flight had done the trick and I was feeling refreshed and wide awake. After what seemed an eternity we were given the go ahead to make our way down the stairway and on to the concrete. I had to put my sunglasses on as I got to the door. It was mid day in Dar Es Salaam and it was blindingly bright outside. Once I got down to the concrete I became aware of the searing heat. It was a marked change from the cool Cape Town climate. I was now near the Equator. There was no bus to take passengers to the terminal. Instead we were told to take the hundred metre walk to the airport building. The thought of a cigarette and the mild excitement of being somewhere new quickened my step and I was the first to arrive. The interior of the building and the immigration section was a typically chaotic African scene. There were no signs telling passengers where to get forms or where to go. Although it was slightly cooler in the building there was no air conditioning and it was humid. There were black and white vinyl tiles on the floor, some of which were missing. I saw a bored looking young man in uniform sitting in a booth behind a grimy perspex window. I stepped over a few rope barriers to get to him.

"Hello, how are you?" I said with a hopeful smile.

"Fine thank you, passport please," he replied.

The other passengers were filing into the hall as he flicked through my passport.

"Tanzania visa for British passport is US$50, you pay here," he said.

Quickly I drew out the cash in a single note and paid.

"Business or pleasure, and how long are going to stay in Tanzania?" He asked.

"Pleasure. I am going to Zanzibar. Two weeks at the most."

He placed a sticker in my passport and stamped it.

"Go to that counter and get your entry stamp," he said, pointing to his right.

"Thanks very much," I said and quickly moved off. An equally bored looking lady stamped my passport without a word and I made my way to the baggage claim. As I waited, I wondered what would happen if my bags were searched. What would the authorities say about the tracking devices and other bits of kit I had brought along?

I decided if it happened I would say I had bought them as samples in South Africa and was taking them back to the UK. Eventually my larger bag appeared on the rickety carousel and I made the tense walk through customs. I had no reason to worry as I walked straight through into the arrivals hall without a second glance. It was a huge cool space with open vents above to allow the fresh air to flow. All around were billboards advertising safaris, trips to Kilimanjaro and other resorts for tourists. Feeling relieved and excited I made for the exit and stepped out into the shaded pick-up area outside. I put my bags down and gratefully lit a smoke. It felt good and gave me a sense of well-being. A short black man in a white shirt and tie approached me.

"Jambo!" he said, "welcome to Tanzania!"

"Thank you," I replied suspiciously.

"Do you see that office over there sir?" he said pointing to a large square glass cubicle near a taxi rank. "That is my office. I am a travel agent. I can help you to get to where you want to go. Anywhere in Tanzania."

I figured I had nothing to lose. The place did indeed look like an official office. It was pasted with flight times and various special offers.

"I need to get to Zanzibar," I said taking another draw on the cigarette.

"Zanzibar?" He asked with wide eyes. Then he looked at his watch and dug in his pocket for his cell phone. He motioned me to follow him to the office as he spoke to the person on the phone. When we arrived at the office he made his way inside and came to speak to me from the counter.

"I have a flight sir, leaving in half an hour from the domestic terminal. The carrier is Tropical Air. It is a light aircraft which takes only ten people at a time. Here is the pamphlet for Tropical Air," he said passing me a glossy print showing the aircraft and logo etc.

"The next available flight is at 4pm, sir. I have spoken to my people from Tropical Air and there is a seat available for you in half an hour from now."

It seemed to be kosher. The pamphlet was real. There was a poster on the glass wall with flight times and prices for the small airline. The price for a one way flight across to Zanzibar was US$55.

"Are you sure you can get me on this flight in half an hour?" I asked, feigning suspicion.

"Yes! Certainly I can. Maybe you will give me something for arranging it for you, sir?" He said with a twinkle in his eye.

"But you are already getting your commission from the airline!" I said, enjoying the African banter.

"Ah ok, no problem sir. Can I write your ticket?"

"Yes go ahead please." He busied himself with the ticket as I drew the cash from my wallet. I asked him if he would accompany me to the domestic terminal to which he agreed. Once everything was done he stepped out of his cubicle and carried my larger bag to a waiting cab. A few words in Swahili were exchanged and we got in. The heat was pounding through the roof of the car as we drove off.

"How far is the domestic terminal from here?" I asked. "It's very close sir. Two minutes."

"And how much will you charge me to drive there?" I asked the driver.

"Only $10 sir!" He replied helpfully.

I smiled and shook my head as we drove off. $10 was an outrageous fee for such a short trip. Africa. It was great to be back. We arrived in two minutes as promised. The domestic terminal was even more ramshackle than the international one - a small building with dark corridors and baggage trolleys stacked high. We were greeted by an official from Tropical Air. She seemed flustered and anxious to check my ticket and get my large bag onto a trolley. I worried about leaving my bag unattended in the dark corridor but she assured me that it was safe and would always be in my view from the front room. I made my way to the front room and sure enough I had a clear line of vision back to the luggage trolley.

It was stuffy and hot inside, and the sun blazed through the bay windows that looked out onto the concrete and the waiting plane. It was a twin engine prop, silver in colour with overhead wings that would give a good view of the trip to the island. A small group of people waited with me. Some dabbed at their foreheads with handkerchiefs to wipe away beads of sweat.

After a few minutes we were all ushered through the doors and out onto the concrete to make our way to the plane. Once again I was acutely aware of the blistering heat as I walked. The large baggage trolley was also on its way out and I noticed my bag on top of it. A few ground crew busied themselves loading the pile of bags into the small storage space to the rear of the aircraft whilst we squeezed in through a small swinging door to the cramped seating area. My seat was directly under the wing next to a large window. I asked a lady who was sat to my left how long the flight was and was told it was only fifteen to twenty minutes. Although I was sweaty, cramped, and uncomfortable I was looking forward to the short hop to the island.

Eventually, the baggage door was closed and a Ray Ban-wearing pilot in his thirties arrived and started his pre-flight checks. Once done he turned around and briefed us all on safety precautions and emergency procedures. His was a strong Afrikaans accent spoken in a very laid back voice. I guessed the heat of this part of the world made everyone appear a bit dreamy and slow. After a few more checks he fired the noisy engines and we began to move towards the runway. Once in position he radioed the tower for clearance to take off and we began slowly trundling down the runway. The plane vibrated heavily and the noise of the engines was deafening. It seemed to me that the small plane was badly overloaded and would never get off the ground, but eventually it did and slowly we made our way skywards. Below me were thousands of tiny shanty houses. Their tin roofs baked brown and rust coloured by the scorching sun. Soon we flew over some more affluent areas with avenues and trees until eventually we were over what looked like the main city of Dar Es Salaam with its large buildings and public squares. We continued north east for a good five minutes and the air in the small plane became cooler and cooler till eventually we were over the sea. I shook my head in awe at the colours of the water. The white beaches gave way to pale blue completely transparent sea, which in turn gave way to the dark shapes of coral reefs.

After this the water turned a deep indigo. I could clearly see the coral and rock formations on the sea bed and the odd Arab dhow sailing vessel making its way across the waveless ocean. I sat there totally mesmerised and stared out for the next ten minutes. My mind was in another place. I could no longer hear the sound of the engines or feel the turbulence of the flight. Perhaps the hectic events of the past days had caught up with me but I didn't care a bit. I felt alive for the first time in ages. I was full of energy. Full of the enthusiasm and vitality that comes with travelling to new and exotic places. I felt a spirit of adventure and discovery. A feeling one gets when travelling into the unknown with no idea what to expect.

I was suddenly snapped out of my daydream by the sound of the engines changing as the pilot dropped the revs and began his descent.

In front of me in the distance was the island. It was lush, green and jungle-like from the air and was surrounded by a perfect white beach. I had been lucky getting the flight so fast after my arrival in Dar Es Salaam. The thought of the later 4pm flight would have meant a long, hot, and boring wait at the airport. Worse still would have been a three hour ferry ride from the docks. I was early and would have time to have a look around and get my bearings. It was all good. The plane made its noisy descent over the impossibly blue water till we were over the island and approaching the airport. I could see palm trees and thick green jungle everywhere with the odd tin roof house squeezed in between. I couldn't see out of the front window of the plane as the nose was raised but a few tense seconds later we made an extremely bumpy landing. The wings on either side of the aircraft bounced up and down like diving boards. We sped along with the engines roaring until eventually we slowed and began taxiing towards some buildings ahead of us to our left. A minute later we had stopped moving and the pilot cut the fuel. The engine to my right sputtered and the propeller stopped with a jerk. The Afrikaans pilot in front removed his bulky headset and hung it on the controls. Still wearing his dark aviator sunglasses, he turned around slowly in his seat to face us. He was slightly unshaven and had obviously styled his black hair with gel. He was a mixture of comical and cool. After a brief pause he spoke with the same lazy, laid back voice as before.

"Welcome to Zanzibar," he said.

CHAPTER NINE

– ZANZIBAR

T he heat had returned before the passengers had time to disembark. When I finally got out and stepped onto the concrete runway I glanced around at my surroundings. Apart from a few light aircraft, the airport was empty. The main building was squat and in need of a coat of paint. The only modern feature was the large darkened window to the front which served as a viewing area for the departure hall. All around the perimeter was lush tropical bush with tall palm trees popping up here and there. We made our way to the arrivals door and entered. It was dark inside and it took a few seconds for my eyes to become accustomed to it. To call the room basic was an understatement. Twenty metres ahead of me was the exit of the building and I could see the taxi and minibus drivers waiting like vultures outside. There were no immigration procedures and only a few official-looking staff sitting around joking with each other. After a while, a large door to my left opened and a hand cart was pushed inside by a sweaty young man. I saw my bags immediately and grabbed them before heading out for a cigarette. I stood outside, smoking and taking in my surroundings.

On my right was what appeared to be the main road into Stone Town. In front of me was the main parking area which had been planted with Japanese cycads and other greenery. Under the trees sat the taxi bosses - Indian and black men in traditional Muslim gowns waiting for business. As the other passengers made their way out they began to ask for destinations and to negotiate fares. A few of them approached me but soon saw that I was in no rush to move and was relaxing with my cigarette. They went on to harass the other passengers.

Slowly they all got into the vehicles. Some agreeing to share a minibus into Stone Town to reduce the fare for each of them. I noticed a thin black man with sunglasses standing in the shade in the distance, leaning on an old Toyota. On the side of the vehicle, the words Taxi Service were painted in bright red. I decided I would give him a try seeing as he was the least insistent of the bunch. I slowly made my way across the boiling tarmac towards him.

"Jambo," he said in a quiet voice. I knew from the guide book that this meant 'hello' in Swahili. I replied accordingly.

"Where would you like to go, sir?" he asked.

"I am going to Paje. How far is that and how much will you charge me?"

Being closer to him I could see that he was in his mid-sixties. He grinned at me with a few missing teeth.

"Paje is fifty kilometres from here, sir and I will charge you US$30. It is the usual fare for this journey, sir. I don't need to be like these guys and try to over charge you," he said, motioning towards the younger, more aggressive drivers. Thirty dollars for a fifty kilometre trip sounded fair to me and it was on the other side of the island.

"Right, that sounds ok to me, let's go," I said.

He quickly took up my luggage and placed it in the boot of the vehicle.

"Would you like to sit in the front or the back seat sir?" he asked courteously.

"I'm happy in the front if that's alright with you?"

"Certainly sir" he replied. I got into the car and noticed the heavy material seat covers in a gaudy burgundy colour. It was going to be a sweaty drive. We reversed out of the shaded area and made our way towards the main road where we turned left.

"Do we drive through Stone Town on the way or is there a road which goes straight across the island?" I asked.

"To get to Paje sir, we will turn right just before Stone Town and cross what we call New Town. There we will find the road which goes to the east coast, Paje, Jambiani and the other towns. But I can take you to see Stone Town if you would like to?" he said hopefully.

"No thanks. Some other time perhaps. I have to get to my hotel and I have things to do."

"No problem sir." I was impressed with his mild manner and careful command of English.

"You speak very good English. Are you from Zanzibar?" I asked.

He turned with the toothless grin again.

"Thank you sir. Yes I was born in Zanzibar. I come from Paje myself so I am very happy to get a fare back home. And by the way my name is Hassan."

"Nice to meet you. My name is Jason," I replied.

We talked as we drove down what was the biggest road in Zanzibar. We passed what looked like a few government buildings, some service stations, and schools. I was struck by the greenery and tidiness of what I had seen so far. The locals seemed to be well-dressed and tidy, especially the women. Being a Muslim island they were required to follow a strict dress code and not reveal any shoulders or legs.

"Mr Jason, sir, we are going to turn right here. Ahead of us is Stone Town. We will now drive through New Town for ten minutes to reach our road."

"That is fine" I said.

So far we had been inland all the way. I had hoped to see some coastline but I needed to get to my hotel and do my job, so I made do with taking in the surroundings from the car. New Town was nothing like the pictures I had seen of the World Heritage site of Stone Town with its intricate narrow cobbled streets and bazaars. It was more of the third world and was obviously where the majority of Zanzibari people lived. There were tatty-looking five storey blocks of flats with peeled paint and broken windows. Shirtless young kids kicked soccer balls made from waste plastic to each other on the sides of the bustling streets. There were a myriad of colourful stalls selling everything from phone cards to generators and bicycles. Loud music blared from crammed shopfronts and vehicles hooted in the dust and chaos. It was what I had expected and I wasn't disappointed. The place was an assault on the senses and I was enjoying the drive. Every few minutes Hassan would take a cloth from the side console and wipe the sweat from his face. I made do with the sleeve of my shirt.

After a while we began to leave the built up area of New Town and move into a more wooded area, where the road began to dip and wind through massive trees. In amongst the trees were scattered dwellings and small factories. Hassan and I smoked and chatted as we gained speed while avoiding pot holes.

"So you live in Paje?" I asked.

"Yes Mr. Jason, I have lived there all my life but I come to Stone Town everyday for work. I will give you my number so if you need me to drive you anywhere I will be available for you, hakuna matata!"

I smiled at his last words. They meant 'no worries' in Swahili.

"Ok," I said, "that's fine."

Our trip continued for another fifteen minutes until we were stopped at a police road block. Hassan slowly pulled the car up to the boom in the road where we were met by an extremely fat and sweaty policeman wearing a white uniform. I sat silently as Hassan spoke warmly to the man, whom he clearly knew. I understood nothing of what they said but it obviously was cordial as we were on our way within a minute.

"Mr Jason, we are now approaching the Jozani Forest. It is a very famous area and is well-known for the red colobus monkey which is found almost everywhere. Maybe one day you would like to stop and visit this place. It is very popular with the tourists." He was playing the tour guide very well.

"Ok, well we'll see about that. Another day perhaps," I replied.

"Hakuna matata," he said. We drove through the forest which was basically a tropical jungle. Dark, green and almost impenetrable. Long vines hung from the canopy and thousands of brightly coloured birds flew in the dappled shade. The road dipped and curved as we drove and I realised that this was probably the highest region of the island. We had been driving for 40 minutes when we started to leave the forest area and began approaching a flatter, drier part of the island.

"Very soon we will come to another road block where we will turn right. Then from there it is only five minutes to Paje. Which hotel will you be staying at Mr. Jason?"

"I am staying at the Paje Village Hotel."

"Hakuna matata," came the reply.

We made our way through the road block and turned right down a sun-baked tar road which was almost white in colour. Five minutes later, as promised, we came to a small village with a line of palm trees to the left.

I could see from the sand on either side of the baked road that we were now near the beach. To my left was a road with a line of shacks and old buildings. On the right under a huge tree were two taxis. Their drivers were sitting on a wooden bench in the shade. They waved enthusiastically at Hassan as we passed. I kept glancing to my left to get a view of the sea but it was obviously a few hundred metres away and I never once got a glimpse. A minute later we turned left onto a dusty road and began approaching a long wicker fence with a gate to the centre. Above us was a mixture of fir and pine trees.

"This is the Paje Village Hotel, Mr Jason. I will drive you to the reception area and drop you there unless you need me for something else?" Hassan asked optimistically.

"I think I'm ok for today Hassan, but please give me your number and I will call you if I need you. Oh, and another thing," I said, "where is the Eden Beach Lodge from here?"

"Eden Beach Lodge is that way sir," he said pointing to our right.

"Ok, that's fine, thanks very much."

I had got lucky once again. I liked the polite and soft-spoken Hassan, and I decided I would use his services in the coming days. As we got to the high wicker gate he hooted briefly and the gate was opened by a Masai security guard in full tribal regalia. He stood tall and dark in his dark red outfit and wore a large panga knife in an animal skin sheath on his side. We drove through the gate on the sandy road and pulled up to a thatched reception area. Hassan passed me a tatty business card which I pocketed as I got out of the car. A smart young man in black trousers and a white shirt came out to greet me.

"Welcome To Paje Village Hotel sir," he said with a smile as he approached me with his hand outstretched.

"Are you Mr Green sir?"

"I am, how are you?" I said as I shook his hand.

"Fine thank you sir, welcome, welcome." Hassan was busy removing my luggage as I entered the reception.

The thatch roof made the interior of the open plan building cooler than the outside, and above us an overhead fan whirred away quietly. The young man who had greeted me walked behind a hardwood reception desk and handed me an arrival form. As I filled it in my bags were neatly planted behind me by Hassan. Once all formalities had been completed I paid the taxi fare and bade farewell to Hassan promising I would call him if I needed him. As he drove away, the receptionist picked up my bags.

"I am now ready to take you to your room Mr Green. Please follow me."

"Thank you," I said and we began walking down a sandy path with white painted rock borders and green grass. Above was a mixture of tall pine and palm trees and on either side bright red and yellow hibiscus bushes were in full flower. The path went up a slight incline and then for the first time I saw the Indian Ocean on the east coast of Zanzibar. I found it harder and harder to concentrate on the small talk the receptionist was making as he walked in front of me with my bags. The path continued ahead of me for 40 metres or so before dropping off slightly down to the beach. Ahead of that, the perfectly calm sea stretched out to the horizon. Had it not been for the thin seam of deeper and darker water at the distant reef there would have been no way of telling where the sea and sky met. I decided at that moment that if this was not paradise on earth then it probably didn't exist.

"Your room is this way Mr Green, sir," the receptionist said turning left down another sandy path.

I fought the urge to take the short walk to the drop-off and take in the scene in front of me. *Patience, Green,* I thought to myself, and dutifully followed the man. On my left were a series of thatched bungalow chalets. Each had a small verandah area with two hardwood chairs and a table. They were set in the dappled shade of the pines and palms above. Various pathways led to each one individually.

"This is number eight, your room Mr Green," the man said, turning left. As we got to the room he placed my bags on the floor and unlocked the room with a key that was attached to a large wooden plaque with the room number burnt into it.

The room was basic, but comfortable and clean. To the right there was a double bed constructed in Zanzibari style with a wrapped-up mosquito net above. To the left were two pedestal fans and a dressing table with plug points nearby. At the far end of the room was a built in cupboard with rustic wooden louvre doors. I walked over to the bathroom door and had a look inside.

It was pretty much similar to the room. Basic and clean with a toilet, shower, basin and mirror. All of this was under thick thatch which made sense, given the oppressive heat outside. The receptionist was busying himself opening windows and switching on the fans.

"This is fine, thank you very much," I said handing him a ten dollar bill. His eyes lit up at the sight of the note.

"My name is Albert, sir. If there is *anything* you need please contact me at reception. There is a restaurant area with a separate bar closer to the beach and there are plenty of activities we can arrange for you. I will be around until 10 tonight. Thank you very much and enjoy your stay."

"Thank you Albert," I replied and he left the room closing the door behind him.

Alone at last, I gazed around the room before taking a look out of the front window. I smelled the salt as the coconut laden palms swayed in the air. Two blonde women in swimming costumes and sarongs strolled up the main path back towards the reception area. They were in animated conversation and looked like they were in their forties. Beyond them the sea stretched out in infinite blue.

"This is fucking paradise Green," I said under my breath. "Fucking paradise."

I had expected to feel tired when I arrived but I was anything but. I set about organising myself, starting by connecting my laptop to see if the roaming internet was working. Thankfully it was, albeit a bit slowly. I took a quick shower and changed before getting on with the day.

Richard's direct flight to Zanzibar had been on schedule and that meant he would already be at his hotel, or hopefully nearby. I needed to make my way over there and have a look at what he was doing. After a cold shower I changed into some long shorts, an old tee shirt, and some beach slops. I glanced into my open suitcase and saw the camera with the zoom lens. *You're a tourist Green. You're not going to look out of place with that,* I thought. I slung the camera around one shoulder, grabbed a towel and headed out, locking the door behind me. One of the Masai security guards was standing diligently under a lopsided palm tree nearby. I nodded in greeting to him to which he responded by doing the same. Still looking at him I pointed with two fingers at my eyes then at the room as if to say 'keep an eye on this place please.' He nodded sternly in understanding.

I made my way through the greenery back to the central pathway and up to the reception area where I was greeted by the beaming smile of Albert.

"Hello Albert. I would like to leave some cash with you for safe keeping please."

"Certainly Mr Green let me give you an envelope and I will lock it up for you, hakuna matata."

I sealed the bulk of the cash in the envelope keeping $100 in small notes, then headed out down the path to the beach. On the way, I passed a large thatch open plan building I assumed was the restaurant. Inside were tables and chairs, drinks fridges and an enclosed kitchen. A few families with young children were sitting around in the shade cooling off with drinks. I continued past the restaurant beyond the tree line and into the afternoon sun. It was like stepping into a sauna. Scattered around in front of me on the pristine white sand were large, thatched umbrella structures on thick wooden poles. Under these were deck chairs and rustic sun loungers made from wood and bark strips. A few extremely sun-tanned guests were braving the scorching heat and lay in the direct sunlight. Beyond that, the powder white sand melted into the pale blue ocean and stretched out to the reef on the horizon. The few guests there were chatting quietly and drank from bottles of mineral water. Some were wading through the sea, others snorkelling. All around me was calm and tranquillity. I stood in awe taking it all in for a good two minutes. It was breathtaking. My mind went back over the events of the previous week, everything that had suddenly happened out of the blue. *Incredible,* I thought.

As I walked down the beach towards the sea I felt the sun melting the ice in my bones from the long dark months of the English winter. I felt the heat of the sand burning through the rubber of my slops and all of my worries gradually slipping away. I carried on in that relaxed, dreamlike state until I was up to my knees in the Indian Ocean. It was like stepping into an infinite lukewarm bath. In the distance someone started playing a dub reggae tune. It fitted the surroundings perfectly. To my left and right the beach stretched away into the distance. The tree line a perfect thirty metres from the sea. Suddenly I was snapped out of it by the sound of a young boy coughing and spluttering in the water. He had inhaled some salt water through his snorkel and was now standing waist high in the ocean removing his mask as he wretched. I glanced at my watch. It was time to go to work.

I waded out back onto the hot sand and turned left in the direction of Richard's hotel.

I recalled the phone call in London and the receptionist saying it was only five hundred metres down the beach. Billions of grains of sand sparkled at me in the afternoon sun. I was grateful for my sunglasses. Eventually

I came to what looked like the boundary of the Paje Village Hotel. The next place was hidden away in the tree line as well but looked a bit shabby with peeling paint and bits of litter lying around. *No wonder it looks empty,* I thought. *No way Richard would stay in a dump like that.* The beaches at Paje were sparsely populated with the few tourists and visitors there sticking to the beach front adjacent to their guest houses or hotels. As I walked I passed the occasional couple sunbathing, the odd group swimming, and a few locals peddling their wares, I kept my eyes open, as the last thing I wanted was to bump into Richard on the beach, but as far as I could see there was no-one with his tall lanky frame around.

I passed a water sports centre which had signs outside the front offering scuba diving and deep sea fishing. There was a group of tourists hanging around outside talking excitedly, obviously making bookings for some excursion. After four hundred metres, I came to a very smart-looking building on my right with light blue pastel walls and green lawns. There was a good chance that this could be the Eden Beach Lodge. There were more people in front of the building than usual so I paused to see if I could spot Richard. He was nowhere in sight. I glanced back to see how far I had come from my hotel and saw an old black man riding a bicycle up the hard sand near the water behind me. He was obviously a local trader as his bicycle was loaded with sarongs, sea shells, and other trinkets. I motioned to him to stop as he approached which he did happily.

"Jambo," he said, thinking I was a customer.

"Jambo. Do you know where the Eden Beach Lodge is please?" I asked. A look of disappointment came over his wrinkled face.

"Eden Beach Lodge is over there," he said pointing south in the direction I had been walking.

"You want to buy something boss?" He asked with wide eyes.

"No thank you, maybe tomorrow," I said.

"Ok, tomorrow for sure," was his reply as he mounted his bicycle and pedalled off unsteadily in the sand.

I carried on down the beach for another hundred metres or so before arriving at what had to be Richard's hotel. It was different from the rest I had seen in that the tree line had been cut away, save for some palms. There were shiny tiled pathways with immaculate manicured lawns constantly being watered by fine mist sprays. The main building was three stories high and designed in typical colonial Zanzibari style. In the front was a multi level swimming pool complete with wet bar at the lowest level. The hotel was by all accounts very busy as there were wealthy looking guests scattered all around, lazing on sun loungers, walking hand in hand. Some strolled on the beach ahead of me, while others sipped bright green and red cocktails served by smart-looking waiters in gold turbans and waistcoats. The outdoor furniture looked comfortable and expensive, and was being well-used by the many guests. On either side of the main building, a series of separate bungalows spread out in a U shape facing the sea. I noticed each room had air conditioning units cleverly hidden to the side.

There were covered walkways to the front of the rooms with small trees and shrubbery between each building to give the occupants an impression of privacy. All in all it looked like the sort of place Richard would book for his holiday. Expensive and luxurious. From where I was standing I had a good view of the main building, the pool and bar area, and the rooms to the right and left. I was reluctant to venture any nearer for fear of running into Richard, so I took off my tee shirt, lay my towel on the sand and got to work. I propped myself up on my right elbow as

I lay down and switched on the camera. I decided that I appeared perfectly normal where I was and would certainly not look out of place or obtrusive by using the camera. After all it was a holiday resort and most, if not all, people visiting would be taking pictures. I started by zooming in on the round bar in the pool at the lowest level. There were a few guests swimming and some sitting on the underwater stools sipping drinks. The powerful lens made a buzzing sound as it zoomed in on the scene. There were five people in the pool. Two couples and the barman. One young couple sat at the bar leaning towards each other in conversation. The woman with her back to me was a bottle blonde and wore a lot of gold jewellery, while the man had long curly black hair and looked Italian. Both were heavily suntanned.

The two swimming in the pool were older and lighter in complexion and spun each other around in the water laughing with each other. *No Richard there,* I thought. I moved the camera towards the barman, who was wearing a similar gold turban to the waiters. He was busy shaking a cocktail for someone and as I zoomed in further, I noticed a sign above him that read Eden Beach Lodge Pool Bar.

"Bingo," I said, under my breath. I turned onto my stomach as if trying to get a tan on my back. All the while propping myself up on my elbows, the camera to my face. I zoomed out and scanned the busy scene in front of me. Next, I decided to focus on the main building. It had a series of archways on each of the three levels to allow the air to flow through. Zooming in, I saw that the lower level was a reception and administration area. It was decorated with what looked like antique furniture, in fitting with the style of the building. I could see a few figures moving around inside, but it was a shaded area and it was impossible to make out any features. *Probably staff,* I thought and moved the camera up a level.

The first floor was the restaurant. Although there was no-one there at that time of day, I could clearly see exotic drapes around the arches and sea view tables with wind-proof candle holders for those romantic dinners. I noticed a waiter setting one of the tables to the left of the building in preparation for the evening service. I was too low on the beach to see into the top level, but I imagined given what I had read about Zanzibari architecture that this would be a plush open air lounge area for guests to relax after dinner.

"Where are you Mr Lewer-Allen?" I said quietly to myself. Next I zoomed in on the top and middle pool areas. There were a number of people lounging around in the late afternoon. Some sitting on the pool sides. Others sprawled out sunbathing and reading. I zoomed in on each one individually, like a sniper, but to no avail. There was no sign of him. I set the camera down on the towel in mild frustration and lit a cigarette. I turned onto my side again and gazed out to sea as I smoked. *Not to worry Green, he's here somewhere, you'll find him.*

After finishing the cigarette, I extinguished it by pushing it deep into the sand. I felt a pang of guilt about polluting such an idyllic place but needs must. Picking the camera up again I decided to have a look at the row of bungalows to the right of the main building. One by one I zoomed in on each, looking for any signs of movement. There was nothing except for some house keeping staff pushing a white trolley filled with sheets. As I zoomed in on the bungalow nearest the reception, I saw the door open and a young blonde woman in a yellow g-string bikini walk out. She was tall and slim, and carried a book and some suntan lotion. It made for decent viewing and I followed her as she walked towards the middle pool area, dumped her belongings on a lounger and dived into the pool gracefully.

That would suit you, Richard, I thought, *I wouldn't be surprised if you followed her out of that room any minute now.* But he didn't.

There was still no sign of him anywhere. Suddenly, behind me I heard a dull repetitive thudding sound that was growing louder and louder. Slowly I put the camera down and turned onto my side to see what it was. It turned out to be an extremely red faced and hot looking jogger. She ran towards me on the hard sand by the water, dripping with sweat. She was in her mid thirties and wore dark blue running shorts and a white vest. The look of steely determination on her face changed for a split second as she passed me.

"Hi!" she said breathlessly.

"Hi there," I replied. I watched as she ran into the distance, never once slowing or changing her pace. I shook my head. *Crazy, why would you want do something like that in a place like this?* I settled back down onto my stomach and brought the camera up to my face again. I decided I would have a look at the rooms which spread out to the left of the main building. The lens buzzed as I zoomed in on the one nearest the reception. The door was open and there was some movement in the darkness inside but there was no way I could make anything or anyone out. I decided to revisit that one later. Then it occurred to me that I could actually just stroll in to the hotel and wander around. Maybe ask if there was a room available although I knew there wasn't from the conversation I had had with the reception from London. I paused and thought about it for a while then decided against it. I was feeling relaxed and quite happy doing what I was doing from a distance and I didn't want to rock the boat too much. I brought the camera up again and started zooming in on the next few rooms. All doors were shut and all pathways were clear. The late afternoon sun had lost some of its ferocious power now, but I could still feel its warmth on my back as I lay there scanning the rooms to the left of the main building. I wondered where he was. Was he inside sleeping? Had he gone out somewhere? After all he had arrived some time before me and probably had an instant transfer to the hotel. I consoled myself with the knowledge that sooner or later he would have to pitch up and then all would be well and I would be earning my pay. I lay there, blissfully, on the beach as the sun slowly went down towards the main building. A good 45 minutes passed before one of the doors to the left opened and out walked Richard. Quickly I raised my camera and focused on him. He was wearing red Bermuda shorts, sunglasses, and a loose grey tee shirt. His curly hair looked ruffled and untidy. He stepped out into the sun and stood yawning and stretching his long arms. Clearly he had been sleeping. Then he scanned his surroundings and decided on the beach. He wore no shoes, carried no towel and made his way down the tiled pathway past the last room and onto the sand.

He was a good fifty metres from where I lay so I was quite happy about staying where I was. The camera clicked as I photographed him on his short walk. Just before he got to the ocean he removed his tee shirt to reveal his tall scrawny frame, and ran the final metres into the water. The sea was shallow all the way out to the reef and Richard took advantage of this by wallowing around floating on his back, pushing himself out with his legs. Occasionally, he paused to take a look around with only his head poking out the water then pinched his nose and went beneath briefly. There were a number of people moving around on the beach and swimming. All at a discreet distance from each other. There was a lot of space in Zanzibar. Space to be alone. Richard was alone.

He swam lazily around for a good ten minutes, until the sun finally started disappearing behind the main building of Eden Beach Lodge. Then he stood up and waded back towards the beach. Once there he shook the excess water out of his hair, picked up his tee shirt, and started back towards the hotel. *A relaxing afternoon for you, Richard my friend,* I thought as I watched him walk up the slope of the beach. Some of the guests who had been lazing around the front of the hotel were now finishing their drinks and collecting their belongings. They were going back to their rooms to prepare for the evening and so was Richard. He made a beeline for his room, opened the door and disappeared inside. I sat up cross-legged on the towel and took a few photographs of the room.

Ten minutes passed with no movement from Richard. There was a steady warm breeze coming off the sea and suddenly I felt thirsty and hungry. I needed to go back to my hotel for a shower and some food before deciding what to do later on. After such a long day travelling, I was feeling surprisingly awake and full of energy. The sleep on the flight from Cape Town to Dar Es Salaam had done me good. I took a slow walk back down the beach in the fading light, my ankles in the warm ocean. I felt cheerful and slightly overwhelmed as I walked past the various lodges and the water sports centre on my left. The grimy building that was next door to my hotel was drawing a crowd early. There were red and blue lights shining through its arched windows and a steady beat coming from a sound system. Inside I could make out a mixture of black and white patrons drinking beer from brown bottles and dancing. Eventually I arrived at the beach area in front of the restaurant of my hotel. I could no longer hear the music from the place next door and the beach was empty. I wrapped the camera in my towel and dumped it on the beach with my tee shirt. The sea was now a bluish grey in the fading light and I walked out until I was waist high in it. I sunk down in the water until it covered my shoulders. It was still unbelievably warm and the powder fine sand squeaked under my feet.

I turned around and took a look at my accommodation. The lights on the pathways and in the rooms were glowing yellow and the palm trees swayed in the breeze. The backdrop to the scene was the burning red of the setting sun.

'Paradise,' I said quietly, 'fucking paradise.' The breeze was cooler as I stepped out of the sea and collected my belongings. I made my way up the slope of the beach and onto the pathway that led past the restaurant and to my bungalow. The Masai security guard I had seen earlier was still in his position and we gave each other the thumbs up as I opened my room and turned on the lights.

Feeling ravenous I took another cold shower and changed into some fresh clothes. I checked my emails before heading to the restaurant. There was nothing of importance. I noticed some mosquitoes in the room and having had malaria three times during the war, I decided to spray some repellent on my exposed skin. It was still early when I left the room. Some of the guests were sitting on the verandahs of their bungalows. I was greeted by the head waiter as I arrived at the restaurant. He was a stern looking tall man in a white shirt with a black bow tie.

"Good evening," I said, "table for one please."

"This way please sir," he said, leading me through the tables to the beach side of the open air thatch building. The lighting was mellow and soft music played through hidden speakers. I sat down and looked out through the palms towards the sea on my right. The moon had come up and had turned the surface of the water silver. The waiter returned with a menu as a family of five arrived. There were three young children who were misbehaving and consequently being scolded by their parents who spoke German. I ordered a bottle of mineral water and browsed the menu as the waiter went off to collect my order. The heat of the day had dehydrated me and I knew I needed some water before trying the beer. I decided to go for the prawn cocktail followed by a main course of Thai green prawn curry. I placed my order when the waiter returned with the water. It was ice cold and droplets of condensation were forming on the outside of the plastic bottle. I poured and drank a full litre, keeping the remainder for later. Other people started arriving and taking their tables as I sat. The stern-looking head waiter appeared again from the closed kitchen area and approached me.

"Your order will take about half an hour to prepare sir, perhaps you would like to go to the bar? I will call you when it is ready."

"Sure, that sounds fine," I said, and he motioned behind me.

I turned and saw where he was pointing. Again, it was a thatch structure set in the trees near the beach, about thirty metres from where I sat. My thirst for water now quenched I made my way across the sand through the darkness towards the building. It was a beach bar set in the sand with rough hewn bar stools and wooden chairs and tables around the perimeter. A string of coloured lights circled the thatch above on the inside and the design was such that the patrons could see the ocean through the shelves of bottles as they sat. Underneath the thick hardwood bar were refrigerators that were screened by grass mats and on either side were tall glass door drink coolers. There was no one there except a young black man in his early twenties who was sitting on a stool behind the bar fast asleep. His head leaning against a drink cooler. I sat on the stool directly in front of him and rapped my knuckles on the wooden surface. Instantly he sat bolt upright with wide confused eyes.

"Ahhh!! Sorry sir! I am sleeping! Very sorry sir!" he cried, jumping to his feet.

"No problem," I said, "tell me young man, what is the best beer in Zanzibar?"

"The best beer in Zanzibar sir? The best one is Safari. Can I get you one sir?" he asked cheerfully.

"Please do," I replied. A good beer it was too. A perfect balance of sweet and bitter served ice cold. It tingled as it went down my throat and was gone in thirty seconds.

"You were right," I said, "that was a very good beer. I'll have another one please."

"Hakuna matata!" he replied happily. The two of us got talking as I sat waiting for my dinner. His English was not as good as the rest of the staff I had met at the hotel but his youthful enthusiasm and good humour were refreshing and I hadn't spoken to a lot of people recently. I enjoyed his company. We sat in limited conversation for a good twenty five minutes until the head waiter arrived informing me that my dinner was ready. I made my way back to the now busy dining area and sat down. The starter and main course were superb and were washed down with another Safari beer. Afterwards I sat and smoked a cigarette gazing out onto the rippling silver of the sea and checking out the other guests. To my left at the far end of the dining area were the two women I had seen earlier from my room. They were red faced and flushed from the sun. They still wore their sarongs.

They were looking in my direction and our eyes met briefly after which they giggled like teenagers and carried on with their hushed conversation and their drinks. *Oh dear,* I thought. As I finished my smoke, the head waiter came with the tab and asked if there was anything else I would be needing. I told him no, thanked him for the dinner and signed the bill. It was 7.30pm and I needed to make a decision on my next move. There was nothing else for it. I would have to take a moonlit walk up the beach and do some snooping around Richard's hotel. I was still thirsty and I decided I would have one more beer at the bar before leaving. Feeling relaxed and full, I took the short walk across the sand back to the bar area. It was still deserted except for the young bar man who was awake this time and pleased to see me.

"Safari, boss?" He asked with a smile.

"Why not?" I replied.

CHAPTER TEN

- AN ACCIDENTAL MEETING

I pulled up a bar stool and sat as the freezing green bottle was handed to me. The young man was now in a talkative mood and asked in his limited English if I would like some music.

"Carry on," I said. He rummaged in a folder of CDs and asked if liked reggae. He was obviously the person who had been playing the music I had heard earlier in the afternoon.

"Sure, no problem," I said. The music fitted the scene perfectly and I sat contentedly sipping my beer gazing out through the back of the bar at the sea. To my left I could see the crowd in the dining area was thinning out as people made their way back to their rooms. A few minutes passed and I was halfway through the beer when I noticed a dark figure walking down the beach behind the bar. I took no notice of this until I saw the person turn left as if to come towards the bar. For a while I couldn't make out any features except that whoever it was, was very tall. Then I noticed the glint of the spectacles. Time suddenly slowed down and my mouth went dry. *No fucking way!* I thought. *This cannot be happening!* But it did happen and my worst fears were realised in a split second. The tall figure of Richard Lewer-Allen ducked under the thatch to my left and walked into the very bar where I sat alone. He was still casually dressed in Bermuda shorts and a tee shirt, his face slightly red from the sun. He nodded in greeting, bright eyed and smiling as he pulled up a bar stool a metre and a half from me and sat down.

"How are you doing?" he said, "I see you've discovered Safari, it's a great beer."

"It's excellent," I replied.

"You from UK?" he asked casually.

"Yup" I said, "just on a bit of a holiday"

"Me too, this place, Paje, it's the best beach in Zanzibar without a doubt. I come here quite often."

My mind was racing at a thousand miles an hour. *How could I have allowed this to happen?* This was way out of my brief and constituted a major fuck up on my part. Richard turned to the barman.

"Robson, how are you!?" He asked. "Ah Mr Richard, welcome back Mr Richard!" Came the barman's reply.

This was turning into a nightmare. The two were obviously friends from a previous visit and knew each other well. They laughed as they shook hands vigorously over the bar. *What the fuck are you going to do now Green?* I thought. *How are you going to explain this?* I sat in stony silence and sipped the beer while the turmoil in my brain continued.

"Robson, please can I have an ice cold Safari, and perhaps another for the gentleman here?" Richard said with a smile.

"Cheers, thank you," I said.

The drinks were delivered as the reggae played on. The very person I had been watching and following across the world for the past week leant forward and offered his hand.

"Richard Lewer-Allen, pleased to meet you," he said.

"Jason Green," I replied as I shook his hand. "Likewise." I told myself there was absolutely nothing I could do in the situation. I couldn't just walk away and hope that he would forget my face by the next day. No. I would have to play it cool and behave like any other tourist on holiday. He clearly hadn't recognised me and was quite happy to sit and have a beer with me. I would just have to go with the flow and relax. It was too late for anything else. Again he turned to me,

"You staying here?" he asked.

"Yup, just got in today."

"I'm staying up there at the Beach Lodge but I usually come down here in the evenings. Don't like the bar up there. No music." He was in a chatty mood.

"You say you come here quite often?" I enquired.

"Yeah about three times a year, it's really good."

"That's for sure" I said as I sipped the beer.

I realised that although this was totally unprofessional and completely out of my brief, it just might work in my favour if I played my cards right. I might be able to get an insight as to what my friend young Richard was up to. How he was able to afford it all.

"Where in England are you from?" he asked.

"I'm in London. I work in insurance," I replied, not lying. "Been through a divorce so I decided to take a break and get away from the cold."

"I hear you mate! I'm in London too," he said, "I run a sports shop." *I know Richard, I know quite a lot about you.* He downed his beer and slammed the empty bottle onto the bar surface.

"Robson my friend!" He said loudly in a posh accent, "let's have another round please. We are very thirsty here!"

"Hakuna matata Mr Richard!" replied the young barman and swiftly delivered the order. At that moment the two women who had been looking at me from across the restaurant walked in. They were both smiling at Richard's boisterous request and they took two bar stools to our left.

"Good evening," they both said in what sounded like a Dutch accent. My new friend Richard and I greeted them in unison as they made their orders. Richard turned to face me again, smiling. He raised his eyebrows as if to say 'look what the cat dragged in!' I smiled and nodded in acknowledgement, now totally accepting my fate. Everything had changed. I was no longer in control of the situation. *Just relax and go with it Green,* I thought, *there's nothing you can do now so just try and enjoy yourself.*

"How long are you here for?" Richard asked.

"Oh I'm here for about ten days, might extend it though. The thought of going back to London isn't really appealing to me at the moment"

"No, I hear you, definitely not, better off here for sure," he said.

"And you Richard, how long are you here for?" I asked, knowing full well.

"Umm, I'll be here for about a week I think. Then it's back to the cess pit!"

The barman was busy mixing brightly coloured cocktails for the women to our left. Richard turned and glanced at them briefly.

"Robson, can you turn the music up a little bit please?" he asked. The barman obliged and Richard began drumming the beat on the bar counter with his fingers. He seemed relaxed and happy as far as I could see. I sat there facing him nodding to the beat softly. *What the fuck have you got yourself into now Green?* I thought. Our conversation went on, and we spoke about our respective accommodation and the quality of the food. We spoke about the island in general and he told me about the capital Stone Town with all its narrow streets and bazaars. He was lively and enthusiastic in his descriptions and I found myself enjoying talking to him. My worries about the accidental meeting were fading as the beer flowed and I resigned myself to the fact that there was nothing I could do. It was as if we were just two buddies having a drink and catching up.

The two women started making conversation with us. "Are you both staying here at Paje Village Hotel?" one of them asked. I knew from the strong accent that they were from Holland.

"I'm staying up the beach at another hotel, but Jason is staying here," Richard replied. He turned in his seat so he faced the bar and could talk to myself and them more easily. They both stood up with their cocktails and leant over to shake our hands and introduce themselves. "I am Ineke and this is Helen. How do you do?Nice to meet you." We shook hands with each of them and introduced ourselves. They were all smiles and giggles although they were in their late thirties or early forties.

"Are you girls here with family in Zanzibar or is it just the two of you?" Richard asked, making polite conversation.

"No it's just us two friends on holiday here, enjoying the beach and the sunshine." was the reply. I sat as the small talk continued. The volume of the music rose steadily as time passed and the scene started resembling a party. Although I joined in the conversation at times, I couldn't help thinking what Gareth Lewer-Allen would think if he could have seen me at the time. The two women were getting through quite a few cocktails and were starting to get quite drunk when Richard came up with a bright suggestion,

"Robson, I think we should have a round of shooters. Let's make it four sambucas please." he turned to me for approval.

"Sure, why not?" I said with a resigned shrug and a smile.

"What is sambuca please?" Helen asked between giggles. She was the darker of the two.

"Sambuca is a very sweet liquorice drink, good for parties. You'll love it!" Richard said, tapping out the beat of the music on the bar top.

"Great, let's try one!" The women said in unison. The drinks were delivered in shot glasses and handed to each of us.

"You have to drink it in one go," Richard said to the girls before raising his glass. "Cheers everyone, here's to Paje Beach!" he said triumphantly. The girls and I all reached forward and clinked our glasses together and downed the strong sickly sweet liquor. It burned my throat. Both of the girls coughed and winced in pain as the drink went down.

"Oh my god that is so strong!" said Ineke, the blonder of the two. But the alcohol was working overtime now and the jokes and laughter got louder and louder. The revelry continued for a good hour or so. More than once I caught the darker haired Helen looking at me with a smile and a glint in her eye. It turned out, through the conversation, that Ineke had recently divorced and had decided to take a holiday to get over it. A story which was very similar the one I had told Richard. Her best friend Helen had come along for support. Both of them came from Rotterdam and worked as systems analysts. More beer, cocktails, and sambuca flowed until the two girls turned to each other and huddled in secret conversation. Then they both turned and faced Richard and myself.

"Helen and I are enjoying ourselves very much. Would you like to dance perhaps?"

I knew that Dutch girls were pretty straight forward but this was the last thing I needed. *Jesus Christ Green, what the fuck.*

"Sure!" Richard said enthusiastically and jumped to his feet. "Come on Jason!" He said bleary eyed, "lets boogie!"

"No, really, I don't think so," I said laughing at the ridiculous scene I had got myself into. "I'm not much of a dancer honestly." The darker woman, Helen, who had been staring at me, was having none of it. She came over to me briskly, grabbed my left arm and pulled me out onto the sand in the middle of the bar where Richard and Ineke were already dancing. It was all smiles, happiness and laughter as we danced. The two women were more than tipsy and thoroughly enjoying themselves. Richard was dancing away awkwardly with his tall lanky frame. He kept smiling at me and winking as if to say, "hey buddy, looks like we are gonna pull tonight!" For me it was the incredibly bizarre situation that I had found myself in at the time. There I was, on a beach in Zanzibar, having an absolute ball, getting drunk, dancing with two Dutch women and the son of the man who was paying me £1000 a day to do it! It was absolutely outrageous but there was nothing for it. I joined the party.

After 15 minutes or so, all of us were pretty hot and thirsty. We made our way back to the bar except this time Helen sat next to me and Ineke next to Richard. More drinks were ordered. I stood up to excuse myself as I needed to go to the toilet. I had noticed there was a gents in the restaurant area. As I left, Helen grabbed my arm and whispered in my ear.

"You are coming back Jason?" she asked.

"Yup. I'm coming back. Two minutes." I replied. I made my way through the darkness under the palms towards the dining area. I felt numb from the events of the evening. *Just enjoy yourself Green.*

The sand that stuck to bottom of my slops crunched on the concrete floor of the dining area as I walked in. I found the place totally deserted and the door to the gents locked. I decided I would find a dark area under a tree and go there. As I walked out into the darkness, I bumped into the tall dark frame of Richard coming towards me. "Jason, Jason!" he said, stopping me. "It's looking good in there mate! What do you reckon?" He had a broad grin on his face and his glasses glinted in the moonlight. "Ya, its looking pretty good Rich," I said smiling.

"Is the toilet open?" He asked pointing at the restaurant.

"No, it's locked, I thought I would find a dark palm tree and go there." I replied.

He paused, looking around. "Umm, do you think we could go to your room instead?" He asked in a hushed tone.

"Why bother?" I said, "we can just go to a dark area somewhere." *Why the hell is he asking to go to my room?* I thought, confused.

"I'll show you when we get there, it'll be quick, I promise, come on!" he whispered, excitedly.

"Ok, if you insist." I said, and we walked together down the pathway past the other bungalows towards mine. On the way, he spoke constantly about the two women in the bar right up until the time I unlocked the door and turned on the light.

"Toilet's through there Richard," I said motioning towards the door at the rear of the room.

"No you first, please go ahead," he replied.

Feeling slightly puzzled at his behaviour, I went through and used the toilet, keeping the door open behind me. He talked away as I peed and only when I stepped out did I realise his motivation for coming to the room. He was hunched over the dressing table, a small glass vial in his left hand, a credit card in his right. He had removed the jug of water and two drinking glasses from the plate on which they sat and was busy chopping two fat lines of white powder with the credit card. He turned and faced me with a broad grin as I walked out.

"Would you like a line Jason? Party all night!" he asked, raising his eyebrows. I had smoked weed in my youth in Africa and occasionally in London, but I had never delved into harder drugs.

"Is that coke?" I asked, stopping in my tracks.

"Yup, one hundred percent pure cocaine," he replied as he rolled up a crisp $100 bill.

"It's not really my thing Richard," I said. He put the rolled up note to his nose, dropped his head and proceeded to snort one of the huge white lines on the plate. Instantly he stood up, sniffing and brushing his nose with his hand.

"Hey no problem Jason, if you don't want it, I'll have it. But I'm busting for a piss, can I carry on?" he asked.

"Sure, sure, carry on," I said motioning again to the bathroom. As he went through, I walked over to the table. Suddenly it all made sense. The dinner plate on the floor of the passenger seat of the Aston Martin. The plate on his bedside table in the flat in Sloane Square, and now the plate in my room in Zanzibar. *Fucking hell. Think fast Green.* I put my middle finger to the right of the line of white powder on the plate and flicked it onto the floor. At the same time I made a loud sniffing sound so he would think I had taken it. I glanced at my finger and saw a residue of white powder. I quickly put my finger in mouth and sucked the residue. Instantly my mouth was filled with a clinical chemical taste. The toilet flushed and Richard walked out beaming from ear to ear.

"Did you have it then?" He asked looking at the plate.

"I did, pretty good stuff."

"Excellent, now let's get back to the ladies." He picked up the vial and the $100 note and we made our way back up the pathway towards the bar. I found it more and more difficult to talk as we went. My mouth was completely numb and cold from the tiny amount of powder I had swallowed. By the time we got back to the bar the ladies were in fine form and they both cheered as we walked in. Helen immediately came up and put her arms around my neck.

"Let's dance again Jason, I love this song!"

"Just a minute please Helen, I need to drink something, my mouth is very dry." I said. I wasn't lying either. If Richard was at full throttle before, he was now in overdrive. He ordered another full round of drinks and shooters and proceeded to turn up the volume and dance with Ineke.

This time it was rave music and he made frantic movements with his long arms as he danced, all the while with a huge grin on his face. The music and dancing continued whilst I sat at the bar and chatted to Helen. She moved closer and closer as we spoke and after half an hour she was sitting right next me brushing her fingers up and down my back. It wasn't an entirely unwelcome distraction, but I kept my eye on Richard and Ineke as we spoke.

Eventually I noticed Ineke begin to tire from the dancing. She dragged the extremely energetic Richard back to the bar and sat down. Richard immediately picked up his beer and drank deeply from it. Ineke had become a bit pale in the face.

"Do you think she's ok? She looks a bit pale." I asked Helen. Immediately she got up and went to tend to her friend. Richard came and sat down near me.

"How are you feeling buddy?" He asked, still nodding to the music with a sweaty grin on his face.

"Feeling good Richard, you?" I replied.

"Hundred percent buddy, hundred percent!" He laughed knowingly. Then I noticed that Helen had put her arm around Ineke, who was now leaning on the bar counter and beginning to slump. Clearly she had drunk too much and was now feeling it. Helen stood up and walked over to Richard and myself.

"I'm very sorry guys, Ineke is not feeling very well, I think I should take her to bed now," she said in her broad Dutch accent. A look of genuine disappointment on her face.

"Oh no, I'm sorry to hear that," Richard said, "do you need any help?"

"No thank you Richard, it will be fine. I think she just needs to sleep. But thank you for an excellent evening, we hope to meet you again."

Then she quickly stepped up to me and whispered in my ear. "What is your room number Jason?"

"Number eight," I replied without thinking. She made her way back to her friend, helped her up and they both made their way out of the bar.

"Goodnight girls!" Richard called as they left, then he turned to face me again.

"That's a damn shame!" he said, "but I reckon you're in there Jase."

"Hmm, I think you may be right." I replied. Our conversation continued for another twenty minutes. Richard was a lot more talkative than usual. A direct effect of the cocaine. Eventually the combination of the drink and the long day caught up with him visibly and he decided that he would take a walk back to his hotel. By then, it was 12.30pm and the barman Robson was not happy about it at all. "Mr Richard, very dangerous to walk alone this time on beach. Please wait. I come with you." I decided that I would offer to take the walk with him.

It would give me a chance to get more of an insight into his life without the distractions of the bar, the women, and the drink.

"Actually I wouldn't mind a walk up the beach Rich, I'll walk with you." I said.

"Ya, let's do that, we can take a beer with us," he replied. Robson the barman had overheard our conversation and was eyeing us both dubiously.

"Robson, I am going to walk with Mr Richard, don't worry please. I will be very careful," I said to him hoping for approval.

"Ok, hakuna matata, but this time late, too many beach boys looking for money!" He retorted with a worried look on his face. Richard ordered two more beers and the tab for the evening. I insisted on paying half. After all it was only fair considering it was his father's money. We left the bar and made our way through the trees and onto the beach. The moon was high in the sky now and the ocean and beach were clearly visible in the natural light. We crossed the soft sand and started walking up the hard shoulder. The night was warm, but a cool breeze was coming in from the sea. Robson had turned the music off and to our right I could hear the constant and ever-present sound of the cicadas in the grass and trees. "Sweee sweee sweeee sweee sweeee sweeee," it was a sound I hadn't heard in many years, a sound of Africa. It brought back mixed memories of my childhood. Some were fond memories of lying awake on camping trips in the bush listening to the sounds of the night. Some were terrible memories of twisted fever dreams whilst in the burning hot and freezing cold grip of a bout of malaria. Then it was a bad sound which seemed to get louder and louder as the parasites periodically burst out of the liver and the hallucinations, craving for water, and sweating started. Soon enough we passed the boundary of the Paje Village Hotel and to our right was the shabby bar I had seen earlier. The music was still playing and although the outside of the building was shrouded in darkness, I could see the patrons dancing and drinking as they had been before. Apart form the distant twinkling lights, the slow left curve of the beach ahead was deserted and I wondered if there had been any substance to Robson's warning. Perhaps he was just over concerned for his customers. How wrong I was.

As we walked I realised that Richard's steam was beginning to run out and the events of the day were catching up with him. He staggered in the sand occasionally and his speech became a little slurred.

"It's been great to meet you Jase, thanks for a good evening, we must do it again," he said.

"Yeah it's been good fun Rich," I said. "We'll play it by ear." 50 metres ahead was the water sports centre. In the dim light I could see that all the signage and kit had been removed and the front had been boarded up for the night. Just before the building on the right was an access road which obviously led back to the tarmac through the trees. I imagined this would be where the boats and equipment would be driven onto the beach. The area was dark, deserted, and totally silent and I glanced at it occasionally as we walked. It gave me a bad feeling. It was a perfect place from which to make a sneak attack or ambush. It also offered a convenient getaway back to the main road through the darkness and cover of the trees. There were no hotels, lights, or security guards in the area. It must have been instinct because as we approached I noticed two human figures emerge from the darkness. They walked quickly and silently across the sand on a path that would see them meet with us somewhere opposite the water sports centre. *Not to worry Green, they could be guards, they could be tourists, they could be anyone!* I thought hopefully. All the while Richard jabbered on, totally oblivious to what was happening in front of us. As we got closer, a cold feeling spread through my stomach and I felt my arms tense up and start tingling as the adrenalin started pumping through my body. I felt my senses sharpening. *What now Green?* After everything that had happened that day, this was the last thing I needed. It was definitely going to be a confrontation of some kind. They were dressed in dark clothes and on a deliberate and planned path to meet us. I poured my half finished beer onto the sand and stuffed the bottle, base first into the back of my shorts. Then I gripped Richard's left arm as we walked to warn him of what I believed was happening.

"What's up?" he said surprised. "Listen, I think we might have a spot of bother here Richard.

Just be calm ok?" I whispered.

"Oh shit!" He replied, as he saw the two men approaching. By then we were no more than ten metres apart and by that stage everything had started to appear in slow motion. They were two black men in their twenties. Both over six feet tall and well built. One wore black shorts and a grubby brown vest. He carried a thick wooden club which was half a metre in length. The other wore dark trousers and what looked like a tracksuit top. Strapped across his right shoulder and his left side was a large sheath.

I had no doubt that this would contain a panga (a crude and deadly blade attached to a rough wooden handle). Everything appeared in slow motion.

"You stop now!" the man with the panga bellowed. I was facing him whilst the other man with the club was facing Richard. We stood two metres apart and I could see the reddened whites of their wide eyes. Suddenly, I heard Richard's breathing to my left. It had become panicked and short. Out of the corner of my eye I noticed his chest heaving in and out rapidly. His entire body was racked with base fear. He raised his hands, one still clutching his beer bottle and stood there shaking uncontrollably. As expected, the man in front of me drew the panga from sheath on his chest. The sharpened section of the ugly blade glinted in the moonlight as he brought it up to point it towards my face.

"You no give us money, we fucking kill you, give money now!" the man with the blade shouted. I smelled home-brewed opaque beer on his breath. Slow motion. I was now gauging the situation every tenth of a second. The man with the club who was standing in front of Richard was obviously the sidekick. The less aggressive and more stupid of the two. His bloodshot eyes were more interested in Richard's expensive watch and the beer in his hand than me. Trying my best to exude an air of calmness, I slowly raised my hands showing empty and open palms.

"No problem," I said quietly, "we will give you money. We don't want any problem with you."

"Shut up!" the man screamed. "Give money now or I kill you now!" Droplets of saliva shot from his mouth as he shouted. He was becoming more and more agitated with every second and his eyes kept darting to his left and down the beach behind us. Slow motion. Red mist. The blade was less than a metre from my face, thick ugly iron hammered flat and fashioned from an old leaf spring.

"Ok, ok, ok," I said, "I am going to take the money in my pocket." I started lowering my left hand to where my wallet was. His eyes followed my hand as it dropped slowly. To my left Richard shuddered in terror, his breathing frantic and fast, both hands still raised in the air. My left hand dug into the deep pocket and found the wallet. "Ok, I have the money now, lots of money ok?" I said nodding, trying to get the man to look into my eyes.

Slowly I drew the wallet out of the pocket. Although there wasn't a great deal of cash in it, it looked full from all the cards and papers I had stuffed into it.

"Ok," I said, "no problem, here is the money, plenty of money here." With a flick of my left wrist, I tossed the wallet into the air between the two men. It flew not more than a foot above their heads but it was what I had planned and gave me the opportunity I needed to neutralise at least one of them. Slow motion. Red mist. My right hand dropped as soon as the wallet was tossed and went behind my back to find the neck of the empty beer bottle. Predictably, the two mens eyes followed the wallet as it flew and their focus and concentration was broken. Both tried to catch it at the same time and as a result, the panga which had been in my face began to move upwards as well. By the time the wallet had reached their eye level my right hand had found the neck of the beer bottle and it was on its way around on a path towards the panga man's temple. Before he knew what was happening the thick green glass of the bottle shattered on the side of his head. It made a curious sound as it connected and I knew the force with which I hit him would be enough to render him unconscious for a while. I used the sideways motion of my right arm swinging and ducking beneath the still slightly raised blade, I barged into his torso in a desperate effort to get to the man with the club. The panga man staggered backwards, blade still raised, and as I passed him I saw the eyes roll up. I never saw him drop as I was on my way towards the man with the club. He was standing there with his weapon raised, incredulous and stunned at what he had seen take place in the second before. Acutely aware that the club could do me some serious damage, I hit him with my right shoulder in the solar plexus while gripping him around his filthy brown vest with my arms. The wind was instantly forced out of his body with a whooshing sound. At that moment the club came down onto my back with force, but I was grateful he had missed my head. He was picked off his feet, carried for a few steps and slammed into the hard sand with another shoulder to the solar plexus. Feeling his body was now limp, I knelt up and looked into his face. His eyes were still wide awake and his mouth was gaping as he desperately tried to get oxygen into his lungs.

As I stood up, a bolt of pain shot across my lower back. Without looking at Richard, I walked over to where the man with the panga was lying. He was flat out on his back, snoring in the moonlight, his head leaning slightly to his right, a peaceful look on his face. A trickle of blood ran down from his head into the sand. It looked black in the moonlight. I pulled the sheath from around his neck and retrieved the panga which was still in his right hand. Then I turned to Richard. He stood where I had last seen him. His hands were not as high as they had been but they were still at chest level. The bottle of beer still clutched in one of them. His glasses were halfway down his nose and he stared at me with a look of confused disbelief on his face. At that moment the man with the club finally got his breath.

He lay where he had fallen with his barrel-like chest moving up and down steadily as he gulped in the precious air with desperate wheezing groans. I put the panga in its sheath as I walked over towards him. I knelt down beside him and was again aware of the smell of home brew beer as I looked into his eyes. They stared up at me, wide and frightened.

"A couple of minutes and you'll be up and out of here won't you?" I said to him as I grabbed the club from his side and stood up. "I'm sorry but I can't have that, buddy. Good night." I brought the club crashing down onto the side of his head. It wasn't a life threatening blow but it was certainly enough to put him to sleep for the night. His eyes rolled up and he was out. I tossed the club as far as I could out to sea then put the panga and sheath over my shoulder.

"Jesus Christ!" exclaimed Richard, "that was incredible! What the hell happened there?"

"Come on Richard," I said, "it's time to go. I don't think they'll be hassling me on my way back but I don't really want to meet them again." We both started walking briskly up the beach again. The adrenalin had woken us both up and Richard turned a few times to look at the two men as we made our way. I was feeling upset about what had just happened and I just wanted to get him back to his hotel safely. As the adrenalin wore off, the events of the day started to catch up with me and the pain in my back grew worse. I swung my left arm around to feel if anything had been broken and was relieved to feel no clicking or crunching of bones. I figured if anything it was a bad bruise.

"Where did you learn to do that sort of thing? To fight like that? It was like a fucking blur!" Richard asked, struggling to keep up with my pace.

"I was in the army years ago." I replied. "They teach you that sort of thing in the army".

"Hey I'm sorry Jason," he said, "that guy hit you pretty hard, are you hurt?"

"I'll be fine Richard, it's just a bruise." I wasn't in the mood for small talk any more so I kept up the pace until we arrived at Eden Beach Lodge and made our way up to the lower pool area. I stopped there remembering I wasn't supposed to know where his room was.

"You'll be ok now. Sorry about that shit back there," I said.

"Hey Jason, I've got to thank you, you probably saved my life! I can't believe it!" he said wide-eyed.

"No, I don't think so" I said, "they were just after some cash. I reckon they would've run off as soon as we had handed it over. The other guy wanted your watch as well."

"Well fucking hell," he said shaking his head, "I owe you one buddy, thank you very very much! I'll see you again for sure. Is that ok?"

"Yup that's fine," I said. He held his hand out and I shook it.

"Unbelievable, unbelievable!" he said, not wanting to let go of my hand. "I'm out of here Richard, take it easy," I said and made my way back down the slope to the sand. I decided to jog the way back. I had hoped it would help me focus my thoughts a bit. I picked up the speed as I hit the hard sand. *Jesus Christ Green. You successfully follow this bloke all around London. You break into his email account and his flat. You follow him halfway around the world to Cape Town and then to fucking Zanzibar. Then you run into him like a fucking asshole and make friends with him! Then you go for a moonlit walk up the beach with him, take two blokes out and become his fucking hero! What the fuck are you doing?* I ran faster still as if to try to get away from my thoughts. Halfway back, I passed the two men lying on the beach. They hadn't moved an inch and were still peacefully asleep. They would certainly feel their hangovers the next morning. The run was helping me and my brain became numb as I focused on the pace and getting back to my hotel.

Eventually I made it to the area of beach in front of the restaurant of the Paje Village Hotel. I was hot, and the sweat dripped from every inch of my body. I paused and leant over with my hands on my knees to catch my breath, the panga still hanging from my shoulder in its sheath. My back ached painfully as I stood there panting in the moonlight. Eventually I stood and started making my way back up the beach, through the trees and towards my room. I hid the panga from the view of the Masai guards by slipping it under my shirt. Finally I came to the room, opened the door and stepped inside. I turned the lights and the fans on. I decided I would take a cold shower and head straight to bed. As I stripped in the bathroom I turned and had a look at my back. There was a thick red blue mark running down the left side. I imagined it would not be a pretty sight by the morning. Gratefully I stepped into the shower and turned the cold tap on to full pressure. I leant forward and put both hands on the tiles beneath the shower rose. With my eyes closed I stood there, motionless and let the cool water run over me. Five minutes later and feeling a lot better I stepped out of the shower and dried myself off. I wrapped a thick white towel around my waist and stepped back into the bedroom. The fans were blowing hard onto my damp skin and I felt cooler than I had done since arriving in Zanzibar. I decided to check my email before turning in. At that moment there was a soft knock on the door. *What now?* I thought, turning towards the door.

"Hello Jason, it's Helen. I'm not disturbing you am I?" she spoke in a soft voice from behind the closed door.

I had almost forgotten about the two Dutch girls what with the incident on the beach with Richard. *Jesus, here we go,* I thought and walked over to open the door.

"No, no I'm awake Helen, come in," I replied, opening the door. She stood in the doorway wearing a blue sarong wrapped around her midriff. Her hair was wet as if she too had just stepped out of the shower. Her eyes travelled slowly down my chest to the towel and back up.

"I came earlier but you were not here, where did you go?" she whispered.

"I took Richard back up the beach to his hotel," I said. "Please come in." I turned slightly to let her in and she saw the rapidly darkening bruise on my back.

"My god, what happened to you?!" she said with alarm, as she moved behind me and ran her fingers lightly down my back.

"We ran into a bit of trouble with some thieves on the beach," I said. "It's fine, there's nothing broken, it's just a bruise."

"Oh my god, it looks so painful!" she whispered. "Is Richard ok? Did they rob you?"

"Richard is fine and no, they didn't get anything." I felt her right hand slowly and lightly make its way around my stomach from behind. I felt her kiss my back repeatedly as her grip tightened. Her left hand came round and travelled up my chest and I felt her breath quicken as she began to pant slightly.

"I want you Jason, I want you now," she whispered. I turned around to see that the blue sarong had been dropped and was on the floor around her feet. She stood there in the light, wide-eyed and totally naked. Her full breasts rose and fell rapidly as her breathing quickened. Her body was slim, tanned and smooth to touch. I turned the lights off using the switch to my right and led her to the bed.

CHAPTER ELEVEN

- THE BIG HOUSE AND THE MARLIN

I awoke at 6am sharp, with Helen's head still on my shoulder. She was fast asleep and hummed quietly as she turned over when I moved silently. I got up and walked barefoot and naked to the window. The morning light was pale and the tide was out revealing a number of pegs in the sand which the seaweed farmers used to harvest their crops. They looked like bunches of brown spaghetti lying on the sand in the distance. When the tide was in they were underwater and invisible. I walked over to the table and poured myself a glass of water from the jug. As I drank, I stared down at the plate that Richard had used to chop the cocaine on the previous evening. I glanced down at the floor to the left of the table to see if there was any of the white powder visible on the floor. There wasn't. It had been dispersed so as to be invisible. I stood there for a while, deep in thought as I drank the water. *A wealthy young chap with a drug habit, gallivanting around the world, living the life of the rich and famous - beautiful women, fine foods, top resorts, first class tickets. Still no answers Green. So many questions and still no answers. Fuck it, I'm going for a jog on the beach.* As I dressed I took a look at my back in the mirror. The thick red blue mark had turned an ugly black brown colour as if a welt was forming. As I twisted my body I felt a dull ache and no more. I was grateful for that. After dressing I wrote a quick note on a piece of scrap paper and left it on the bedside table nearest where Helen was sleeping.

'Helen, I have gone for a run, if you wake up before I get back and you need to leave, please drop the keys at the reception, Jason,' it read. I picked up my shoes and sneaked out of the door making as little noise as possible. I nodded a greeting to the Masai guard and made my way down the pathways towards the beach. To my right there was a bit of movement from the family rooms. Otherwise the place was fairly quiet. The beach was almost deserted save for a few seaweed farmers who were way out beyond the high tide mark. *Left or right Green?* Curiosity forced me to turn right in the direction of Richard's hotel and the unfortunate incident of the previous evening. The morning air was comfortably cool and as I started running, I smelled the salt in the air and it felt good. As I ran, I glanced to my right at the scene of the party in the shabby resort next door. There were beer bottles in the sand but the music was gone and the place was deserted. I got myself to a fast but comfortable pace and persevered.

Within a few minutes the sweat had started and I felt the poisons from the previous night start to leave my body. After a while I reached the water-sports centre to find that the front had been opened and the staff were busy placing the sign boards and flags out. Some of them were carrying aqualungs and other dive kit to the front for display while others were busy placing colourful windsurfers. Soon I passed the sand road that the two thieves had used for cover the previous evening. I had been right about it leading to the main tar road. A small, very old and rusty tractor was making its way slowly down toward the beach towing an ocean-going ski boat. I imagined it would be used for deep sea fishing or diving expeditions. I passed the area where the two thieves had attacked us. There was no sign of them. I tried to look on the beach for the shattered glass of the beer bottle but saw nothing. I felt a pang of guilt for the small boy who would probably cut his foot and scream as he walked over it. The sun was gradually getting higher to my left and I pressed on, keeping up the pace. The events of the previous day were neatly stored in the back of my mind and all I could think of was the run. Eventually after passing the other buildings I reached the Eden Beach Lodge where Richard was staying.

There was very little activity at the hotel save for a few staff who were busy preparing for the day. I focused on Richard's room as I got closer. The curtains were closed and all was quiet. Eventually I passed the boundary of the hotel and was into fresh unseen territory. I decided to myself that I would do another five hundred metres or so then turn around. That would give me a two kilometre run and I would be fine after that. To my right the jungle became thick and there were no buildings at all. To my left the tide was gradually coming in along with the occasional seaweed farmer carrying his crop for the day. By then my legs were starting to feel heavier and my breathing was hard and steady. For the rest of the five hundred metres there was absolutely nothing except thick green jungle and palm trees. The beach was totally deserted. I was about to turn around and run back to my hotel when I noticed a large white building begin to appear in front of me. It was set high up to the right and looked grand to say the least. My curiosity got the better of me and I decided to run another hundred metres or so to have a look. *Probably another expensive hotel.*

As I got closer, more and more of the building came into my vision. It was vast, with varying levels and patios with furniture and umbrellas. All around was a huge stone wall built into the beach. It must have been four or five metres high. To the right within the wall was a stairwell with a heavy black metal gate. It was then I saw a sight which I had not seen for many years. It sent a shiver down my spine and the adrenalin started pumping. Sitting on a rock to the base of the wall was a man with an AK.47 assault rifle resting against his chest.

He wore cheap sunglasses and his head was tilted back leaning on the wall behind him. He made no movement and didn't appear to see me at all. Knowing the beaches were public I decided to keep running. He made no movement as I passed him. He was clearly fast asleep. The stone wall was at least two hundred metres long and from what I could see, the building or house above was unlike most in Zanzibar. It looked like it was of Spanish or Mediterranean architecture with perfectly whitewashed walls. *Unusual, must be someone important.* I stopped to turn around. The sleeping guard made no movement as I passed him on my way back and eventually I was back into the area of thick green jungle and palms. Ahead of me the beach was still quiet as were most of the hotels. Thankfully there was no running into Richard and eventually I reached the water-sports centre. The rickety old tractor had managed to position the ski boat for when the tide came in and the shop front was resplendent in colour. When I finally made it back to the beach front of my hotel I was dripping with sweat and panting heavily. I threw off my shirt and took the hundred metre walk to where the tide was coming in. I wallowed in the warm clear water which was only a couple of feet deep and got my breath back. Once done I made my way back up the beach towards the hotel. Hoping that Helen would have woken and seen my note I walked down the pathways towards the reception.

"How are you this morning, Mr Green?" the receptionist asked cheerfully. "I'm fine thank you, was my room key dropped here by any chance?"

"Yes sir I have them," he replied handing them over.

"Thanks," I said.

"Will you be needing me to arrange anything for you today sir?" he asked.

"I'm not sure yet but I will let you know, see you later."

"Have a good day, Mr Green." I took the walk back to my room. I was glad that Helen had left. I needed to gather my thoughts and do some work. The heat was starting to kick in and I needed a cold shower to wash away the salt and cool off. After my shower I dressed and checked my emails. There were a few from various insurance companies wanting me to investigate some dubious injury claims. I replied, telling them I was busy. I decided I would send an email to Gareth Lewer-Allen informing him of my progress so far. There was no way I would mention that I had accidentally run into his son. Neither would I mention the fact that he was using cocaine.

I would leave that for later when and if I managed to find out what he had hired me to do. For all I knew that might be weeks.

Having finished my business I glanced at my watch. It was 7.30am and I was feeling ravenously hungry. I locked my room and made my way out to the restaurant. As I arrived, the restaurant was busy and I saw Ineke and Helen sitting where they had been the previous evening for dinner. I smiled and waved at them as I made my way to my table. Ineke waved shyly, obviously feeling slightly embarrassed about getting ill the previous evening. Helen gave me a huge smile and looked particularly rosy cheeked and flushed. I helped myself to fruit juices, cereal, and a full English breakfast followed by coffee and a cigarette. As I sat at my table, I had the strange feeling that something was missing. It was only after a few minutes that I realised what it was. *You're missing your fucking newspaper, Green. Take a look at the view to your right and ask yourself if you really need a newspaper!* I did just that. Across the grass and through the dappled shade of the palms the sun was getting higher. The tide had come in and the calm blue expanse of the Indian ocean spread out before me. In the distance, a dhow sailed silently.

"No, you don't need a newspaper," I said to myself under my breath. After a while I decided to go back to the room to make my plans for the day and check my phone for any missed calls. I avoided the glances of Ineke and Helen as I made my way out of the dining area and back to the room. I turned the fans on when I got there. There was only one text message. It was from Tracy Summerfield.

'Dear Jason, hope this message finds you well. I was thinking about you and I just wanted to say hi. Tracy." I lay on the bed in the breeze of the fans and read the message again. I thought about her, the tall, poised, and beautiful Tracy Summerfield, no doubt feeling lonely and sad, sitting in her flat in the freezing cold darkness of north London. I closed my eyes and drifted off to sleep. I hadn't been asleep for more than fifteen minutes when there was a loud knock on the door. I woke suddenly, it was unlike me to fall asleep in the day like that. Perhaps it had been the run, or perhaps I had eaten too much breakfast. *What now? That was too loud to be Helen, maybe house keeping?* I got up and opened the door only to be greeted by the beaming face of Richard Lewer-Allen. He was wearing sunglasses, a crisp white cotton shirt, and long khaki shorts. On his head he wore a cream coloured panama hat.

"Good morning sir! How are you today?" he said, still smiling.

"I'm well Richard, and you?" I said. *Jesus not again! After last night you are this man's hero Green! What the fuck?*

"I just wanted to say thank you again for last night," he said, "I've never seen anything like it. Also I've arranged a fishing charter this morning and I was wondering if you would like to come along? There's barracuda and sailfish out there, and it would be a nice way for me to show my gratitude. Those guys were pretty scary!"

He stood there with an expectant look on his face, I could see he had set his mind on this and it would be difficult to refuse.

"Umm, sure Rich, why not?" I said lifting my hands up resignedly.

"Excellent!" he said loudly, "excellent, well the boat is ready and waiting so, whenever you're ready. Oh, and I've also arranged some alternative transport."

"Ok, well let me sort some things out in here and I'll see you at the restaurant in a minute," I said.

"Brilliant, see you in a minute," he said and made his way back up the pathway. I shook my head as I gathered some supplies. Sunglasses, sun cream, camera. Then I locked the room and left. When I arrived he was sitting at the table I had been using. I was glad that Ineke and Helen had left the restaurant.

"Do you think we should take some water or drinks on the boat Rich?" I asked.

"All of that is taken care of Jase, all we have to do is get to the boat, and down there sir, is our chariot!" He pointed triumphantly towards the beach where a large and powerful looking quad bike was parked.

"I've hired it for the next few days. Those bastards from last night will have a hard time catching me on that baby!" We made our way down towards the bike.

"Jump on the back Jase!" he said as he swung his tall skinny frame over the seat. *This gets worse and worse Green.* I sat on the back and the engine roared into life. We sped on up the beach and in what felt like a few seconds we had arrived at the water-sports centre.

Richard parked the bike in the shade near the front and we got off.

He pointed towards the large ski boat which was now floating in the water. "There's our boat, fully stocked with bait, rods, reels, drinks and food. Shall we go fishing?"

"Let's go fishing!" I replied and we started walking towards the boat.

As we arrived and boarded the huge boat, I noticed that it was indeed fully kitted out. There was a fighting chair bolted into the rear, and a plethora of huge rods and reels in holders running down the side. All the rods were fitted with large deep sea lures and there was a captain and a deckhand on board. Within a few seconds a crew of workers had arrived and began to push the boat out to deeper water. The captain, who was standing on the raised deck turned to greet us. He wore tatty browned clothes and a straw hat. His skin was blacker than most due to the nature of his job and his white teeth showed in stark contrast.

"Good morning gentlemen. I am Austin, and I will be your captain today. Please sit down and relax, there are cokes in the cooler boxes. We will be leaving just now and going out beyond the reef to do some trawling. Let's hope we have some good luck today." The inboard motor gurgled into life as Richard and I looked around the boat and made small talk. Eventually the ground staff had pushed us out far enough to turn us around and we faced the reef. Slowly we made our way out through the shallow protected waters. I took a seat on the side of the boat and looked down into the crystal clear water. As we travelled, I noticed myriads of tiny fish and hundreds of huge red starfish on the sea bed. Richard was in a jovial mood and was busy familiarising himself with the layout of the lower deck and the fighting chair.

"How far to the reef, Austin?" he asked.

"Not far sir, three hundred metres now. Only one place to go out and come back. Straight ahead." Richard climbed up the chrome ladder to where the captain had the wheel.

"Ah this is great! Come up here and have a look Jason," he called. I followed suit and the three of us stood on the top deck watching our progress through the now deepening water towards the gap in the reef. Although there was a breeze from the movement of the boat, I could feel the sun beating on the fibreglass roof above and reflecting off the sparkling water all around me. Behind us the figures on the beach at the water-sports centre were tiny and the thick green jungle hung low and humid in the distance.

"So what will we be catching today Austin?" asked Richard.

"Fishing, yes, catching, not sure sir. But with luck, maybe barracuda, sailfish, even marlin."

"Marlin!" Richard said, "that would be something hey Jase?"

"It certainly would Rich." As we approached the reef the captain stood in concentration to ensure we made it safely through the right spot. Sensing he would prefer us not to be there I motioned to Richard as if to say 'let's go down.' He dutifully followed me down the steps to the fishing deck. The young deck hand was busying himself attending to the equipment, testing drag strengths, and polishing the massive reels. I opened one of the cooler boxes and found it full of ice, bottled water and soft drinks. I pulled out two waters and offered one to Richard.

"Cheers Jase, after last night I think I need it," he said.

"True story Rich. Was quite a party." We sat on the bench seats and gazed back at the slowly receding land, the powerful engine steadily rumbling and gurgling below us. Suddenly the boat started rocking more than before and the engine became louder.

"Through the reef now, hold on please, we go!" shouted the captain from the wheel deck. With my right hand I gripped the rail and braced my body as the rear of the boat sank, found its footing, and we roared off into the open sea. The front of the huge boat crashed violently but solidly through the breakers for a good two minutes, before the water calmed and the captain turned left. He made a parallel run with the now distant coast and we were finally on the plane, the wind blowing our hair. I turned to look at Richard. He was sitting on the opposite bench seat grinning at me from behind his sunglasses.

"This is great!" he shouted over the engines. I smiled and gave him the thumbs up. It was difficult not to like Richard Lewer-Allen as a person. He was exactly as his father had so painstakingly described in the red file I had been given. Spontaneous, full of jokes and laughter, an easy smile, definite ladies man, adventurous, wealthy. *Yes, wealthy Green. And don't forget that you are here to try and find out how he got that way.* I decided that when we finally reached the fishing grounds I would make some conversation and try and find out something about his business.

See if I could glean any information from him. *After all, we're now the best of friends, and friends share their secrets. Don't they Richard?* The water around us was calmer and a much deeper blue now. We travelled for a good twenty minutes at full tilt until the driver puller back the throttle and we came to rest.

"How long have you booked the boat for Rich?" I asked.

"I wanted the full day Jase, but they told me at the water-sports centre that it gets too hot and the fish don't bite at midday. So I guess we'll go back at around lunch time. Is that ok?"

"That's fine by me," I replied. "I think we should start trying to catch some fish."

"Yeah. Let's do that," he replied enthusiastically. With the engine chugging slowly, the captain turned the boat around so we were facing south.

"Right," he said, "now we are in very deep water, we are going to cast all of the rods and slowly make our way along the coast back towards Paje. The deck hand will help you with everything. Good luck gentlemen." We spent the next ten minutes casting the eight heavy rods out to sea behind us. We allowed for at least two hundred metres of line to drift out with the lures behind us so as not to spook the fish with the sound of the engine. The captain and deck hand were helpful and knowledgeable and eventually all the lines were out and the rods placed in the angled holders at the rear of the boat. We were both fitted with harnesses and given instructions on what to do in the event of a big strike. The fish would be allowed to run and the base of the rod would be fitted into the tough plastic cup of the harness. Then whoever had the fish would be strapped into the fighting chair and the battle would commence. I had to admit to myself that even given the strange and highly unusual situation I had found myself in, I was thoroughly enjoying myself. And so was Richard. He constantly questioned the captain about what to do in all manner of situations. How would we land a sail fish? What happens if we hooked a shark? Etc etc.

Fifteen minutes passed and he began to quieten down. The boat rocked gently in the swell and slowly we made our way along the coast with the deep, hypnotic rumble of the engine beneath us. We both sat in silence, smoking, drinking the iced water, and taking in the scene around us.

"So I guess it's a case of sit around and wait?" Richard said, looking at me.

"Yup, I guess it is, Rich." Suddenly I heard the captain get off his seat and walk to the left of the wheel deck. I turned to see him holding a pair of binoculars to his eyes and staring out to sea.

"Whale and dolphins to the left!" he shouted. Richard and I got up and walked out to the back of the fishing deck to have a look. In the far distance I made out the shape of the whale. Its body and huge tail surfacing, its spout occasionally blasting water high into the air. Then literally out of the blue, we were surrounded by a pod of dolphins. They were black in colour and shot around the boat like bullets.

"Wow look at that," said Richard, "that's amazing, I've never seen dolphins here before." They cruised through the water like guided torpedoes, occasionally tilting their heads to take a look at us. Then, just as quickly as they had come, their curiosity satisfied, they were gone. We sat back in the shade of the overhang and I decided it was time to start on Richard Lewer-Allen.

"So what do you do in London Rich? For work that is," I said casually. "Umm I run a shop," he replied, "a sports shop. We sell snowboards, skate boards, surfboards. That sort of thing. Been going for a few years now."

"Oh right, I think you mentioned it last night," I said, "is it your place or do you run it for someone else?"

"No, it's my place. I've got a few staff who are pretty good and they help me out." He was relaxed and talking easily. I had been worried that he might be reluctant to speak about his business, but it appeared not. "It's actually down near Liverpool Street Station, called The Boardroom, do you ever get down there?" he asked.

"No, not a lot," I said. "Working in insurance I don't get to move around as much as I'd like. Nope, it's pretty much a nine to five I'm afraid. Stuck in the office." "Yeah." he said dreamily, "but at least we're *here* and not in *that* shit hole."

"Oh I hear you," I said nodding, "have you been in London all your life?" I said.

"Yeah, I've lived either close to, or in London all my life. My father works in London. He's a banker. And a bit of a wanker for that matter," he grinned, "I like to travel though. And you Jase, have you been in London long?" It seemed I had his full trust and he would talk about most things. Maybe not the incident with the switching of the bags at the restaurant in Notting Hill. But most things. I figured I had no reason to lie to him.

"I was actually born in Rhodesia, and I was in the army there. I left after the war and came to London, been there ever since, so coming out to Africa now for me is great."

"Rhodesia" he said with interest, and paused, "is that Zimbabwe now?"

"That's right" I replied.

"Oh right, I thought your accent sounded a bit different."

We carried on making small talk like this for a while. It was all part of getting to know each other and I decided that given the situation, there was nothing else for it. It seemed he was slightly reluctant to let me know he was from a wealthy family. As if in some way it embarrassed him. What was clear to me was that there was no love lost between him and his father and when asked about his family he skilfully steered the conversation away from the subject. It all fell in place with what I had learned so far. Another thing that struck me was although he would talk freely about The Boardroom, he made no mention of any other 'sideline' - whatever it was that he was doing was clearly a secret. The boat chugged its way along the coast slowly. Richard and I talked and joked for at least an hour until suddenly the peace was shattered by the loud and alarming sound of screaming reels. Two of the massive fishing rods, one on my side, and one on Richard's side were bent over facing the rear of the boat. They jerked violently, seemingly in unison and I felt certain that one would surely break under what had to be enormous strain.

"Two fish on now, take the rods please!" The captain shouted from the wheel deck. The pitch of his voice had gone up a few octaves with excitement. Suddenly the deck was a flurry of activity. The quiet deck hand leapt into action and was frantically reeling in the other rods to save ours from getting tangled with them. Richard and I both went for our respective rods and yanked them out of their holders. The force pulling on my rod was unbelievable. It felt like a tug of war with a small car. In my youth I had fought the vicious tiger fish of the Zambezi Valley but this was something completely different. I jammed the base of the rod into my right lower belly, held it low for a second and then struck hard twice yanking it upwards to embed the hook properly. Whatever was on the other end felt it and the huge golden reel began to scream like a banshee. Any attempt to wind in the reel in this situation would have been totally futile.

"How much line is on this reel?" I shouted to the captain. "Two thousand metres sir, just let the fish run a while." the pain in my back from the beating with the club was starting to return as I held fast. I glanced to my left at Richard who was in a state of panic shouting questions at the deck hand continuously. I didn't pay it too much attention as I had my own set of problems. Eventually the captain and the deck hand managed to get all of the remaining rods reeled in and the fight began in earnest. The captain spoke to me in my ear above the noise and chaos,

"Right boss, I am going to fasten this fighting belt around your waist, when I tighten the drag the fish will pull hard and you must put the base of the rod into the cup. Ok?"

"Ok, I'll do that" I panted. The deck hand was busy telling Richard the same thing. The deck was now a confusing place of thudding footsteps, frantic shouting, and the high pitch screaming of the reels. I felt the heavy leather belt as it was fitted and fastened by the captain behind me. He shouted commands to the young deck hand in Swahili at the same time. He came up to my left and spoke to me, perspiration dripping from his face. "Ok boss, I am going to tighten the drag on your reel now and I want you to be ready ok?"

"Ok, let's do it," I replied. Keeping the giant rod at forty five degrees to the ocean, I put my left leg forward to brace myself and leant back slightly. Thankfully the end of the rod was now firmly in the leather and plastic cup of the fighting belt and no longer digging into my groin. The captain leant down and in a second had tightened the drag on the great reel. It was only then that I felt the true power of the monster that was on the end of my line. Although I kept my braced position I was dragged at least a metre towards the back end of the boat. I could feel the captain holding on to my fighting belt from behind me. I guessed in a fleeting thought that the last thing he needed was a client pulled overboard into the shark infested waters of the Indian Ocean.

"Fucking hell!" I shouted, "Jesus that's a strong fish!" At that moment the great beast leapt out of the ocean and soared majestically into the air. I saw it all as if it was slow motion. It was at least four hundred metres away but even then it was an awe-inspiring sight. Eight feet of sinuous, shiny black and blue muscle with a sword in front and a sail on its back, blasting frothy white spray behind it as it burst from the water twisting and jerking frantically.

"Marlin, boss. Big one!" screamed the captain behind me. The fish went under and started to dive, pulling to my right.

"Keep the rod up and try to reel in now boss!" shouted the captain.

I glanced at Richard to my left. He was hunched over his rod and groaning with the strain, his glasses half way down his sweat-soaked nose. I noticed that his line appeared to be pulling to the right as well. Suddenly the fish made a left turn and both rods bent in the same direction. Sensing something wrong, the deck hand shouted to the captain in Swahili. Richard asked above the chaos, "what's going on here?"

"One fish only, boss!" the captain replied, "one line tangled for sure, dunno which one!" At that moment I heard the twang and hiss of a line breaking. The brutal force on the end of my rod was still there and I heard a series of thudding sounds behind me. I turned briefly to see the figures of Richard and the deck hand spread eagled on the wooden deck. He had broken his line and had tumbled backwards onto the poor chap.

"Sorry, Rich!" I shouted shaking my head and straining as the fish made another run. The captain pulled me backwards towards the fighting chair. "Time to strap you in boss, this is gonna be a big fight!" Eventually I was manhandled into the seat and strapped in. There was an angled foot rest which helped take some of the strain off my now deeply wounded back. Through the chaos I felt for Richard, would he be disappointed or angry at losing the fish? It turned out he wasn't at all and he appeared to my left shouting encouragement and demanding advice from the deck hand. I was glad about that. By then the baking sun was high in the sky and I was soaked with sweat. It poured from my arms, my hands, my feet, my face. More than once I had to ask for assistance to push my sunglasses back up to my eyes. I knew in my mind that what I was going through was the equivalent of a workout at the gym three times over, but the adrenalin was coursing through my veins and keeping my burning muscles strong.

For the next half hour straight, the fish ran, then slowed. Ran, then slowed. I reeled in a bit, then it ran again. This pattern repeated itself countless times and I began to wonder if I was fighting a losing battle. All the while the captain fed me bottled water and Richard shouted excitedly. Then I saw the tail break the surface of the water. It was only a hundred metres away. I had been wrong and I was actually bringing it in slowly. Fish close now boss!" said the captain. I could feel my hands starting to develop blisters from the squeezing and pulling on the rod but seeing the great fish so close to us helped to put that out of my mind. As the fish began to tire it made great sweeps from the left to the right and I was being slowly turned with it as it moved.

Fifteen minutes, and a lot of pain and shouting later, I had brought it to within fifty metres of the boat. "Brilliant!" Richard shouted, "fucking brilliant! You're doing it Jase, keep it up!" The captain was on the radio excitedly informing the boss at the water-sports centre that we had hooked into a blue marlin and to prepare for a trophy weigh in.

"More water please!" I said to the captain who obliged by pouring it from the bottle into my mouth and over my shoulders to cool me down. The cycle of pain and progress continued until the fish was only twenty five metres from the boat. Thinking I had won the battle, I pulled and cranked the huge reel as hard as I could, snarling as I did it. The fish responded with its own anger and aggression and made another run. Again the reel which had started to quieten down, screamed, but this time with a sense of urgency. I imagined that somehow it knew, deep in its primitive mind, that the end was near, and that it was going to die. Thankfully the run only lasted for forty metres or so before it tired again and began its pattern of arcing from left to right, turning me in the chair with it. Through all the chaos, the heat, the pain and the sweat, I felt like I knew the great fish, and it knew me. Two old friends, or maybe enemies, pitted against each other in a deadly battle of wills. From then on I knew that the fish was exhausted and that with every time it turned back on itself whilst it made its arc, I brought it in another five metres. Richard stood on my left hunched over with his right fist clenched. His face was red with excitement and he was shouting, "come on Jase! Just one more pass and he'll be here, keep going mate! Keep going!"

The pattern continued until the fish was only ten metres from the boat. I could see its long dark shape under the water. Its relaxed and slow swimming motion only betrayed by the immense forces that were bending my rod at forty five degrees. Sensing that death was imminent, it broke its pattern and swam to my right as if to move to the front of the boat. "Must get out the seat now boss!" Screamed the captain. "Fish wanna go round to the front, you gotta bring him back now!" He quickly freed me from the seat and I stood for the final chapter of what had become an epic battle. Bracing myself with my left leg, and leaning back into the strain, I slowly moved to the side of the boat in the middle of the deck. I gave another monumental pull on the rod. I felt a long slow, ever-increasing burn in my left arm as I pulled him round for another pass. Slowly he turned and came. The captain had grabbed an eight foot long, thick metal pole with an ugly hook on the end of it. He stood next to me holding it out ready for the pass. "I'm gonna get him with the gaff now boss!" he whispered. "Deck hand and me gonna hold him, then we bring him in." I brought the great fish slowly back towards me from the front of the boat. Again everything appeared to be in slow motion.

He was two metres away from where I stood and was attempting to make another arc. It was then that I saw him for the truly magnificent creature that he was. Through the crystal clear water I saw the serrations on the sword. I saw the beautiful luminous shades of green, blue, and black running the entire eight foot length of his perfectly formed body. I saw the huge spiny fin and tail break the water. Then I looked into his eye and he looked into mine. His eye was the size of a tennis ball, but black and flat. *What are you thinking?* I thought, feeling almost delirious with exhaustion, *you're looking death in the eye, what are you thinking now?* The captain put one foot on the side of the deck and held the gaff out ready to impale the fish. All the while I stared into its seemingly emotionless eye. Then, as if to say, "thanks, but this is not going to happen today," the fish made a sharp movement to the right with his head and the thick wire trace that attached the lure to the nylon line snapped. The great fish moved off at an angle into the deep. I watched it go for a good four metres through the clear water. It moved with slow, graceful, dignified sweeps of its tail until it disappeared into the blue. For some reason I felt a huge sense of relief. Not because the fight was over but because the fish had got away. It had fought with immense strength and bravery. It had looked death in the eye and won. "You go boy," I said out loud, "you deserve it." I handed to rod to the captain who had tears in his eyes by that time. I guessed he thought he would miss out on a very large tip. Both Richard and the deck hand were both standing shaking their heads. Their lips were moving and they were speaking but at that stage I couldn't hear a thing. I walked over to a bench seat that was situated in the shade at the back of the cabin and slumped down onto it on my back. I lay there breathing heavily, soaked with sweat, for a good ten minutes as the sounds of the engine, the lapping of the water, and the chatter of the others gradually returned. The next thing I knew was Richard had sat down near me and heard the sound of a bottle opening.

"I think that deserves a beer, Jason. That was fucking amazing. Sorry you lost it mate!" I opened my eyes and reached up to grab the bottle he was holding out for me. The icy coldness of the bottle soothed the red and raw callouses of my right hand.

"Tell you the truth Rich, I'm not upset it got away at all," I said, "I'm glad. It was too beautiful to kill."

"You're right" he said thoughtfully, "it was. What a fucking amazing day huh?" "That's for sure." I lay there, recovering and chatting to Richard for a good ten minutes before eventually sitting up. We spoke at length about the fight and the fact that we both thought we had hooked into a fish at the same time.

We laughed about his line breaking and him falling into the deck hand. He wasn't bitter about anything and instead was happy just to have been there for the experience. I had become fond of Richard Lewer-Allen despite who I was and what I was doing. It was impossible not to be. As he passed me a second beer we toasted the blue marlin that got away. As we drank my mind slipped back to the sad fact that I was there in a professional capacity. *Another fine bonding experience for you and Richard today, Green. How are you going to extricate yourself from this? How is this going to come to a conclusion?*

The captain, who had been busying himself on the wheel deck climbed down and addressed us both. "sorry bosses, time is late now," he said in his Swahili accent, "think we should start to head back to Paje."

"That's fine Austin," Richard said, "let's go". The captain climbed back up the chrome ladder to the top deck and revved the engines slightly. Richard and I took seats on either side of the boat so as to take in the view as we went. The sky above was completely cloudless and the dark green slab of the distant shore looked like a thick carpet.

"We go!" shouted the captain. The powerful inboard engine growled like a singer in a thrash metal band and we were off. Richard and I didn't talk very much as we sped down the coast back to Paje. There was too much noise from the engine and the wind. Instead we sat, enjoying the view and the cooling effect of the spray and the wind. Eventually we neared Paje and the captain made a wide circle to the right with the boat as if to show off to the tourists on the beach. It was then that I noticed the large, white Mediterranean house I had seen that morning on my run. It looked even more imposing from out on the sea, stretching for hundreds of metres along the coast. Surrounded by jungle on either side. The whole expanse of it protected by the four metre stone wall. Then the captain slowed the engine so we would be able to safely navigate through the breakers and the reef to the calm water beyond. Finally the noise of the motor and the wind were gone and we were able to talk again. I stared at the house blankly as I sipped my beer. "I saw that place this morning when I went for a jog," I said pointing at it. "What is it, is it a hotel or a house? Looks pretty big."

Richard turned to see what I was pointing at. "Oh that?" he said, "that's a house. Belongs to a friend of mine. Carlos. Yeah, it's huge for sure."

"Impressive place!" I said.

"Carlos," replied Richard, "oh he's a business man. You know the bottled water we were drinking? He bottles that stuff. Sells it all over Zanzibar and Tanzania. He's also got a surfboard manufacturing business on the mainland in Dar Es Salaam. Ships them all over the world including to my shop in London."

"Oh right." I said and thought nothing of it.

"I'm actually going to a party there tonight," he said, "you should come with me Jason. Bring Helen along." I sipped my beer and thought about the offer for a few seconds. I had screwed up enough and been with him the previous night and that day. It couldn't harm any more. "Will you take Ineke?" I asked.

He turned and looked at me. "Um, no," he said thoughtfully, "no I don't think so."

"Well we can't separate them" I said, "they *are* on holiday *together.*" The boat chugged along for a few more seconds. "well let's just you and me go together." he said. He had the same look on his face as when he had invited me on the fishing trip in the morning. *Go on Green, you might learn something, you never know, and you're already in the shit here.*

"Yup ok, I'll come along Rich," I said reaching for my cigarettes.

"Excellent!" he replied. "Considering what happened last night, I think we should go by taxi," I said.

"No need!" he said smiling, "I'll pick you up on the quad bike!" I nodded, lit my cigarette, and stared back at the water sports centre. Eventually we made it safely back through the reef and into the calm water beyond. The driver revved the motors briefly just before we got to the beach and boat surged forward. The sand made an abrasive sound on the fibreglass below as we stopped.

"Very sorry about the fish bosses," said the captain mournfully. "That's fine Austin, we had a good time," said Richard as he passed him a $100 bill.

"Oh thank you boss, thank you very much, thank you."

I thanked the crew and got off the boat. "What are you doing this afternoon Jason?" Richard asked.

"No real plans Rich," I said, "thought I might go back to the hotel and catch up on some emails, do some work."

"Yeah," he said thoughtfully, "I've actually got some stuff I need to take care of as well. Can I give you a ride back to your hotel?"

"Thanks, but I think I'll take a walk Rich." I said.

"Ok, well, I'll be with you at about 6pm, there's no need to have dinner at the hotel. There'll be plenty of food at Carlos' place, should be a great party." He said.

"That's fine," I said, "I'll see you later Rich and thanks for the fishing, it was a lot of fun."

"Pleasure mate, see you later," he said and I made my way back down the beach in the blistering sun. The walk took the usual ten minutes and I was grateful to get into the shade when I arrived at my hotel. There was no sign of Ineke or Helen anywhere, and I made my way straight to my room to the cool of the fans. I was covered in dry sweat and sea salt so after a quick cold shower I felt a lot better. I stood in the breeze of the fans and stared out of the window wondering what to do next. Richard had said that he had some work to catch up on. What work was he talking about? Richard didn't work very hard even when he was at home in London so what work would he possibly have to do here on the east coast of Zanzibar? It would be foolish of me to go up to his hotel after just having spent the entire morning with him. He might see that as unusual if, by accident, we were to run into each other. After all, we did have a bad habit of doing that. I decided that I would eat some lunch in the restaurant and then take a taxi ride around the area, perhaps down to the next town, Jambiani, for no other reason than just to have a look around. The thought of lying on a sun-lounger all afternoon doing nothing didn't appeal to me. Before I left, I replied to the message I had received from Tracy Summerfield. I kept it polite and business-like telling her where I was and the fact that I was on business and would return to London within ten days or so. I watched the message go, then stood in the breeze of the fans, staring out the window at the scene outside. I still found it hard to fathom the incredible colours of the place. The dark lush green of the lawn and the trees against the stark whiteness of the sand. Then the incredible tanzanite blue of the ocean with paler sky above. I walked back to my bag and dug out the number for the taxi driver, Hassan, from the previous day. I dialled the number and it rang immediately. "Taxi service, Hassan speaking, can I help you?" came the reply.

"Hello Hassan, this is Jason Green, you gave me a ride from the airport to Paje yesterday, how are you?"

"I am very well Mr Jason, how are you sir?"

"Good thanks," I said, "I was thinking of going on a bit of a drive today, maybe down to Jambiani, just to have a look around. Are you available?"

"Sorry boss, I am in Stone Town now," he said sounding disappointed, "but I can come there if you like. It will take me thirty five minutes only." I thought about it for a second then I decided that I would prefer him to drive me rather than anyone else. He had struck me as being honest and helpful and I had enjoyed talking to him. Plus he smoked cigarettes. "Ok that's fine," I said, "I will pay you extra to come from Stone Town. I will have some lunch now and when you arrive please tell the reception to call me from the restaurant."

"Ok boss," he said, "I will see you very soon, thank you very much for calling me."

"No problem, see you shortly," I said and hung up. I packed a small bag with my camera and a few other bits and pieces, and headed out to the restaurant. I had been hoping to avoid the Dutch girls, Helen and Ineke, but as I arrived I was greeted by their smiling faces and waves.

"Please come and join us!" they called, as I walked in. It would have been rude not to so I agreed and sat down with them at their table. We made small talk and laughed as we ate a seafood feast and drank mineral water from plastic bottles. All the while Helen kept looking at me with a mischievous smile and a sparkle in her eye. I decided that it was an appropriate time to let them know that I would not be there that afternoon or evening. I told them both that I had some business to attend to in Jambiani and that I would only return later that night. After all, I wasn't lying to them, and in reality I was actually on business. The disappointment in their faces, especially Helen's, was tangible. It was as if in some way they thought that we were on holiday together and shouldn't be separated. It made me feel a little bit guilty especially after what had happened the previous night with Helen, but Richard had said that he would not invite Ineke to the party and who was I to argue with that? I consoled them by saying that I would do my best to join them both for a drink later that evening to which they seemed to cheer up. Soon after a waiter approached to inform me that my taxi had arrived. I signed for the meal, bade my farewells to the two ladies and headed towards the reception.

I arrived to find Hassan waiting for me in a shady spot near his car. He was wearing similar clothes as he had been the previous day and as he stood to greet me, he gave me his familiar toothless grin. "How are you, Mr Jason?"

"I'm well Hassan, thanks for coming to collect me."

"No problem at all," he said as he opened the front passenger door,

"Where would you like to go today?"

"I thought we would take a drive south along the coast, maybe to Jambiani. I have some hours to kill so I thought I would take a look around."

"Hakuna matata!" he said cheerfully. He made a U-turn in the parking area and we drove through the big reed gates and down the sand road that led to the tar. When we got there we took a left turn and trundled off slowly. "So, how is business?" I asked, making conversation.

"Ahh it's ok Mr Jason, up and down sometimes you know. But then if I get lucky I get a customer like you and things are a bit better." Once again I was reminded of the stifling heat of the taxi as Hassan wiped the sweat from his brow with a dirty looking cloth. To my right was scrubby bush and to my left was the lush green belt of palms and jungle. In front of us the road stretched ahead, baked a light grey colour by the scorching sun. We smoked and talked as we had done the previous day. A few minutes later I noticed another sand road to the left. It was wide and seemed well-used.

"Is that the road to the water-sports centre Hassan?" I asked.

"Yes Mr Jason, that is the one. Did you see it from the beach?"

"I did," I replied, remembering the unfortunate incident with the muggers the previous night. "So where do you live?" I asked.

"I live back there in Paje," he said pointing his thumb in the direction we had come from.

"If you drive a few hundred metres up the road past your hotel, you will come to the village of Paje. That is where most of the people live. My house is up there"

"Ok," I said, "I haven't seen the village yet. Perhaps you can show me on the way back?"

"Hakuna matata." He replied. We carried on talking as we drove and I noticed the various entrances to the lodges and hotels I had seen from the beach. I also noticed the particularly grand entrance to the Eden Beach Lodge where Richard was staying. "So this taxi" I asked, "is this your only vehicle or do you have others?"

"This is my only taxi Mr Jason, but I do have a small dhow."

"A dhow?" I asked with interest, "a sailing boat?"

"Yes, a sailing boat. Thirty feet long. It stays in the harbour at Stone Town."

"So is it a working boat?" I asked. "What do you do with it?"

"Sometimes we carry tourists to Prison Island for snorkelling. Sometimes we carry spices and coconuts to Dar Es Salaam. It just depends on who wants to hire it," he said, wiping his forehead again with his cloth.

"Ok, that's interesting," I replied. As we carried on down the coast, the jungle on my left became thicker and there were hardly any buildings to be seen. It was then we came to a tall stone wall and a sharp right turn. "And what is this here?" I asked pointing to the wall in front of us.

"This is the property of Mr da Costa," he said, as he turned the vehicle.

"Mr da Costa. Is he the owner of the big house I saw on the beach?" I asked.

"Yes, that is the one. This is his property here behind this wall," he replied, "a very very big property this one."

"Why is there such a big wall Hassan?" I asked. Hassan shook his head and smiled. "Ahh this man, Mr Jason, he doesn't want people to come into his property. When this man came here ten years ago, he bought this land from the government, then he put this wall around the whole place. We as children, we used to play inside there many years ago. Inside there you can find fresh water caves and water springs."

"So he is the person who bottles the drinking water that I've seen all over the place?" I asked.

"Yes," he replied, "he is the very one." We carried on driving until we got to the boundary of the huge property and turned left. We drove alongside the imposing wall until we passed a huge black electric gate. Sitting outside was a security guard similar to the one I had seen sleeping in the early morning outside the front of the property on the beach. Strapped around his shoulder was an AK.47 machine gun. Hassan waved at the guard who responded by smiling and waving back.

"Why does this man have so many guards Hassan?" I asked as we drove past the gate. Again he shook his head. "Ahh this man, Mr da Costa," he said, "sure, he doesn't want anyone to get inside that property. He is too cheeky!"

"Is he?" I asked.

"Very cheeky, very cheeky." I shrugged my shoulders and we drove on beyond the stone wall and back onto the main tar that led down the coast to the next town. Ten minutes later we arrived in the small fishing village of Jambiani. It had a similar feeling to Paje with the main population's housing to the right and the hotels and lodges to the left. "Where would you like to go Mr Jason?" asked Hassan.

"Just take me for a bit of a drive around and then maybe a hotel where I can have a drink." I replied. He did just that and we drove around for a while before he dropped me at a beachside resort called Jambiani Paradise. Hassan insisted on waiting in the taxi while I went inside. I told him that I would send a Coca Cola out to him with one of the waiters, to which he agreed happily. Although the resort was clean and well maintained, it was different to Paje in that there wasn't as much vegetation between the main road and the sea. Still, there was a pleasant round bar set under thatch, which I decided would suit me fine for a few hours. I ordered a Safari beer for myself and a coke for Hassan. I told the waiter to take it to him in the cab. There were a few German tourists sitting on the opposite side of the bar but they were deep in a conversation I couldn't understand, and I was quite happy to sit in the breeze and quietly drink my beer. I spent the afternoon there, occasionally talking to the barman, and taking in the scenery until I looked at my watch and saw that it had just gone 4pm. It was time to head back to Paje and get ready for the evening with Richard. I paid my bill and made my way back to Hassan who was by then asleep in his taxi. I woke him and we slowly drove back up north, passing the big stone wall and eventually arriving in Paje.

He showed me the main village with all its stores and tiny houses set amongst the palms and then I told him it was time for me to return to my hotel. We drove through the reed gates and parked at the reception. I gave Hassan three US$20 notes to which his eyes almost bulged out of his face. "Thank you, Mr Jason. Very kind, thanks very much," he said gratefully. "Thank you Hassan, I'll call you if I need you again," I said as I got out of the car. Cautiously, I made my way up the pathways towards my room. I really didn't want to run into Ineke or Helen again, especially as I had told them I wouldn't be back till later. Thankfully I didn't see them and I made it back to my room alone. By the time I had showered and changed it was 5.40pm and starting to darken outside.

If the previous evening was anything to go by, the two ladies would only arrive at the bar after dinner so I made my way down there to have a beer and wait for Richard to arrive. I was greeted by the smiling face of Robson, the barman who had been there the previous evening. He greeted me in his broken English and offered me a cold Safari which I accepted. We sat quietly talking to each other until I heard the sound of the quad bike racing down the beach towards us. The sound of the engine got louder and louder until it stopped nearby. Twenty seconds later, Richard Lewer-Allen stooped his tall frame under the coloured lights of the beach bar and stepped in. He was looking particularly smart that evening and was beaming from ear to ear. "Good evening gentlemen!" he said as he stepped up and pulled out a barstool.

"How're you doing Rich?" I asked.

"Very well thanks," he replied. He glanced at his watch briefly. "Well, I think we should have a quick drink before we leave," he said, "is that ok with you Jase?"

"That's fine Rich, let's do that," I replied. He ordered two more Safaris and as we sat there chatting I couldn't help notice that he looked a little flushed and excited. *Perhaps he caught the sun this morning when we were fishing?* I thought, *or maybe he's just had a fat line of coke?* He drummed his fingers impatiently on the bar as we sat and before I knew it he had finished his beer. "Ready when you are Jase!" he said, as he plonked the empty bottle on the counter.

"Are you sure we don't have to take anything with us Rich?" I asked, "perhaps a bottle of something?" "

Jase, we're going to Carlos da Costa's house," he said smiling, "I can assure you, everything is taken care of at his parties."

"Ok then," I said, "let's do it." We said our goodbyes to Robson the barman and made our way down to the quad bike which was parked on the beach. Richard fired up the engine, I hopped on the back and we were off. In the rapidly fading light we passed the various hotels and the water-sports centre. I glanced briefly up the sand road from where the muggers had come. There was no one in sight. To my left, the expanse of the sea had gone from dark blue to gun metal grey. I knew when the moon rose it would turn silver again as it had done the previous night. The breeze from the ocean along with the wind from the speed of the bike blew in my face and hair as we rode. Soon we came up alongside Richard's hotel. He revved the bike harder and we sped off up the beach towards the big house of Carlos da Costa.

CHAPTER TWELVE

- THE PARTY

There was no slowing Richard down as we sped through the semi-darkness. On our right was the thick, lightless jungle that I had run past in the morning. Eventually, we rounded the bend and the lights of the big house began to come into vision. As we pulled in and stopped at the base of the corner of the great stone wall, I noticed the guard who had been stationed there in the morning was back for his night shift. Instead of being asleep, this time he was leaning against the wall smoking a cigarette. He crushed it out as we arrived and stood to attention. All along the base of the wall were weather-proof spotlights at ten metre intervals. They shone upwards making it look all the more imposing. We got off the bike and walked toward the guard.

"Good evening, can I help you?" he said in a thick Swahili accent.

"Yes please," said Richard, "it's Richard Lewer-Allen and guest, for the party this evening."

"I was not told anyone was coming this way," the guard said nervously, "please wait while I radio Tintin to check if it is ok"

"That's perfectly fine," said Richard, "please go ahead." The guard swung the AK47 around his shoulder and reached for a hand-held radio that was strapped to his waist. It crackled and whistled as he spoke into it in rapid Swahili. "Your name again please?" asked the guard. The upward shining lights at the base of the wall gave him a spooky appearance as he spoke. "Richard Lewer-Allen and guest." There was a brief exchange of words with whoever was on the other side and the guard put the radio back into his belt. "Tintin says it's OK for you to come this way, please follow me."

"Thank you," said Richard, and we began walking up the sandy slope toward the heavy black metal gate I had seen in the morning. "*Tintin?*" I said to Richard as we walked. He turned and smiled, "Tintin works for Carlos, he's in charge of security here, sort of a right hand man." We eventually arrived at the gate, it was ten feet tall with ugly spikes at the top. The guard immediately started fumbling in his pockets searching for a key. When he eventually found it and unlocked the gate, it squeaked as it opened. "Please enjoy yourselves," said the guard as we walked through. "Thanks," said Richard, "we'll see you later."

I followed Richard up a steep and winding set of tiled stairs until we got to the first landing which was level with the front wall. It was only then that I saw the true scale of the place. To my left was an infinity pool tiled with marble that stretched for at least thirty metres along the top of the wall. All around was luxurious garden furniture and thick, white cotton covered loungers. Tall white classical statues of semi naked ladies stood at intervals along the length of the place. The house itself was staggered into three separate levels and the whitewashed Mediterranean architecture of the bottom level, where we stood, was at least a hundred metres long. We paused to look out to the sea and back at the house which was lit by cleverly hidden lights. All around the bottom level were huge terracotta pots that held meticulously pruned palm trees. The place was without a doubt, the very last word in luxury. Somewhere in the distance I could hear what sounded like a live band playing along with the constant chatter of a group of people. I shook my head in amazement at the sheer scale of the place. "Wow," I said quietly, "this is some house."

"It certainly is," replied Richard, "and this is only the bottom. The party will be on the second level and the top is Carlos' private area."

"Oh right," I said, "so how many people are expected?"

"Usually about fifty or sixty," Richard said, "live band, full spread, you name it. Carlos' parties are the best in Zanzibar, come along Jase, you ain't seen nothing yet!" I could see he was excited and was eager to get going. I followed him past the back of the infinity pool and along the huge building towards a grand sweeping, double staircase that obviously led up to the middle level. As we made our way up, the sound of the music and the chatter of the guests got louder and louder.

When we arrived at the middle level, the scene in front of me was pretty much what I imagined an 'A' list Hollywood party would be like. All around was lush green lawn dotted with flaming bamboo torches for lighting. Beyond that was yet another marble tiled pool with thousands of water lilies floating on the surface for effect. To the right of the pool and stretching out with a wooden balcony was a paved seating area. Again, the expensive looking tables and chairs were covered with crisp white linen. Silver champagne coolers and cutlery adorned each table which were individually lit by windproof candle lights. To the left of the seating area was a purpose built stage and dance floor. Above the seven piece band hung a large glitter ball on a custom-built lighting rack. It spun slowly, sending a sparkling effect over the entire scene.

The band was playing mellow lounge music and a few guests were shuffling and turning on the dance floor. To the left of the dance floor was a huge bar area which was manned by at least four barmen in uniform. Their waiters moved effortlessly between the bar and the seating area delivering bottles of champagne to the many well-dressed guests of all races, who mingled around clinking crystal glasses and made small talk. To the left of the bar area, and near the main building of the second level of the mansion were the food tables. Although it was obvious that they were not yet serving anything, I saw at least three chefs, complete with uniform, fussing over what I imagined would be a very impressive dinner. We stopped to take in the scene in front of us. Richard turned and smiled at me, his hands out stretched. "Well Jason, what do you think?" Again, I noticed his excitement and responded accordingly. "Well Rich, I've got to say, it's pretty impressive."

"I think we should go get ourselves a drink and a table!" he said. We walked across the grass and through the seating area. A few of the guests nodded politely in greeting to us. We both reciprocated and I could see that Richard was unfamiliar with the majority of the guests. Eventually we found an undisturbed table near the dance floor and took our seats. Somewhere in the distance, sticks of incense were burning. The combination of the smell, the music, the lights, and the dancing was intoxicating. Someone had gone to great effort to create the atmosphere and it had worked extremely well. "I'm off to the bar Jase, what would you like?" asked Richard, looking pleased with himself.

"I think I'll have a Scotch please Rich," I replied, "somehow I don't think a Safari would fit in here."

"You're right," he said standing up, "I'll be right back." He made his way across the dance floor to the bar area to order. I took a look at the people around me. There was a mixture of white, black, Indian, and mixed race.

They all seemed to be between the ages of forty and seventy. Some of the men were overweight and sat like toads with sweaty scowls on their faces. I imagined they would be government officials or hotel owners. The party was very obviously for the crème de la crème of Zanzibar society. The men were all dressed smart casual while the women wore elegant evening gowns. At that moment, a waiter approached me with two bottles of champagne on a linen covered tray. "Good evening sir, I have brought you some champagne, Cristal or Dom Perignon?" I chose the Cristal and he carefully placed the bottle in the silver cooler in the centre of our table. Richard returned to the table with the drinks and took his seat. As he sat, he glanced around at the guests like I had done. I lit a cigarette and held my glass up to toast him. "Well thanks for inviting me Rich, and cheers," I said.

"It's a pleasure Jase, thanks for coming along with me," he replied as our glasses met.

"So," I said, looking around at the guests, "where is the man of the house? Is he around?"

"No," he replied, "I can't see him anywhere, I'm sure he'll be down shortly though." At that moment I noticed a huge black man appear from the darkness behind the stage. He had long dreadlocks tied behind his head and he wore a full tuxedo. In his hand he held a two way radio and he was busy talking into it as he walked. He must have been at least seven foot tall and he had the build to match his height. His huge shoulders were almost splitting the material of the tuxedo as he made his way between the stage and the bar area towards the dance floor. He stopped just short of the dance floor and spoke into the radio once again. Although I was mesmerised by the sheer size of the man, I noticed that Richard had also seen him arrive. "That's Tintin," said Richard raising his hand and waving in an effort to catch the man's attention. It obviously worked because the man waved back as he continued speaking into his radio. I could see he had a deep scar running from his right temple down to his chin and his dark, unsmiling eyes met mine briefly as he spoke. A few seconds later, the radio conversation finished and the huge man made his way over to greet Richard. Richard stood to greet him and even with his six foot something frame, the man towered above him. "Hello Tintin, how are you? Long time no see!" said Richard smiling.

"Yes Richard, long time, I am fine thank you," the man's voice was deep and loud. Once again his dark eyes darted at mine. "This is my friend Jason Green, he is my guest tonight," said Richard. I stood up to shake hands and was again aware of the colossal size of the man. "Pleased to meet you," I said holding my hand out. His hand enveloped mine like a bunch of bananas. His grip was tight and his flesh was cold and sweaty. "Welcome Mr Green, I hope you enjoy yourself," he boomed. As he spoke he looked at me once again and for a brief moment everything appeared in slow motion. His eyes were dark and cruel. The deep and menacing scar on his face shone with sweat and I knew, by pure instinct, that this was a very dangerous man indeed. Our hands parted and the moment was over. "So where is Carlos, Tintin? I haven't seen him yet." said Richard cheerfully. At that moment the radio the man was carrying squawked and he paused to listen to the message.

"He is coming now, Richard. I must tell the band, please enjoy yourselves," the man turned and made his way to the band. He bent over and spoke to the leader, who was playing an alto saxophone. The musician immediately motioned to the other band members who promptly stopped the music. Suddenly they restarted with a slightly louder volume and a new song. I instantly recognised it as the old Frank Sinatra Broadway hit New York, New York.' Then the band leader spoke into his microphone as if he was introducing some famous personality.

"Ladies and gentlemen," he said, "please welcome your host for the evening, Mr Carlos da Costa!" I looked around me and saw many of the guests clapping, a few of them cheered politely, all of them seemed to be focused on a stairway near the food tables that obviously led to the upper level of the mansion. Then I saw Carlos da Costa for the first time. From a distance he struck me as a slightly comical figure dressed in a white suit over a colourful tropical shirt. He made his way down the stairs at a quick pace, waving at the crowd with his right hand. In his left hand he held a large cigar. He reached the end of the stairs and immediately went to greet the guests at the bar shaking hands with the men and kissing the women on their cheeks. I was struck at how short the man was. Even with the heels of his white shoes, he was no higher than five foot. Richard turned to me, grinning and shaking his head. "What a character," he said above the music.

"He certainly is," I replied, "he made quite an entrance there."

"He always does that," said Richard, "he's a great chap." I sat there sipping my whisky, enjoying the atmosphere, and watching the host as he moved from guest to guest. He made his way slowly, from the bar through the dance floor and to the tables behind us. Richard kept turning and watching the man as he greeted his guests. It was as if he was anxious, almost desperate to see him. Eventually Carlos da Costa finished with the tables behind us and started making his way back to the bar in our direction. Richard stood up and turned to face him as he came nearer. He stopped dead in his tracks when he was two metres away and held his hands up in a welcoming gesture of recognition. "Epa Reeechard, my friend, long time! Why you no come to see us?" The man had a thick Portuguese accent and a loud, deep gravely voice. The voice of a showman. It sounded like he had been a very heavy smoker most of his sixty-something years. I was struck once again at how short he was.

It was as if he had no neck at all and his fat bald head was attached directly to his shoulders. His face was very sun-tanned and it showed up against his white suit and tropical shirt. His short body was not overweight but was squat and solid and thick black hair was visible on his hands. The flesh around his eyes was dark and shiny in the lights and as he made the final steps towards Richard, I saw that he walked with duck feet.

He stopped short of embracing Richard and instead gave him a warm two-handed handshake. It was as if he was slightly intimidated by Richard's tall frame. "How are you Carlos?" asked Richard, beaming from ear to ear, "it's great to see you old friend!"

"Yes, yes, fine, fine!" said the short man, his small eyes darting around constantly. "Always good Reechard, always good to see you my friend." Their hands parted, and Richard motioned towards me. "This is my friend Jason Green, I brought him here this evening as my guest." Carlos' face turned to mine. Although he gave the impression of being a jovial clown, an eccentric and entertaining host, my instincts told me that he was not to be trusted. His constantly darting eyes unnerved me somewhat and left me feeling cold. I put on a pleasant, happy face and stood to shake hands with the man. His hand was dry and warm and as I had expected, his grip was firm.

"Welcome, welcome," the man said in his heavy Portuguese accent, "a friend of Reeechard, is a friend of mine."

"Nice to meet you, Carlos," I said with a smile, "it's a great party." His eyes held mine as we spoke as if he was reading me, as if he was somehow looking into my soul. Then the moment was over and he addressed us both with his usual flamboyant showmanship. "Please, enjoy gentlemen. Good food, good champagne, the stars in the sky, music, beautiful people."

"Thank you Carlos," said Richard, "will you be singing for us tonight?" The short man feigned embarrassment, "maybe later Reechard my friend, I have bad throat." As he spoke he turned to look at the staircase he had just come down. "Epa Reechard, see," he said motioning towards the staircase, "my beautiful wife, she comes now. I go to greet her!" I turned my head to glance at the staircase, half expecting a short, fat, Portuguese woman in a black dress. What I saw left me gob- smacked. My lower jaw almost hit the floor at the sight of her, and immediately alarm bells began ringing loudly in every corner of my mind. She was tall, dark, and stunningly beautiful. She glided down the stairs with effortless grace and serenity. Hers was a face I would never forget in my entire life. Just like the last time I had seen her, she seemed to have a mesmerising effect on everyone that laid eyes on her. She wore a backless white dress that was cut just above the knees revealing her long, slender, silky smooth legs. A diamond wedding ring sparkled on her left hand as it slid down the bannister as she descended. Her huge, perfectly white smile was in stark contrast to the milky coffee complexion of her face.

Her long dark hair was once again tossed over to one side, revealing the diamond necklace and the tendons of her neck. She was the woman I had seen in the restaurant in Cape Town. The woman who had caused such a stir when she met Richard for dinner in Kalk Bay. The woman who had accompanied him to the club and danced the night away. She was the woman Richard had skilfully seduced and taken back to his guest house. And she was the wife of Carlos da Costa. I sat down pretending to show no interest and immediately reached for the glass of Scotch. I needed it by then. *Jesus Christ Green, talk about a can of fucking worms!* With his duck feet walk, Carlos da Costa made his way over to base of the stairs to greet his wife. Dutifully she stooped her six foot frame over and kissed him on both cheeks. I glanced at Richard to see his reaction and found him standing there, staring at her with a half smile on his face. For a moment, he was totally dumbfounded. Speechless, and unable to move at all. I cleared my throat in an effort to snap him out of it. He shook his head briefly, blinked once, and sat down. Like I had done, he reached for his Scotch, took a large sip, and looked around at the guests. Then he turned to me and raised his eyebrows.

"So", he said, "what do you think Jase?" I knew he was referring to the party in general but I couldn't help the thoughts that were racing through my mind.

What do I think Richard? You don't want to know what I think. "Great party Rich, thanks for the invite." I sat there, tapping my foot to the music, trying to look like I was enjoying myself. Out of the corner of my eye I could see that Richard was watching the woman as she walked slowly through the crowds with her mismatched husband. I tried to make some light conversation with him and spoke about the fishing trip earlier that day, but he was clearly distracted by her presence and was a bit vague with his responses. Then I saw his face light up and he waved enthusiastically at the couple who were now behind me. I turned to look and noticed that Carlos da Costa was busy talking to an elderly man in a tuxedo while his wife stood nearby. She was smiling, her head slightly tilted, and was waving back at Richard. She had a sparkle in her eyes and was also clearly pleased to see him. It was a tense moment and I thought briefly that she might recognise me. Thankfully, she didn't and the moment passed. My head started to fill with questions. *How long had this affair been going on? Apart from meeting with Richard, what had the woman been doing in Cape Town? Why was there so much security at the house of Carlos da Costa? Why had I felt so uneasy in the presence of Tintin and Carlos? How could one man accumulate so much obvious wealth by bottling mineral water? How would this man react if he found out that Richard was having a clandestine affair with his wife?* So many questions. I decided that there was only one thing for it and the best thing I could do was watch and learn. There was the nagging thought that things were not as I would have wanted them and that the situation was out of my control. But at the same time there wasn't a lot that I could do about it. *Go with the flow, Green, go with the flow.* Seemingly relieved by the woman acknowledging his presence, Richard was filled with new zest for life and began to laugh and joke with me again. He swung his chair around to face me as he spoke but I knew the reason he had done so was so he could follow the progress of the couple as they made their way through the crowds behind me. He spoke with a half smile and his eyes constantly flicked towards them. Noticing Richard's glass was almost empty, I finished mine and stood up. "Would you like another Scotch Rich?" I said casually, "I'm off to get one."

"Yeah, please Jase, same again," was the reply. I made my way slowly to the bar area, nodding greetings to the various guests I passed on the way. I got to the bar, made my order, and turned as if to watch the band and the guests in the seating area. By then Carlos and his wife were in amongst the tables shaking hands with the guests and generally being pleasant hosts. When my eyes went to Richard it was as I had expected. Although he was making great efforts not to make it obvious, he was watching her like a hawk. Carlos da Costa and his wife stood in the crowd with their backs to me. He was obviously trying to get a point across to one of the guests, and was gesticulating with his short arms as he spoke. She on the other hand stood by his side dutifully, a glass of champagne in her hand. Her long dark hair cascaded over her shoulders and down her exposed back. At that moment, she turned in a girlish sort of way and flashed a smile directly at Richard. It was as if she had been trying to force herself not to but the urge had become overwhelming and she had given in. *Jesus, why not get a megaphone and tell the world?*

The barman delivered the drinks, I topped them up with water and made my way back to Richard. After the smile he had got he looked even more flushed and pleased with himself.

"Cheers Jason," he said as I passed him the glass, "great to have you here with me!" As I sat, I turned my chair slightly to face him. By doing so I could also see the crowd to the left in my peripheral vision. The band played on and I made light conversation with Richard. We spoke about Zanzibar in general and laughed about the foul weather back in England. I played the part of the clueless tourist and Richard was only too pleased to impart his extensive knowledge of the island to me. He pointed out a few important personalities that he had recognised amongst the guests. There were hotel owners, local businessmen, the Zanzibar police chief, even the Mayor of Stone Town.

I realised that whilst doing so he was also able to keep his eye on Carlos' wife when the tall woman once again leant over to whisper in her husband's ear. With a nod and a movement of his hand, their greetings and welcomes now finished, he dismissed her. He was still deep in conversation with a guest and seemed quite happy for her to move off on her own. I predicted her next move precisely and I was not wrong. She turned and started making her way towards our table. I watched her approach us and for a moment, just like before in Cape Town, I was completely mesmerised. Her expression was a mixture of happiness and embarrassment and I could tell that all she really wanted to do was to run into Richard's arms. Thankfully she exercised some restraint and kept her composure as she walked. Richard did the same and we both stood up as she arrived. "Hello Angelique," he said warmly as he held out his hand, "it's great to see you again."

"Hello Richard," she said as she shook his hand, "it's nice to see you too." Her voice was gentle with a strong French accent. "This is my friend Jason," he said politely, "Jason, this is Angelique, Carlos' wife."

"It's a pleasure to meet you," I said as I took her hand. It was slender, warm, and dry to touch. Her presence was nothing short of electrifying and I had to strongly remind myself that I was there in a professional capacity. "It's a pleasure to meet you too Jason," she replied. She smiled and tilted her head slightly as she spoke to me and I was again aware of the genuine warmth and happiness in her eyes. At that moment I understood completely why Richard had fallen in love with her. Like her name suggested, she was an angel. She was astonishingly beautiful. We stood there, making polite small talk for a few minutes, then I felt my cell phone vibrate in my pocket. I excused myself from the conversation and walked over to the staircase to take the call. It was an agent from one of the insurance companies I worked for and as we spoke I leant on the wooden railings and watched the party from a distance. The warm breeze coming off the sea blew on my back as we talked. It gave me an opportunity to have a good look at the house and the guests as I spoke.

Eventually we finished our conversation and I made my way back to the table. I explained that it had been a call from London and sat down leaving Richard and Angelique standing and talking. I had to give it to them. They were doing a good job of keeping things formal and had I not known that they were lovers, I wouldn't have suspected anything. They kept a polite distance from each other as they spoke in hushed tones. All the while the guests mingled and danced to the band.

As I sat, tapping my fingers to the music and pretending to enjoy myself, I realised that the three of us were all playing a complex game of deception. It was then that Carlos da Costa turned around briefly to look for his wife. Without Richard or Angelique knowing, and with dark, beady eyes, he watched them for a second before turning back to his conversation. It gave me an uneasy feeling in my stomach and I could only hope that Richard's game of deception would not turn out to be a dangerous one. Then Angelique leant over to speak to me. "Please excuse me Jason, I have to attend to the dinner now," she said in her lilting French accent, "I will come to talk to you both later."

"Thank you Angelique, see you later," I said as I stood up. She flashed a smile at both of us and then walked off towards the buffet area. We stood for a moment and watched her go. The elegant evening dress accentuated the slimness of her waist and the way her buttocks moved as she walked. "She's gorgeous," I said as I took my seat. "She certainly is," said Richard dreamily as he sat down, "and she's a really lovely person too. You know Jase," he paused, "most women as beautiful as her, they won't even give you the time of day, and yet her, she's friendly, she's approachable..." His sentence trailed off and he sat there, shaking his head slightly, watching her go. It was clear that his feelings were getting in the way of his common sense. From what I had seen in Cape Town, the affair was a fairly new thing.

When they had met at the restaurant there had been an obvious attraction but nothing like the chemistry I was seeing that evening. I decided to dig a little. "So how long have you known them Rich?" I asked casually. "Carlos and Angelique?" he asked, "oh about two years I think. I met Carlos through a friend here in Zanzibar two years ago, and then Angelique about a year ago, just after they got married."

"Oh right," I said "business or just friends?" Richard's eyes quickly went to the floor and then back up to mine. It was as if my last question had made him slightly uncomfortable. "Ah, just friends," he said, nodding unconvincingly. Sensing this I changed the subject and began talking about the band and the music. "I heard you ask Carlos if he would be singing tonight. Is this his band?" His face lit up again. "No, no," he said with a laugh, "as I'm sure you noticed, Carlos is a bit of a showman. He likes to sing at his parties and he's actually got quite a good voice. He says he used to sing in a hotel in Las Vegas but I'm not too sure if he did or not. Still, he's got a good singing voice."

"Oh ok, "I said, "well I'll look forward to that." We sat around for the next half hour talking and people watching. All the while Angelique moved around the buffet area, organising the staff. Although I was facing the opposite direction I knew she was there because Richard's eyes constantly followed her as we spoke. Then I heard someone tapping on a microphone behind me. I turned to look and saw the diminutive figure of Carlos da Costa standing on the stage removing a microphone from a stand. "Ladies and gentlemen, friends, and guests, the dinner is now ready. Please help yourself from the buffet and the bar and most of all, enjoy yourselves!" There were a few cheers and claps from the crowd and people began making their way over to the buffet tables. "Shall we?" asked Richard.

"I think I'll wait a few minutes for the rush to finish Rich," I said sipping my drink.

"Yeah, you're right," he replied. The guests busied themselves with what looked like rich pickings from the buffet and slowly made their way back to the tables to eat. When the crowd had died down a bit, Richard and myself headed over to see what was on offer. For a private party it was a mind boggling spread to say the least. For starters, there was a choice of oysters, fishcakes, calamari strips, snails, mussels, prawn tempura, and cheese and crab-stick spring rolls. For the main course there was hake, calamari, dorado, kingklip, sole, salmon, giant prawns, and crayfish. To top it all there was an extensive choice of French and South African wines. "Carlos' wife certainly knows how to throw a dinner party," I said turning to Richard.

"Oh yes, she does indeed," came the reply. We made our choices and headed back to the table to eat. I noticed that Carlos and his wife were sitting on a table to my left with some friends. She ate quietly at his side while he joked and made toasts, clinking wine glasses. By the time we had finished, there was no room for dessert and Richard and I sat back and smoked a cigarette. A waiter came across, removed our plates, and asked if we would like coffee. We refused and opted for another drink from the bar, which Richard went to collect. Alone and feeling full and satisfied, I looked at the scene around me. The candles flickered in the moonlight and the band played softly. The food and the entertainment so far had been superb. I wondered if the uneasy feeling I had got from Carlos and Tintin had just been paranoia. Perhaps Carlos was just a colourful, eccentric character who liked to show off and have a good time. Maybe I had been wrong about him and his excessive security. After all, Richard and I had been through an attempted robbery the previous night. Maybe Robson the barman had been right and Paje was full of thieves. All of the hotels and resorts had security guards, so perhaps there was nothing out of sorts with this man having his big wall and his armed guards.

Then my thoughts went to Richard and Angelique.

There was no escaping what I knew was going on between them. I had seen it with my own eyes and I had followed them, in the middle of the night, to Richard's guest house in Cape Town. They were lovers, pure and simple, and she was married to this man. I hoped that they would play their game of deception sensibly and not rock the boat too much. Richard returned as the band started playing louder and some of the guests got up to dance. Carlos and his wife were still sitting at their table and as if like clockwork, Richard kept looking over at them. I tried to put myself in the position of the person I was pretending to be; someone who didn't know that there was an illicit affair going on. A 'happy-go-lucky' tourist who happened to save Richard from a mugging. *Surely it's obvious Richard?* I thought, *surely you shouldn't keep looking over at her like that? But then again, who could blame you? And with a wife as good looking as she is, I'm sure the man is used to it.*

We sat in the warm sea breeze, talking occasionally and listening to the band. Despite all that had happened in the past week I had that familiar mellow feeling I always got after a good meal. A sense of satisfaction and control. Then, from behind Richard, I noticed a tall dark figure coming up the staircase we had used when we arrived. As the person got closer I realised it was Tintin, the head of security. I watched him as he walked along the wooden railing around the seating area and headed behind the stage. He was clutching a radio to his ear and although I couldn't hear him, he was speaking rapidly to whoever was on the other side. He looked agitated, almost angry, and he walked quickly taking giant strides as he went. I watched the huge man with mild curiosity as he went but as soon as he had disappeared I figured that he was probably just doing his job and soon forgot about it. The music was getting progressively louder with each song and more and more of the guests were getting up to dance. Then I noticed Richard's eyes again. Instead of crossing to where Carlos and Angelique were sitting every thirty seconds or so, they were locked onto something else and I turned to see what was going on. Carlos and his wife had got up from their table and were making their way to the now crowded dance floor. When they arrived, the two of them began shuffling to the music. Again I was aware of the striking difference in height between the two of them. She was at least a foot taller than him and the couple looked awkward to say the least. *Now that's a pretty comical sight,* I thought to myself as I watched them. Then they turned as they danced and through the crowd, I saw Angelique glance at Richard briefly. Although she wore a smile, for a split second, I saw what looked like a certain sadness in her eyes.

It was as if she was trying to tell Richard that she was unhappy, that she was trapped and desperate to break free from her husband. *How the hell did they get together in the first place?* I thought. H*e's short, bald, frankly quite ugly, and she, well she's a goddess! How the hell did that happen in the first place?* My thoughts were stopped by a dull ache coming from my bladder. I turned back to face Richard who was by then in a semi dream-like state as he watched her through the crowds.

"Do you have any idea where the toilets are, Rich?" I asked.

"Toilets, uhh yes," he said snapping out of it, "they're behind the stage in an ablution block. Can't miss them, you go around that way.." He pointed out a route that led around the seating area and along the wooden railing.

"I'll see you shortly," I said as I stood up and made my way through the tables. Before long I had passed the stage and in front of me was a dimly lit grassed area with a wide, single storey building on the other side. I crossed the grass and saw the building had two entrances, each had a metal sculpture depicting stick figures on the wall outside. The one on the left was clearly for the ladies while the one on the right nearest the wooden railing was the gents. The building was in keeping with the main house and was in a Mediterranean style with large rectangular, vertical holes set high up in the walls every metre or so to allow air to flow through. I made my way inside and noticed there were no urinals but there were three showers followed by three toilets to the far end of the building.

The building was empty so I chose the first and stood there gratefully relieving myself. When I had finished, I reached forward to flush the toilet but just before I did, I heard an unusual sound coming from behind the building. I paused to listen but there was nothing except the distant sound of the band playing and laughter from the crowd. Then again, just as I was about to flush I heard the sound again. It was very faint but it reminded me of a wounded animal. Something that was shot and unable to move. Something that was in fear for its life. I looked up and saw the rectangular air vent in the wall above me. I decided that I would hear the sound better if I could get up there so I put the toilet seat down and stood on top of it. By then, I was a lot closer and when the sound came again I knew it was from a human being. Then there were two voices, both speaking in Swahili. One in anger and one pleading in fear. Then there was the sound of a slap followed by more wailing and pleading. I looked up at the air vent again. I needed to get higher so I could have a look at what was going on. Quietly I put my right foot on the cistern and with my hands on the top of the walls of the cubicle, I hoisted myself up.

For a few seconds I only saw darkness through the vent but as my eyes became accustomed, it became clearer. Behind the building was a steep slope made up of grass and rocks. Far to the left beyond the ladies changing room was a well-lit stone staircase leading down the slope to what looked like an office or some utilitarian building. It was surrounded by trees and darkness and was certainly not part of the main house. A tall shadowy figure moved to the left and the right of a stationary seated figure. Then there was shouting followed by another loud slap that sounded like a gunshot. More wailing and pleading followed. It was clear that someone was getting a severe beating. I stood there, straining to see for a good minute but it was too dark and basically all I had was the soundtrack. I let myself down, wiped off the top of the cistern with some toilet paper and the faint sound was gone as I flushed the toilet. *What the fuck was going on there?* I thought as I washed my hands. At that moment, two guests entered the changing rooms, they were laughing and talking with each other and I passed them on my way out. They had clearly had a few too many drinks and I very much doubted they would hear anything. As I left the building and stepped onto the grass I looked to my left at the corner of the building and the wooden railing. Between the two was a half metre space and I realised that there was a good chance that I would be able to get around the back of the block and have a closer look at what was going on. Apart from the two men inside the toilet block, there was no one around. Curiosity got the better of me and I took the opportunity and dashed into the dark space between the building and the railing. To my right, beyond the railing, was an almost sheer drop of about five metres. Beyond that was the massive perimeter wall that surrounded the property. Feeling safe in the darkness I crept along the wall of the toilet block and out onto the grassy slope behind. Although I still couldn't see clearly, the sound of the beating was much clearer now. The pattern repeated itself. The deep voice shouting, the other pleading, the meaty crack of a slap to the face followed by terrified wailing. Although I couldn't understand the words, it was a sound I was familiar with. I had heard it many times before, years ago during the bush war. It was an interrogation and a brutal one at that. Crouching in the darkness and using the boulders for extra cover, I slowly made my way down the slope towards the noise. Finally I reached the bottom and it was then it became clear what was going on. The building was set in a dark space amongst trees and bushes. On the inside, behind iron burglar bars and a small window burned a paraffin lamp. To the front was a small area of concrete on which a tall dark figure paced from left to right. I could tell from the booming voice and the sheer size of the man that it was Tintin. In the dim light, I could make out the shape of a man sitting on the floor. As he squirmed and pleaded, I saw the glint of handcuffs attaching his right wrist to the metal bars of the doorway to the building.

There was no sea breeze down in that dark place, only hot, damp humidity. Beads of sweat formed on my brow and forearms. Then there was the squawk of a radio which coincided with a flashing red light on Tintin's belt. He removed it, put it to his ear and snarled something in Swahili to whoever he was talking to. When he finished talking, he lunged down at the crouched man and again there was the deafening crack as his huge hand struck the side of the other man's head.

"Aaaaaaiii!" came the terrified wailing again. *What in hell has this person done to deserve such a beating?* I thought to myself. Suddenly there was movement to my left and I had to quickly move around the boulder in front of me for cover. Safely in the darkness again I saw a man trotting down the stone staircase I had seen from the toilet block. It was Carlos da Costa. There was no mistaking his short stature and white suit. When he reached the bottom he made a beeline towards the building with his duck foot walk. I was surprised he could move so fast but he obviously knew exactly where he was going and he was in a hurry. As he approached the concrete area where the other two men were, he quickened his pace even more.

"Filla da porta!" He growled as he picked up speed, "carralio!" I knew that what he had said in Portuguese was 'son of a bitch, cunt,' and as he stepped onto the concrete he kicked the sitting man square in the face with such brutal force I heard the dull clunk of the man's head as it slammed into the rough brickwork behind. There was no more wailing from the seated man, only a dreadful moaning sound.

"You think you can steal from my party!?" Carlos screamed in a voice that sounded like he had been gargling crushed glass and caustic soda. "I give you fucking job here and you fucking steal from me?! Carralio! Put torch Tintin, I want to see this fucking thief!" The towering figure of Tintin pulled a torch from a pocket and shone it at the man's face. What I saw shocked even me. The man sat with his head flopped to one side. Blood trickled from his right ear down his neck and onto his ripped collar. A mixture of blood and dusty sand covered his face and hair and his mouth hung open, dribbling, as the space between his teeth and his bottom lip slowly filled with dark liquid. His eyes were half closed from concussion, he was barely conscious. "I don't believe this fucking thief Tintin!" he shouted, "show me what he steal." Silently, the tall figure of Tintin leant over and retrieved a dark coloured canvas bag. He unzipped it to reveal what looked like about six bottles of champagne and a pile of food wrapped in a white table cloth. Filla da porta!"screamed Carlos, as he saw the stash. "I pay you fucking good money and you steal this? From my party?! Carralio!" I saw Carlos step back to prepare for another kick.

Not in the face, please not in the face again, I thought as I watched. Thankfully the powerful blow from his right foot landed in the sitting man's stomach instead. The man jerked violently and let out a long low moan as half a cup full of blood and saliva poured from his mouth. The torch shone on the man's face and at that moment the image was burned into my mind. "Give me torch please Tintin," said Carlos in a surprisingly calm voice. Tintin complied and Carlos shone the beam onto his right trouser leg and shoe. "Fuck!" he shouted, "look Tintin, the blood of a thief spoil my clothes! I go to change now, we deal with this carralio later." "Ok boss, no problem," said Tintin. I sat silently and watched as Carlos made his way back towards the light of the staircase. Instead of going up, he disappeared around a corner. There was obviously another access point to the house and his private quarters where he would change his clothes. After he had gone Tintin continued walking silently back and forth on the concrete in front of the semi-conscious man. Realising it was time to move, I quietly made my way back up the slope in the darkness towards the building. Once there I slipped into the narrow space between the wall and the wooden railing and poked my head around the front. It was all clear and I walked out onto the grass checking my clothes for any grass or leaves I might have picked up whilst crouching in the darkness. My mind was numbed by what I had witnessed, and I found myself idly preparing an excuse for why I had been away so long.

The party was in full swing when I returned with the majority of the guests dancing to the band who were in the middle of a cover of a Buena Vista Social Club tune. There was no sign of Carlos da Costa but his wife was seated at our table talking to Richard. She sat at a respectful distance from him with her legs crossed and was laughing and sipping champagne. "What took you so long Jase?" Richard asked as I arrived.

"Oh I got talking to some people around the corner," I replied. "How are you doing?"

"Fine, fine thanks. I was just telling Angelique about our fishing trip today." She turned to me smiling. "And I was laughing about Richard falling down on the boat! I wish you had a photograph of that." The sadness in her eyes had gone and the sparkle had returned. "Yes," I said smiling as I reached for my drink, "it was quite a funny moment." Then both of their eyes went to the staircase behind me. I turned to look and saw Carlos making his way down back to the party. I watched him as he reached the bottom and saw that he had indeed changed his trousers and shoes. He looked perfectly normal and happy as if nothing had happened and all was well.

As he made his way to the bar area, he gave a quick wave and a smile towards our table. The three of us reciprocated by doing the same. *How can someone go from such extreme violence and furious anger back to this seemingly charming host in a matter of minutes?* I thought. *It's fucking bizarre!* The Cuban music ended as he received his drink and I watched him as he made his way to the stage. I saw him have a quiet word in the ear of the lead musician and the revellers clapped as he took the microphone from the stand. "Looks like we're going to get a song," said Richard.

"Yes, I think so," said Angelique with unsmiling eyes. I turned my chair slightly so I could watch the man. I found myself strangely fascinated by him. His shortness, his duck feet, the way his large ugly head seemed to fit onto his stout body with no visible neck. His dark eyes and his hairy hands. *Ok, the bloke had clearly stolen from you but was that reaction really necessary?* The band broke into a familiar Broadway tune. It was 'New York, New York' by Frank Sinatra and the horn section played it to a tee. The delighted crowd clapped away from the dance floor and Carlos began to sing. "Start spreading the news, I'm leaving today..." Like a true showman he blew kisses at the delighted crowd and walked back and forth along the front of stage. Although he sang with a pronounced Portuguese accent I had to give it to him, his voice was very good indeed. Gone was the rasping hatred he had been spitting out only minutes before. I sat there, still feeling somewhat numb, and a thousand questions I couldn't answer filled my mind. I turned to look at Richard and Angelique who were both staring at the stage.

"Pretty good isn't he Jason?" Richard said clapping along.

"Excellent," I replied. Angelique was clapping as well although not with as much enthusiasm as Richard. The sadness had returned to her eyes and I felt a pang of sorrow for her. After a while, the song ended and to much applause Carlos bowed and left the stage. This was the cue for Angelique to leave. "Excuse me Richard, Jason I must go now, I will try to talk to you later," she said with polite charm. Richard and I stood as she left. She made her way back the table where her and Carlos had sat previously and again, I was acutely aware of Richard's eyes following her as she went. I sat down feeling somewhat drained. I needed time to think. Time away from the music and the crowds of people. Time to process everything that had happened and try to make sense of it all. It was extremely unusual for me to feel so emotionally involved in what was after all, just another job. My usual formula of impersonal detachment seemed to be lost on this one. *Maybe it's the unexpected bonus of the travelling?* I thought, *maybe you're tired? Maybe you're just getting fucking old Green.*

I decided I would wait till I got back to my hotel. I would be alone to think things through once I was there. Richard and I sat there sipping our drinks and smoking for the next hour. We sat mostly in a comfortable silence, like old friends, talking occasionally.

The revellers were starting to leave and the party was winding down. "Shall we make a move Rich?" I asked. "Umm, yeah well I was hoping to have another word," he paused, "with Carlos and Angelique. But maybe you're right." His eyes went again to the table where she sat with her husband. He picked up his glass and drained it. "Shall we go and say goodbye to our hosts?" He asked.

"Sure, let's do that," I replied. We both stood and made our way towards the table where they were sitting. Both of them turned to face us in their seats as we arrived. "Epa Richard!" said Carlos with wide eyes that flicked between Richard and myself. "We're going to get going Carlos," said Richard politely, "we just wanted to thank both of you for a brilliant evening."

"I hope you and your friend Jason enjoyed," he said with his gravelly voice. Both of them stood and I had to make a concerted effort not to look at Angelique for too long. I was afraid that the sadness I had seen in her eyes would return and betray her. I prayed it wouldn't.

"Very nice to meet you both and thank you very much for a great night." I said. Handshakes and niceties were exchanged and I felt a deep sense of relief as Richard and I made our way across the lawn, past the pool and towards the wide staircase that led down to the wall. Richard spoke constantly as we walked down the stairs, across the bottom level of the mansion and down towards the large security gate near the beach. It was as if he too was somehow relieved to get away. The guard with the AK47 was sitting nearby and obviously heard our approach. He unlocked the gate and we stepped out onto the sand of the beach once again. We both thanked him and Richard got onto the waiting quad bike to start it. The engine roared into life, I jumped on the back and we sped off down the beach into the night. The air was warm and smelled of salt. It blew my hair back as we gained speed and eventually cleared the dark jungle to our left and passed Richard's hotel. A few minutes later we arrived at my hotel. Richard stayed on the running bike as I got off and went to say goodbye. "It was a great day Rich, thanks a lot," I said shaking his hand.

"It was a pleasure Jase, I'll be in touch. Sleep well!" With that he was off and speeding back up the beach.

I made my way through the trees and down the pathway towards my room. I felt relieved to be alone. There had been an information overload and I needed to sift through it and sort it out in my mind. I unlocked the door to my room and stepped in to the breeze of the running fans. Feeling lazy, I brushed my teeth, poured a glass of water and flopped down onto the bed with the lights on. I lay there with my hands behind my head and stared at the ceiling for a good five minutes before the knock on the door came. "Jason, Jason," the soft voice said. "Are you awake?" It was Helen. I opened the door and let her in. Before I could even close the door, she lunged forward and kissed me, dropping her sarong to the floor. Aware of the presence of the guards outside I fumbled for the light switch, turned it off and led her to the bed. Afterwards she fell asleep quickly with her head resting on my right shoulder. I lay awake listening to the whir of the fans for ten minutes before I too drifted off into a restless slumber. The dream came quickly and it was not a good one. I was back on the grassy slope behind the toilet block at the big house. I was making my way down towards the sound of the beating, crouching in the darkness. The sound of the slapping and the wailing were more pronounced and louder in the dream. The stuffy heat and humidity were choking me as I moved closer. Then I saw the figure of Carlos da Costa approaching. He was raging, and he delivered the kick to the face of the seated man with the same brutal hatred I had witnessed. Again I heard the sickening thud of the man's head as it hit the bricks and I heard Carlos rasping voice, "I give you fucking job here and you fucking steal from me?! Carralio! Put torch Tintin, I want to see this fucking thief!" Just like I had seen it the man sat with his head flopped to one side. Blood trickled from his right ear down his neck and onto his ripped collar. A mixture of blood and dusty sand covered his face and hair and his mouth hung open, dribbling, as the space between his teeth and his bottom lip slowly filled with dark liquid. His eyes were half closed from concussion, and he was barely conscious. But it was not the face of the waiter I had seen. In my dream, it was the face of Richard Lewer-Allen.

CHAPTER THIRTEEN

- A DEATH IN THE AFTERNOON

I was woken at around 6.30am by the sound of Helen leaving my room and shutting the door. I felt angry with myself. It was unlike me to sleep so late and I could only put it down to the bad dreams. I found a short note she had written and placed on the bed where she had slept. "Darling Jason, you were tossing and turning all night and I was worried about you. I decided to leave you to rest for now and I also have to get back to Ineke. I hope to see you later and if you would like to talk about anything, I am there for you. Helen xxxx." I tossed the note onto the bedside table. My head was fuzzy and my body felt grimy as if I had been sweating during the night. I got up and took a shower. Afterwards I stood and gazed out of the window drinking water and smoking a cigarette. Finally I was alone and able to formulate a plan. I lay down on the bed and closed my eyes to think. From what I had seen, Richard and Angelique were playing with fire. There was no doubt about it. Was Richard so naive to think that this Carlos character was just some harmless buffoon who liked to sing Frank Sinatra songs and impress his friends with lavish dinner parties? Was it not obvious to him that the man was powerful and clearly dangerous? One only had to look at the strangely named Tintin, the huge perimeter wall, and the armed guards to know that the man was paranoid. It was also plain to see that he was *extremely* possessive over his wife. *Surely* Angelique would have told Richard about this? Surely she would have told Richard that her husband had a violent temper and there would be some very serious trouble if he were to find out. After all they had spent the night together in Cape Town. Had she not warned him? I knew that Richard was a persuasive person and by all accounts, quite a womaniser, but she must have told him that it would be a very bad idea to start an affair. And how long had this affair been brewing? I couldn't blame him for falling in love with her, any man would, but even before I had seen the waiter receive the savage beating, I had got a very bad feeling from both Carlos and Tintin. Another thing that worried me was how Carlos afforded such a lifestyle. The house alone was certainly worth millions and Richard's story about him making surfboards and selling bottled water surely couldn't have paid for it. The sheer size of the place, the location, the marble pools, the statues, the staff. I had no doubt there was a great deal more to Carlos da Costa than met the eye and I would have to find out exactly what. But I was also plagued by feelings of guilt and worry. Guilt because I had screwed up by running into Richard in the first place. Guilt that he had somehow worked his way into my life and that I had broken my golden rule to keep things distant and impersonal. To steer clear of all emotions and treat the job for what it was. A fucking job. Nothing more. Guilt that I had still failed to find anything out about how he afforded his lifestyle.

Guilt that I had actually grown fond of him, his easy laugh and his carefree attitude to life. Then there was the worry. I was worried for his safety. Perhaps he really couldn't see the wood for the trees? Perhaps he was totally blinded by his love for the woman? Questions. So many questions.

I got up and, as I dressed, I formulated a plan for the evening. I would need to get into Stone Town to do some shopping so before I left the room I called the taxi driver Hassan. He recognised my number and greeted me enthusiastically. "Hello Mr Jason! How are you today?"

"Fine thanks Hassan," I said, "listen I need to get to Stone Town this morning to do some shopping, are you available?"

"I can be there in thirty minutes, is that ok for you?" he replied.

"That's perfect, see you then." I left the room and made my way to the restaurant.

I could feel the heat of the day starting as I walked. I arrived to find the restaurant empty and was happy about that. I was in no mood for small talk with Helen or Ineke that morning and I still needed to think about what I was going to do when I got back from Stone Town. I ordered a cheese and ham omelette with toast with fruit juice and coffee. Soon after a waiter approached and informed me that the taxi had arrived. I made my out to meet it. Before I got to the car I was approached by the receptionist. "Good morning Mr Green," he said with a grin, "I have a message for you."

"Oh really?" I replied, surprised. "Yes sir, here it is." He pulled a folded piece of white paper from his breast pocket and handed it to me. I stopped to read it. 'Morning Jason,' it read, 'I came to see you but you were obviously still in your room. Helen perhaps? I hope so! I was wondering if you would like to come scuba diving this afternoon. I have booked a boat for 2pm from the water-sports centre. Don't worry if you don't have a dive licence, there is brilliant snorkelling as well. Would be great if you could come along. Bring the Dutch girls if you like. Hope to see you later, Richard." I pocketed the note and walked off down the pathway shaking my head. *Another fine day with your mate Richard then Green?* Hassan was waiting for me near his car. He was his usual cheerful self and as we drove out of the complex on the sandy road, I felt my spirits lift a bit. Even at that early hour it was sweltering hot in the car so we opened all the windows in an effort to catch a breeze. We smoked as we drove up the sun-baked road and then took the left turn towards Stone Town.

Without going into too much detail about my requirements I told him that I needed to find a market. Somewhere the locals would do their shopping. I didn't need to waste any time browsing the curio and trinket shops the tourists would visit. He told me he had the perfect place that was situated just outside Stone Town in a municipal centre where the locals went. It sounded fine to me and I was sure that I would be able to get what I needed. I felt I had formed a friendship with Hassan. He no longer tried to sell me the regular tourist fare like spice tours and dolphin trips. The jungle around us became thicker as we drove and soon we entered the Jozani Forest once again. This time there were troops of red colobus monkeys leaping through the trees above us. They stared at the car with comical shocked looks on their tiny faces.

Roughly thirty minutes later and we had reached the semi industrial border of New Town. We drove slowly through dusty, chaotic streets that were crammed with vendors, blaring music, and children playing. Eventually we arrived at a large fenced off factory with no walls. There was a buzzing mass of humanity on the inside. "Mr Jason, this is the market I was telling you about." said Hassan wiping his brow with a stained rag. "If you cannot find what you are looking for inside there I can take you to Stone Town, hakuna matata."

"Thank you, Hassan," I said, "will you stay here with the car?"

"Yes I will be waiting here." he replied. I got out of the car and took the short walk in the sun to the gate of the market complex. Clearly the locals were not used to seeing white people there, and immediately I was surrounded by a bunch of excited kids who shouted "Muzungu! Muzungu!" repeatedly. I knew from reading the Zanzibar travel guide that this was a non-derogatory word for white person. As I arrived at the main gate I was met by an ancient woman with a shrivelled wrinkled face. She was carrying a huge bundle of brightly coloured but strongly made, woven plastic carrier bags. She held one of them out to show me and said something in Swahili. I decided it would be perfect to carry my purchases and bought one for $3. I made my way under the shelter of the huge roof and into the noisy darkened chaos within. Hassan had been right. On offer was everything from skin lighteners and mosquito coils to double beds and fly covered cow's heads. As I moved, there was confusion and constant shouts of "Jambo! Muzungu!" Had I not been familiar with such scenes, it would have been intimidating. I knew what I was there for so I moved from stall to stall purposefully, until twenty minutes later I emerged with a bag full of supplies.

As I stepped into the sunshine, the heat of the day hit me like a jet blast. I put my bag into the boot of the waiting car and as I got into the cab I noticed my feet and legs were covered with dust. "Did you manage to get what you were looking for Mr Jason?" asked Hassan in his polite Swahili accent.

"Yes I did, thanks," I replied. I looked at my watch. It was 11am. I had some time to kill before getting back to Paje and I was feeling hot and thirsty. "Hassan can you take us somewhere we can get a drink and maybe some food? I said, "I have an hour or so to play with before I have to get back."

"Certainly Mr Jason, I will take you to Explorers'. It is very popular and is right on the sea so there is a breeze."

"Excellent," I said, "let's go." We took the drive through the littered streets of New Town, past the football field and the dirty five storey blocks of flats. Eventually we arrived at what I assumed were the outskirts of Stone Town. The buildings were obviously ancient and were mostly four stories tall. They were ornate and crammed together tightly with only narrow alley ways between them. On their windows were wooden shutters in typical Zanzibari style and the intricate iron bannisters on each floor were tightly woven and Arabic in style. We turned right and headed down a bustling street that was filled with mini buses, scooters, and cyclists. All around there was the sound of cars hooting, music, and the shouts and laughter of the locals. We carried on through the chaos until we arrived at a T junction. In front, there was a large green building behind which I could see the masts of at least a hundred ships and dhows. To my left was a long street lined with palm trees and the sea to one side.

"That is the harbour and the fish market Mr Jason," said Hassan pointing ahead. "To the left is one of the only roads that runs through Stone Town. It goes right around, along the sea front, past the fort, and out the other side. Most of Stone Town is only passable by foot or by scooter. One can get easily lost in there but either way you end up by the sea." We turned left and drove down the waterfront road. Like everywhere, it was crammed with traffic of all kinds. As we drove I stared out of the window at the buildings to my right. They were beautiful and I found myself wishing I had the time to stop and explore the place. We passed a huge banyan tree which must have had some significance as there were groups of tourists all around taking photographs of it. Slowly we made our way past the grand old dispensary with its set of decorative balconies.

Then we passed a very large square-shaped building with several stories. It too was surrounded by tiers of pillars and balconies and topped by a large clock tower.

Hassan couldn't help being the tour guide.

"This is the House of Wonders, Mr Jason. It was built in 1883 as a ceremonial palace for Sultan Barghash and was the first building in Zanzibar to have electric lights and a lift. That is why the locals called it 'beit el ajaib', the House of Wonders."

"Yes I've seen pictures," I said.

"Up ahead is the Arab fort," he said, "it was built between 1698 and 1701 by the Busaidi group of Omani Arabs. A very old building." As we passed the huge building I gazed at its high dark brown walls and the huge cannons on the outside. The walls were topped by castellated battlements. They reminded me of the big house on the beach in Paje. That too was a fort of sorts. We then passed through an ancient archway and took a sharp right into a shaded taxi rank that was filled with local traders selling their wares to the many tourists. "Explorers restaurant is just ahead on the sea front Mr Jason," said Hassan as he parked the vehicle.

"Why don't you come in with me Hassan?" I said, "I'll buy you a coke and something to eat. I'm sure the car will be safe here with the other taxi drivers." He looked around nervously. It was clear that he was not used to being invited in to places by his customers. "Ahh, ok Mr Jason, thank you very much," he replied. We locked the vehicle and took the short walk on the cobbled street to the entrance. The interior was dark, packed with tables, and busy with tourists. They sat talking amongst themselves, eating and drinking. On the walls were blackboards showing the choices of meals and drinks.

Although there were ceiling fans, it was hot and stuffy inside. I pointed towards an exit that led onto the white sand outside. We walked through and found a sealed off area of beach right on the sea. All around were tables, umbrellas, and comfortable safari-style chairs made from dark wood and cream canvas. We chose an empty table and sat down in the welcome breeze. In front of me was the expanse of the Stone Town harbour. There were Arab style dhows of all sizes, some sailing, some parked for loading. Near where we sat were at least twenty wooden tourist boats with orange canopies for shade. Each one had an amusing name painted on the side. Gladiator, Mr Bean, Promise, Jambo. Out to the right and parked at the port was the large and fast tourist ferry from Dar Es Salaam. Moored far out to sea was a huge ocean going cargo ship. The blue paint of its hull and funnel were rusted and baking in the sun.

Its decks were deserted save for a few old shipping containers and its tall white bridge had turned a dirty beige colour. Although the immediate area around the tables was guarded by security, young local kids splashed and played in the sea in front of us and wily traders passed by trying to catch the eyes of the tourists. A waiter approached and took our order, he recognised Hassan and was mildly surprised to see him in the restaurant normally reserved for tourists. I ordered some burgers and cokes and we sat quietly in the shade waiting for our order to arrive. The food was good. Afterwards we smoked and chatted about the busy maritime scene that was spread out in front of us.

"Where do you keep your dhow Hassan?" I asked.

"It stays near the port over there Mr Jason," he said pointing to our right. "It has gone to Dar Es Salaam with spices this morning. I hope it will be back later this evening. Sometimes we carry tourists to Prison Island."

"Yes, you told me. Where is Prison Island?" I asked.

"Prison Island is about five kilometres past that big ship," he replied pointing at the massive cargo vessel I had seen, "but you cannot see the island right now, the ship is blocking our view." He was right, I hadn't noticed but the great vessel was only anchored to the front and it had slowly swung round in the wind. The rust and decay I had seen earlier was even more evident now I was seeing its full length from the side. "What is the story with that ship?" I asked. "It seems to be abandoned and it looks like it's falling apart."

"That ship came from China five years ago now," he replied, "there were some problems with the hull and it was condemned as unfit for Tanzanian waters by the port authority. The insurance company has not paid for any repairs to this day so the cargo was removed and the crew have all left."

"So it's a ghost ship?" I said with a smile. "Haha!" he laughed, "yes, it's a ghost ship. But many people are unhappy. They want it to be removed, but it just stays there." We sat and smoked another cigarette. I realised it was time to go. I paid the bill and we both made our way out to the car.

"Thank you very much Mr Jason," said Hassan with a look of real gratitude on his old wizened face.

"No problem Hassan," I replied, "let's get back to Paje."

Driving in the car at that time of the day was like sitting in a steam bath. There was nothing I could do except open all the windows and sit back as we passed the winding alleys, the bustling bazaars, the mosques and the grand Arab houses of Stone Town. As we drove, my thoughts returned to Richard and what I had seen the previous evening. As much as I tried I couldn't get the image of the face of the waiter in the torch light out of my mind. Pathetic, bloodied and broken from the savage beating he had received. Once again, the thought sent alarm bells ringing in my head and the memory of the bad dream where the waiter's face was replaced by Richard's only served to worry me more. Eventually we made it through the traffic of the waterfront road and took the right turn at the port. I sat in silence for most of the journey through New Town and only started talking to Hassan once we had reached the forest and picked up some speed. Thirty minutes later and we had made it through the two permanent roadblocks and turned right on the coastal road. We were five minutes from Paje in an open bushy area when I noticed a large crowd of locals in the distance on the right hand side of the road.

There must have been at least a hundred of them, young and old, all crowded together. "What do you think is going on there Hassan?" I asked.

"Ahh!" he replied leaning forward and screwing up his eyes to see, "I don't know what is going on Mr Jason, maybe some trouble? Maybe some people fighting?" We cruised slowly in third gear towards the crowd until it became apparent. There was indeed some trouble up ahead. A group of older women were trying to restrain a younger one who was clearly very upset. She was screaming in anguish and kept falling to the ground. Her arms flailed about, and as we drew closer I saw the tears running down her cheeks. I had seen this sort of thing many times before during my youth in Africa, usually at funerals. "Ahh! I think maybe someone has died?" Said Hassan in a quiet voice, "I better take you back to your hotel first Mr Jason."

"There is no rush Hassan," I said, "you can stop and find out what is going on if you like." We passed the group of women slowly and pulled up near a crowd of men and boys who were standing and talking amongst themselves. Hassan leaned out of the window and said something in Swahili to the men. They all responded together and pointed into the bush to our right. There was an exchange of conversation that I didn't understand then Hassan turned and spoke. "Someone has died Mr Jason. Some young boys were hunting for birds in the bush and they have found a dead man. The woman who was screaming was the wife of that man."

"Has anyone called the Police?" I asked. "Yes they are on their way," he replied, "but the police are no good Mr Jason, they can take some hours to come.

I want to see who is this man. I will take you to your hotel and I will come back."

"There is no problem Hassan," I said, "I'll come with you, we can go and see." We both got out of the car and made our way across the road towards the group of men. Behind us the wailing and screaming continued. Hassan barked something in Swahili to the men and they responded by immediately assigning two of them to lead us through the bush to the site of the tragedy. It was clear to me by the men's response to Hassan that he was a well-respected elder in the community.

We followed the two men silently through the scrub and thorny bush. We passed boulders and giant anthills that were baked hard and white from the sun. Eventually after walking for a good three hundred metres, we arrived at a dried up river bed and the two men in front of us stopped. They turned around, wide-eyed and nervous, spoke something in Swahili and pointed to the left. Thirty metres away, under a thorny bush that overhung the sand of the river bed was the figure of a man. The two men refused to go any further and left it to Hassan and myself to go on. We both clambered down the steep sandy bank and made our way towards the body. I had seen a lot of death in my time as a soldier in the bush war but nothing could have prepared me for the sight I witnessed as we arrived and squatted down to look at the body. It hit me like a wrecking ball and stunned me into silence. The man was sprawled out on his side, facing us. His left arm was outstretched towards us, fingers curled up in agony. His right arm was clearly broken and flopped out behind him. It was blocked from sight by his body. He was a young man, in his late twenties or early thirties. He wore only ripped black trousers and no shirt. His upper body, face and head, were covered with dried, congealed blood and sand. A long thin line of tiny black ants were making their way across the river bed and were busy climbing his exposed shoulders. Swarms of ugly green flies were buzzing around his swollen eyes, mouth and nose, and the air was thick with the distinct and pungent stench of human faeces. I moved around slowly to have a look at the man from behind. It was then that I saw that his right hand had been neatly hacked off at the wrist. The hand was nowhere in sight and only the white bones and tendons of the wrist were visible. Hassan looked at me wide-eyed.

"Are you alright Mr Jason?" He asked solemnly. "I'm fine Hassan. Do you know this man?" I asked

"I recognise him from the village but I do not know him." He replied. I moved around and looked at the man's face again. It was not the horrific sight of the dead body that had shocked me. It was the fact that, like Hassan, I too recognised him. The image of his terrified face had been burned into my mind not twenty four hours before. The dead man was the waiter who had been caught stealing from Carlos da Costa at the big house on the beach. The man I had witnessed getting a savage beating and pleading for forgiveness. Carlos and Tintin had finished the job We both backed off and stood up. Sweat ran down my temples and my brain felt like it was full of cotton wool. *What the fuck are you going to do now, Green? You pretty much witnessed this man's murder. But you were alone. Who would believe you? The chief of police was there at the party along with the mayor. This is turning into a fucking zoo! Best to walk away from it and keep quiet for now. Carry on with your plan for the mean time.* I turned to Hassan. "Well I'm glad he is not a friend of yours Hassan. I think it's a police matter."

"Yes Mr Jason" he replied, "you are right. We should leave this place now." We turned back and made our way up the river bank to the waiting men from the road. The four of us walked in silence through the bush and back to the crowd. When we arrived the distraught woman was still wailing in anguish nearby. Hassan said a few stern words to the waiting men and we made our way back to the car. Both of us sat in silence as we drove back to my hotel. "It is no good for a tourist to see that Mr Jason," said Hassan, shaking his head as he parked outside the reception. "It's ok Hassan." I replied, "don't worry, I have seen that sort of thing before." I retrieved my bag from the boot and paid him for the trip. I watched him as he drove slowly out of the reed gates and back to the road. I slung the bag over my shoulder and started walking up the pathway towards my room. By then all of the euphoria I had felt when I had arrived was gone. The idyllic beauty of the island, the palm trees, the white sands, the blue of the sky and the ocean were all gone and replaced by a dark cloud of intense worry and fear for Richard. My instincts had been right. The men at the big house were stone cold killers. I needed a plan. I unlocked my door and stepped into the breeze of the fans. I felt grimy from the market and the sweaty trip in the car so I stripped off and stepped into a cold shower. As the cool water poured over my body I decided what I would do. I would take Richard up on his offer of a diving trip that afternoon and I would confront him about Angelique. I wouldn't tell him who I was or who I was working for. There was no need to blow my cover. I would simply say that I had got a feeling at the party that there might be an attraction between the two of them and warn him that I thought there might be serious consequences should he be found out. Advise him to back off. *Surely he'll see sense in that?* I thought, *he looks up to you Green. He trusts you and he'll listen to you. He thinks you saved his life for fuck's sake!*

I stepped out of the shower, dried myself off and dressed. The diving trip was booked for 2pm and I had a little time to kill before I made my way to the water-sports centre. I decided to check my emails and set about booting up the laptop. I felt a little happier that I had decided to confront Richard. I would still carry out the plans I had made for later that evening but at least I would have some time to talk to him and try make him see some sense. As I was receiving my mail I heard some female laughter coming from outside my room. I glanced out to see Helen, Ineke, and Richard making their way down the pathway. I closed my laptop and went to open the door. "Guess who I ran into, Jason?" said Richard with his usual smile. "The ladies are joining us on our diving trip. You are coming with us aren't you mate?"

"Sure I am, Rich," I replied after greeting the girls. There was a sparkle in Helen's eyes. "Well, shall we go then?" said Richard, "ok, I'll just get some things together and I'll meet you at the restaurant," I said. They agreed and I was left to gather my belongings for the afternoon.

I took my camera and binoculars and left the room. As I made my way up the pathway I realised that I would probably not have the opportunity to talk to Richard seeing as the Dutch girls were coming along. I would have to wait till afterwards and see if there was an opportune moment to do so. It was absolutely imperative that I did speak to him. The haunting sight of the dead man in the river bed weighed heavily on my mind as did the worry I was feeling for both Richard and Angelique. I arrived at the restaurant to find Richard and the girls waiting. The girls both wore their sarongs and straw hats.

"We'll take a walk up the beach to the water-sports centre then," said Richard.

"Great," I said, "shall we go then?" The four of us made our way out across the beach and into the heat of the day. The sun was blistering hot on my skin and we made our way up the hard sand with Richard entertaining the girls with stories of our fishing trip the previous day. We arrived to find the same boat we had used waiting in the shallows. It had been kitted out for diving and had ten sets of scuba bottles and various equipment on board. "We have a new captain today, Jase," said Richard as we climbed aboard. "Carlos' wife, Angelique owns this business so she'll be taking us out."

"Oh right," I said, "where is she then?"

"She should be arriving anytime now." Richard replied looking at his watch. *Jesus* I thought, *definitely no chance of having that word with Richard then Green. This just gets worse and worse!* The two Dutch girls chatted away excitedly as they explored the boat. At that moment I saw a yellow Hummer coming down the sandy access road towards the water-sports centre. It parked near the thatch building and two figures got out. One of them was Angelique and the other was the unmistakeable huge frame of Tintin. He was obviously the driver for the day and he stood in the shade scowling at us as Angelique made her way across the sand towards us. "Hello!" she called with a cheery wave as she approached the boat. She was wearing a loose fitting yellow summer dress and had her hair in a pony tail. The Dutch girls were clearly taken aback by her beauty but we all exchanged greetings nonetheless. She climbed aboard nimbly, shook hands with the Dutch girls and in true French fashion, kissed both Richard and myself on each cheek once. I could smell Chanel No 5 on her skin. I glanced at Tintin. He sat on a white plastic chair in the shade, his legs crossed, chewing on a straw of thatching grass. Even through the dark glasses I felt his stare and his suspicions.

"Where are you taking us today Angelique?" asked Richard, looking pleased with himself.

"Today we will dive at Seven Mile Reef," she replied. "the best scuba diving in Zanzibar. Is everyone ready?"

"I think we are," said Richard. It was clear to me that my presence on the boat that day was a clever plan of Richard's to give the impression that we were on a completely innocent day trip. We were supposed to look like a group of friends simply getting together for an afternoon of diving. Nothing more. But the memory of the dead man in the river bed and the cold stare of Tintin watching us unnerved me and made me very uncomfortable. A group of workers made their way across the sand to push the boat out so we could get going. One of them jumped aboard as a deck hand and busied himself checking the dive equipment. The two Dutch girls spoke amongst themselves.

"We are afraid of sharks and we do not have a diving licence," said Ineke with a worried look on her face.

"There is no problem," said Angelique with a reassuring smile, "you can go snorkelling, and I don't think we will see sharks."

"Oh good, we are very afraid!" said Helen, with a nervous giggle.

"You're in safe hands ladies," said Richard, "Angelique is a true professional." The boat was turned around and Angelique climbed the ladder to the wheel deck. Richard couldn't help himself and watched in awe as she climbed. She fired up the motor and revved it with confidence before turning around to speak. "Everyone ready?" she shouted above the motor. Richard gave her the thumbs up and we were off. She drove the shallows with more confidence than our driver from the previous day and before long we had cleared the reef and were speeding through the open sea. I took my binoculars out and took a brief look at the water-sports centre.

Tintin was still sitting staring at us as we went. "I think I'll go up to the top deck and talk to Angelique," said Richard, "see you guys in a bit." *Of course you will Richard,* I thought, *just try to control yourself.* I watched his tall skinny frame climb the ladder. Although I couldn't hear them over the noise of the engine, I could see that they were immediately in animated conversation with Angelique pointing her route out to Richard on the horizon. They both looked flushed and happy. *If only you knew what I know,* I thought, as I sat down to talk to the Dutch girls. The spray from the engine sparkled in the sun and the wind took some of the power from the relentless beating sun above. After a good fifteen minutes the sound of the engine subsided and I saw we were approaching an area of calm sea. The land was now far and low in the distance and the expanse of the ocean was all around us. The sun was like a grill above us in the cloudless sky. The two Dutch girls and I stood up and had a look around. It was the first time we had been able to stand since breaking the reef. Richard and Angelique were still on the top deck but were no longer talking. She was deep in concentration trying to guide the boat to the diving spot. She was using a GPS device that was mounted on the front near the wheel. I took a look over the side and saw that we were slowly cruising over a massive coral garden five metres below. The water was crystal clear and already there was a myriad of colours beneath us. Richard climbed down the chrome ladder to join us again.

"I think we're almost at the dive site," he said, "Jason do you have a dive licence?"

"I do Rich," I replied. I had done a fair bit of diving before and during the war and had more recently dived whilst on holiday. Then I heard Angelique call the deck hand. He clambered up to the top deck quickly and listened intently as she gave instructions. The two Dutch girls were talking nervously amongst themselves with Helen occasionally giving me nervous looks.

Then the engines were cut, the deck hand climbed down the ladder and tossed an anchor over the side from the front of the boat. Then, as required in open water diving, a bright red buoy was tossed overboard as well. "Right my friends, are you ready to have some fun?" came a lilting voice from above with a French accent. It was Angelique. She was leaning on a rail looking down at us with a huge smile. She was a picture of radiant youth and beauty and I could tell she was happy to be away from the big house. Her mastery of the boat was impressive as was her nimble descent from above as she gracefully climbed down the ladder. Thankfully it turned out that the two Dutch girls had some experience snorkelling and were familiar with the equipment that was handed to them by the deck hand. There was no need for wetsuits in the warm water so Richard, Angelique and myself busied ourselves preparing our equipment. It was difficult not to notice when Angelique removed her yellow summer dress. Her body was slim, lithe, toned, and tanned. She wore a modest, sky blue bikini and her strength surprised me as she easily lifted a scuba bottle to prepare the regulator. Eventually we were all fitted with our equipment and the three of us who were going underwater sat on the left hand side of the boat ready to go over backwards. The two Dutch girls were still fully dressed and preparing their masks as Angelique, Richard and myself did a last minute check of our dive signals. "Ok," said Angelique, "this place is like an aquarium. Helen, Ineke, enjoy yourselves and don't worry about sharks."

"Thank you Angelique," said Helen, "we will be right above you, enjoy." With that, we fitted our masks and mouthpieces one final time, gave each other the 'ok' sign and tumbled over backwards into the sea. Instantly the weight of the cumbersome equipment was gone and we were plunged into another world. Gone was the burning of the sun and the glare of the surface. It was replaced by the warm embrace and silence of the sea. There was a visibility of at least fifty metres all around us and the only sound was that of my breathing and the dull thuds of the three who remained on the boat as they moved around. Five metres below, the coral garden spread out as far as the eye could see.

I looked around at my dive buddies and saw that Richard was having a few problems with water in his mask. He was obviously familiar with the method of clearing it whilst underwater and was busy attending to it. Angelique, however, was having no such worries, and I watched as she descended towards the reef below. She was as graceful underwater as she was on dry land and her long slender legs were perfectly straight as she slowly finned away. It was only when she had reached the coral below that she turned to check up on Richard and myself. By then he had sorted out his mask and gave me the 'ok' sign. I reciprocated and we began our descent.

As we neared the coral, I became aware of just how intricate and colourful it was. There were literally thousands of fish of all sizes and colours. Some darted away in fear as we approached while some faced upwards at us, their mouths gawping. There was a steady backward and forward movement to the sea. I noticed that Angelique did not fight the current but rather hovered a few feet above the coral bed and allowed the current to carry her forward a metre or so at a time. Richard however seemed to be constantly finning and looking around anxiously. Above us the surface of the sea was like a huge pulsating silver mirror while all around us was alive. I became aware of a scratching sound and saw a parrot fish crunching away at some dead coral with its tough, beak like mouth. All around were huge examples of plate coral that had taken thousands of years to form. It would only take one touch to break so I carefully avoided touching. Every now and then, there was a gap in the coral and I saw that it was at least a metre and a half from the top to the perfect white sand below. Huge red starfish hunkered down lazily in groups on the sand. As we passed one of these bare areas I noticed a huge moray eel poking its head out of its coral lair. Its razor sharp teeth exposed in a warning not to approach any more. The myriad colours were accentuated by the bright sun above us and gave the place a mystical, other worldly feel. It was without a doubt the most impressive dive site I had ever visited in my life. Angelique once again took the lead and Richard and I followed. Soon after I felt a tap on my right shoulder. It was Richard and he was signalling for me to look above us. I complied and saw the two Dutch girls four metres above us. They were both kitted out with their masks and snorkels and fins. As far as clothing they wore only their bikini bottoms and the whiteness of the their breasts was in stark contrast to the rest of their tanned bodies. They waved frantically at us and gave us the OK sign. Clearly they were enjoying the spectacle as much as I was. I glanced back at Richard. He was nodding approvingly and giving me the thumbs up sign. I reciprocated by doing the same. We carried on like that, hovering a few feet above the coral and slowly moving over its infinite shapes and hollows, its bridges and archways. There were lobsters and sea bass, octopuses and giant clams. Tiny, almost neon bright blue cyclids. Clumsy-looking slow-moving grouper. There were huge yellow and black angel fish. The sight of them made me think of the sight of Angelique walking across the beach with her yellow summer dress and her dark hair. She was an angel just like her name suggested. There was no doubt. She was a lot more than a pretty face as well. She handled the boat like a true professional and was quite adept at handling the heavy equipment as well.

I stopped my progress to closely inspect an interesting coral formation and allowed Richard to carry on ahead of me. When I looked up, I saw that Richard had caught up to Angelique.

They were parallel with each other and I saw their hands briefly brush together. I wondered if they would be able to contain their feelings now they were in a completely secluded place. There were no prying eyes. No Tintin, no Carlos, only a couple of dumb tourists brought along as tokens for their game of deception. A few times, I heard the engine of the boat above us start as it caught up to where the buoy was floating. The deck hand was doing a good job of staying near his precious cargo underwater. Obviously the current on the surface was very different to the one we were riding underwater. All around us the incredible cycle of life continued as it had done for thousands, if not millions of years. The reef was truly untouched and unspoilt and for a while my mind was taken off the shocking events of the day and the burden of my knowledge of the danger Richard was in. I glanced ahead again at Richard and Angelique. Their feelings had now gotten the better of them and they floated, hand in hand as they glided across the stunning vista below. As far as they were concerned there was absolutely no danger of being caught here. It was a clever plan of Richard's to invite me firstly to the party as a distraction and secondly myself and the Dutch girls on this day excursion. Perhaps he thought it gave him credibility in the eyes of the powers that be. But it gave me a bad feeling. I knew Richard was no fool but his love of Angelique was clouding his judgement. Those people, Tintin and Carlos were no fools either. No man acquires that much wealth by being a fool. But then how was Richard acquiring his wealth? Even underwater and surrounded by the beauty of the reef, I was still obsessing over the job. To a certain extent it had taken over my life. Completely sucked me in and caused me to act in a most unprofessional way. I would remedy that that evening and would find out what I needed to know for sure. *You just enjoy your dive, Green. You enjoy the coral and the swaying breasts of the Dutch girls above and you will satisfy your curiosity later.* Eventually I noticed Angelique grabbing Richard's oxygen gauge. She made some signs informing him that he was running low and looked back at me as if to ask how I was doing for air. Obviously Richard's initial struggling against the current had caused him to breathe a lot more than I had, as I had plenty left. She made a motion that it was time to surface. We all agreed by giving the 'ok' sign and slowly swam to the surface. The two Dutch girls were still above, still topless. Breaking the surface was like being suddenly tossed into the real world again. Gone was the cool cocoon of the ocean with all its wondrous colours and creatures and we were all back in the glaring sunshine. Sea gulls squawked overhead and the water slapped against the hull of the boat thirty metres away. "That was amazing!" said Ineke as she removed the mask and snorkel.

"I have never seen anything like it!" said Helen, treading water, her mask in hand.

"Yes," said Angelique, "it's a pity that Richard had run out of air, we might have had a bit longer, but it was a great dive." The deck hand fired the motor and slowly drove the boat towards us. The two Dutch girls were the first to board using the chrome ladder to the rear of the boat. They immediately donned their bikini tops much to the relief of the embarrassed-looking deck hand who tried by all means to avert his eyes. Next was Angelique followed by Richard and myself. The deck hand removed our scuba bottles as we boarded. Once we were all on deck there was an air of exhilaration amongst the party.

"Well, thank you very much Angelique," said Richard diplomatically as he wiped his face with a towel, "I think everyone was impressed. Such an amazing reef to dive!"

"Yes" she replied, as she pulled her summer dress over her bikini, "like I said, the best in Zanzibar." The sun was slowly starting to descend in the sky but still packed a punch. The sea breeze helped as it evaporated the water from my skin and cooled me down a bit. The four of us sat down on the lower deck and chatted about the dive for a few minutes until Richard suggested we drink a beer. This was met with approval by all and he set about cracking open some ice cold Safaris from the cooler box. We sat, seven miles out to sea, the boat gently swaying in the swell, while the conversation flowed. Although I tried to keep a cheerful disposition, I suspect that Helen realised that there was something troubling me. She kept glancing over at me with a concerned look in her eyes. I nodded slowly at her and gave her a half smile to reassure her. But her instincts were right. I had seen and done too much in the previous few days to cover my feelings fully. I felt my role had changed from being an observer to being a protector. It was a role I didn't want or need. It was supposed to be a fucking job, clean and simple. Instead I had been sucked into a bizarre scenario that I had little control over.

My plan of having a quiet word in Richard's ear had been blown out of the window for the moment. Still, I had my plan for the evening and I hoped it would answer a few questions. If not, I hoped I would eventually have a chance to talk some sense into Richard. *Dear Richard, dear naive, stupid, wealthy Richard.* The happy chatter on board continued for half an hour as the sun slowly descended towards the steamy green land mass that was Zanzibar. It was then that I noticed a wistful look come over Angelique. Her smiles and laughter disappeared

269

and I saw the sadness return to her eyes as she stared out towards the coast. "I wish we could stay out here all day and night," she said softly.

"Well why don't we?" Richard said loudly to much laughter from the Dutch girls, "we could have a party!"

"I wish we could," she said with a sad smile, "unfortunately I have to get back." I thought I could cut the tension with a knife. It was then that I realised that it was only me who knew anything about what was actually going on. I quickly put myself in my assumed role and moved to sit nearer Helen. This pleased her no end and she duly shuffled closer to me on the seat. As we finished our beers, Angelique stood up and said something in perfect Swahili to the deck hand who had been silently sitting on the top deck. Suddenly there was movement as he prepared the boat to leave our idyllic ocean spot. "Ok my friends," said Angelique, "I go upstairs to drive us back to Paje."

"I'll join you," said Richard standing as well, "you folks ok?"

"Fine thanks, Rich," I said watching him. The two of them climbed the ladder to the wheel deck as I opened another three beers for the Dutch girls and I. The engines were fired up and we were on our way back. The deck hand came down and busied himself quietly packing away the scuba equipment. I noticed we were travelling a lot slower than we had done on the way out. I stood up to have a look at the top deck. Richard and Angelique stood alone, their backs to me, deep in conversation. Their arms were around each other's waists. Although I couldn't hear what they were saying I could see that Richard appeared to be pleading with her. She looked ahead and then at him, shaking her head occasionally. I knew she was taking the boat back slowly in an effort to spend as much time as she possibly could with him. It was a sad sight and I felt for them. I decided to leave them to their conversation. I hoped that she would have the good sense to speed up as we got closer to the beach and revert to normal behaviour. This was something that Tintin certainly did not need to see. I sat down again with the Dutch girls who were thoroughly enjoying themselves by now. The sun was slowly setting and there was a cool breeze coming in from the ocean. "we have had such a wonderful day Jason, thank you" said Helen with a glint in her eye.

"Well it was Richard who arranged it all, girls, but yes, it was excellent. I'm glad you enjoyed it." About a mile before the reef, the motors revved up and the boat picked up speed. I looked out to my left and once again saw the big house of Carlos da Costa in the distance. Its fortress-like wall imposing and jutting out of the beach and the jungle like a prison. It was a prison. It was a prison for Angelique. I wondered if she knew the penalties for breaking the rules of the prison.

The dead waiter certainly hadn't bargained on his punishment being so brutal. Lying there covered in blood and flies and shit. His right hand chopped off and gone. *Fucking hell. What kind of gangsters were they?* I was going to find out. Obviously Richard had realised the importance of the excursion appearing innocent and he climbed down the ladder to be with us as we passed the reef and entered the calm waters beyond. From there, Angelique skilfully piloted the boat until we heard the sand scrape beneath us and we were back on land in front of the water-sports centre.

The crew of workers were waiting for us and they spun the boat around to allow us to disembark into the shallow water near the hard sand. I allowed the Dutch girls to climb off first, followed by Richard and then myself. I glanced up the beach towards the thatch building and saw the ominous sight of Tintin. He was standing now, his great black arms folded in boredom. A piece of straw still jutted from his mouth and he stared unwaveringly at us from behind his dark glasses.

The Hummer was parked just as it had been. He had been waiting there all along. I wondered what was going on in his mind. Did he suspect anything or was I just being paranoid? I hoped dearly for the latter. We all stood in a group on the beach and waited for Angelique. She fiddled with the sat-nav and flicked a few switches before sliding down the ladder and jumping off the back of the boat to join us.

"Well my friends, thank you for a wonderful afternoon once again!" She said gaily. There was a chorus of thanks from the three of us. She stepped towards me and kissed me lightly on each cheek and then did the same for Richard. *Good thinking Angelique,* I thought. *Kiss me first to keep Tintin from thinking too much.* Then she did the same for the Dutch girls who couldn't stop thanking everyone from the staff to the deck hand. "I must go now" she said calmly, "goodbye!" She started off up the beach. The two Dutch girls were busy talking and I noticed Richard staring at Angelique as she walked up the sand. "So Rich," I said, desperately trying to snap him out of his lovesick daze, "what are you doing now?" He turned to me suddenly. "Oh, umm," he said, "I'm not sure, shall we go for a beer somewhere?"

"We can do," I said, "but I have a lot of work to catch up on tonight so I can't have too many."

CHAPTER FOURTEEN

- A NOCTURNAL FORAY

L ater that night I was finally alone in my room. The breeze of the fans was a relief as the night was hotter and more humid than it had been previously. I took a cold shower and walked back into the room with a towel around my waist. Although the events of the day were fresh in my mind, I felt a sense of relief that I was eventually going to take back some control and hopefully get some answers to the many questions I had to answer. There had been too much fooling around and too much uncertainty. I had to actually do my job. When the knock on the door came, I knew it wasn't Helen or Richard. I opened it to find a waiter standing there with my dinner on a tray. I signed for it, thanked him and took the tray inside. I had time to kill, so I browsed the internet and checked emails as I ate. There was nothing of great urgency to attend to so I spent the time catching up on news. When I had finished, I closed the curtains and emptied and sorted the contents of the bag from the trip to Stone Town on the bed. There was a fifteen metre length of heavy duty nylon rope. It was black in colour. It had been a job to find black rope but Hassan had been right, anything and everything was available at that market. Next there were three small tins of black shoe polish and brushes, and a small black rucksack. There was a black tracksuit top as well as a black woollen skull cap. The skull cap had the name of a popular rap artist woven into the front but I would turn that inside out when it came time to use it. Next there was a pair of trainers. I sat quietly as I brushed the thick black polish onto the shoes. The polish held well and instantly they became dark in colour. The next item from my shopping trip was a foot-long section of wooden pole. It was 3cm in diameter and was made from hard pine. I used the panga I had taken from the muggers on the beach to cut it in half. The blade was surprisingly sharp and cut through the wood easily. I was left with two equal length sections of wood and around the middle of each I carved a circular groove. Next I picked up a one-metre section of heavy duty fishing trace. It was similar to the trace we had used on the boat with Richard. It was made from thick but extremely flexible steel wire, and was covered with a smooth layer of plastic. I wound the end of the trace around the groove I had carved in one of the sections of wood. Then I twisted the wood at least ten times to give a tight immovable fit. Using my lighter I burned the twisted trace near the wood. The plastic melted immediately and the wire trace was fixed for good. I repeated the exercise with the other section of wood till finally I was left with what was a highly effective and silent killing machine. I had made a garrotte. It was a bit extreme but I was fully aware of the potential danger I would face later. These were dangerous men. Killers. I looked at myself in the mirror briefly when I had finished making it. *Pray you don't have to use this Green,* I thought grimly. I held a section of wood in each hand and pulled at the wire violently.

It made a twanging sound as the tension hit the wire but there was no way it would break. The wire was of at least 300kg breaking strain. Slowly and methodically I packed the black rucksack with my supplies.

Then I went to my main travel bag and retrieved a pair of night vision goggles, my camera, and some tracking devices. The goggles were an expensive bit of kit I had only needed to use twice before during insurance jobs in London. I tested them quickly in the bathroom to make sure they were working. I tossed the kit into the rucksack along with a pair of black jeans. I did a quick mental checklist of the equipment and then buckled the rucksack closed. My plan was simple. I would walk out of the hotel dressed like any other tourist and take a slow walk up the beach in the moonlight. There would be no suspicious movements or behaviour. Nothing out of the ordinary. I would have a look at Richard's hotel and hopefully his room. Finally I would take a walk up the beach to the big house. I needed to get inside the property and have a good look around. My main worry was the armed guards, but I had extensive experience in such activities and I felt sure I could move around unseen and unheard.

I sat quietly on the bed and smoked a cigarette. All my feelings of guilt and fear for Richard and Angelique were gone. They were replaced by a low and constant buzz of adrenaline and excitement. The stakes were high and the danger was very real indeed, but I was ready. I crushed out the cigarette in the ashtray and looked at myself in the mirror once again. "Right Green," I said quietly, "let's go." I stood up and slung the small black rucksack over my shoulder. It was heavier than I had expected. I made my way out and locked the door. The old Masai security guard saw me from a distance and gave me a nod. I waved at him and made my way through the palms and down to the beach front. I would have used the pathway past the restaurant but I didn't want to run into any of the guests. Helen was already upset by my insisting that I needed time alone to work. I felt bad but there were far more important fish to fry that evening. I made it down to the hard sand of the beach unseen and turned right. The lights of the Paje beach resorts curved out to the left in the distance. There was not much of a breeze that night and beads of sweat formed on my forehead as I walked through the darkness. I passed the hotel bar unseen. There was light music playing but I couldn't make out if there was anyone there or not. The next door resort was quiet as well and all I heard was the soft repetitive crunching sound of the damp sand underfoot as I walked. I carried on at that pace until eventually I approached the water-sports centre. As expected it was closed and boarded up. I glanced up the sand track that led to the main tar road. I was half expecting to see the crouching figures of the muggers Richard and I had run into. But there was no one and the area was dark and quiet. Eventually I arrived in front of Richard's hotel, the Eden Beach Lodge.

The beach in front was all quiet but there was a fair amount of activity in the main grounds. I paused in the relative darkness near the ocean and gauged the scene. There were a few lights on in the rooms that stretched out on either side of the main hotel building but Richard's room was dark. I wondered if he was eating dinner or perhaps having a drink in one of the bars. I could see the pool bar clearly from where I stood. There were a few figures there but none that resembled Richard. I decided I would stash my rucksack and walk into the hotel like any normal tourist and have a look around. People were free to walk up and down Paje beach and I imagined there would be no problem in doing so. I opened the rucksack and removed the torch which I put in my pocket. I decided that if I was unlucky enough to run into Richard I would merely say that I had finished my work and had decided to take a walk and stop in for a drink. I approached the hotel from the right knowing that there would be very little chance that Richard would venture to that wing of the premises. As I walked up the slope of the beach towards the rooms I noticed a security guard. Unlike the Masai guards at my hotel he was dressed in dark overalls and wore a peaked hat. Around his waist hung a black rubber truncheon. I walked straight towards him and smiled in the dim light of the tiled pathway. "Good evening," I said.

"Good evening sir," came his reply.

"Can you tell me where the bar is please?"

"Yes sir, there is one near the pool, and one in the main building at the restaurant." I thanked him and moved on. My presence was not going to be a problem. Feeling relieved by this I made my way towards the pool bar. I had been unable to find a hiding place for the rucksack but I guessed it was small enough to look like any other day bag. I took a seat at a table in a dark area near the pool and motioned to the barman. Immediately I was approached by a young waiter in full uniform. I ordered a bottle of mineral water which arrived promptly. I sat there watching the scene around me as I drank. There were a few stragglers still sitting waist high in the water near the bar. They were deep in conversation and not interested in what was going on around them. I looked to my left and saw that there was still no lights on in Richard's room. It was time to make a move. I stood up and waved at the barman. He acknowledged and I moved on. I decided I would walk past the main building and down the left wing past Richard's room. If I ran into Richard whilst doing so I would just have to deal with it. The reception on the lower level of the building was plush and well fitted. Various guests and staff were moving around and talking inside as I passed but there was no sign of Richard.

There were the sounds of clinking cutlery and hushed music and conversation coming from the upstairs area. Eventually I had passed the main building and was making my way down towards Richard's room. I was about four rooms away when suddenly one of the doors nearby opened. A couple of overweight and very sunburnt Americans stepped out and walked towards me. "How are ya?" said the man. "Very well thanks, how are you?" I replied.

"Great!" they both said as we passed each other. I had not expected that sudden meeting and it had pumped up my adrenalin a notch. I was relieved to see there was no more activity in front of me and I glanced behind me briefly to find the same. No movement. The rooms at the Eden Beach Lodge were each separated by an area of green foliage and small trees. The area between Richard's room and the next was no exception. I ducked quickly into the dark cover of the bush. I had to crouch down low under the leaves as I made my way to the far corner of his room. When I got there I stopped and turned around to look behind me. Again there was no movement and I waited for a minute or two in the darkness. I dumped the rucksack on the ground amongst some dead leaves and, still crouching, made my way along the back section of the room to the first window. I could tell from the drainage pipes that protruded from the lower part of the wall that I was directly outside the bathroom. Above me was a double window. Slowly I stood up and noticed that, like most hotel bathrooms, the glass of the windows was dimpled and had a misted effect for privacy. The heat of the evening was oppressive and the sweat ran down my temples as I moved along the wall towards the bedroom windows. I arrived to find that he had neglected to close the curtains at the back of the room and one of the windows was wide open. Having been in the dark for a few minutes, I could make out a large double bed with tables either side. Opposite was a lounge area with a low table and to the right was a dressing table and mirror. There were a set of ornate but heavy burglar bars that were set in from the window. I removed the torch from my pocket, put it through the window and held it low as I switched it on. The room was cool from the air conditioner that was obviously left on. I moved the beam around the room and saw nothing out of the ordinary. It was clearly an expensive hotel with plush fittings and decor but there was nothing to set Richard apart from any other wealthy tourist. Like in my own room down the beach there was a laptop on the dressing table. I switched off the torch and quietly made my way back through the darkness to the bathroom windows. The only sound I was aware of was my breathing and the crunching of dead leaves underfoot. I arrived to find one of the windows had been left open slightly. I slowly pulled at it. The screw latch on the window had been left a little tight and it groaned as it moved. I squeezed my right arm through the tight gap and loosened it so it would make no more noise.

It worked and I was able to open the window wide. Like in the bedroom area there were heavy burglar bars and because there were no other windows the room was pitch black. I grabbed the torch, held it into the room and turned it on. The large bathroom was tiled from floor to ceiling. There was a bidet, a shower, a bath, and directly below where I stood was a double sink. The toilet was to the rear of the room behind a low wall. I shone the torch down onto the sinks and noticed a drinking glass that held a tube of toothpaste and a single toothbrush. *Nothing out of the ordinary again, Green.* I flashed the torch around the room again. It was then that I noticed a white dinner plate sitting on the counter of the right hand sink.

In the harsh light of the torch I could see the residue of white powder on the surface of the shiny porcelain. Like the plate that was hidden under the seat on the passenger side of the Aston Martin. Like the plate that I had seen in Richard's bedroom in his flat back in London. Just like the plate he had used in my hotel room on that fateful first night in Zanzibar. *You been coking it up again Richie boy?* I thought, *haven't you heard drugs are bad for you?* I switched off the torch, closed the window, and made my way, crouching, back to where I had hidden my bag. Once there I replaced the torch and stopped to have a look at the scene in front of me. Apart from some laughter in the distance there was no sound and I could see through the dense foliage that the pool bar was now deserted. I sat there for a minute watching and thinking. I felt disappointed. I had thought that I might have found something. Anything that would set him apart and give me a clue as to what made young Richard Lewer-Allen tick. But apart from being an obvious womaniser, a party animal, and a casual drug user, there was nothing. My thoughts were disturbed by the sound of heels on tiles approaching. I could tell the person was walking slowly down the pathway from the left in front of me. I froze in position and waited. The sound got steadily louder until I saw the dark overalls of the security guard appear from the left. Although I could not see his upper body I imagined it would be the same one I had met on the way into the hotel. I could see the truncheon attached to his belt. He stopped right in front of me and for a brief moment my heart sank. I saw his feet turn. He was obviously facing the pool bar and the other wing of the hotel. He stood there for a good minute before I saw his feet turn again and he made his way back in the direction he had come from. I breathed a sigh of relief and waited a few minutes until the sound of his footsteps disappeared. I made my way, still crouching in the undergrowth, towards the mellow light of the pathway. I paused to look and listen just before I got there, heard nothing, and quickly stood up and started towards the beach. Although I had found nothing of major importance, I had once again looked into Richard's private world. I walked casually past the remaining rooms with my bag slung over my shoulder until I reached the sandy slope that led to the beach.

There was a slight breeze coming off the sea and it made me aware of just how much I had been sweating in the undergrowth behind the room. My back was dripping with perspiration which was now drying in the salty air. I made my way to the darkness of the hard sand near the ocean. I stood and looked back at Richard's hotel. I felt slightly frustrated and puzzled but there was not a lot I could do. I shrugged my shoulders, and started off down the beach towards the big house of Carlos da Costa.

As I walked the low buzz of adrenaline I had been feeling gradually got more and more intense. It heightened my senses, quickened my breathing, and gave me an electric feeling in my arms and legs. It was a feeling I had not had for a long time and I savoured every moment of it. I passed the remaining buildings on the right within ten minutes and the shroud of darkness between Paje and the big house enveloped me. For safety and cover I decided to move onto the soft sand near the line of jungle. There was a lot more debris on the beach there. Things like washed up coconuts, palm fronds, and drift wood. They were a bit of a worry in that they were obstacles and might make a noise if I trod on them but I could make them out pretty clearly as I walked. The soft sand underneath my feet looked grey in the gloomy light and the breeze I had felt was subsiding leaving a humid fug all around me. When I was sure I was within five minutes of the corner of the wall of the big house I sat down and opened my bag. I pulled the pair of jeans on over my shorts and then replaced my rafters with the now blackened trainers. Then I put on the black tracksuit top and zipped it up. It had a flap of material that covered the entire length of the zipper. I opened a tin of black shoe polish and proceeded to smear it on my forehead, cheeks, nose, chin, and neck. Finally I pulled the woollen skull cap from the bag, turned it inside out, and pulled it over my head.

With all the layers of clothing, the heat was stifling but it was absolutely essential that I would be unseen. I packed the bag and made my way slowly down the beach. The guard I had seen sleeping on my morning run and then later with Richard would no doubt be there. With any luck he would be drunk and sleeping on the job again. The sight of his AK47 had unnerved me both times I had seen him. I walked slowly and quietly keeping an eye on the grey sand in front of me. Eventually I rounded the last section of jungle and the light at the corner of the wall surrounding the big house came into view in the distance. I could see the guard clearly. He was sitting in the same spot I had seen him sleeping in on the morning of my run up the beach. In his right hand, he held a cigarette that would glow bright every twenty five seconds or so when he took a draw from it. I decided to stop for a while and watch him. I had learned a long time ago that a bit of patience could save your life.

I sat down slowly in the darkness of the vegetation. I was aware of the sound of my breathing and the gentle lapping of the sea to my left. Along with the constant whistling of the cicadas, there was the occasional sound from the darkness of the jungle to my right. A coconut falling, a small animal shifting as it slept. The creaking of a tree. The guard never moved from his seat. He leant back against the base of the wall and although I couldn't see his gun, I knew it was there. He finished his smoke and flicked the butt out onto the sand. I watched until the tiny glow extinguished itself. Then the man sat up straight, stretched his arms, and slowly got to his feet. My pulse quickened slightly as I realised he might take a walk down the beach towards me. If he had done so I would have moved a few metres into the jungle and laid low while he passed. Thankfully he moved off in the opposite direction and it was then that I saw the weapon. He walked slowly for about ten metres and then stooped down to retrieve something from a hiding place in the wall. It was only when he had come back into the light of his favourite spot that I saw he was carrying a bottle. The man leant his weapon against the wall and sat down in his favourite position. I watched him as he slowly unscrewed the top of the dark plastic bottle and took a swig. I imagined it would be some toxic home brewed spirit. The man lit another cigarette and took turns between smoking and sipping his drink. *That's right, buddy,* I thought, *you carry on and get hammered, it's fine by me.* The heat was starting to get to me now the breeze had gone and with all the layers of clothing my entire body was sweating profusely. Still, my eyes never left the man until he had finished the cigarette and was concentrating solely on the bottle. Finally I felt satisfied that the man had settled in for the night and I decided it was time to move. I got up and backtracked for fifty metres or so down the beach. My plan was to cut into the jungle for a hundred metres and then make my way to the wall and try to get over it. A hundred metres would put me a long way behind the big house and the scene of the beating I had witnessed. I would decide on what to do once I was over the wall.

The jungle was totally black and seemed impenetrable. I squatted down, opened my bag and retrieved the night vision goggles. It took a few minutes to get them fitted comfortably but when I turned them on, the foreboding blackness of the jungle was transformed into a monochrome green and white obstacle course. It looked like the graphics of a primitive computer game. Every branch and frond was clearly visible, along with all the dead vegetation on the ground and the vines in the trees. I was impressed. Flicking the goggles up, I took one last look at the guard in the distance. He had not moved an inch. I pulled the goggles over my eyes and started making my way into the undergrowth. I was surprised at how quietly and quickly I was able to move in the alien green and white world the night vision produced.

I kept a mental note of each step I made as I climbed over fallen trees and ducked under hanging vines. Ten minutes later I was satisfied I had gone at least a hundred metres back from the beach. I knew from memory that if I turned left and crossed the wall, I would be safely behind the house and the out building I had seen.

The heat and humidity of the night was intense and I felt like I was roasting. I paused and flicked the goggles up to see what my surroundings looked like without night vision. All around me was totally black and I could not even see my hand outstretched in front of me. Gratefully, I pulled the goggles back over my eyes and paused to listen. There were no sounds apart from the usual. It was time to head to the wall. Turning left I started off in the direction I knew it to be. The green and white maze of the jungle was just as it had been on the way in and it was only my sense of direction that reassured me I was on the right track. Ahead of me a snake slithered away into the undergrowth. The adrenalin was humming constantly in my body and it helped me to overcome the claustrophobic green and white sauna I found myself in. I moved slowly and carefully, counting my steps for a good ten minutes. I stopped and looked around. There was no change and worryingly, no stone wall anywhere near. I had a brief moment of self doubt and I wondered if I had erred somewhere. *Fuck all, Green,* I thought, *it's there, you know it's there. Carry on and you'll come to it.* I followed my instincts and proceeded. It was not a minute later that I became aware of a looming grey mass with intensely bright, pin prick lights above it. I flicked the goggles to the upright position and saw that I was indeed at the wall and the bright lights above were stars in the night sky. I was out of the canopy of the jungle and in the clearing that had been cut when the wall was built. The wall was at least four metres high, jagged and imposing in front of me. I squatted down quietly to watch and listen. My eyes once again had become accustomed to the night and the stars above gave me enough light to gauge the wall. It was made up of jagged coralline rock with cement mortar in between. It towered above me. I stood up and ran my hand across the surface. The coral was as sharp and dangerous in the air as it was in the sea but it was lumpy and would offer some grip for me to climb it. What I needed was a strong tree to attach my rope to.

This would guarantee an exit from the property no matter what the surface of the wall was like on the inside. I turned right and walked slowly in the clearing between the jungle and the wall. It wasn't long until I came across a tall palm tree that was two metres from the wall. Its surface was smooth and as thick as a beer keg. I ran my hand up the wall opposite it and was pleased to find it was as jagged and rough as I had found it earlier. I squatted down, removed the coiled rope from my bag, and tied one end firmly around the trunk at shoulder height. I pulled at the rope violently and felt the knot tighten reassuringly around the trunk.

Then I slung the remainder of the coiled rope as high as I could over the wall. It flew silently and disappeared, leaving only the section between the palm and wall at a forty five degree angle. Once again I sat to watch and listen for any movement. There was nothing except the sound of the cicadas. My entire body was dripping wet with sweat by that stage. It felt like the polish on my face was preventing my skin from breathing. It was time to go. After donning my gloves I stood up near the wall and felt for hand and foot holes. There were quite a few but some were too sharp and jagged. Eventually I found some that were suitable and with the bag on my shoulders, I started climbing. It was a slow process of finding a hand hold, pulling myself up, then finding a foot hold. My arms ached as I moved half a metre at a time but I was getting there. At one stage I had to move to the left as the rocks above me were too jagged but I managed, and eventually I pulled myself, panting and sweating, onto the top of the wall. It was a metre thick at that point and the surface was as rough as the sides. I paused, squatting, and caught my breath. I was half way there. In the distance to my left I could clearly make out the house and the various out-buildings. The house towered above the tree line. There were a few lights on including on the top floor which I knew to be Carlos and Angelique's living area. Quietly I moved to where the rope was hanging over the wall. I gave it a pull and was relieved to see it hanging all the way to the ground on the other side.

After pausing for a moment, I took hold of it and began abseiling down into the property of Carlos da Costa. Half way down I heard a crunching sound under my right foot. A loose piece of rock had become dislodged and tumbled to the ground noisily. It landed in amongst the vegetation with a thud and for a moment I hung there suspended. My arms burned from the strain but I remained calm and waited to see if there would be any reaction. There was none. I carried on descending till I reached the bottom. My heart was beating loudly in my ears and I was panting from the exertion. I laid low for a while to recover. The vegetation around me was not as thick as the jungle on the other side of the wall but it was equally dark. I retrieved the night vision goggles and fitted them. I decided I would first move towards the house and the outbuildings to have a look around. I had seen very little on the night of the party and I needed to get a clear idea of the layout of the property. I made a mental note of where the rope was hanging and moved off slowly through the darkness, pausing every four or five metres to check my surroundings. The adrenalin was pumping freely through my body at that stage and my limbs felt like coiled springs. There were no pathways, only thick bush and palm trees. Eventually, through the night vision goggles, I became aware of burning white lights ahead of me. I flicked the goggles into the upright position and saw that I was approaching a building.

Inside were dim lights but I saw no movement at all. I realised that I was behind the building where I had witnessed the waiter get his beating. Staying in the darkness and using the limited light from the building, I skirted around to my left. Eventually I could make out the dark shadow of the wall and the back of the ablution block from where I had heard the cries of the waiter. In front of me was the dark, rocky slope I had come down, and to my right was the side of the mansion. The lights were still bright on the top floor. There was no movement and nothing to see so I decided to skirt around the building to the right behind the main house. I moved off silently with the goggles in the upright position until I arrived at a large flat clearing. In front of me was the back of the mansion. Its three stories towered above me and I was once again aware of the sheer size of the place. It was clearly the business end of the house and I could see various stairways and entrances to kitchens and other utility rooms. Still in the relative darkness and cover of the bush I squatted down to get an idea of the layout.

The clearing was huge and immaculately manicured with green lawns and palm trees. Cleverly hidden lights shone on the lawns and back of the building. To my right near the house were a line of six shaded car ports. All were occupied and I could see the shape of the Hummer I had seen Angelique and Tintin arrive in at the water-sports centre. To the rear of the carports was a tarred driveway with a roundabout to the centre. There were dim lights on either side of the driveway at twenty metre intervals and I saw them stretch off to my right until the bush of the tropical garden obscured them. I had no doubt that it led back to the main entrance to the property. The manicured green lawn stretched off on the other side of the driveway and appeared to continue all the way around the other side of the house. I decided I would stay in the safety of the darkness and carry on skirting the house to the right. I would, at one stage, have to cross the driveway but that didn't worry me too much. What puzzled me was there was no movement. No people. No guards patrolling and no staff. A house of that size would require a lot of workers to keep it running, but apart from the guard house I had not seen any staff quarters at all. Staying in the darkness I moved on. It was only when I was approaching the tarred driveway that I became aware of a buzzing sound behind me. It was different from the constant sound of the cicadas and I was sure it was a machine of some sort. I stopped to listen. The sound went quiet and then repeated itself every few seconds or so. *What the fuck is that?* I thought, *and in the middle of the night?* I shook my head and decided to continue.

The noise got louder as I went and it was when I was only metres from the driveway that I noticed a pathway leading off into the jungle behind me. There was no doubt the noise was coming from that direction.

I looked up the pathway and although it was well trodden I could see no lights. The tarred driveway stretched off into the distance to my left. My curiosity got the better of me and I shelved my plans of skirting the main house. I decided to investigate the source of the noise. I replaced the night vision goggles and started following the pathway while keeping at least five metres away from it to the right. As I moved, the sound got louder and louder as the pathway wound its way around huge trees and bushes. By that stage I was certain what I was hearing was machinery of some kind. Suddenly, as I rounded a thick bush, I was blinded by a bright light that shone white hot in the green monochrome of the night vision. I stopped immediately, squatted down, and flicked the goggles upright. Through the vegetation, in a clearing not twenty metres away, was a large building. It had a steel frame and corrugated walls and roof. The metal of the walls were grey in the moonlight. To the front of the building was a large sliding door that was in the closed position. Bright lights shone from the inside through the crack between the sliding door and the wall, and the noise of the machines continued. I paused to watch and listen. The building was well-hidden in the jungle. Had it not been for sound of the machines I would never have known it was there. There were various spots around the building where the metal of the walls were joined and the light shone through. It would be too risky to approach the main door so I decided to move around to the right of the structure and see if I could have a look inside from there. The sweat ran down my body as I crept through the darkness and the undergrowth to the right of the building. As I reached halfway, I noticed there was a half centimetre gap between the corrugated iron sheeting of the wall. It ran all the way up to the roof and the light shone through brightly. I decided that I would approach and have a look at what was going on inside. I felt dangerously exposed as I moved from the cover of darkness into the clearing that surrounded the building. As I approached the wall, I noticed a small white piece of paper on the ground. It was only three centimetres square but I picked it up as I crept forward. It felt like a small packet that contained tiny plastic balls but I didn't bother examining it as I was only a few feet away from the gap in the wall. Slowly and very carefully I moved my right eye into position not an inch from the wall and looked inside. It took a while for what I saw to sink in but once it had, I was totally mesmerised.

Bright industrial lights hung from the roof of the building, illuminating the interior to almost daylight. On the far side of the building, and covering the entire wall, there were a series of metal racks that went up as high as the ceiling. On each shelf lay white surfboard blanks. There must have been at least fifty of them. To the centre of the room, standing near a work bench, stood a black man in a brown dust coat. On his face, he wore goggles and a protective mask.

His hair was full of white dust. In his hands he held an electric router and using a template, he was in the process of neatly removing a section of body from a surfboard blank that was held in a large padded vice. The dust sprayed out as he finished the job before placing the router on the bench to his side. When the dust had settled I noticed a large man pacing up and down near the sliding door to the left. There was no mistaking him, it was Tintin. He was smoking a cigarette and he looked impatient as he walked. The man in the dust coat then picked up a rubber air hose and sprayed compressed air into the neat rectangular hollow in the centre of the surfboard blank. Once the dust had settled Tintin stubbed out his cigarette, picked something up from a table to his left and walked towards the machine operator. My heart beat a little faster as he approached. He was carrying a tightly wrapped rectangular plastic package. The plastic of the package, although thick, was transparent and there was no mistaking the contents. It was a white powder. He handed the package to the machine operator, who then placed it into the hollow made by the router.

It was a near perfect fit and the package only required a few taps with a rubber mallet before it was neatly embedded in the hollow. Tintin nodded grimly in approval to the machine operator. He then manually loosened the padded vice grip that held the board, and carried it to another work bench on the right. There were at least five surfboards that had been through the same process on the bench. I guessed that the next part of the job would be the sealing of the boards with fibreglass and the job would be done. I couldn't believe my eyes. It was starting to make sense. I had stumbled across a highly efficient and mechanised cocaine smuggling operation. I watched in amazement as Tintin returned to his observation spot and the process started again. The machine operator walked around the workbench and collected another surfboard blank from the shelving. He then carefully fitted it in the padded vice and set to work again with the router. As the dust flew I remembered the small paper packet I had picked up as I approached the building. It was still in my right hand. I was barely able to take my eyes from the scene that was playing out in front of me, but I forced myself and held the tiny packet up to look at it. There was printed blue lettering on one side. It read 'Silica gel. Do not swallow.' It made sense. Silica gel was a drying agent. In the tropical humidity of Zanzibar it would be essential to keep the product free of moisture. I imagined there would be a lot of it around. I had seen enough. My head was spinning and I needed to gather my thoughts. I realised that I had been standing there for some time and I was exposed. I backtracked through the clearing and made my way into the cover of the jungle behind me. Once I was safely in the darkness again, I squatted down to think. What I had seen explained a great deal. It explained the source of Carlos da Costa's immense wealth.

It was a lot more than the manufacture of surfboards. It certainly had nothing to do with the bottled spring water and everything to do with him being an international cocaine smuggler. It also explained the connection to Richard and the source of Richard's wealth. He was a cocaine importer. There was no doubt in my mind. The Aston Martin. The luxury flat in Sloane Square. *His business for fuck's sake, The Boardroom.* It all made sense now. It explained the nervous exchange of bags he had made with the two Indian men in the restaurant in Notting Hill in London. Cash for cocaine, it had to be. London. London seemed a million miles away. It felt like I had been away for years. So much had happened since I had even thought of London. It also explained Richard's own drug use. His father had been one hundred percent right. He was up to something illegal. Very fucking illegal. More importantly I was now absolutely certain that Carlos da Costa was an incredibly dangerous, powerful, and ruthless man. There was no doubt. Through all the steamy heat of the undergrowth I felt a dreadful cold chill spread through my stomach and my mouth went dry. Richard and Angelique were treading on fucking thin ice. If they were to be found out, who knows what the consequences would be? Considering a simple waiter had been savagely beaten and killed for stealing some food and drink. *What would Carlos do to Richard? For that matter what would Carlos do to Angelique? Were they fucking crazy? Were they complete idiots? Perhaps their love for each other had totally blinded them? But what the fuck should I care? I was doing a job. It was simple. Do the job, answer the questions, and get the fuck out.* This had become very dangerous indeed. But no, it wasn't that simple. This was no ordinary job. Through my stupidity, I had become fond of Richard. In some way he was like a son I had never had. For some strange reason I felt an urge to protect him. And what of Angelique. Who could not be fond of her. Who could not love her for that matter. A cold black cloud of fear and worry descended on me and for a moment I felt desperately helpless. All the good feelings of myself regaining some control were now blown out of the water. I would have to confront him. If necessary I would beat some sense into him. It had gotten to the point that I didn't even care if I had to tell him everything.

Tell him that I had been hired by his father and followed him halfway around the world. Tell him I knew everything and threaten him if necessary. Tell him I was no friend of his. Make him see sense. I decided that was what I needed to do and I would do it immediately. I needed to get back to the clearing and then make my way to where I had left the rope. I flicked the night vision goggles down and took a look around. It was then that I noticed a light in the distance to my right. It was coming from an area to the back of the factory. I stared at it for a moment wondering what it was. I put the goggles in the upright position and realised it was very dim and would hardly be noticed by the naked eye. It was late.

I had made my mind up on what I was going to do but my curiosity got the better of me and I decided to go and have a look. I moved around the building in the undergrowth until I was directly behind it. When I arrived, I noticed another pathway heading in the direction of the light I had seen. Staying in the bush, I made my way parallel to the path. It wound off to the left and then to the right. I passed a few large boulders as I went. I had not seen any rocks on the premises since I had seen the waiter get beaten on the night of the party. Eventually I arrived at what appeared to be a large rocky outcrop. A small hillock covered with boulders and bushes. The source of the light I had seen appeared to be coming from within it. From where I was I could only see a faint glow emanating from what appeared to be an entrance to the base of the hillock. I stared at it feeling somewhat puzzled for a while. Then I remembered that Hassan had mentioned the fresh water caves that were on the property. He had told me he used to play in them when he was a kid, before the government had sold the property to Carlos. I could only imagine that this was what I was looking at. There was no sound except for the machinery from the factory and there was no movement from the caves. It would be risky but I decided to have a closer look. I crept out of the bushes and into the clearing in front of the entrance. The path under my feet was well-trodden but the entrance was naturally concealed by vegetation. I paused and looked inside. There was a gap in the rocks that must have been seven foot wide and ten foot tall. Below me were a series of stone steps that led down to a small natural pool. It was completely still and silent inside and had I not known it was water one would imagine you could walk on it. The source of the light was on the other side of the pool. It was brighter there and had it not been for the night vision goggles I would never have known the place existed. I felt an overwhelming urge to go in and look closer at what was there but there was also a feeling that once inside, I would be trapped. I had no idea if there was a way out on the other side. What if someone was to come in behind me. It was dark inside, and I was blacked up, but if someone was to come in, they would surely be carrying a torch or would activate some kind of lights. Again my curiosity got the better of me and I decided to go further into the cave.

I noticed a well trodden walkway hewn from natural rock to my left. It led all the way around the silent pool of water to the source of the light. There was no other way there except through the water. There were huge stalactites hanging from the roof of the cave. I took one last look behind me. There was no one in sight and there was no noise at all from inside the cave. Silently I made my way down the rock pathway that skirted the water. The only sound I could hear was that of my heart beating and my breathing. The light got brighter as I approached it and I saw that in front of me was another natural entrance to another cave.

It was only when I walked through and turned right that I saw the source of the light. I couldn't believe my eyes. I was in a subterranean office and the light came from a simple desk lamp that had been left on. There was a telephone, a carpet, a fan. There was a desk with pens and writing paper as well as an electronic calculator. I was flabbergasted. I pulled the torch from my bag as the glow of the lamp only illuminated the desk area. The walls and ceilings were all rock that were yellowed and melted by a million years of running water.

The desk had a comfortable chair behind it with two positioned in front of it. It was bizarre to say the least. My instincts told me to keep out of the light so I moved around the space keeping close to the wall and made my way around the cave. It was when I got behind the desk I saw a wrought iron barrier that had been built into the walls of the cave in concrete. There was an access gate but there was a strong-looking lock to the latch. The area inside was completely dark. I walked towards it and when I arrived I flashed the torch on to see what was behind. The fact that there was an underground office in a freshwater cave was astounding to say the least, but what I saw behind the gate came as no surprise. In front of me was a storage area with wooden pallets all over the floor. Neatly packed on top of the pallets were telephone book-sized packages of cocaine. They were stacked up on top of each other and were at least three foot high. Packed all around them were thousands of tiny bags of silica gel and covering them was a large sheet of thick transparent plastic. I had found the factory where the product was concealed and made ready for shipping and I had also found the office and storage department of the entire operation. I stood for what seemed like an eternity, staring in amazement at the sheer quantity of the deadly white product in front of me. There must have been at least half a tonne of the stuff. In my mind I saw then how it all worked. Carlos and Tintin would run the admin from the cave. Then the product would be moved, bit by bit, to the factory where the the machine operator would perform his duty of preparing the surfboard blanks, loading them, and sealing them. What happened after that was a mystery but I could only imagine the finished boards were shipped out to the big factory on the mainland in Dar Es Salaam, combined with standard unloaded ones, and then on to various destinations around the world. Richard would only be a small fish as far as the scale of the operation went. I was certain that he would have no idea of the existence of the Zanzibar factory or the cave. He would simply receive batches of surfboards, remove the important ones, open them up and then act as a wholesaler to the packers and dealers of London. A dangerous but extremely lucrative business. I turned around wanting to have a look at the desk. The sight of the light made me feel exposed once again. Darkness was my friend and the light a deadly enemy. I decided against it. I had seen enough and had been in the cave for too long.

If someone were to come I would have to either attack him and put him to sleep or I would have to kill him. None of these appealed to me. It was time to leave. It was then I felt a light breeze on my face. I had not seen any holes in the walls and I wondered where it might be coming from. I shone the torch around me and saw nothing. It was when I shone the torch above me I saw an opening in the roof of the cave. It appeared natural and was roughly a half metre in diameter. I imagined that it would be a good source of light during the day as well as a good source of ventilation for the office. It was in the centre of the ceiling of the cave about five metres above and I could see the stars in the night sky through it. I felt a sense of being trapped. It was definitely time to go. What if Tintin were to return to collect more product? There was no way out except the way I had come in.

Quickly and quietly I made my way out of the office and back into the freshwater pool area of the cave system. It was reassuringly dark, but I knew I had a good thirty metres of walkway to cross before I would finally be out in the open. As I walked I prayed that I would meet no one. There were no lights or noises as I made my way, and eventually I was out and hearing the sound of the machines from the factory once again. I flicked the night vision goggles down and hastily crept into the undergrowth. My mind was blank as I skirted the pathway back towards the factory. I passed with no trouble as the two swing doors were still shut. Panting slightly and sweating profusely I tracked the path back towards the clearing where the car park and driveway were. From there it would easy to cut through the bush and make my way to the perimeter wall.

It was when I was only metres from the clearing and the drive that I flicked up the goggles to have one last look at the house. Suddenly I heard an engine turn over and start running. It sounded like a small car. Reverse lights were turned on. Someone in the carports was going somewhere and I was in an exposed position. The car reversed rapidly and I heard the crunching of its tyres on the tarmac. There was no time to retreat back into the jungle and I was only metres from the driveway. There was nothing else for it. I lay down as flat as I could and removed the goggles from my head. In the light of the driveway I saw a small silver car moving forward around the roundabout. Whoever was driving seemed to be in a rush. I felt like a rabbit in the headlights as the car accelerated towards me. The only consolation was the sparse bush that surrounded me and the fact that I was as low as possible on the ground. I was sure that there would be very little chance that whoever was driving the car would see me. It felt like an age but eventually the car was up along side me. I looked up briefly and saw the unmistakeable silhouette of the driver. The long hair flowed out behind the driver's head. It was Angelique and she was driving alone.

Where the fuck is she going in the middle of the night? I thought. *I've got I good idea!* In an instant the car was gone and the sound of the motor faded away as she drove. There was no time to waste hanging around. I flicked the goggles back into position and started off through the jungle to my left. My mind was still numb as I walked and the adrenalin was surging through my body from the close encounter with the vehicle. The jungle seemed thicker than it had when I had first arrived. I was sweltering and frustrated. I needed to get over the wall and back into the beach where I hoped there would be a breeze. From there I would decide on my next move and how I would go about it. After what seemed an age I reached the clearing and the wall. Again there was enough light to remove the goggles. I realised that I was probably a fair distance from the rope and I would have to move back towards the main house and beach before I reached it. The feeling of being trapped was ever present although not as bad as it had been in the cave system. I walked slowly and carefully until I saw the figure of the huge palm tree towering above me to the left. It was a welcome sight and soon enough I came across the rope. It was exactly as I had left it. It was my ticket out of that hell hole and I felt a huge sense of relief as I began pulling myself upwards. My arms ached as I went and I was extra careful with my footing. The memory of the falling rock was still fresh in my mind and I didn't want to make a mistake like that so late in the game. Eventually I reached the top and I stopped to catch my breath. As I sat, I looked at the main house. It no longer looked grand and beautiful. It was now dark and sinister. I could only imagine the secrets it held within its whitewashed walls. The tantrums and abuses it had witnessed. But there was no time and I needed to get well away from the place. I pulled the rope up and quietly dropped it over the other side. Then I carefully lowered myself down the other side until I found what felt like a good foothold. It took longer to descend than it had coming up as I struggled to find decent foot and hand holds but eventually I made the one-metre drop and was back on the other side. I untied the rope, coiled it up and packed it away in my bag. Without pausing to rest I flicked the goggles over my eyes and made my way north through the green monochrome maze of the jungle. When I was sure that I had walked at least a hundred metres I made a right and headed towards the beach. Once again it felt like the jungle was endless. The deafening screech of the cicadas combined with the maddening heat and humidity was enough to drive a man insane, but eventually I saw the end and the pinpricks of the stars come into view. When I finally got to the beach I was totally exhausted. I sat on a fallen palm tree for a break. All I wanted to do was to get out of the heavy clothes and run into the water. To scrub the boiling polish from my face and neck and be done with it. Just to feel cool again would be like a re birth. But I realised that there was a very good chance that Angelique would be visiting Richard.

I needed to find out but it was very late at night and it would not look good for a random tourist to be seen wondering around Richard's hotel at that time. Especially a non-resident. No, the polish and the heavy black clothes would have to remain until I had seen what was going on there. Then and only then would I be free of them. After a few minutes, I got to my feet and started walking back up the beach. The guard from the wall was out of sight as I had come a fair distance through the forest. As I walked I thought of the winter in London I imagined how it would feel with the howling wind and freezing rain on my face. I decided I would rather be warm in the cold than sweltering and unable to do anything about it in the heat. Finally I had made it past the jungle to my left and was approaching the outskirts of Richard's hotel. The lights were forty metres in front of me as were the last of the rooms on Richard's side of the hotel. Once again I made my way into the bushy jungle to my left. The one consolation was that the property was a lot smaller than the big house and I would only have to travel a short distance until I was parallel with Richard's room. The lights of the first two rooms were off and the residents obviously asleep but there was a dim light coming from Richard's room and the lights of the bathroom were bright. Slowly I crept towards the room. It was when I was within twenty metres, that I heard the un mistakable sound of two people having wild and passionate sex. For a moment I wondered if the female I was hearing could be someone else, one of the Dutch girls perhaps, but then I heard the unmistakeable voice of Angelique. She cried out his name in her French accent. I needed no further evidence of what they were doing so I retreated back into the jungle until I was out of earshot. I paused to decide what to do. There would be no approaching Richard now. It would be shocking and embarrassing for both of them. It was out of the question. Then it struck me that I was carrying the tracking devices. I had seen the car she had been driving and I decided it wouldn't be such a bad thing to keep tabs on her movements. I had not seen the car park for the Eden Beach Lodge but I could only guess that it would be directly behind the main building. I flicked the goggles back into position and made my way inland until I had passed where the main building stood. Through the bush, I could see the light of the car park. There were not many vehicles there and the small silver one I had seen Angelique driving was conveniently parked near the edge of the clearing. Feeling relieved that I wouldn't have to venture into the semi light of the car-park I made my way through the bush and stopped just short of the clearing. There was a guard house with a dim light near a wooden boom that was the entrance. It was all quiet so I wasted no time in retrieving a tracking device. I activated it, dropped my bag and crawled over the dead leaves towards the car. I had to cross a low wooden pole but I arrived near the front wheel arch unseen and the magnets made a quiet clunk as they attached themselves to the body of the car. I could feel the engine bay was still warm from the drive there.

I crossed back into the darkness of the bushes, retrieved my bag and, using the goggles once again, made my way through the jungle and back towards the beach. When I finally arrived I walked up the dark side until I was at least a hundred metres from the hotel. It was a feeling of massive relief when I removed the tracksuit top, the jeans and the skull cap. The shoes were last followed by my shirt which was totally drenched. I was desperate to sprint into the water and absorb its coolness for hours but I restrained myself and walked slowly across the sand. I would have been a strange sight to anyone had they seen me. An undressed black and white minstrel having a midnight dip in the ocean. Eventually I made it to the water and lowered myself into it. Slowly I pushed myself out into slightly deeper water and the temperature dropped around me. It was like finally being free from a terrible fever.

The relief was unbelievable and I lay floating, staring at the stars for a good five minutes, my mind totally blank. Using the wet sand from below me I scrubbed the polish from my face and neck. After doing this I made my way out of the water back up the beach to where my bag was hidden. I packed the heavy black clothes into a separate compartment of the bag and started walking up the beach towards my hotel. It was late and I passed Richard's hotel and all the others on the way unseen by anyone. Thankfully there was no trouble near the water-sports centre either and I arrived safely at my hotel. I was exhausted and all I wanted to do was make my way up the lighted pathways to my room but I was worried that there might be residue of polish on my face, so instead I walked until I was parallel with my room and made my way through the palm trees and over the grass to my door. I unlocked it and stepped into the cool breeze of the fans. Without thinking I dropped my bag onto the bed and headed straight to the bathroom for a well deserved cold shower. Usually I would stand in the shower and think things through but I was weary and just enjoyed the cool water running over my naked body instead. When I finished I dried myself off lightly, walked back into my room and slumped onto the bed. The fans were blasting and the evaporating water from my skin acted like an air conditioner. I felt like I had died and gone to heaven.

After a few minutes I had cooled down sufficiently. I got up and drank a full two litres of Carlos da Costa's mineral water. It left a bitter taste in my mouth but it was wet and that was what I needed. I pulled on some clean shorts and opened my laptop to check the tracking device I had planted. It took some time for the programme to load, but eventually the screen showed a map of Paje and surrounds. Angelique's car was exactly where I had seen it with the blue light flashing on the screen. I positioned the screen so I could watch it from the bed.

My plan was to sit upright whilst I watched and smoke a few cigarettes whilst I ran through the events of the day in my mind. I sat back on the bed and smoked. The last thing I remember was a feeling that my mind was drifting away from my body and I fell into a deep dreamless sleep.

CHAPTER FIFTEEN

- BAD DAY IN PAJE

My mind woke up before my body. That quiet peaceful feeling of having had a good night's sleep. I felt cool and comfortable. Without opening my eyes, I turned over wanting to drift back into the place I had been. Suddenly, and with a shock, it all came back to me. The face of the dead waiter covered with flies in the river bed. The diving trip with Richard and Angelique. The blazing heat of my nocturnal trip into the jungle and over the wall of the big house. The incredible sight of the cocaine packing factory and the even more bizarre subterranean office and storage facility. My eyes opened like a shot and I looked at my watch. It was 7am. "Fucking hell!" I cursed out loud and jumped to my feet. I was furious with myself for falling asleep so quickly. I consoled myself with the fact that it had been a hell of day and I must have been absolutely shattered. I drank some water, lit a cigarette, and went to the laptop. Angelique's car was no longer at Richard's hotel. Instead I saw the blue light flashing in an unmarked but large piece of land between the road and the ocean. I knew she was back at home at Carlos da Costa's place. I opened a smaller window on the screen that showed the log and times of the car's movement. It showed she had left Richard's hotel at exactly 3.30am and had driven south down the main beach road straight home. *At least you know where she is, Green,* I thought. Still angry with myself, I put on a tee shirt and some shoes and headed out for a run on the beach. I crossed the lawn and headed to the beach without looking around. I wanted to be alone that morning. Instead of turning right, I made a left and ran faster than usual up the soft sand for a full two kilometres. My mind was still numb and I was happy to leave it that way for the duration of the run. I stopped and leant over on my knees for a minute to catch my breath and then repeated the same fast run on the way back. I hardly took any notice of my surroundings and instead concentrated on the sand directly in front of me. There were a few clouds in the sky that day but when I finally got back to my hotel I was once again burning with heat. Burning with heat, but feeling better. Angelique's car was still in the same place it had been when I awoke. I drank a litre of water, stripped off, and took a cold shower. As I washed I knew it would be the day I would confront Richard. My plan was to have some breakfast and go directly to his hotel and have it out with him. It had all gone too far. It had been become personal and too dangerous for me to continue this charade. I had had enough. I dressed, put on my sunglasses and headed out to the restaurant. Most of the hotel guests were busy eating as I arrived, so I slipped around to the left of the building hoping to get my usual table and be left alone. As luck would have it my table was free and I made a bee line for it, avoiding looking at anyone as I went. All around me were the cheerful sounds of children and parents talking and laughing and cutlery clinking on porcelain.

As I sat down, my usual waiter approached me. I ordered a large glass of chilled orange juice, a pot of coffee, and a full English breakfast. As I waited for the order to arrive, I noticed a figure approaching from the left out of the corner of my eye. I knew it was Helen. I had been hoping to avoid her that morning especially after seeing her disappointment with me the previous evening. I braced myself as she arrived.

"Good morning, Jason, how are you today?" she asked cheerfully, her face beaming, an expectant look in her eyes. She put her right hand on my shoulder as she spoke. "Oh hi Helen," I said, "I'm fine thanks, and you?"

"I missed you last night," she said quietly, "Ineke and I were wondering if you would like to go on a spice tour with us today?"

"I'm sorry Helen, I can't. I have some very important things to take care of this morning." Her expression dropped into one of worry and sadness. "Did I do something to upset you?" She asked in a shaky voice, tears welling up in her eyes. This was the last thing I needed. It was yet another example of how I had screwed up on the job. I looked her straight in the eyes. "Listen Helen," I said quietly, "you have done nothing to upset me. Please just believe me. I have to do this. Maybe I will see you later, ok?"

More tears came and her bottom lip began to tremble. "Ok, Jason," she said, "I'm sorry I bothered you." She turned and left. I stared grimly out to the sea on my right. "Fucking hell" I said under my breath. The breakfast arrived and I ate without averting my gaze once from the table. When I had finished I signed the tab and without looking around, headed back to my room. As I walked in, I lit a cigarette and walked over to the laptop to check on the tracking device. The flashing blue light indicated the car was still at the big house. I sat down and stared at the screen as I smoked. I was about to crush out the butt when suddenly the blue light began to move. *What now?* I thought as I watched it slowly approach the main road. The car turned right and there was no surprise when five minutes later I saw it turn and park in the grounds of the Eden Beach

Lodge. *You couldn't keep away could you?* I thought to myself. 'Fuck it!' I stood up, closed the laptop and walked straight out of the door. There was no time to waste. I would drag Richard away from her if I had to, and beat some sense into him. There would be no more pussy footing around. I walked out over the grass, through the palms and onto the beach which was then in full sunlight. I felt a great sense of relief as I walked, a feeling that the whole situation would finally be brought to a conclusion shortly and I would finally finish the job I had been given.

I knew the outcome would come as a huge shock for many people, but at least I would know that I had ultimately done what I was being paid for. It was with that same single mindedness that I took the fifteen minute walk down the beach to Richard's hotel. I paid no attention to my surroundings or the various people on the beach but instead walked swiftly with very little on my mind other than what I had planned. When I arrived, I made my way up the right hand wing of the hotel and walked past the main building. There were very few people in the lobby and I carried on walking down the other side towards Richard's room. When I arrived, I knocked firmly on the door. "Richard!" I called, "Richard, it's Jason." There was no response. The curtains were closed and there was only silence from inside the room. I looked around frustrated and noticed two ladies from the house keeping staff at the next room. "Excuse me," I said to them impatiently, "have you seen the man from this room?" They looked at each other with an alarmed look on their faces and then back at me.

"Sorry sir," said the older of the two, "we have not seen him today." I started walking back in the direction of the main building. When I arrived I went quickly up the stairs to the restaurant. There were two couples eating a late breakfast but no sign of Richard or Angelique. With frustration building, I went back downstairs and made my way to the reception. It occurred to me to walk out side into the car-park to see if Angelique's car was there or not. I stepped out of the cool shade of the lobby to see there was no small silver car in sight. "Fuck!" I said under my breath. I wondered if she had left alone or if Richard had accompanied her. I walked back into the hotel lobby and went straight to the reception. There was a tall thin man in a black suit behind the counter. "Good morning sir, how can I help you?" He asked with a smile.

"I'm looking for Mr Lewer-Allen," I said, "I'm a friend of his, I've been to his room, but it seems he's not here?"

"Oh that's right sir," the man said, "he left about ten minutes ago."

"Did he say where he was going or when he would be back?" I asked impatiently. "I'm sorry sir, he didn't say anything at all," the man was non committal and he could sense my growing anger. There was no point in asking who he had left with. I knew full well that he had left with Angelique. "Thank you," I said to the man and began walking out the front of the hotel. As I walked I made a call on my mobile to my taxi driver Hassan. He answered quickly with his usual cheerfulness. "Hello Mr Jason, how are you?"

He said. "I'm fine thanks Hassan. Listen, are you available to drive me around today?"

"Yes sir, I am actually in Paje now, I can come to the hotel anytime."

"Good," I said, "will you please stay in Paje. I will call you when I am ready. Please don't take any other fares, I will make sure it's worth your while. Is that ok?" Hassan seemed to sense the urgency in my voice.

"Hakuna matata boss. Just call me and I will be there."

"Thank you, Hassan," I said. "I will call you soon." I walked out of the hotel and back onto the beach. The sand and the water sparkled in my eyes as I turned left and started making my way back to my hotel. When I arrived fifteen minutes later I was sweating from the heat of the day. I opened the door and went straight to the laptop to see where Richard and Angelique had gone. To my surprise the flashing blue light that was Angelique's car was still showing in the car park of Richard's hotel. I shook my head in disbelief. *Had I missed something?* It was then I noticed that the computer was no longer connected to the internet. *No service.* "Fuck's sake!" I cursed loudly. I unplugged the laptop and moved around the room with it hoping it would pick up a signal but it was futile. The system was obviously down. I put the laptop on the bed and pulled out my mobile phone. The screen showed full signal. 'I'll phone him,' I thought. I pulled the red file from my case and found Richard's cell number. I was certain he would be roaming. I dialled the number and stood at the window tapping my foot impatiently for the connection to go through. It took ages and eventually I was greeted by a pre recorded. "The subscriber you have dialled is not reachable. Please try later." I shook my head in frustration. I knew there was a computer with internet for the guests in the reception of the hotel. I thought there might be a chance that their service would be working and I might be able to locate the car from the tracking device manufacturer's website. I locked the room and took the short walk through the shady gardens to the reception. When I arrived I was told the bad news that the internet everywhere was down. Apparently it was a regular occurrence and there was no telling when service would be restored. As I walked back to my room I was reminded how frustrating Africa could be. The fact was that there was little point in losing one's temper with it and it was best to sit it out and wait. But that was the last thing I felt like doing. I had started the day out with all the gung ho intention of finally putting an end to the whole nightmare scenario I had found myself in. Only to be felled at the last hurdle by a pair of love birds and a broken internet service. To say I was angry and frustrated was an understatement.

I glanced at my watch. It was 11am. I walked to the window and stared unseeingly at the ocean through the palms and the hibiscus flowers. *Where had they gone?* I thought. There was no doubt that their relationship was building in its intensity. She had left Carlos house in a hurry the previous evening and had only returned after 3.30 in the morning. That in itself was surely an escalation of things between them. I wondered if there was any point in calling Hassan and trying to drive around the island looking for them. I decided that there would be very little point in doing that. I knew for a fact that apart from being a good fifty kilometres to Stone Town, the island itself was much bigger from north to south. It would be like looking for a needle in a haystack and would probably only serve to spoil my day further.

I lit a cigarette and continued staring out the window. The feeling of helplessness growing all the time. I spent the next three hours pacing my room, checking the internet connection every fifteen minutes. I called Richard's hotel on the hour, every hour to see if he had returned. Each time I called I was told he had not and was asked if I would like to leave a message. I declined. At 2pm I had had enough of being cooped up. I called Hassan and told him to collect me at the reception of my hotel. He arrived within five minutes and a waiter was sent to call me. I picked up my laptop and walked briskly through the grounds of the hotel on my way out.

I hoped to avoid running into the Dutch girls and luckily I made it to the waiting car unseen. "Where would you like to go Mr Jason?" Hassan asked as we drove out of the grounds and onto the tar road. "Umm let's go down to the Eden Beach Lodge first please, Hassan. I need to check something there." He turned and looked at me as I spoke. A concerned look on his wise old face.

"Is everything ok Mr Jason?" He asked quietly. "Not really Hassan," I replied, "not really." We drove in silence until we reached the gate to Richard's hotel. As we drove through the boom into the car-park I could see immediately that the car was not there. I called the hotel on my mobile once again and was told that Richard had not returned. "Let's drive down to Jambiani please, Hassan," I said. We drove out through the boom and headed south. Eventually we arrived at the point where the big stone wall of Carlos' property cut into the path of the old road. We turned right and followed it around past the heavily guarded gate and beyond. As we passed it, I had a sudden, uneasy, liquid feeling in my stomach. It was the knowledge that not three hundred metres from where we were, hidden in the jungle, was the cocaine packing factory and the old fresh water caves that had been turned into a storage facility. It still seemed a little surreal in my mind. As if it had been some kind of weird dream.

My fears were growing with every hour of the day. "Where would you like to go in Jambiani, Mr Jason?" Hassan asked, wiping the sweat from his face with his cloth. "Take me to the same place you took me last time please Hassan." He knew full well there was something badly wrong but kept quiet and dignified as he drove. We arrived to find the resort pretty much deserted. To kill a bit of time, I went inside and sat at the bar near the beach to check if the internet was up and running again. It was still down. I was in no mood for drinking so I ordered a bottle of water and a coke for Hassan. I tried once again to call Richard on his mobile and then at his hotel but it was to no avail. I returned to the cab and we drove around the small fishing village of Jambiani aimlessly for a while. Eventually I decided to head back in the direction of Paje. There was a tense silence as we drove through the oppressive heat of the afternoon. We stopped briefly at the Eden Beach Lodge on the off chance that Richard had returned but he had not. It was 4pm when we arrived back at the car park of my hotel. I knew that Richard had not checked out and at some stage he would definitely return to his hotel. I was in no mood to walk up and down the beach again so I asked Hassan if he would wait close by for a call. He agreed happily and I made my way back to my room. I spent the next three hours in my room. Like before, I checked the internet connection every fifteen minutes and called Richard's hotel every hour. At around 6pm as the sun was setting, I ordered some food to be brought to the room. It was good but I didn't have much of an appetite. It was at 6.45 precisely that the internet service was finally restored and the small icon at the bottom right of the screen showed there was full service. After so long it felt like Christmas had come. I drummed my fingers on the surface of the dressing table as I waited for the tracking program to load and refresh. When it finally did I saw the flashing blue light that was Angelique's car moving down the main road from Stone Town towards Paje. They were in the middle of the Joziani Forest and appeared to be driving relatively slowly back in my direction. *Thank fuck for that,* I thought, *finally. Finally I am going to get to speak to Richard and finish this!* With an immense feeling of relief, I called Hassan and asked him to drive to the reception and wait for me to come out. I lit a cigarette and smoked as I watched the blue light move and turn on the map on the screen. As I sat, I imagined the reaction I would get from Richard when I finally spilled the beans and told him what I knew. I was sure he would be completely flabbergasted and probably very upset. I really didn't care at that stage, I just wanted the whole thing to finally be over. Eventually the flashing blue light made the right turn on the beach road towards Paje. I had a good idea but I needed to know exactly where they were going.

The perfect scenario would be that Angelique dropped Richard at his hotel and then went home herself.

That would give me the opportunity to talk to him alone and not have to drag him away from her and embarrass him. I didn't really care though. Either way, he was going to be told the whole story that night without fail. A knock came on the door, it was a waiter informing me that the taxi had arrived. I thanked him and told him to tell Hassan that I would be out shortly. After such a frustrating day I realised that the last thing I needed was to lose track of the car again. I prepared the bag I had used the previous evening to carry the laptop with me when I was to leave. I watched the flashing blue light pass my hotel and eventually stop in the car park of Eden Beach Lodge. I sat for a few minutes hoping it would leave, but it stayed put. There was nothing else for it. I packed the laptop away in the bag and headed out towards the reception and Hassan. The night was warm and still as I took the short walk to the waiting car. I slung the bag and its contents onto the back seat and we made our way up the sandy drive, through the gates and out onto the road. "Eden Beach Lodge please, Hassan," I said staring ahead into the darkness.

"Hakuna matata, Mr Jason," he replied. A few minutes later we turned off the darkness of the main road and through the boom into the car park of Richard's hotel. I saw Angelique's car parked exactly where it had been the previous night. I told Hassan to park his taxi to the left of the main building. As he parked I turned and faced him in his seat. Once again he wiped the sweat from his brow with his cloth. "Listen Hassan," I said, "as I'm sure you have guessed I have a bit of a problem on my hands. Now I have to go inside and speak to someone, but hopefully after that everything will be sorted out." He nodded understandingly. "I might be a while, but please wait for me ok?"

"No problem, Mr Jason," he replied. As I turned in my seat to retrieve my bag that I noticed the headlights coming through the gate of the hotel behind me. They were large and square and far apart from each other. As soon as I saw them I had a very bad feeling. It was like a premonition, as if I knew very well what car it was and who would be driving it. My fears were realised in an instant as I saw the hulking square mass of the yellow Hummer as it pulled up and parked next to Angelique's car. I froze in my seat. "Just a moment," I said quietly to Hassan as I watched. It was as I had feared. In the dim light of the car park I saw the huge dark shape of Tintin as he got out of the car. He was talking on a mobile phone and he walked slowly and ominously around the small silver car as he spoke. In my mind I knew who he was talking to and what he would be saying. He had found them. Eventually he hung up and pocketed his phone. I watched as he walked towards the main arched doorway that led to the lobby. He paused for a moment and then started walking inside. "Shit," I said under my breath. "Shit, shit, shit. I'll be back Hassan. Just wait ok."

I waited until Tintin had stepped into the hotel before I got out of the car. I slung the bag over my shoulder and cautiously walked towards the entrance. *Please,* I thought, *please let them be doing something innocent like having a drink or some dinner.* I paused at the entrance to the hotel and saw that Tintin had gone to the reception. He was talking to the same man I had seen in the afternoon and his massive frame towered above the desk as he spoke. The receptionist motioned with his arm towards the right wing of the hotel. Clearly he was giving directions to Richard's room. Tintin nodded and without looking around started off in that direction. When he had left the lobby and turned right I walked in. I tried my best to look like a happy go lucky tourist as I walked in. It was extremely difficult given the chaos that was going on my mind. I walked through the lobby and into the dim lights of the outside area. I could see Tintin walking down the right hand side of the hotel. I decided to head to the relative safety and darkness of the pool bar to watch from a distance. *Please let them be in the restaurant or the bar,* I prayed as I walked. I arrived at the bar area to find a party in full swing.

For a moment, I hoped that Richard and Angelique would be sitting there innocently enjoying a drink. I could then join them as if by accident and give them being together a semblance of normalcy and innocence. Sadly they were nowhere to be seen and instead there were a group of couples cavorting, drinking, singing and swimming. I chose a dark table and sat down. The music and laughter blared but in my mind there was nothing but near panic as I watched Tintin finally arrive at the door of Richard's room. He paused for a moment and then I saw him knock five times on the door. I could not hear a thing through all the racket but I could see that he had knocked with considerable force. Thirty seconds later I saw the door open and a slightly dishevelled Richard appear in the light. It looked like he had just pulled his shirt on and I saw him smile with wide eyes and try to look normal and innocent. I could not see Tintin's face but I saw him nod a few times and the smile disappear from Richard's face. Then I saw Richard point into the room and shake his head. I could only imagine what was being said but even from the distance I could see that the meeting had turned tense and unpleasant. At that moment I was approached by a waiter who greeted me and asked if would like to order a drink. I shook my head quickly and told him I was waiting for someone and to come back in five minutes. Slowly, and right in front of me, my worst fears were being realised. It was then I saw the slim elegant shape of Angelique step out of the door from behind Richard. She wore a loose green summer dress and sandals. Her hair was in a pony tail behind her head. Again I saw Richard smile and then I saw him raise both hands in a gesture of innocence. I saw Angelique pointing at Tintin and speaking. She didn't seem to be shouting but she seemed determined to get her point across as she spoke.

All around me the party continued and no one took any notice of the drama that was unfolding nearby. It was at that moment that I thought I would take a walk over and attempt to diffuse the situation. Perhaps if I pretended to have been with them all day it might give them being together some credibility in Tintin's eyes. I got up off my seat and started to walk around the pool towards them.

At that moment I saw Tintin raise his left hand in front of Richard's face as if to say 'no more.' The smile left Richard's face once again and Tintin took Angelique by the arm gently but firmly and they both left together and walked towards the lobby. I watched helplessly as they left and saw Richard staring after them as they went. Richard scratched his head in confusion and then shook his head. He stood there as they walked and then closed himself in the room and was gone. I followed Tintin and Angelique from a distance. It was clear he was under instructions to return her to Carlos and nothing would stop him. I could see her protesting and gesturing at Tintin but he kept his vice-like grip on her arm and shook his head as he walked. As they approached the lobby and the reception she seemed to gain some composure and walked without protest. I waited in the semi-darkness until they had both exited the front of the building and turned left towards the parked cars. I casually walked through the well lit lobby and paused at the entrance to see what had transpired. What I saw filled me with fear. Angelique's protests had started again and the last I saw was her being forced into the front seat of the Hummer and the door being locked. Tintin moved quickly around the car and got in the driver's seat. The vehicle started, reversed quickly and was gone in a cloud of dust and sand. It had happened. Everything I had feared had just happened right in front of my eyes and at the time there was little I could have done to prevent it. I looked to my right and saw Hassan staring at me with a worried look from the window of the cab. Although he knew nothing of what had transpired he could clearly tell from the alarm on my face that something was badly wrong. I was suddenly faced with a terrible decision. Was I to ignore what had just happened and go back to Richard's room to confront him? Tintin had been sent to find Angelique and not Richard so he was more than likely safe where he was.

I watched as the lights of the Hummer disappeared south down the beach road towards the big house. *What the fuck are you going to do now, Green?* I thought. I had no idea the sort of relationship Carlos had with his wife but I was under no illusions. He was an extremely dangerous and violent man. *Richard is safe where he is Green. For fuck's sake you have to go and check if she is safe as well. This is a fucking nightmare!* I turned and looked at the lights of the lobby behind me and then back to the road in front. If Angelique had been allowed to drive herself home I might have considered leaving it.

But she was taken by force and her car left behind. My mind was made up. I would go to the big house to check on Angelique. Once I was sure that she was safe I would go back and confront Richard about the whole shit show. I had no choice. I had to go and see that she was alright. I ran towards the the car and noticed again the worried look on the face of Hassan as I jumped in the front seat. "Hassan," I said with urgency in my voice, "I need you drive towards Jambiani and I need you to drive as fast as you can. This is very important, ok?"

"No problem, Mr Jason I have seen you have been very, very worried all day," his voice was shaking as he spoke. We reversed and drove through the gates before taking a left turn. I was mildly surprised by the speed at which he drove the rickety old car. The road was dark and completely deserted. "Now you are going to see some unusual things and I am going to ask you to drop me in an unusual place, but I need you to trust me Hassan." He nodded as he drove and the sweat ran down his temples in the light of the dash board.

"There are some very bad people behind that big wall. Now I have been sent to find out about these people. I have come all the way from England to find out about these people. Do you trust me Hassan?" I asked loudly.

"I trust you Mr Jason," he replied. "Right. I am going to change my clothes and I am going to ask you to drop me near that big wall, ok?"

"Ok,"

"Then I want you turn around and drive a few hundred metres and wait for me on the side of the road. If anyone asks you why you are there, you tell them you are having trouble with the car and you are waiting for someone to come and help you fix it. Do you understand?"

"I understand and I will do as you ask Mr Jason."

"I know what I am asking is unusual but I will make it worth your while ok Hassan?"

"Hakuna matata Mr Jason I will do as you ask, hakuna matata."

"Thank you Hassan, now I am going to change my clothes." I pulled the bag from the back seat and opened it. I removed my shoes and then pulled on the black jeans. They were still damp from the sweat of the previous evening.

Next I pulled on the black tracksuit top followed by the beanie and the blacked up trainers. Hassan watched in amazement as I did it. Last was the black polish that I smeared onto my face and neck. We were approaching the wall when I took the laptop out of my bag leaving only the rope, the panga, the night vision goggles, and the garrotte. Hassan slowed the car as we reached the wall. "This is fine here Hassan," I said, "turn the car around like I said and wait up the road there. I don't know how long I will be but I promise I will be back."

"I am afraid Mr Jason," he said gravely, "what is happening here?"

"I promise I will tell you everything, Hassan but I have no time now. Just trust me and wait for me ok?"

"I will do it," he replied. I trusted him. I grabbed the bag and jumped out of the car. Immediately I ran to the clearing between the thick jungle and the wall. I turned left and made my way as fast as I could. My plan was to reach the palm tree I had used to cross the wall the previous night. There was scrappy bush and tree stumps and more than a few times I stumbled over low lying vines and fell. Eventually I decided to stop and put on the goggles. When I did, it was a massive help and my journey was made a lot quicker, quieter and safer. I had no idea if there were guards patrolling but the sense of urgency was too much and if I had run into one, I would have dealt with him accordingly. Adrenalin rushed through my body in surges every ten seconds and I was completely oblivious to the steaming heat that enveloped me.

A few minutes later, I arrived at the familiar palm tree. I wasted no time in fastening the rope around it as I had done the previous night and tossing the other end over the wall. I climbed the wall as I had done to the best of my memory and before long I was squatting on the top panting and surveying the scene in front of me. My plan was to go to the main house and move around until I was sure that no harm had come to Angelique. If there was a shouting match, I could deal with it and I would leave once I was certain she was safe. But deep inside I feared the worst and my instincts told me there was a good chance it would come to more than that. *Just go and see, Green. Deal with whatever happens when and if it happens.* I climbed down the rope as quickly and quietly as I could, replaced the goggles and headed towards the clearing and the car park at the back of the house. From there my plan would be to skirt around until I found a suitable place from which to get closer. From what I had seen the previous night there wasn't very much security on the inside of the premises, probably due to the nature of the business being conducted there.

I felt sure I would be able to get close enough to establish what I had come for. Eventually I arrived at a place near the guard house. To my right I could see the car ports and back of the house. The Hummer was parked and all seemed to be quiet. I looked around and decided that I would gain entry to the main ground by going up near the guard house and through the darkness that surrounded the entertainment area. I felt sure that Angelique would be upstairs in Carlos' private quarters and it would be relatively easy to gain access from there. It was at that very moment that I heard a door open and slam shut.

What followed chilled me and made my heart sink. The towering figure of Tintin and the much thinner and shorter frame of Angelique appeared from a door to the centre of the rear of the house. She was visibly angry and struggling against the vice like grip of Tintin who held her by one arm and was force marching her across the car park. "Let me go, you bastard!" she shouted. "You have no right to touch me like this!" There was more anger than fear in her voice and this was a small consolation to me as I watched from the darkness of the jungle. Tintin said nothing and continued his march across the clearing. It was then that I saw in his left hand he was carrying an AK47 automatic machine gun. *Oh Christ,* I thought, *Jesus, no. No, no, no.*

"You take your hands off me, you bastard. Do you hear me Tintin!?" she shouted. Then I saw her punch his arm and chest with her free hand. There was no reply or reaction from Tintin and he continued to drag her kicking and screaming across the clearing. I froze as I watched them pass me. *Where the fuck is he taking her?* I thought. If it hadn't been for the gun, I would have ambushed him and cut his throat but it was impossible at that point. Instead I decided to follow them and see what I could do when they got to their destination. Using the goggles, I moved with them, staying slightly behind them in the darkness. I was making a fair amount of noise in the bush as I went but it was nothing compared to the angry protestations of Angelique. She gave a spirited fight but there was no stopping Tintin. Within no time they had reached the other side of the driveway and I saw Tintin stop in his tracks. I wondered if they were going to walk up the drive to the main gate but then, using the hand with which he carried the gun, he flicked a switch that was hidden on a nearby palm tree. Instantly a series of low lights illuminated the path that led through the jungle. It was the path that led to the packing factory. The screaming and shouting continued as they made their way up the path. All the while, I followed from a distance like a predator in the night. The lights of the pathway glowed like phosphorous in the goggles but I avoided looking at them and instead concentrated on keeping up with them as they walked. My mind was racing all the while.

I knew there was nothing I could do until they reached wherever they were going. Once they were there I would assess the situation and deal with it accordingly. The only weapons I was carrying were the panga and the garrotte. I kept calm and followed.

The two of them arrived at the factory. Unlike the previous night, there were no lights coming from the inside. Clearly they were not going there. I saw its tall square shape as a grey block in the goggles. The path of lights followed around the other side of the structure and I knew that they continued to the fresh water cave system. My heart was beating fast and the adrenaline coursed through my veins.

The two of them continued past the factory, following the lights, until they arrived at the entrance to the cave system. I could see a glow of light coming from the inside. All the while, Angelique kicked and screamed, but it was to no avail. There was no stopping Tintin and he made no sound at all as he pulled her through the entrance and they both disappeared from my sight. *Please just lock her up,* I thought, *lock her up and leave her in the storage facility. I'll get her out and take her to a safe place.* I paused for a moment and thought about my next move. There was sufficient darkness in the first chamber of the cave system for me to hide myself. I imagined they were heading to the second cave where the lights and the office were. I thought I considered hiding in the shadows near the entrance to the 'office' and ambushing him as he left. Then I remembered the hole in the roof of the second cave. I had seen it the previous night and remembered clearly seeing the stars through it. It would give me a better vantage point from which to plan my next move. Every fear, every worry, and every scenario I had imagined was playing out right in front of my eyes but there was no time to cry over spilt milk. There was no time for blame or regrets. The situation demanded action. Immediate action. I skirted around the hillock that was the roof of the cave system until I was far enough from the entrance not to be seen. Then I started climbing. I knew that the opening was at the highest point so my first move was to get to the top. The rocks were sharp and the hillock completely covered with thorny scrubby bush. It made my progress slow and painful. More than once my tracksuit top and the skin underneath were torn by long sharp acacia thorns. Eventually I arrived at a clearing and I noticed a dip in the rock formation that was the opening at the top of the second cave. I paused briefly to catch my breath and remove the goggles. I placed them in the bag and put the bag down carefully. In the moonlight I lay on my stomach and, being careful not to shift any loose rock, I snaked my way towards the hole.

As I got closer and closer I became aware of shouting and cursing beneath me. A few seconds later I managed to pull my face over the edge of the hole in the rock and I was finally able to see the entire horrific scene beneath me. Angelique stood against the metal gate of the storage area. Her hands were behind her and were clearly shackled to the steel with handcuffs. Her chest was rising and falling rapidly, her face red with rage and pure hatred. Her ponytail was gone and her sweaty hair clung to her cheeks in thin strips. Carlos da Costa paced calmly up and down the length of the room two metres in front her. From above, his squat podgy frame looked like that of a bullfrog and I could see the moist bulges of flesh on his neck above his barrel-shaped body. To the left, leaning against the wall near the entrance to the second cave stood Tintin. His face was expressionless and he made no movement at all. The gun was still in his left hand with the butt resting on the gritty floor. In that moment, I wished to God that I had had a gun. The two of them were like sitting ducks and I could have ended both of their miserable lives in a second. "Five years, my darling wife," said Carlos calmly. "Five years we are married and happy together."

"Five years of hell, you bastard!" screamed Angelique, tears running down her face. Carlos voice grew louder. His accent more pronounced. "Five years my darling, I give you everything you need. I give you beautiful house, I give you beautiful things. I give you everything you want, and now, you do this to me?"

He started to pace faster as his voice grew louder. Angelique watched him as he walked, a look of resigned disgust on her face. "I never loved you Carlos," she screamed, "can't you see that? You disgust me! The sight of you makes me sick to my stomach!" My world went into slow motion. Carlos da Costa's voice grew louder still and began to rasp like it had the night of the party. "Five years I try to make a good life for you and me, my darling wife! I work hard to make sure you happy! I pay for everything. I buy the clothes! I buy the jewellery! I fly you all over the fucking world and now I find you playing with another man?" Carlos was working himself into a frenzy. His short arms were shaking and gesticulating wildly as he walked. Then he stopped midway, directly in front her. "But no!" he screamed, "not just any man. No, no, no! I find you with the tall young carrallio from London! A customer of mine! You fucking whore!" He lunged forward and slapped Angelique on the right hand side of her face with such force that it sounded like the crack of a whip. At that moment I had never felt so helpless in my entire life. I felt my head was about to explode with rage and the entire scene below had filled with a red mist. If I could have, I would have jumped down from where I lay and ripped the little man to pieces with my bare hands. Never in my entire life had I felt such burning rage and hatred towards another human being. Angelique's head dropped to one side but she still stood. Carlos gripped her by the chin and held his face to hers. I saw a trickle of blood run down the left side of her mouth onto her chin. Carlos tilted his head to one side and spoke kindly as if he was talking to a child. "What you do now my darling wife? What you do now?" Her beautiful lips parted and turned into a snarl with the blood welling in between her white teeth.

"I am leaving you, you horrible little man. I love him and I am leaving you. Do you understand? You disgust me. It's over. I never ever loved you," she said calmly. Then she spat a gooey mixture of blood and saliva which landed directly in the right eye of Carlos da Costa. I saw the right hand of Carlos da Costa bunch up into a fist. "You fucking bitch!" he screamed as he slammed his fist into the side her head. Her body slumped unconscious immediately and I was sure that her arms must have broken behind her. I needed to close my eyes but I could not. My mouth filled with bile and I was overcome with nausea. I had never witnessed anything so cruel in my life. War was savage but this was different. Carlos da Costa stood there and looked at the slumped body of his wife. Then he turned his head skyward and for a split second I thought he might see me. His face contorted into an obscene mask and from his mouth emanated an ungodly screaming wail of rage. The sound was like a freight train smashing through a bottle factory. Then, with an air of calm serenity, he turned and walked towards the standing figure of Tintin.

"Give me the gun Tintin." Carlos took the gun and walked back towards the pathetic slumped body of Angelique. I watched as the barrel was raised and then I closed my eyes. Bam, bam, bam, bam. Four rapid shots. My body shook with each shot and I smelled the cordite rising through the gap in the rocks. I opened my eyes and saw the horror below. A pool of dark red blood was steadily gathering around her slumped body. I was truly grateful that I could not see her beautiful face. Tears filled my eyes and the vomit sat in my throat. Carlos stood there staring calmly at the body of Angelique. "Tintin," he said.

"Yes boss," came the calm reply. "I want you to take this bitch to the boathouse. I want you to put her in the boat. Tonight my beautiful wife will swim with the sharks. Do you understand?"

"Yes boss."

"Tintin," said Carlos, "afterwards I want you to go get that carrallio Richard and I want you to bring him here quietly. I don't want any problem.

I want you to take him quietly, and bring him here quietly. Tonight he will swim with the sharks as well. But first he will meet me and explain what he has been doing. Do you understand Tintin?"

"Yes boss. I understand. First the boathouse, then I go to get Richard."

"Good, Tintin," said Carlos calmly, "you go now." The last thing I saw of the cave below was Carlos turning around and Tintin walking towards the body of Angelique.

I pushed myself backwards until I was clear of the hole and then got up in a state of complete shock and disbelief. I pushed my way through the scrappy bushes and over the rocks until I reached the bottom of the hillock. I pulled the night vision goggles over my eyes, and stumbled off in the direction of the wall. It was not long before I started to feel faint and dizzy, as if I might pass out. My brain was spinning and my mouth filled with bile and saliva. I leant against a tree and then suddenly it came. I fell to my knees and vomited violently four times in a row. I had never been affected so profoundly by the sight of a person being killed or indeed by death in general as I was that night. As I spat the last of the foul taste from my mouth, my brain began to clear itself and I started to think straight. She was dead. There was nothing that would change that. Although I was sickened by the fact that I had witnessed her death there was no way I could have saved her. It had all happened too fast and like most of the shit storm I had been in, it was totally beyond my control. *Richard*. Richard was the only priority for me at that time. I had no idea how long it would take Tintin to get the body of Angelique to the boat house. I had no idea where the boat house was, but I knew then that I was in a race against time. If I failed, I knew that Richard's death would be considerably more painful and drawn out than Angelique's had been. Carlos had demonstrated his inane cruelty very well and I knew that I could not let that happen to Richard.

The nausea had gone and was replaced by a blazing red mist of rage and a desperate sense of urgency. I pulled the goggles down, got to my feet and started off in the direction of the wall as fast as I possibly could. *Got to get to Richard! Got to get to Richard!* was the only thing going through my mind as I ducked branches and jumped over dead trees. Eventually I reached the clearing near the wall. I knew I was a fair distance up from the rope so I turned right and jogged. I arrived at where the rope was hanging within a few minutes and wasted no time climbing it. A few loose rocks fell and landed noisily but I paid no attention to that.

I climbed half way down the other side and jumped the final two metres to the ground below. As I landed my right foot bent at an angle on a rock and a sharp pain shot through my ankle. I fought the urge to shout out in pain and sat down to feel it. How it did not break was sheer luck but I was sure I would have a bad sprain. I untied the rope and packed it into my bag. It was time consuming but I didn't want to leave any sign that I, or anyone else for that matter, had been there. When I was done I made off up the rough clearing towards the main road. I hopped and limped in pain as I went but I was grateful the ankle had not been broken. A few minutes later, I had reached the tar road. I paused to look around and listen for any vehicles. There was no movement or sound. I made my way on the right hand side of the road. I had told Hassan to wait a few hundred metres away, but I needed to be close to the cover of the jungle beside me in case of a vehicle from behind. I prayed that Tintin would still be busy with Angelique's body but I had no idea how long that would take, and there was a very real chance that the lights of the Hummer might appear from behind me at any time. I walked as fast as I could with my injured ankle, my eyes straining to see into the darkness ahead of me but I could not see any waiting car. *Had he abandoned me? Surely not. Hassan, I trusted you.* Perhaps the whole scenario earlier had frightened him and he had fled. *Where would that leave me, and more importantly where would it leave Richard? Please, please be there Hassan. Oh god please be there.* I was panting wildly with exertion and thought I might collapse when I saw the dim reflection of the number plate of Hassan's cab. It was a massive relief. Hassan got the fright of his life when I suddenly burst into the front seat of the cab. My face blacked up with polish, bleeding, clothes torn, panting uncontrollably and smelling of vomit. "Jesus, Mr Jason! What happened?"

"No time Hassan, we must go, I will tell you later. Please start the car and we go to Eden Beach Lodge now!" As the car drove off and I got my breath, I glanced at him. His chest was rising and falling rapidly as he drove and I saw the sweat running down his temples in the yellow and blue lights of the dash board. I glanced behind me praying that I wouldn't see the lights of the Hummer approaching.

"I want you to drop me just before the hotel please, Hassan. Then I need you to do the same again please. I need you to pass the hotel, drive for a couple of hundred metres and park the car. Like before, if anyone asks you what you are doing you say the car is giving you problems and you are waiting for someone to come to help you fix it. Will you do that for me, Hassan?"

"I will do it, Mr Jason but I don't want any trouble, I am an old man with a family and I don't…" I cut him off as he spoke.

"Trust me Hassan, it will be ok, I promise, I need you to trust me and do this for me ok?"

"Yes Mr Jason, I trust you and I will do as you ask." Up ahead I could see the light of the entrance to the Eden Beach Lodge. I told Hassan to slow down and drop me in the darkness. I could hardly drive in in the state I was in at the time. Dressed in black, covered with shoe polish, bleeding and limping. I would go in through the bush to the side and watch Tintin as he arrived. I had a feeling that he would park close to where he had parked before and that would give me the opportunity I needed. So far I had been lucky but I had the distinct feeling that time was running out. I knew that at any second I would see the lights of the Hummer behind me and if I failed that would be the end of Richard and would mean a total and compete failure on my part. I could not and would not let that happen. I picked up my bag, got out of the car, nodded at Hassan and made my way into the bushy jungle that surrounded the hotel. Once again, I was surrounded by darkness and jungle. I pulled the goggles into position and started making my way as fast as I could towards the lights of the car park. It was when I had just become parallel with the main building and Angelique's car that I heard the sound of a vehicle on the road. I turned around, and I knew that Tintin had arrived. As instructed, he drove slowly and calmly as he approached the hotel. He took his time coming through the gate and as I had expected he parked right next to Angelique's car. My heart thumped in my chest as I watched him. He made no movement and simply sat in the driver's seat watching and waiting. I decided that I would retreat towards the back of Richard's room. It wasn't far from there and I would still have access to the Hummer if I needed.

Slowly and painfully, I moved backwards through the undergrowth. All the while, I kept my eye on the Hummer and the seated figure of Tintin. When I was almost parallel with Richard's room I squatted down to catch my breath and choose a weapon. The panga was extremely effective but it was messy and more importantly it would be noisy. If I cut his throat or stabbed him there would be a lot of fuss and I was too close to the hotel to allow that to happen. I squatted down, opened my bag and retrieved the garrotte. I placed the bag behind me and waited. Five minutes passed. It felt like days to me but still I sat and watched the Hummer and its occupant in the dim light of the car park. All the while, my brain kept repeating the same thoughts. *This cannot and must not go wrong Green. You cannot allow this to happen. You must save Richard!*

It was then that the door of the Hummer opened and I saw the huge man step out. I watched as he walked around to the rear of the car and stopped. It was as if he was trying to think of a way to carry out the task at hand. Carlos had told him to take him quietly and without any problems. I could almost hear his thought processes. I watched him as he stared at the the front entrance to the hotel and then looked in my direction. It was as if he were weighing up his options on how to get Richard out. Eventually, after glancing around, he made his decision. He walked around Angelique's car and stepped into the very same bushes I was hiding in. I had to remind myself that he could not see me as I watched him carefully pick his way through the foliage towards me. As he came, I moved backwards slowly. I knew then what his intentions were. He was planning on going through the back windows of Richard's room and taking him from there.

He had no idea that there were thick burglar bars. Neither had I the first night I had come to take a look. I kept moving backwards until I was directly parallel with Richard's room and stopped against a tree. Through the goggles I watched the green monochrome scene in silence as the huge man quietly felt his way over and under the branches and foliage. He knew full well where the room was and was steadily coming directly towards me. I knew that I would have to take the opportunity as soon as it arrived. I knew that it would not be easy but it was my only chance to save Richard. I gripped the wooden handles of the garrotte firmly and stood my ground. Everything was again in slow motion and the wait was agonising. He took a few steps and then stopped to look around. On more than one occasion I was sure he could see me as he appeared to look straight at me but the camouflage was working well. Tintin was only metres away from where I stood and I realised that this was it. Within a small area there were three people. One or two of us were going to die that night. Tintin, or myself and Richard. Closer and closer he came and I started to hear his breathing. It was slow and calculated as he moved methodically through the trees. Ten metres from me and I was again aware of the sheer bulk of the man. Through the goggles I could see his pale green eyes as they moved from left to right. Still he came slowly. Five metres away and I knew that I could no longer move and the next time I did would be to make the attack. Three metres away and I was overcome by a strange feeling of serenity. A feeling of acceptance and understanding. I hated the man but it was nothing like the hate I felt towards Carlos da Costa. Tintin paused, and I saw him realise that he was almost parallel with Richard's room. He knew that a few steps more and he would be able to turn left and arrive directly at Richard's bedroom window. My breath slowed to almost nothing and my body froze completely as he started walking again straight towards me.

In the last metres I realised that he might walk right into me and that attempting to get the garrotte around his neck while he faced me could be a problem. Doable, but a problem. My fists clenched like a vices around the handles of the weapon as he took his last step. The man stood less than a metre from where I stood and I could smell garlic on his breath. He stopped in his tracks and stood there looking around. Everything appeared surreal and in super slow motion at that stage. Then the big man turned and faced the window of Richard's room. I knew then that it was time.

In a split second my right hand shot up, and passed to the left over the dreadlocks above his head. The trace wire made a soft whistling sound as it travelled through the air and landed on his throat just above his Adams apple. I jumped up as it landed, as if I was getting a piggy back from him and with all my strength I pulled the wooden handles apart. The crossed wires tightened and dug into the flesh of his neck. There was a crackling, squelching sound as his wind pipe was crushed followed by a dull ticking sound as the tendons in his neck snapped one by one. I pulled tighter and tighter, my legs wrapped around his waist. Instinctively his hands came up to try to free himself, but I pulled harder and I knew there would be no way that he would be able to loosen the wire that was now digging and cutting through his flesh. I pulled with such force my arms burned but I knew that if I loosened my grip for a second it would mean a terrible death for me. I could smell Vaseline on his skin as my face was right up behind his neck. The great man lurched forward and almost stumbled. I thought that I might be flung over his head so I tightened my legs around his waist some more. Then he started to swing from side to side in a desperate effort to fling me from his back. It was to no avail. I was going nowhere. Apart from a few grunts from me and the shuffling sounds of his feet in the dead leaves on the ground the whole episode had been quiet till then. Then the man stood upright and started stumbling backwards. Both of us crashed into the tree I had been standing at. The force of the weight of his body knocked the wind out of me and instantly, I too was unable to breathe.

I hung on as he stumbled forward and tried once again to shake me loose. I was acutely aware that if I passed out and loosened my grip there was a very good chance that I would wake up dead. I clung on desperately trying to inhale as we floundered. I forced one last burning effort and pulled the wire like it was the last thing I would do. Again the big man stumbled backwards and once again my upper body was slammed into the trunk of the tree behind me. It was at that point that my world turned black. The darkness came from my periphery vision and gradually closed in. The last thing I remember before passing out was a feeling of us both slowly falling to the right and then there was nothing.

I awoke gasping for air. It came in loud whooping rushes and felt like it would never be enough. I realised that I was lying down behind the still body of Tintin. My left leg was pinned under the weight of his torso and the handles of the garrotte were still in my fists. We lay there like two lovers spooning, as I caught my breath and listened for any sounds. Apart from my wheezing, which was gradually abating there was nothing but the constant whistling of the cicadas. I loosened my grip on the handles of the garrotte and the great weight of the body in front of me was still. In the struggle my goggles had been flung from my face. I felt around for them, found them and pulled them on. Then I removed my left leg from under the dead weight of the man and kneeled at his side. I reached over to his right shoulder and pulled him so he lay flat on his back and I looked at his face. The wire of the garrotte had sunk so deep into the flesh of neck it was no longer visible. His mouth was wide and gaping in a silent scream and the capillaries in and around his terrified eyes were ruptured and bloody. It was a grotesque sight but I had succeeded. I was alive and the big man was dead. I leaned over and began to remove the garrotte. I had to lift his head as I did it and I saw the now dark wire as it came from an inch below the flesh of his neck. As the wire came free from around his windpipe I heard and smelled the last breath that had been trapped in his lungs for so long. Garlic. I had given Richard a reprieve. For how long I had no idea. Tintin and Carlos were a tight and personal operation and from what I had seen at the house, there were very few others. I guessed that eventually Carlos would decide that Tintin had run into problems and would wait to find out what had happened. It was decision time again. There were two priorities. The first was to get rid of Tintin's body and the second was to get Richard off the island and safely back to London. I could hardly knock on Richard's window with my face all blacked up and tell him the news, so I stripped off the shoes, the jeans, and the torn tracksuit. I stuffed it all in the bag and removed my torch. Using the night vision goggles I started making my way towards the beach. My plan was to head slightly to the right so I would emerge on the beach in a dark area away from the hotel grounds. It took a good few minutes but eventually I arrived. I put the goggles and the torch in a safe place and made my way to the water. I stood knee deep and started to wash the polish from my face and neck. The salt water stung the deep scratches on my arms and shoulders. I didn't mind the pain as it brought home the seriousness of the situation I found myself in. Until then it had all been a bit of haze.

When I was satisfied I had removed the majority of the polish and blood I walked back to the where I had left the goggles and the torch. My plan was wander into the front of Richard's hotel from the beach and walk straight to his door and knock. The ocean was calm and peaceful in the moonlight as I walked.

It betrayed the savagery of the evening so far. I arrived at the left wing of the hotel where Richard's room was and walked straight up the beach and onto the tiled walkway that led past the rooms. As I walked I scanned the place for any sight of a guard but it seemed the place was deserted. I paused and took a deep breath as I reached Richard's door. I wondered how he would take the news of Angelique's death. More so I wondered how he would react to seeing his friend Tintin lying dead only a few metres from his room. I knocked firmly on the door three times. There was a pause, followed by a shuffling sound from the inside.

"Yes, who is it?" came the voice from behind the door. "Richard it's Jason, open up please."

"Jason?" came the reply. I heard the door unlock from the inside and the sound of the light switch. Then the door opened and Richard stood there wearing only shorts. He had a confused look on his face as he put his glasses on and blinked at me.

"Jason what are you...?" His sentence was cut short as I lunged forward and pushed him in the chest with my left hand. With my right, I slammed the door shut behind me. He stood there with a startled, confused look on his face, his glasses sitting at an awkward angle on his nose.

"What's going...?"

"Listen to me Richard!" I said as I gripped his bare shoulders and looked him in the eye. "I am not who you think I am. I was hired by your father Gareth Lewer- Allen to follow you. I've been following you for a while now "

"What?" He said with a mixture of fear and confusion on his face.

"That's right, Richard I've been following you since London. I followed you to Cape Town and then here to Zanzibar. I am no friend of yours do you hear me? I am here doing a fucking job!" He shook his head in disbelief and I knew that the next bit of information I would give might send him into a panic. "Shut up and listen to me Richard!" I said, almost shouting. I gripped his shoulders harder and looked into his now terrified eyes.

"Angelique is dead, Richard," I paused to gauge his reaction. There was none. "Angelique is dead, Richard. Do you understand? Carlos killed her, Richard. He knew about you and her and so did I, you fucking idiot!

There was nothing I could do, if there was I would have, believe me!" His mouth hung open and he began to shake his head from left to right. "No, no, no," he said quietly. "No, no, no, no!" His voice grew louder until he began wailing as he repeated himself. His face turned from disbelief into the realisation that what I had said was all true. He stumbled backwards with me still gripping his shoulders. A look of terror crossed his face and his head fell backwards, his mouth opened wide and he let out a wail of anguish. "Noooooooooooooooo!"

It was too loud and there was nothing else for it. I slapped him hard on his right cheek and the glasses flew from his face. I shook his shoulders and guided him backwards towards the bed so he could sit. The slap had stunned him and he sat there looking at me with a blank unseeing look on his face. I picked up the glasses and helped him put them on, then I pulled up a chair and sat down in front of him. I reached forward and held his shoulders again. "She's dead Richard, I saw it happen. There was nothing I could do. I would have saved her if I could have Richard, I'm sorry." He sat there with his mouth still open and stared at me blankly. "Get up and look at this Richard." I growled as I pulled him to his feet by his right arm. I dragged him to the back window and pulled the curtains open with my left hand. I dug the torch from my pocket and shone it into the darkness outside. The body of Tintin lay where I had left it not six metres from the window. Richard stood there staring at the lifeless body for a few seconds while the enormity of the situation sunk in. I swung him around and gripped him by the shoulders again. "That is Tintin, Richard. He's dead as well. I killed him. Do you understand?" He nodded and I saw tears welling up in his terrified eyes.

"Carlos killed Angelique and he sent Tintin here to get you. Luckily I was able to stop that happening Richard, but if you stay here for one minute longer than you have to, you are a fucking dead man! Do you hear me? You are a fucking dead man!" He started panting uncontrollably as he stood there staring at me. "Don't make me slap you again, Richard!" I said with my finger pointed at his face. This seemed to jolt some sense into him and again he nodded at me. "There is no time to talk now Richard, you listen to me, ok? I want you to pack your stuff and get ready to check out of the hotel. You don't leave this room or make a fucking sound. You wait here until you get a call from me and then you walk with your bags to the reception and check out. Do you understand?" He nodded.

"I am going to get you off this island Richard. If you do as I say, there is a chance you will live to see tomorrow morning but believe me, if you don't do exactly as I say, there is a very good chance that you will die tonight. *Do you understand?*" Again he nodded.

"I want you to lock the door, wash up, pack your stuff, and sit here calmly. If you hear any noise outside the window that will be me ok? I will call you. You walk to reception, check out normally and I will be waiting for you in a car outside. Is that understood?"

"Yes Jason, I understand," he replied in a stunned, deadpan voice. "Good. Now I'll be watching you Richard, and if you step one foot out of line, or do anything other than what I've told you to do, so help me I'll come and sort you out myself. Understood?"

"Yes Jason," he said, "I understand"

"Good" I said, "now get to it." I walked out of the room and closed the door behind me. He was in a state of shock, but I was sure that I had stressed the seriousness of the situation to him sufficiently. As I walked towards the reception I caught the eye of a guard who was seated near the bar area. I gave him a casual wave as I walked. My ankle throbbed painfully. The reception was deserted and I made my way out and across the car park to the boom and guard house. There was another security guard sitting in the guard house. He was fast asleep and I ducked under the boom and made my way out onto the tarred road without any hassle.

To all intents and purposes, I was a wandering tourist, probably drunk, trying to get back to my own hotel. The walk to Hassan's waiting car took a few minutes through the darkness and again he was surprised to see me arrive at the passenger door. "Mr Jason, are you ok? You have changed again."

"I'm ok, Hassan," I replied, "but I need your help..."

CHAPTER SIXTEEN

- ESCAPE FROM ZANZIBAR

The negotiations with Hassan took a full half hour. At first he was terrified and almost burst into tears, as I told him what I wanted him to do for me. It was only after I had pretty much told him my full story and promised him the sum of $10 000 in cash the very next day, that he reluctantly agreed. I assured him that in doing what I had asked he would be doing the world a favour and would probably be helping to save a great many lives. First we drove to my hotel where I checked out and retrieved my bags. After that, we drove quietly past the entrance to the Eden Beach Lodge. When we had cleared it by half a kilometre, we turned around again. Slowly, we drove back until we were about a hundred metres from the entrance. "Just park here and wait for me Hassan. Any problem, you just use the same story as before. When you hear me call you, open the boot for me ok?"

"OK Mr Jason, but for sure, I am afraid." I looked him in the eye. "If you do what I say, everything will be alright, I promise, and you will get your $10 000 in cash tomorrow. Just trust me Hassan." I left him nodding and crossed the road. I pulled the goggles into position and made my way through the undergrowth towards where I knew the body of Tintin to be. A few minutes later, I arrived. There was the glow of the light coming from behind Richard's curtain. I removed the goggles and tapped on the window. The curtains opened after a few seconds to reveal the shocked pale face of Richard peering out. I could see that his bags were packed and that he was ready to go. At least he had listened to me and I felt that there might just be a chance of getting him safely off the island. I looked him in the eye and brought my forefinger up to my lips. "Shhhhhhhh," I said and I pointed towards the bed, signalling him to sit tight. He nodded at me with wide eyes and closed the curtains. I turned to look at the body of Tintin and realised the gargantuan task ahead of me. 120 kgs of dead weight to move through the jungle and into the boot of the car was not going to be easy. I decided that a fireman's lift would be best. I leant over and grabbed the dead man's left arm with mine. Just the effort of pulling him into a seated position was hard enough and his head sagged backwards to show a deep black line on his neck filled with congealing black liquid. It dribbled slowly down his back. Next, I knelt down and swung his arm over my shoulder. Tintin's head thudded onto the top of my back as I attempted to lift his body from that position. Half way through the manoeuvre I was once again reminded of the back injury I had sustained during the mugging on the beach with Richard, and a bolt of red hot pain shot through my lower back. For a moment I wondered if it would be easier to simply drag him feet first through the jungle to the road. But that would have made a lot of noise and would have been difficult due to the ground vines and fallen trees.

I persevered and after a few minutes, a lot of pain and grunting, I managed to get to my feet. It was a good thing I had kept up my gym membership as it felt like he weighed a tonne. It was not only the weight but it was the height of the man that caused me so many problems. With the goggles in position, I stumbled off into the darkness of the jungle. On more than one occasion I almost fell as I stepped on a rotten piece of wood or I had to duck slightly, but after what seemed an eternity I made it to the edge of the road and the waiting car. "Hassan," I whispered, "open the boot." Without a word he got out of the car, walked around and opened the boot. On my instructions he immediately got back into the driver's seat and closed the door. I could tell that he was terrified but somehow I knew that I could trust him. Perhaps it was my gut feeling about him or perhaps it was the cash incentive, but I knew that he would try his best to go ahead with my plan. As I stumbled out of the undergrowth I almost fell again as my shoes slipped on the gravel at the side of the tarmac.

I managed to stay upright, and made my way to the rear of the car and the open boot. I leaned forward and dropped the torso of the dead man as best as I could in the direction of the open boot. As he fell, his knee crashed into the back of my head which then knocked into the boot lock. I felt warm blood oozing down my temple, and for a moment everything went red again in my vision. *You can fucking walk away from this now, Green,* I thought. But it was too late. The body of Tintin was in the boot, but his legs and arms were poking from various sides. I wiped the blood from my head on my sleeve and started the difficult task of fitting the huge man in. With a bit of pushing and shoving, I managed and I staggered backwards in exhaustion as I slammed the boot closed. My bag? As I slumped into the passenger seat of the car, Hassan turned and saw the gash on my head. "Jesus, Mr Jason, this is a very bad situation."

"Bad, but getting better now Hassan. Do you have any water?" He produced a grimy plastic bottle of drinking water. I drank half of it and used the rest to clean the wound on my head. The cuts and scratches on my arms were wet with sweat but at least they were not bleeding. I was shattered, and all I wanted to do was sleep but there was no time. I knew that Richard might lose it at anytime. I had seen the look on his face and I knew that his shock could turn without warning. I pulled the mobile phone from my pocket and rang the number for the Eden Beach Lodge. It took almost a minute before a sleepy-sounding man answered.

"Please put me through to room number eight," I said. There were a series of clicking noises, and then Richard picked up the call. "Hello?" he said.

"Get your bags and walk calmly to the reception. If they ask you why you are checking out so late, you tell them that you need to get to the south of the island and that a cab is waiting for you. I want you to act as normal as you can, Richard. Don't fuck this up! I will be waiting in a taxi in a dark area to the left of the car-park ok?"

"Ok Jason," he replied and hung up. I told Hassan to start the car and we headed off towards the gate. The guard was still sleeping when we arrived and he lifted the boom with one eye open to let us through. We parked where I had said and waited for Richard to emerge. I sat there nervously watching the arched entrance to the hotel until I saw the tall frame of Richard step out. He appeared confused and looked around for a few seconds before seeing the car. Then, dragging his bags behind him, he started walking towards us. I glanced back at the road praying that no car would approach. The prospect of meeting Carlos da Costa at that stage would have been too much for me. Thankfully, there were no cars and Richard arrived at my window with a vacant look on his face.

"Put your bags in the back seat and get in!" I growled at him. Without a word, he did as I said. The air was electric with tension as we drove out of the gate of the hotel and turned right towards the main road to Stone Town. Richard sat quietly in the back as Hassan wiped the sweat from his forehead with his cloth. The night was still and humid and every inch of my body was wet and aching with exhaustion. "Open the window, Richard," I said as I lit a cigarette. The old car moved off slowly into the night and I realised that the rear of the car was sitting low on the road. The weight of Tintin in the boot had compressed the old springs to near breaking point. "What about the police road block, Hassan?" I said as I took a draw from my cigarette.

"Ah, they will be drunk at this time, Mr Jason. We will drive straight through I am sure." Understandably he sounded nervous and unsure but I had no choice but to go along with him. Out of my peripheral vision I saw Richard leaning forward to speak to me. "Where are we going Jason?" he asked blankly.

"Shut the fuck up, Richard," I said raising my forefinger. He immediately sat back in his seat. I was angry for so many reasons. Angry with Richard. Angry with myself. I was angry with everything. But as we drove off into the darkness in silence, I felt a pang of guilt for shouting at him. After all, he had just been told that the woman he loved was dead and within the space of a few hours, his entire world had been turned upside down. Still, I wasn't ready to talk to him and we had a lot to do before I could relax.

The 50 kilometre drive across the island went slowly but thankfully without a hitch. Hassan had been right and we drove through the roadblock without seeing a single policeman. We passed only three vehicles as we travelled that were driving in the opposite direction. I stopped Hassan five times during the journey when I had seen a suitable lump of coralline rock on the side of the road. These I picked up and dumped on top of the body of Tintin in the boot. The extra weight made the car sit even lower on the road but somehow the springs maintained and we managed to continue. The entire journey was spent in an anxious silence, and I smoked as I made my plans. We arrived at the road that led to the port. Thankfully the streets were deserted at that time. Hassan paused at the turning.

"Right, what do I do Hassan?" I asked.

"You drop me at the port, Mr Jason, then you turn right and drive down the ocean road for five kilometres. When you see a sign which says Baya Beach, you stop and park the car under a big banyan tree. The place is deserted. When you see the boat coming you flash your lights once and I will come."

"How long will you take Hassan?" I asked.

"I will be there within one hour and then we go."

"Good," I said, "trust me Hassan, everything will be alright. You will have your money tomorrow morning and your life will return to normal. Ok?"

"Ok, Mr Jason, we go." Hassan turned right and drove down the dimly lit street towards the port. At the intersection of the ocean road he jumped out of the car and I moved across to the driver's seat. He turned to look at me and we gave each other the thumbs up sign before he crossed the street and was gone. I crunched the gears into first and made a right as instructed down the ocean road. After a while we had passed the populated area of Stone Town and the surroundings became dark and quiet. Eventually, as Hassan had promised, we arrived at a rusty sign that read Baya Beach. I turned left onto a sandy patch of ground and immediately I saw the huge banyan tree he had spoken of. It was gnarly and eerie-looking in the moonlight. I parked the car, turned off the lights and the engine, and sat as I lit a cigarette. Apart from the occasional shaky sigh, Richard sat in complete silence behind me and I never turned to look at him once. Hassan had been right. Not one vehicle passed. The place was indeed deserted. Fifteen minutes passed without movement. I decided it was time to let Richard know what my plan was.

Before I spoke, I took a deep breath. "I am going to tell you what we are going to do, Richard. We are sailing to Dar Es Salaam by boat tonight. It would be too dangerous for you to leave the island by any other means. I'm sure you know, Carlos is too well connected and powerful here, you would be stopped for sure."

"Ok," he said with a shaky voice.

"When we get there, the three of us will go to a bank and you will withdraw some cash. I will pay Hassan for kindly helping us, and then I will put you on a plane to London. Before you get on that plane, I will take your SIM card from you and destroy it. When you get to London you will buy a new SIM card and you will call me on a number that I will give you." I paused to let my instructions sink in.

"Now listen to me, Richard," I said turning to face him, speaking slowly so he would understand. "You do not go anywhere near your home. You do not go anywhere near your work. You do not contact your family or even your best friend. You do not even use a credit card. In fact I want you to stay away from London. You take a train to Brighton. I want you to go and book into a guest house and sit there until you get a call from me. It might be a few days, it might be a week, but I don't want you to contact anyone or do anything until you hear from me. Do you understand?"

"Yes, Jason." I looked him in the eye.

"Now, Richard, if you slip up once, if you don't do exactly as I say, I will come back to England and drop you in so much shit, your feet won't even touch the ground. I'm not talking about your family Richard, I'm talking about the law. And in your business, I'm sure you really don't want to be dealing with the law."

"I understand, Jason, I'll do what you say, I promise."

"Good" I said and I turned back to look at the silver surface of the ocean in front of the car.

"It's not my job to look after poor little drug dealing cunts like you, Richard. I don't even know why I'm doing this." But of course I did know why I was doing it. I liked him and I had no choice but to help him. Still, there was no way I would let him know that. We both sat in silence for half an hour until I heard the distant thudding of a diesel engine. I got out of the car and walked onto the beach to look. To my left in the distance I saw the shape of a boat approaching.

"Hassan, you fucking beauty," I said under my breath. I walked back to the car quickly and flashed the headlights once. I saw a light on the boat flash once in response and I knew my plan was working.

"When the boat gets here Richard, I want you to take your bags and get in ok?"

"Ok Jason," he replied. We sat and waited. Ten minutes later, the shadow of the big dhow came into full view and Hassan cut the engine. It drifted until I heard the sand crunching beneath its wooden hull and it came to rest. "Right, go," I said to Richard and he immediately did as I had said. Hassan jumped off the boat and walked up to the car, passing Richard as he came.

"I must help you Mr Jason, you are very tired."

"Thank you, Hassan," I said gratefully. We started by carrying the rocks I had collected from the road. Between the two of us this was easily done and we dumped them into the boat near where Richard sat in the moonlight. Hassan and I walked back to car and looked down at the curled up body of Tintin.

"You do not have to help me with this, Hassan," I said.

"No Mr Jason, I will help you," he replied soberly. I leant forward and grabbed the body from under the arms. It was starting to stiffen with rigor, but thankfully was still flexible enough for me to haul the upper part of his body out. Hassan took the legs under the knees. For a man of his age, and considering his skinny frame, I was impressed by his strength. Tintin's head lolled to one side and once again I saw the deep line where the wire of the garrotte had been. The muscles in my back screamed, but slowly we made our way to the waiting boat. The body hit the deck like a sack of potatoes and Tintin's face lay wide-eyed, his mouth still open in agony, facing Richard. "Oh Christ, oh Christ!" said Richard as he looked in horror at the spectacle. I leaned over the bow to get my point across to him.

"Shut up!" I growled. He turned and vomited over the side of the boat. Hassan and I walked back towards the car. He locked it and tossed the keys into one of the hollows between the branches of the banyan tree. "I will tell my brother to collect the car tomorrow. I will phone him in the morning. It will be safe here."

"I need water Hassan," I said, "I am very, very thirsty."

"Don't worry Mr Jason, I have plenty on the boat. We go now."

The dhow was a lot bigger than I had expected. It took Hassan and myself a while to get it off the sand and floating again but once done, we both jumped in and Hassan fired the old diesel engine. It made a slow thudding sound that was reassuring, as Hassan manned the rudder and turned the boat around to the left and out of the harbour. Richard sat just in front of me. He looked constantly out to the right in an effort to avoid seeing the grotesque sight of Tintin's face staring at him in death. I noticed a dirty bit of tarpaulin lying beneath me and I picked it up and covered the upper half of the body with it. Richard saw what I had done and nodded at me briefly in acknowledgement. The boat chugged slowly across the harbour in the moonlight and we all sat in silence. Eventually we came towards the edge of the harbour, and the giant shape of the ghost ship I had seen with Hassan came into view. It had drifted, so its stern was facing the port and I could see its entire length as we passed it. Even in the dim light I could see the rust and decay on the hull. A faded name The Star of Guangzhou was painted on its side. A huge, lonely, deserted hunk of steel with peeling paint and rotting decks. The sight of it made me feel uncomfortable, but I stared at it constantly as we passed. The top deck towered ominously above us in total silence and solitude. In the moonlight it was an eerie sight.

Eventually we passed the huge ship, left the protection of the harbour and started out to sea. The stretch of water between Zanzibar and the mainland was protected by the island, so there were no heavy waves on the east coast. Hassan bound the keel with some old rope and got up to raise the sail. There was a good westerly breeze and I watched him as he skilfully raised and bound the triangular sail. Once done, he cut the motor and I was surprised to see that we were making good headway and appeared to be moving at a firm, fast pace. I got up, leaving Richard staring out to sea, and went to have a word with Hassan. "I'm looking for a deep channel, roughly halfway between here and the mainland. Do you know of any?"

"Yes Mr Jason, there are many and I know them very well. Even at night, I can tell by the way the water looks."

"So you will let me know when we are at a suitable spot then?"

"I will do that, Mr Jason." His wise face looked even older in the moonlight and I could tell that although he had agreed to what we were doing, he was in no mood for conversation. I went back and sat down. The adrenaline and tension I had been feeling for so many hours, was starting to subside and was rapidly being replaced by an overwhelming feeling of physical and mental exhaustion.

The gash on my head was drying in the cool breeze of the open sea, but I was sticky and grimy from the sweat of the night. I turned to look at the island of Zanzibar and the silhouette of the buildings of Stone Town. It was a great relief to see them gradually getting further and further away with every second. I knew that every metre we sailed was a little bit closer for the safety of Richard's life. We were half way there. Dar Es Salaam was a big enough city to disappear in, and I knew that Carlos would only start monitoring the port and the airport in the morning in an effort to find Richard. He would hopefully have no clue as to what had happened to Tintin. Hassan had told me it would take between three and four hours to reach the mainland if the wind held up. That would put us there at about 7 o'clock in the morning. It was a good time to arrive and we could hopefully go about our business without hassle. An hour passed and the three of us sat in complete silence. The only sounds were the water lapping at the bow of the boat and the occasional ruffling of the sail. The moon made the calm sea look as silver as liquid mercury, and the sky was full of stars. It was surreal to think that I was enveloped in such a tranquil and beautiful scene after what had been a night of such horrific violence and death. More time passed and I watched Richard constantly from behind. He seemed to be staring out at the ocean, deep in thought. Occasionally I saw his head drop and his shoulders jerk, as he sobbed quietly to himself. After this had happened three or four times, I started to feel sorry for him. Sorry for his loss. I decided to go and have a quiet word with him. I had been harsh up until then but that had been for his own safety, and mine. I had known that every second spent on that island was a second closer to his, and perhaps, my own death.

I lit a cigarette and went to sit beside him. We spoke for a good hour in hushed tones. I told him how sorry I was for his loss and how sorry I was that there had been nothing I could have done to prevent it. I told him it had come as a surprise and a shock to me as well. I explained that for me the whole thing had gone wrong from the moment he had walked into the beach bar at the Paje Village Hotel. I made no apologies for doing my job as instructed by his father and explained that I thought he had been incredibly naive to think that he could get away with what he had been doing with Angelique. Richard was no fool and he acknowledged that he had been wrong and that they both had been foolish to even contemplate an affair. He told me it had been building up over a long time and such was the nature of love. He told me that the two of them were planning to elope. They had planned to run away together and leave both of their lives behind them. To disappear. It came as no surprise to me. In an effort to get him off the subject for a while I asked him how the operation had worked.

He opened up completely and explained that shipments of loaded surfboards would travel from Zanzibar to the main factory in Dar Es Salaam. They were then combined with regular boards, containerised and shipped out from there. He told me he had been running the imports for three years without a hitch. He explained that once the shipment had arrived in the UK, he would remove the loaded boards and dismantle them at a lock-up he had rented in north London. It was an elaborate and highly secret, one-man operation. And it had been extremely profitable. I had to agree that it was a brilliant scheme. He told me that Carlos had been shipping cocaine all over the world in that manner for over ten years and that through an elaborate system of forged documents of origin and bribery at the port of Dar Es Salaam, it had proved to be an almost fool-proof system. On more than one occasion as we spoke, he broke down and sobbed. I consoled him with the very fact that he was alive and stressed the importance of him following the instructions I had given him. I told him that somehow I would try to ensure he and his family were safe where they were. In my mind, I had absolutely no idea how I was going to achieve this but it helped to calm him down and take his mind off what had happened. I knew full well that if Carlos wanted someone dead he could make it happen anywhere in the world. I had no doubt that his reach would easily extend to England, but at that time I had only one priority. My priority was to keep Richard safe and get him back to England in one piece. My mind was overloaded and exhausted and I could think no further than that. At the end of our conversation I told him words to that effect, and I left him to grieve on his own.

As I went back to my seat, Hassan broke his silence. "Deep channel coming up in ten minutes, Mr Jason. See the water is different ahead." I looked ahead, and sure enough the surface of the water appeared a little rougher.

"Richard," I said, "if you don't want to see this, I advise that you look away now." He did so immediately and I set to work. Using the knife and the nylon rope from my bag, I began tying the heavy coralline rocks to the body of Tintin. I attached one to his neck, three to his torso, and one to his knees. It was a difficult and time-consuming job. Once I had finished I stood up and looked at my handiwork. I was pleased. There was no way that any of the rocks would come undone anytime soon and I felt sure that the sharks and the various sea creatures would ensure that no part of the cruel man would ever see the light of day again. With

Richard still staring out to sea to the right, I motioned for Hassan to help me throw the body overboard. We wrestled with the awkward load for a good minute until finally the body lay lengthways on the thick wooden side of the dhow. The weight of it combined with rocks made the boat sit slightly skew in the water.

I checked my bindings one more time, and then with an unceremonious shove, Tintin disappeared into Davey Jones' locker for eternity.

I sat down feeling satisfied that with each passing minute I was getting nearer and nearer to my goal of getting Richard safely back to England. The next two hours were spent in silence. My entire body was screaming for sleep, but it was impossible. On more than one occasion I found my head dropping, only to snap up suddenly with the realisation of the enormity of what had happened that night. As the sun rose behind us and we drew closer to the mainland, the cool, peaceful tranquillity of the journey was replaced by the rising temperature, and the knowledge that soon we would be in a highly populated area and we would be an object of interest. I stripped off my torn and bloodied clothes and bathed using sea water. Once I was dry, I dressed in clean clothes and attempted to make myself look as normal as I possibly could. I told Richard and Hassan to do the same. Up ahead the huge bustling city of Dar Es Salaam was coming to life and I could see various fishing boats making their way out for the day. There was full mobile signal, so I asked Hassan to call his brother on the island to make sure the car was collected as early as possible. I asked him where we would be mooring the boat, and if there was any chance of the sight of two white men disembarking causing a stir. He replied that he would find a quiet spot in his usual harbour and that he would have a taxi waiting for us when we arrived. He explained that if anyone asked any questions he would say that we had had a problem with the sails and that we had been stuck at sea all night. He explained that it was a busy place and that everyone there would be too busy getting on with their own business to worry about us arriving. The sun rose as we approached and I heard the sounds of the city. Trucks engaging gears, vehicles hooting, and the shouts of sailors and commuters as they began their day. Hassan got up and dropped the big triangular sail. He bundled it carefully and locked it away in a large wooden box in the centre of the boat. He started the diesel engine and we began making our way around a long curving concrete pier and into the harbour. Even at that early hour, the sun was fierce and I could tell it was going to be a scorcher of a day.

"I call the taxi now, Mr Jason," said Hassan as he dialled.

"Thank you Hassan." The port was extremely busy with dhows and fishing vessels of all shapes and sizes coming and going. The sailors shouted greetings to each other and teased the women on the shore who were busy carrying the night's catch up to the fish market. Hassan navigated the boat skilfully to a mooring on the right hand side near the outskirts of the port. A group of six young children clamoured down towards the boat and shouted to Hassan for a chance to tie the ropes.

He spoke back to them in Swahili, and proceeded to toss out three thick lengths of hessian mooring ropes. Richard sat watching with his prescription sunglasses on. His face was pale and drawn. We sat for a few minutes as Hassan performed his various chores, until he stood and faced me.

"We can go now, Mr Jason."

"Right," I said, "let's do that." We all picked up our bags and climbed off the boat onto the smooth boulders on the side. From there, it was a steep climb up a broken concrete staircase to the top and the main pedestrian area. The place was alive with activity and heavily littered. Already the flies had arrived with the smell of the fish market ahead, and I had to constantly swat them from my face. I leant over to have a word in Hassan's ear. "We need to get out of here as soon as possible Hassan."

"No problem Mr Jason, follow me." I made Richard walk in front of me and we made our way through the crowds and past the fish market. Young snotty-nosed kids dressed in filthy rags ran along side us as we walked. They shouted excitedly in Swahili, but no one really took any notice of us. The fish auctions had begun and everyone there was far too busy shouting their bids and trying their best to get a bargain. Eventually we passed the chaotic market and emerged onto what looked like a main road. From what I could see we were in an industrial area. There were factories and refrigerated trucks everywhere that were busy reversing and loading with fish. They hooted at each other constantly in the confusion. By then my eyes were stinging with fatigue and my limbs felt like lead. We carried on walking until I noticed a taxi waiting under a tree. "Our cab," said Hassan pointing at the car.

"Good, let's go," I said. The young driver was obviously waiting for us. He wore fake Ray-Bans and was leaning on the side of his car drinking a can of Coca Cola. He nodded at us, and greeted Hassan in Swahili before opening the boot so we could dump our bags. We all bundled into the car with Hassan taking the front passenger seat. Instantly I was annoyed. There was loud rap music coming from the sound system and the interior smelled of pungent body odour. The driver said something inaudible to Hassan who then turned to face me.

"The driver, he wants to know where we are going Mr Jason!" He shouted over the music. I leant forward and raised my right hand in a stop sign.

"Just tell him to turn this fucking music off please Hassan," Words were exchanged and the driver complied immediately.

"Right," I said, "we need to get to a bank. An international bank. I imagine there will be plenty in the centre of town so let's start there." Again, words were exchanged. The driver started the engine and we were off. I looked at my watch. It was 7.30 in the morning. "What time do the banks open, Hassan?" I asked.

"8 o'clock, Mr Jason. We have arrived in good time." Satisfied, I sat back in my seat and looked at the scene around me. The traffic was heavy and chaotic with most of the drivers happy to hoot at each other constantly. Hoards of pedestrians crowded the pavements and there were men grappling with overloaded push carts everywhere. The interior of the car was uncomfortably hot. That combined with the crowds started to make me feel slightly paranoid. I felt exposed and that eyes were watching us. I told myself it was just the exhaustion, and tried to put it out of my mind. Eventually we left the heavy industrial area and joined a highway that obviously led to the city centre. Unfortunately for us, we were in the middle of the rush hour and again it was a case of stop, start, stop, start. It was 8.20 by the time we left the highway and entered the city centre. Grand old colonial buildings lined the busy streets and colourful billboards stood at the edge of the tree-lined pavements. Richard sat to my right in silence. His face was shiny with sweat and was still as pale as it had been when we arrived. He looked like he was in a bad way. I started noticing the obvious signs of the various financial institutions on either side of the road. I turned to Richard. "We need to draw a lot of cash, Richard, and quickly. Can you see anywhere we can go?"

He spoke for the first time in ages. His voice sounded weak and shaky. "Um, Barclays," he said pointing ahead, "there's a Barclays over there."

"Tell the driver to stop at the Barclays Bank please, Hassan," I said. The driver was told where to go and we pulled into a side street to park. "Right," I said, "let's go. Hassan are you coming?"

"I will wait here with the bags, Mr Jason," he replied. I agreed and Richard and myself got out and started walking down the street towards the entrance of the bank. "I Want you to draw $20 000, Richard," I said, "I'll return anything I don't use but I am not going to be short." He nodded solemnly in agreement. We walked through a large glass revolving door and stepped into the spacious, air conditioned banking hall. Pleasant music was being piped through hidden speakers and the customers formed orderly queues within blue rope boundaries. We walked to the enquiries desk where we asked to see a personal banker. The lady at the desk looked at the wound on my head and the scratches on my arms with a worried look on her face.

She picked up a telephone and spoke to someone on the other side in hushed tones. Again, I started to feel paranoid and exposed. I looked around the room for cameras, as we waited for her to finish. Eventually she hung up and directed us down a wide corridor to a booth on the left. We were greeted by a smart young man who spoke perfect English and invited us to sit down at his desk. There was a fair amount of red tape, a few forms to fill in, a phone call or two plus a hefty bank charge, but an hour later I emerged with two bundles of $10 000 each in my pocket. When we got back to the waiting cab, I told Richard to take the front seat and Hassan to get in the back with me. When everyone was in and the doors were closed, I turned to face Hassan. "Thank you my friend," I said quietly as I shook his hand, "you have no idea how much I owe you, this is nothing." I removed one of the bundles of crisp $100 notes and handed it to him, keeping it low so no-one could see. His wise old face broke into a toothless smile as he took the money and tucked it into the front of his dirty trousers. "Thank you Mr Jason" he said, "I have never had a taxi fare like you and I hope not to have one again."

"We will leave you here then?" I asked.

"Hakuna matata, Mr Jason. I wish you and your friend good luck." I smiled at him as he got out of the car. He walked down the street and never once looked back. I got out of the car and moved to the front seat telling Richard to move to the back. He did so and sat in silence. "We need to go to a travel agent please driver," I said, "take us to the best one you know where all of the tourists go, ok?"

"No problem, sir," the man replied in a fake American accent. We drove down the busy streets of the central business district of Dar Es Salaam until we reached an area of tree lined avenues. Five minutes later, we arrived at a walled three storey colonial building with a large sign outside that read Orbit Travel.

A security guard opened a boom and we drove into a shaded car port and parked. "Let's go Richard," I said. On the way to the door I motioned to the security guard to keep an eye on the cab and the driver. He understood immediately and saluted as we walked through the door and into the offices. "I'll do the talking ok?" I said to Richard as we were ushered to a desk and asked to sit down. The lady behind the desk was fat and bubbly. She greeted us with a huge smile and asked how she could help us.

"My friend here needs to get to London as soon as possible," I said. "Any flights you have, first class, economy class, any airline is ok, as long as it's the soonest flight you can do please."

"Ok, no problem," she said with a musical voice, as she turned to her computer. "Let me see what I can do for you." I drummed my fingers anxiously on my knee as I waited. All I wanted was to see Richard get on a plane out of there. A minute later she turned and spoke. "I can get you on Kenya Airways to Nairobi at 1pm today, connecting to London Heathrow leaving at 10pm this evening. Will that be alright gentlemen?" I glanced at my watch, there was plenty of time.

"Excellent, thank you very much. Please go ahead." It was a huge relief to know that finally the end was sight and I would have a chance to sleep. The air conditioning in the office was making my bloodshot eyes sting and itch and I felt like I was ready to drop. Five minutes later, the formalities were done and the tickets issued. We made our way out of the office and into the baking heat of the day. "The airport please," I said to the driver as we got into the car. We drove out of the pleasant leafy avenues and back into the city before joining a busy motorway. Once again it was a stop, start affair and the drive was uncomfortable, hot, and tedious. Ten minutes before we arrived at the airport I became aware that the driver was chewing gum. He did so noisily and with his mouth open. This annoyed me intensely but I kept quiet and waited it out. I realised that the exhaustion had made me very quick tempered. On the way I took Richard's SIM card from him and threw it out the window. I wrote my number on a piece of scrap paper and handed it to him. "Look after that," I said, "and call me as soon as you land in London ok?"

"I'll do that, I promise," he replied. After what seemed an eternity we arrived at Dar Es Salaam International Airport. Once again, my clothes were wet with sweat as we pulled the bags from the boot of the car. I paid the driver without thanking him and told him to go on his way. Richard's flight was checking in as we walked into the airy terminal. I watched as he stood in the queue and checked his baggage in. Once again I felt eyes watching me as I waited. I had to tell myself that my overtired mind was playing tricks on me. When he had finished, he turned and walked towards where I stood. "I better get going," he said.

"Yes, you better." We took the short walk to the main departure gate where only passengers were allowed to pass the yellow line on the floor. Richard stopped and turned to talk to me. "Jason, I just wanted to say…"

"Get the fuck out of here Richard," I said quietly, "and do not forget to do exactly as I told you."

"Right" he said quietly, as he nodded with a small smile on his face. He held his right hand out to me. I was never one to refuse a man's handshake so I took his hand firmly and shook it.

"Go!" I said. Richard walked away and arrived at the passport control desk. The man in the wooden booth stamped his document quickly and he proceeded to the security area with the metal detectors. I watched as he removed his shoes and sent his hand luggage through the x-ray machine. He walked through the metal detector without a hitch and I continued watching as he sat and put his shoes on. Finally he stood and looked back at me. He held his right hand up in a wave to which I responded by doing the same. Then he walked off to the right and was gone. I took a deep breath and turned around to make my way to the exit. Once outside, I lit a cigarette and stood in the shade of the drop off area. Richard's flight was due to leave in an hour. I decided that I needed to be one hundred percent sure that he had actually gone so I opted to stay until I saw the Kenya Airways flight take off.

I walked to a grassy area at the end of the drop off zone near a security fence. From there I could see the various planes parked and I had a view of the runway. I spent the next torturous hour walking up and down the drop off zone and glancing at my watch until the departure time. Thankfully the Boeing 737 Kenya Airways plane left on time, and I watched as it taxied down the runway in the shimmering heat. After what seemed an eternity, I heard the engines roar in the distance and I watched as the plane took off into the cloudless blue sky. The heat and smell of aviation fuel added to my dull thumping headache. "Thank fuck for that," I said under my breath as I walked off towards the taxi rank. Richard was safe. He was out of the reach of Carlos da Costa. Not for long, but for now at least. I found a modern-looking taxi and got inside. "Have you got air conditioning?" I asked.

"No sir, no air con sorry," the driver replied. "Take me to the best hotel in Dar Es Salaam please," I said, "and make it quick." We drove out of the airport and back onto the busy highway that led to the city. The drive took half an hour and on more than one occasion I became semi delirious with fatigue. We arrived at the hotel. It seemed to be one of the tallest buildings in Dar Es Salaam. It was at least twenty floors high and looked very expensive indeed. The driver took us through the car park and up to the main entrance. There was a fat doorman dressed in a suit and cap to welcome me. On his jacket were hundreds of metal badges from hotels around the world. "Welcome to the Dar Es Salaam Sun Hotel, sir," he said with a beaming smile. I stepped out of the cab slightly dishevelled and obviously wounded.

"Thanks," I said, "bags in the back." I paid the driver and walked into a huge marble-covered reception area. I was in no mood for pleasantries as I approached the receptionist. "I'd like to check in please. One night for now, I will see you tomorrow if I need to stay longer."

"No problem at all sir," said the receptionist, "I'll need you to fill in this form and see your identification or passport please." I pulled a $100 note from my pocket and slid it across the cold stone surface.

"I don't have any identification with me. My name is John Smith." The man glanced around briefly before he carefully took the note from the counter and pocketed it.

"Of course, Mr Smith, that's no problem at all. We have a porter who will carry your bags up to your room. I have put you on the top floor where you will have a view of the city. Please enjoy your stay at the Dar Es Salaam Sun Hotel."

"Can you please have room service send up a full English breakfast as soon as possible?" It was more of an instruction than a question. "Certainly sir, I will do that immediately, have a good day." I turned to see a young porter with a cap waiting with my bags. We walked to a set of elevators and took one up to the twentieth floor. From there it was a short walk to my room. The porter opened the room using a key card and escorted me inside. The room was fully carpeted and extremely plush. The porter politely showed me the bathroom and the controls for the air conditioning and the television. I paid him with a twenty dollar note and he left me alone. I was desperate to lie down on the sumptuous looking bed but instead I adjusted the air-con to a cool twenty two degrees and put the kettle on to make some coffee. I tried to gather my thoughts but my brain was swimming hopelessly. Instead I walked over to the huge tinted windows. The receptionist had been right. There was a spectacular view of the sprawling city beneath me and the sea beyond. I stared out to the east trying to see the island I had just come from. I couldn't see it through the haze but I knew it was there. *Zanzibar,* I thought, *Zanzibar.* A few minutes later, there was a knock on the door. I shouted for the person to come in and was pleased to see a trolley with a huge spread of toast, eggs, sausages, mushrooms, bacon, beans, etc. I sat at the table and ate, while drinking the coffee. I had no idea how hungry I was and I scoffed it down quickly. Afterwards I walked up to the window again and tried to see the island. The haze had blocked it out of sight. The air-con was working well and the room was cool. My skin felt sticky and grimy. *Have a quick shower, Green* I told myself.

"Not a fuck," I said as I flopped onto the soft duvet of the king-size bed. "Not a fuck," I whispered to myself again, and within seconds, I fell into a deep dreamless sleep.

CHAPTER SEVENTEEN

- SPRING THAW

I awoke in darkness feeling confused and disoriented. Then it all came back to me; the appalling violence of the previous evening followed by the strange serenity of the dhow ride back to Dar Es Salaam in the night. I reached to my right and found a light switch. The room was still a cool 22 degrees and all was quiet. I got up and went straight to the bathroom for a hot shower. Afterwards, I walked out with a towel around my waist and stood by the huge windows to gather my thoughts. The lights of the city sprawled out into the distance in front of me. It was 1.30 in the morning and still there were cars moving silently on the streets below. My body ached all over from the exertion of the previous night and I ran through the events again and again in my mind. Richard would be aboard the Kenya Airways flight to London, but his future safety and that of his family was in serious jeopardy. My mind constantly went back to the brutal killing of Angelique, the way she had been punched so savagely by Carlos and the sight of her arms breaking behind her. The image had upset me deeply. It had made me physically sick at the time and even then I felt the bile rising in my throat at the thought of such a beautiful creature coming to such a terrible end. *What sort of monster could do such a thing?* It really was the stuff of movies and I found it difficult to believe. But it had happened. It was real, and I knew that I would have to return to Zanzibar to deal with Carlos da Costa. I knew that I would find it difficult to continue with my life knowing that Richard or his family could come to harm. Even if it was due to his own incredibly stupid actions, it would be a constant burden to me. I was furious. But I was not angry with myself or Richard any more. What was done was done and there was no turning back the clock. My anger was directed at one man and one man only. Carlos da Costa.

In my mind, I saw him as a malignant growth. A cancer. A little toad of a man. Sweaty, volatile, powerful, and extremely dangerous. He was poison. His very business was poison and he sent that poison all over the world. I knew that I had to stop him. But I had to do more than stop him. I would kill him. But simply killing him would not be enough. It would be too easy and generous of me. It was at that moment as I stared out at the lights of the city below that I knew I had to punish him. And punish him I would. I walked over to the telephone and called room service. I ordered some food and coffee to be brought up to my room. I set up my laptop as I waited for the food to arrive and I surfed the web for a good two hours as I ate and drank the coffee. When I had finished, I had formulated a basic plan on how I would deal with Carlos. Feeling satisfied and tired I went back to the bed and lay down in darkness. I was asleep in five minutes.

I woke up at 7am, still feeling sore but refreshed. I took another shower, packed my bags and headed down for breakfast. It was a standard buffet but the food was good, and afterwards I walked to the reception to settle my bill for the night. Whilst I was there, I made enquiries as to how to travel back to Zanzibar by private charter. It turned out that there were many deep sea fishing vessels that could be hired at anytime for an island transfer. They came at a price but I needed to get back to the island unseen and on the quiet. I felt sure that Carlos would have eyes and ears operating at both the harbour and the airport looking for Richard and perhaps even myself so there was no way I would risk being seen at either.

After I had paid, I was given glossy brochures for five different companies that offered these services. I asked the receptionist to call me a taxi and, as I sat waiting in the foyer, I called to enquire if it was possible to transfer back to Zanzibar that afternoon. Three of them were busy but two told me they had boats available for me. I made a provisional booking with one of them to leave Dar Es Salaam at 4 o'clock that afternoon. The receptionist was slightly puzzled by my request for such a late departure time, but agreed nonetheless. When the taxi finally arrived, I was pleased to see it was a modern car with air conditioning. In my pocket was a list of companies and addresses in and around the city that I needed to visit before leaving for the island. I had gotten them from the internet the previous night. I put my sunglasses on as we drove out of the hotel grounds and onto the bustling streets of Dar Es Salaam. My shopping list included a few items that I knew I would have some difficulty buying, but I knew that I was in Africa. With a few hundred dollars, anything was possible. The companies I was to visit were veterinary suppliers and pharmacies. Two hours later, I returned to the Dar Es Salaam Sun Hotel with everything on my shopping list having been ticked off successfully. The first part of my plan was coming together and I felt satisfied as I booked in to the same room for the rest of the day. I told the receptionist that I would be checking out at around 3pm and I paid in advance. As I was walking towards the lifts, my mobile phone rang, showing an unrecognised UK number. I answered it to hear the sullen voice of

Richard Lewer-Allen on the other side. "Hello Jason, it's Richard," he said.

"Where are you Richard?" I asked.

"I'm in Brighton like you told me. I got the train down straight away."

"Good, have you got a place to stay yet?"

"Yes I'm in a guest house."

"And you haven't called or spoken to anyone?"

"No I haven't."

"Right, I want you to sit tight like I said and wait for my call. I will call you in the next few days, ok?"

"I'll do that Jason but..." he paused.

"But what?" I said quickly.

"I'm scared Jason, I'm shitting myself!" His voice trembled.

"You sit tight and don't worry Rich, I'll call you, I promise.

"Ok, ok I'll do that," he replied.

"Right," I said, "talk to you soon." I hung up feeling sure that Richard's fear would keep him where he was for the foreseeable future. It was one less thing to worry about. I took the lift with the porter to the top floor and walked into my room. Once he had left, I opened my bag and spread out my purchases from the morning's shopping on the desk near the window. On the left was a fifty millilitre bottle of liquid ketamine. A short acting but powerful animal tranquilliser sometimes used by junkies. It had been easier than I had thought it would be to buy the stuff. I had been refused by the first company on the grounds that I had failed to produce a valid veterinary licence. The salesman at the second and smaller company had been more accommodating and my story of having a wounded animal on a nearby game ranch, combined with a hundred dollar bill slipped under the table had worked a treat. On the right hand side was a transparent plastic box containing five large syringes with a smaller packet containing hypodermic needles. I stared at the items on the desk in front of me before lifting my eyes to look out towards Zanzibar. The air had cleared and in the distance I could just make out the green mass of the island. I called the boat charter company and confirmed that I would be taking the 4pm trip across to the island. They told me to be at their launch at 3.30pm to make payment and complete the necessary formalities. After that I called reception to arrange for a taxi to collect me at 2.30pm sharp. I had learned my lesson about traffic on the chaotic streets of Dar Es Salaam so booked the car early so as not to be late.

I packed my bags and made ready for the trip after which I lay on the bed and watched the news channel on the television. I tried not to think of what might happen back on the island. I only had half a plan. Still it was better than no plan at all. Three hours later and it was time to move. I gathered my bags and took the lift down to the reception to check out. I was pleased to find that the waiting taxi was from the same company I had used in the morning and was air conditioned. It made the hour long journey through the city and to the port area a lot more comfortable in the heat of the afternoon. The boat charter companies offices were in a private harbour not far from where Hassan, Richard and I had landed on the dhow the previous day.

The receptionist gave me a puzzled look as I made the payment for the trip. I explained that I had been in meetings all day and I had an important dinner appointment in Stone Town. She accepted the explanation happily and escorted me down a concrete pier to a waiting fishing boat. The captain was a tall burly black man in a white uniform. He and the deck hand loaded my bags on board for me as I stood on the pier. I climbed aboard and made my way to the wheel deck as the deck hand untied the moorings.

"How long does it take to get to Stone Town?" I asked the captain.

"I can have you there in one hour sir," he replied, "the boat is very fast."

"No," I said, "I would like to take a slow trip please. Even if we get there just after dark, that will be fine for me." The captain raised his eyebrows, "whatever you wish sir." We cruised slowly out of the harbour with the giant inboard engine gurgling beneath us. Eventually we cleared the pier and the captain pushed the throttle forward until we reached a comfortable speed. I made my way down to the lower deck and smoked as I watched the skyline of the city behind us recede. I was feeling a mixture of emotions. There was anger, anticipation, and anxiety all rolled into one. I spent the next two hours in quiet contemplation and I watched as the sun set over the mainland like a giant fire ball growing larger and more intense in colour as it descended. As we neared the island I climbed up once again to the wheel deck. Up ahead in the fading light was the skyline of Stone Town in the distance. The grey silhouette of the House of Wonders was partially obscured by the ominous shape of the Star of Guangzhou at the mouth of the harbour. The captain reduced speed as we approached the rusting hulk of its hull and we gave it a wide berth to its port side. I stared silently at the huge ship as we passed and I noticed a brown steel gangway that had been lowered to just above the water level from the deck.

It creaked on its chains and made a metallic scraping sound as it swung slowly from the side of the ship. It was then I noticed a few abandoned shipping containers scattered on the deck. Their doors were all open, their contents long since removed when the ship had been condemned and the crew had left. The sight of the abandoned containers gave me an idea and I decided that I would investigate some possibilities later that night.

"Where would you like to go sir?" asked the captain.

"If you can drop me anywhere near the Explorers' Restaurant that will be fine." I replied.

"No problem" he mumbled in reply. We cruised slowly into the harbour until I saw the lights of our destination in front of us. The captain cut the motor and we drifted silently until we hit the sand of the beach. The deck hand set about removing my bags immediately. I pulled out a hundred dollar bill and handed it to the captain as a tip. His eyes lit up and he thanked me profusely.

"Sorry for making you late, captain," I said, "it's just I enjoy boat journeys. Thank you very much." After saying my goodbyes, I jumped from the front of the boat and onto the sand of the beach. I grabbed my bags and walked towards the lights and music of the Explorers' Bar and Restaurant. By the time I had reached the outdoor seating area and found a free table, the charter boat had gone. I glanced around at the various patrons at the other tables. They all appeared to be tourists and were all busy in their own private conversations and listening to music that was coming from the inside area. I ordered a Safari beer from a bored looking waiter and I stared out at the eerie shape of the abandoned ship in the distance as I waited. The beer was ice cold, crisp and bitter to taste. I pulled out my mobile phone and called the only person I trusted on the island. "Hello Mr Jason," Hassan answered in a shaky and surprised voice. Mine was probably the last voice he had expected to hear. "Hello

Hassan, is everything alright with you?" I asked. "Yes Mr Jason, everything seems to be fine. And with you?"

"Everything is fine like I said it would be Hassan. I am in Stone Town again and I have another small job for you tonight if you like. As usual it will pay very well and it is not dangerous at all." There was a long pause on the other end and then he spoke.

"Yes Mr Jason."

"I need a small motor boat, just for myself. I would like it to be waiting at Baya beach at 12 o'clock tonight, and I would like you to drive me there. I will travel on the boat alone and I will be gone for no more than one hour. Can you help me with this? I will pay you $1000 in cash." Again there was a long pause and I sipped the beer as I waited. "I am sure I can arrange this Mr Jason I will take my small boat there tonight and I will ask my brother to collect me in my taxi when I arrive. Where would you like me to collect you Mr Jason?"

"In the car park behind the Explorers' Restaurant at 11.45pm tonight. And not a word to anyone."

"No problem Mr Jason, I will see you there." We said our goodbyes and hung up. I made an enquiry from the waiter as to which was the best hotel in Stone Town. He recommended the Livingstone which was only a hundred metres down the beach from where I was sitting. I thanked him, paid the bill, and headed off down the beach towards the hotel. The night was humid and I was sweating by the time I had arrived at the reception. I checked in under a false name and booked a room with a full sea view. The waiter had been right. It was a plush five star establishment in true grand Zanzibari style. My spacious and elegant third floor room opened out onto a private balcony from which I ordered dinner. I sat there as I ate and stared out at the harbour and the distant black shape of the Star of Guangzhou in the moonlight. After dinner I stayed out on the balcony and drank a few cold beers from the mini bar. At 11.30pm I packed my bag of equipment and headed downstairs. I walked out the front of the hotel, past the swimming pool and onto the beach. Ten minutes later I arrived at the car park of the Explorers' Bar to find Hassan waiting in his taxi as promised. There was a party with a live band in full swing in the pub with a couple of hundred tourists dancing and singing. "Hello Hassan" I said shaking his hand.

"Hello Mr Jason, everything is ready for you."

"That's good." We drove down the main waterfront road past the House of Wonders and the old dispensary. The streets were mostly deserted by that time as were the waters of the harbour. We passed the port building and eventually arrived at the secluded Baya Beach. Hassan parked near the big banyan tree as we had before.

"I will show you how to operate the boat Mr Jason " he said as we both got out of the car. He was clearly not interested in what I was doing and I couldn't blame him after what we had both been through the last time we had met.

We walked down the sand towards the sea where we found a small, four person boat fitted with a 15 HP Yamaha motor. The dented aluminium hull of the boat looked ancient but the motor seemed fairly new. "It is a pull start, Mr Jason, and there is a full tank of fuel on board." said Hassan.

"That's fine Hassan," I said, "are you going to wait here for me?"

"Yes I will wait here. I will flash my lights every five minutes so you will see where to come back." I thanked him and climbed aboard the battered vessel. Hassan gave the boat a shove and it floated slowly away from the beach. The motor was still warm and it fired on the first pull of the starter rope. I sat at the rear with the steering arm and the controls in my right hand. The motor was surprisingly fast and I sped off into the night at a good speed. My destination was clear ahead of me in the moonlight. The dark shape of the star of Guangzhou had shifted in the breeze and I saw its full length side on as I travelled. Slowly its shape grew larger and larger until ten minutes later I dropped the revs and cruised slowly alongside its rusted hull. The light of the moon was obscured by the ship so I pulled the night vision goggles over my head and switched them on. Up ahead of me was the swinging gangway that I had seen earlier. It hovered seven feet above the surface of the water and it creaked and groaned as it scraped against the hull. I cut the motor when I was twenty metres away and allowed the boat to drift closer until I was able to move to the front and grab it. In the green light of the goggles I could see it had been damaged by the sea air. This was confirmed when I felt the crispy roughness of rust under my palm on the steel. I attached the small boat to the gangway using a nylon cord that was attached to a metal ring on the side. Two frayed lengths of filthy rope hung down into the water near the gangway. They were attached to a pulley that hung over the deck above. Their purpose was to lower and raise the gangway from the water level. After some effort I managed to lower the gangway to the level of the boat. The process was noisy as the ropes had not been moved in a long time and the pulley was almost seized with rust. The ropes left my hands smeared with grease. I climbed onto the heavy mesh of the gangway and looked up. It seemed to stretch forever and I estimated that it was at least thirty metres long. I had expected there to be some kind of barricade to prevent people like myself from boarding the ship but there was none. The well trodden mesh gangway with its two rickety bannisters stretched up ahead of me at a forty five degree angle to the deck of the ship.

Treading carefully I made my way up, passing the thick chains that held the metal sections of the gangway. I heard them scrape the hull of the ship three times as I climbed.

It was a sound not unlike someone scratching a blackboard with long finger nails. Apart from that unsettling noise there was nothing but an eerie silence all around. The moon shone bright in the goggles as I stepped off the gangway and onto the deck. All around were the tell-tale signs of a hurriedly abandoned ship. There were empty and dented barrels strewn around and piles of greasy chains in great heaps. I could see the smashed windows of the conning tower and broken glass along with mounds of bird droppings and general litter everywhere. It was a mess, and a hazardous one at that. Twisted and jagged metal machinery lay scattered around and the deck itself was slippery with grease and oil underfoot. I stood there taking in the scene of destruction around me. I was sweating from the climb up the gangway but there was a cooling breeze coming in from the ocean. I turned my attention to the centre of the deck and saw what I had come for. There, sitting at random angles were three damaged and abandoned shipping containers. The one in the centre grabbed my attention immediately. It was the least damaged of the three, and apart from a large dent to the rear, it appeared intact. On its rusted side the words Mediterranean Shipping were printed in faded lettering. I smiled to myself and made my way through the litter and junk to have a closer look. Twenty minutes later I was chugging along in Hassan's small boat past the darkened coastline towards what I hoped was Baya Beach. The lights of Stone Town were in the distance to my right, so I knew I was headed in the general direction. True to his word, I saw the lights of Hassan's car flash twice ahead of me and I revved the boat until I landed at the exact spot from where I had left. Hassan and I drove in silence back to Stone Town. I counted $1000 in cash and handed it to him in the car park of the Explorers' Restaurant. He took it gratefully and we said our goodbyes. The party was still in full swing as I walked past the outside seating area and up the beach towards my hotel. My mind was totally pre-occupied with the plan I was formulating. It stayed that way after I turned the lights off and lay on the bed in my room. The large arched windows were wide open and the sea breeze constantly blew at the curtains on either side. I lay there staring out at the moon for a full hour before I drifted off to sleep. I spent most of the next day in my room planning and preparing for the night ahead. I ordered breakfast and lunch from room service and ate on the patio while I watched the boats and dhows in the harbour. I ventured out only once that day in the late afternoon for an hour and wandered the narrow cobbled streets of Stone Town until I found a hardware shop. I purchased a one metre length of thick chain and a heavy duty lock which I stuffed in my bag. I returned to my hotel immediately. Once I was back I spread the tools I would need for the night in front of me on the desk. I ticked them off one by one from a hand written list I had made earlier in the day.

Black jeans, black tracksuit top, shoes, gloves, skull cap, shoe polish, night vision goggles, rope, panga, liquid ketamine, syringes, hypodermic needles, lock picking tools, garrotte and head torch. I gazed at the array of equipment in front of me and I felt the adrenaline start to buzz in my limbs. *It might just fucking work, Green,* I thought. Next I called Hassan. He answered in the same nervous tone as he had the previous evening but agreed to meet me after an hour in the car park of the Explorers' Restaurant. I waited until it was time to leave, left through the front of the hotel and walked up the beach. There was an easy route out the back and down the street but I needed to keep a low profile on the island. When I arrived at the car park, Hassan was waiting and I climbed in the front seat to talk to him. The trauma of the previous few days had taken their toll on him. He was nervous and jumpy to say the least, but in the end I convinced him that by helping me he would be doing the world a favour. That and earning another $10 000 cash of course. I explained that if all went well, there would be no dead bodies this time and all he had to do was to drive me to Paje, drop me in the bush near the wall of the big house and wait for me to return with my cargo. From there he would drive me back to Stone Town and to Baya Beach, where his boat would be waiting once again. I knew full well that what he had earned from me already was considerably more than he would make in a year. Eventually, he agreed and we made an arrangement to meet at the same place at 11pm that night. I felt the excitement and adrenaline building as I walked back down the beach in the setting sun. My plan was starting to come together and if it worked Carlos da Costa would get his comeuppance in a big way. It was dark by the time I finished packing my bag in the room. I knew I had to eat although my appetite was non existent due to the building excitement and anticipation. I ordered a small dinner from room service and ate slowly on the patio as I watched the movement in the harbour wind down for the night. I spent the next three and a half hours alternating between pacing the room and watching news on the television. A frustrating and anxious time that seemed to take forever. I smoked and glanced at my watch repeatedly until I saw it was 10.45pm. It was time to go.

Leaving everything but the bag I had packed, I left the hotel and walked down the beach to the Explorers' Restaurant. As usual there was loud music and crowds of tourists enjoying themselves inside. Hassan was parked in his usual spot and greeted me soberly as I arrived. We drove off down the now familiar sea front road and turned right at the port building. We stopped once in Stone Town to pick up one last item on my shopping list. I packed the three five-litre bottles of mineral water in the foot well of the back of Hassan's cab and we drove off out of Stone Town towards Paje. Hassan and I smoked and spoke in hushed tones on the journey.

As usual, the road was deserted at that time of night as were the police road blocks. Had it not been for those road blocks I would have hired a vehicle rather than used Hassan, but I knew he was friendly with the policemen and I decided that it would be best to have him with me in the event I was stopped. The Jozani Forest was dark, oppressive, silent, and humid as we wound our way through it. My heart rate was slightly increased and my hands sweaty, as we neared the turn off to Paje. My instructions to Hassan were almost exactly the same as the last time. He was to drop me near the wall, drive for a few hundred metres and wait quietly until I returned. In the event of a car stopping or any questions being asked he was to say that he was having car trouble and was waiting for assistance. I saw the whites of his eyes in the dash lights and I knew he was scared. I told him to slow down a bit at the turn off to give me time to black up and get changed. We passed the various hotels on our left and by the time we had cleared the Eden Beach Lodge I was ready. Five minutes later we arrived at the tall stone wall and Hassan pulled in to the left slowly to park.

"I'll be back as soon as I can Hassan. Just relax. Everything will be fine," I said reassuringly. I wish I had been able to believe myself at that moment. In reality, I had no idea if it would be fine at all. I had no clue as to what sort of obstacles I would be facing and I was more than aware of the sheer audacity of what I was planning. But I was certain of one thing. I would deal with Carlos da Costa that night. One way or another it was going to happen. Hassan reversed the car and drove off slowly as I made my way left down the rough clearing near the wall. Before long I was once again surrounded by the dark, oppressive stickiness of the jungle. The tension had levelled out and I felt the tingling buzz of the adrenaline in my limbs as I pulled the night vision goggles over the skull cap. After a while I reached the familiar palm tree where I had crossed before. Slowly and methodically, I went through the motions of attaching my rope and throwing it over before starting the climb. I paused at the top to catch my breath and study the scene in front of me. The big house loomed in the distance to my left. It looked even more ominous that night, and for a brief moment I doubted myself and the crazy and dangerous plan I had hatched. I shook the thought from my head and remembered Angelique and Richard. I was there for a reason and a very good one at that. With that thought in my mind I grabbed the rope and started the climb down. The first part of my plan was to visit the caves and the cocaine storage facility. I very much doubted there would be any packing of surfboards that night what with Tintin having gone missing. I made my way through the thick bush and jungle until I arrived near the car park and the pathway to the packing building. I paused to look and listen for any activity. There was none and everything was quiet.

One thing I did notice was both Angelique's car and the Hummer had been returned. I guessed Carlos would have reported them missing and had them brought back from Richard's hotel. Keeping a good distance from the pathway I made my way towards the packing factory. As expected, there were no sounds of machinery that night and the building was silent in darkness as I passed it. I was less certain of the cave system so I exercised extreme caution as I made my approach to the entrance. When I arrived, I was surprised to see a heavy gate blocking the way. It had obviously always been there, but had been hidden from view by the foliage on either side. There were no sounds or light coming from the inside so I dropped my bag, removed the lock pick set and set to work.

The sweat dripping made the job difficult but ten minutes later I slid the gate open, picked up my bag, and stepped into the darkness of the first chamber of the caves. I stopped and held my breath to listen. Apart from my breathing and the occasional plop of water dripping into the still pool, it was silent. Slowly I made my way around to the left towards the opening of the second chamber. I looked up for the hole from where I had witnessed Angelique's killing and saw the bright green pin pricks of the stars through the goggles. On the desk in front of me lay a snub nosed .45 calibre revolver. I picked it up and saw it was fully loaded. I pocketed it and moved on. There was a patch of discolouration on the floor of the cave from Angelique's blood. It turned my stomach when I saw it but I put it out of my mind and concentrated on the second gate which led to the storage area. Again it was sweaty, difficult work opening the lock, but eventually I succeeded and stepped inside. The pallet with the pile of cocaine was smothered with tiny sachets of silica gel. I brushed the small sachets away and picked up the top packet. It was packed incredibly tightly and had the consistency of putty to touch through the tough plastic. Its contents were a creamy greenish colour in the light of the goggles. I put its weight at two kgs. At that moment I heard a rustling sound behind me. I spun around on my heels with my heart racing, but saw nothing. I realised the sound had come from the hole in the top of the caves. A small animal perhaps? Relieved I took my bag from my shoulder, opened it, and put it on the ground. My heart pounded in my chest as I placed five two-kilogram packets of cocaine in the bag and closed it. *I'm sure it'll be enough.* I closed the gate as I left and made my way back to the first cave. I paused at the entrance to listen but everything was quiet.

It was a huge relief to step out of the confines of the caves and back into the relative safety of the open. Immediately, I turned left and walked into the jungle to take cover and rest. But there was little satisfaction as I squatted down in the cover of the jungle. I had completed the second part of my plan but it was the third and most dangerous part that worried me.

I pulled up my tracksuit sleeve and glanced at my watch. It was 12.30pm, I was making good time at least. Following the path from a distance I made my way back past the packing factory to the car park. Once again I stopped to survey the area and look at my options. My entire body was itching from the prickly heat and humidity of the night. The shaded carports were full of vehicles as usual and I saw that if I crossed the driveway and approached from the right I would have good cover of darkness. I crept slowly through the foliage towards the driveway and pulled the googles into the upright position. I looked up the drive to my right and saw it wind off into the distance. I guessed it was a good few hundred metres to the gate so I quickly dashed across into the bushes on the other side. My brief moment of exposure had gone unseen and I was once again hidden by the darkness. I knew I needed to be extremely careful in my approach to the house. Treading lightly, I made my way through the undergrowth and on to an area of dark lawn to the right of the carports. Being so close to the house gave me an extra boost of adrenaline. Every sense was heightened as I crawled out in front of the vehicles. I was most interested in the Hummer. Assuming the next part of my plan was successful, the tinted windows of the vehicle would offer me the invisibility I needed to clear the gate and escape from the property. I crawled on my hands and knees along the front of the line of parked vehicles until I reached the Hummer. Then I moved onto the tarmac until I was below the front driver's door. *Surely there won't be any need for vehicle alarms given the amount of security on the perimeter of the property.* With that thought in my mind, I stood up and tried to take a look inside the tinted window. It was to no avail as it was completely blacked out. I took a deep breath and gently opened the door. To my relief there was no siren and the door opened with a soft click. Keeping the door only slightly open I felt inside with my left arm for the ignition. Eventually I found it to the right of the steering wheel and I heard the clinking sound of the keys as my hand brushed against them. *Excellent*. I closed the door as quietly as I could and crouched down to crawl back to the lawn in front of the vehicles. Keeping low and staying in the darkness I moved off towards the far side of the house. Eventually I arrived at a thickly wooded area and I decided it would make a good place to prepare to enter the house. I dumped the bag and then using the goggles once again, I retrieved the syringes and the bottle of ketamine. I realised I was breathing heavily as I opened the plastic box of syringes so I closed my eyes and sat for a minute in an attempt to control it. Once it was under control, I peeled the silver foil away from one of the hypodermic needles. After placing the used foil safely in my bag, I pushed the needle onto the nozzle of the syringe. A mixture of sweat and shoe polish ran into my right eye and I had to lift the goggles to rub it away. It stung fiercely and I blinked a few times before pulling the goggles back down. I held the bottle of horse tranquilliser up and looked at it.

The contents were a thick translucent green in the light of the goggles. I pushed the end of the needle through the rubberised top of the bottle and drew the plunger out until I had retrieved twelve millilitres. Then I removed the needle and placed the bottle carefully back in the bag. I held the syringe close to my face and squeezed the plunger until the liquid squirted from the end of the needle. The needle was designed for livestock, and for that reason it was extremely thick. I was certain it would be incredibly painful for a human to be jabbed by such a thing. *Perfect*. I squeezed the liquid from the syringe until there was exactly ten millilitres left and then placed the plastic cover on the needle. My research had told me this was the preferred dosage for junkies and was sufficient to render the user near unconscious. There would be hallucinations and distortions of objects and although the user would be able to see and hear most things, he or she would be unable to speak or move at all. There would also be a complete loss of body sensation. I removed the garrotte which I wrapped up and placed in one of the tracksuit pockets. Then I took out the panga and strapped it on my back. I looked around in case there was anything I had dropped and then closed the bag. I took a deep breath and looked up at the south side of the mansion. *This is it, Green.* I strapped the bag to my shoulders, got up and walked slowly until I reached the front corner of the house. Stretching out to the right below me were the various tiers and levels that led down to the wall and eventually to the sea. In front of me was the level where Carlos had held his party. There were hidden spotlights shining all along the front of the house to the pool area. It was far too bright. I decided that I would descend one level and make my way in the darkness around to the pool and the staircase that led to Carlos' private quarters. I crept slowly down the grass until I reached the base of the retaining wall and the second level of lawn. As I had expected it was much darker there and the lawn stretched all the way around the front of the house. I pulled the goggles over my eyes to see if there was anyone patrolling the area but saw nothing. Crouching low I crept along the retaining wall until I reached the staircase that Richard and I had used to get up to the party. It was well-lit and I knew there would be a tense moment as I crossed. I looked around once again and then as quick as I could I darted across the tiles into the darkness on the other side. I reached the end of the retaining wall and stood up straight to have a look at the pool area.

It looked a lot bigger without the crowds of people and all the party lights. To the left behind the pool, I could clearly see the stairway that I knew led to Carlos' quarters. There were five windows, all open, and only one of them had a light on. The area from where the food had been served and the band stand were in semi-darkness. I knew that I would have to approach from there and make a dash to the staircase to get in.

I looked up at the third floor and wondered what I would find when I got inside. I had no idea what sort of hours Carlos da Costa kept. I had no idea what to expect. *Perhaps the plan was just too audacious, too risky?* I had no idea but I had come this far and I was committed. One way or another I knew that I had to stop Carlos da Costa. One, if not many lives depended on it. I climbed up to the pool level using the wooden railing. I made my way around the seating area until I arrived at the lawn that led to the ablution blocks. Thankfully, the area was dark and I crossed easily and stopped with my back to the main house. The breeze coming in from the sea did nothing to cool me down and I stood there with my heart pounding and sweat streaming from every pore. Keeping my back to the wall I moved around towards the front. Ahead of me was the band stand and the pool. Around the corner and to the right was the food serving area and beyond that, the staircase. I stood there watching and listening. It dawned on me that this was it. The time had finally arrived and there was no turning back. *Fuck you must be crazy, Green. This is insane! You've got no idea what the fuck is up there! Turn back and go home. This is not your problem!* But it was too late. I knew I was going up those stairs. Subconsciously I felt for the gun, the garrotte, the panga, and the syringe. They were all there. Feeling strangely calm I made my way into the semi-light of the rear of the bandstand. Keeping my back to the building I carried on moving through the area where the food had been served. The staircase was on my immediate right, and I noticed a dark area underneath. I decided to pause there for a moment near a large pot plant. All was quiet and a minute passed as I prepared myself to climb the stairs and enter the building. Finally, I decided it was time to move and I emerged from the darkness and crept to the base of the stairs. As quickly and quietly as possible, I made my way up to the arched doorway.

The door was made from heavy carved wood and was decorated in traditional Zanzibari style with large brass studs. I was all too aware that at that stage, I was clearly visible to anyone who might be looking at the front of the building. At the same time I was completely oblivious to what lay beyond the door. My left hand felt once again for the gun as my right hand turned the heavy door knob and pushed slowly. The right hand side of the huge door opened with a soft click and the door swung inwards silently. As quick as I could, I stepped into the darkness of the room and closed the door behind me. To my right, across the dark room I noticed a few tiny green and red lights that I imagined were electrical appliances. This was confirmed when I pulled the goggles over my eyes and the room in front of me suddenly became visible. I was standing in a huge lounge area with low couches set around a large and ornate table. To my right was a massive flat screen television surrounded by various hi-fi equipment and speakers.

To the far side of the room was a large dinner table and a bar, complete with stools and overhead storage. To the left of the bar was a staircase that led down to the lower levels of the house. At that moment I felt something soft brush across the shin of my right leg. Startled, I looked down to see what it was and saw a huge Siamese cat. It was purring loudly as it wound around my feet. Its eyes bright and yellow through the goggles as it looked up at me longingly. I pushed it away gently with my right foot and continued studying my surroundings. To my left was a long wall decorated with a huge painting of Stone Town. Beyond that was an archway to a wide corridor that I assumed led to the sleeping quarters. The inside of the building was air conditioned and cool but it did nothing to stop the streams of sweat running down my temples around the goggles. Making a conscious effort to control my breathing I stepped onto the carpet and walked slowly towards the entrance to the corridor. When I arrived I was instantly aware of a light coming from the first door on the left. The corridor stretched off ahead of me towards what looked like another staircase leading down. There were doors on either side but all of them were closed except the first one to the left which had been left slightly ajar. I decided that that room would be my first port of call and I crept slowly towards the door. As I got closer, the light from the inside of the room became too bright for the goggles and I shifted them into the upright position. It was then that I heard the snoring. It became louder and louder the closer I got to the door and I was certain that I had found the bedroom of Carlos da Costa. When I arrived at the door I saw that the light I had seen from the outside of the building was from an en-suite bathroom. The door to the bathroom had been left slightly open making the inside of the room light enough for whoever was inside to be able to see. In front of me were a series of arched windows that would have spectacular views of the sea. All of the curtains were closed but they glowed in the light from the hidden spotlights that shone on them from the front of the house.

I paused to listen. The snoring was coming from the right hand side of the room which I could not see. It was the loud and repetitive snoring of a person in a deep sleep. Silently I stepped through the door and looked to my right. The huge room stretched off to the right. To the centre, against the back wall I could clearly see a very large double bed with an ornate headboard and side drawers. There was what looked like a human figure on top of it. With the light from the bathroom behind me, I pulled the goggles over my eyes and looked. Carlos da Costa lay on his side fast asleep with his back to me. There was no mistaking his fat bald head and the folds of flesh of his neck. His squat body heaved under the satin sheets as he snored. To the front of the bed between two arched windows was another flat screen television and to the far of the room was what looked like a walk in wardrobe.

Silently I pulled the syringe from my pocket as I stepped closer to the bed. Every nerve in my body tingled as I removed the plastic cover from the needle and placed it in my pocket. The needle glowed green in the light of the goggles as I stepped closer still to the sleeping lump in front of me. At that moment I felt the soft fur of the cat as it rubbed past my leg once again. It had followed me silently from the lounge area into the bedroom. In my mind I cursed myself a thousand times as it started purring loudly. I took my eyes from the sleeping man in front of me and looked down at the cat in desperation. It sat there looking up at me with an expectant look on its face and let out a loud 'meow.' Instantly the sleeping figure in front of me snorted in reaction to the noise and I watched as Carlos shifted from his side onto his back, his shiny face leaning slightly towards me. Instinctively my right hand came up and gripped the handle of the panga behind my neck. Carlos da Costa never knew how close he came to having his throat cut that night. If he had opened his eyes for a second the blade would have descended and cut the flesh to his spine. It would have been too quick a death for such a vile monster. Instead I watched as he opened and closed his mouth making a clucking sound below me. All the while his eyes were closed and I stood there absolutely electrified. I released my grip on the panga and once again I gently pushed the cat away with my foot. Then the snoring started once again but this time it was louder. It was a wet, gurgling sound, like air being forced through a burst inner tube. I realised then that I had to move and move immediately. I leapt into the air and landed on the stomach of the sleeping man below. My knees pinned his upper arms to the bed and my left hand slammed onto his mouth as I landed. His eyes opened with a look of abject terror as I sunk the needle into the right hand side of his neck and squeezed the syringe. His lower arms came up and gripped my biceps with an incredible vice-like strength. He rammed my back repeatedly with his knees and I felt the hot air of a muffled scream on my left palm. The ketamine took effect in seconds. I felt the iron grip of his fingers loosen on my arms and his legs stop moving. I knew the drug would leave him fully conscious. Able to see and hear, but unable to feel any pain or move at all. The look of terror in his eyes remained as his body became totally limp. I moved my face inches from his and whispered through clenched teeth, "You just relax my friend, we're going to go on a little trip. You and me." I removed my left hand from his mouth and studied his face. His mouth hung open and his jaw twitched in a silent scream. His eyes became dilated as the hallucinations began. I wondered if by that stage he knew who I was. Perhaps, in his now drug-addled brain he imagined he was dreaming. A malevolent, dark figure with mechanical eyes who had stabbed him in the neck. The look on his face told me it was probably the latter. I paused for a moment watching him and wondering what was going through his mind. I was feeling a mixture of intense exhilaration and anxiety.

I had carried out half of one of the most audacious missions of my life. The next step was to get Carlos out of the house and off the property. Satisfied that he was completely immobilised, I got up and left him lying there as I walked back into the lounge area. Not wanting to create an unusual situation with the lighting I kept the goggles on and made my way down the stairway I had seen when I had entered the room. Realising that the exit to the car park would be two flights down I skipped the middle floor completely and arrived in what looked like a service area. There were washing machines and dryers to my right and an archway leading to a huge kitchen to my left. The kitchen had a series of windows from which the lights from out side shone in. I shifted the goggles into the upright position and made my way to the last window to have a look at where I was. When I arrived I could clearly see the carports outside to my left. There were two doors, one leading to a hallway and the main entrance to the house, and another staff entrance.

I opted for the latter and to my surprise I found it open. I realised that the entire house must have been air-conditioned as I felt the heat and humidity of the night hit me as I opened the door. There was no movement on the outside and I noticed a dark pathway to my left that led to the carports. It was looking good so far. There was no time to waste so I made my way back into the kitchen and upstairs to the top floor.

As I walked through the lounge I saw the cat again. It had climbed up onto the back of one of the couches and it purred loudly as it watched me walk past. Carlos da Costa was in exactly the same position I had left him. The only thing that moved were his eyes as he watched me approach and lean over him again. "Time to go, big guy," I whispered as I grabbed his left arm with mine and pulled him into a sitting position. His head flopped back as he came up but his eyes kept staring at me. With my right arm I pulled his legs until they flopped over the side of the bed and the satin sheets fell away. I could see he was wearing boxer shorts and I noticed the thick black hair that covered his huge belly and shoulders. I groaned as I lifted his awkward shaped body into a fireman's lift. Although he was nowhere near as heavy as Tintin he was of considerable weight and my lower back twinged with pain as I straightened up. I was aware of the sickly sweet smell of his body odour as I made my way out of the room and through the lounge. Carefully I made my way down the stairs to the ground floor. Occasionally he would make a wheezing sound as if he was battling to breathe but I paid no attention to that as I made my way to the window closest to the kitchen door. As I paused to look out the window for any signs of danger I realised that no one in their right mind would ever dream such a thing could happen. Considering the amount of armed security on the perimeter of the property it would seem completely outrageous and pretty much impossible. Perhaps it was for those reasons that I was actually succeeding. Having seen it was all clear outside I opened the kitchen door and stepped outside. The last step down to the pathway was a big one and the fat man on my shoulder grunted involuntarily as my right foot landed. In front of me was a clear tiled pathway that led to the carports. Most of it was in semi-darkness except for the carports themselves which were bathed in the glow of a hidden spotlight. I realised that I would need to be quick getting him and myself into the Hummer. *Any sound Green, and you drop him like a stone, duck for cover and reach for the gun.* I walked as quick as I could with the grunting lump on my shoulder and arrived on the driver's side of the big car. Using my left hand I opened the rear door and then unceremoniously dumped the sweaty body onto the back seat. I closed the door as quietly as I could and got into the driver's seat. It was a blessed relief to be finally concealed by the tinted windows of the big car and I sat there panting heavily from the exertion and the nerves. I turned around in the seat to look at Carlos. He had landed badly on his side and his right arm was extended behind his head. I could see his eyes watching me, his mouth still open with a steady dribble of saliva running onto the seat. "Are you ready to go?" I asked. "Let's do it then." I knew there was no point in trying to be quiet from that point on so I turned the ignition key and revved the engine loudly. My hope was that the security personnel at the gate to the property would naturally assume that it was either Tintin or Carlos driving and would open the gate quickly. Failing that, the car was big and heavy enough to smash its way through easily and I would hopefully have time to make the transfer to Hassan's car. Still revving loudly, I reversed the vehicle and engaged first gear. The tyres squealed as we took off down the winding driveway with the lights on full beam. Thick jungle surrounded us as we drove and I hooted continuously to warn the staff at the gate that we were leaving and we were in a hurry. In front of me the driveway veered off to the left. I rounded the corner at speed and came face to face with the grey facade of the perimeter wall with the gate to the centre. Two very sleepy looking security guards were frantically attempting to unlock the gate and they almost fell over themselves as they slid it open for me. They stood to attention and saluted and I saw the whites of their eyes as I drove the big car out and onto the main road. My plan had worked superbly. It had been far too brazen and outrageous to fail. I swung the car to the right and headed up the road parallel to wall. A few hundred metres later, the road made a sharp right at the end of the wall and the tyres screeched as I took the corner.

I was praying that Hassan had kept his nerve and was still waiting for me beyond the wall. I took the left turn and left the wall behind me. To my relief in the distance I saw the reflectors of the waiting taxi. I pulled up behind Hassan and jumped out of the vehicle. "Stay in the car please, Hassan," I said as I noticed him getting out of the cab,." I will deal with this. Just open the boot for me please." He did so and I heard the click of the boot as he pulled the latch.

As quick as I could I opened the back seat of the Hummer and roughly pulled the limp body of Carlos into another fireman's lift. I pushed the door closed and walked over to the open boot of the waiting cab. I figured there was no need to be gentle with my load so I dropped the fat man into the boot like an animal carcass. There was a loud metallic thud as he landed and I had to bend his left leg at the knee to get him in properly. Without wasting time I slammed the boot closed and returned to the Hummer. I removed the keys and threw them as far as I could into the jungle on my left. "Right Hassan," I said as I got into the front of the car, "we are almost finished now. Let's take a slow drive to Baya Beach."

"You want to pick up rocks again, Mr Jason?" he asked.

"No Hassan, there will be no need for that tonight." As we drove off into the night I used the tracksuit top and some of the water from one of the bottles I had bought to wash the polish from my face. I knew the authorities would recognise the abandoned car the next day and attempt to return it but by that time it would be too late. Carlos da Costa would have literally disappeared. The adrenaline started to fade and my body started to cool down as we took the left turn towards Stone Town. I was feeling exhilarated and calm knowing the cargo in the boot would be totally quiet and still should we get stopped at one of the two road blocks. As it turned out the police posts were deserted and Hassan and I drove quietly through the winding roads of the Jozani Forest all the way to the port road turn off.

"Are you sure the boat is at Baya Beach Hassan?" I asked.

"The boat is definitely there Mr Jason. I have filled the petrol tank for you." I was sure that even with the huge payout Hassan was getting, he would be happy to finally see the back of me.

"When we get there Hassan, I will handle everything. You wait in the car, we drive back to town, you get paid, and then I promise, you will never see me again."

"Ok, Mr Jason," he said quietly. I moved to reassure him. "I want you to know that what you are doing now will help thousands of people around the world. This man is a killer and a criminal of the worst kind. Believe me."

"I know he is a bad man, Mr Jason," he replied, "and I trust you."

I left it at that as we took the right turn at the port building and headed off towards Baya Beach.

Five minutes later we arrived and pulled up under the familiar banyan tree. "Ok Hassan," I said, "I'll be back as soon as I can." I collected my bag and the three water bottles from the rear of the car and walked across the sand in the moonlight to the waiting boat. The night was humid and the only sounds were that of the ever present cicadas and the water gently lapping on the metal hull of the small boat. "Open the boot please Hassan" I said as I walked back past the car. I heard the click and saw that Carlos da Costa lay exactly where I had dumped him. It was a difficult and painful job lifting his bulk back onto my shoulder but after a bit of manoeuvring I managed. I walked quietly from the car over the sand and to the boat. I didn't want to break his neck so I leaned over as far as I could and dropped him onto the floor of the small vessel. He landed with a thud like a sack of potatoes. I felt the urge to pause and look him in the eyes, to witness his terror, but time was short and there was still a great deal to be done. My back ached intensely as I heaved the boat off the sand and into the shallow water. Eventually it floated and I jumped in to pull start the motor. It fired after three attempts and I lifted the small tank to confirm there was sufficient fuel. True to his word, the faithful Hassan had filled it. I sat down, twisted the throttle and we sped off into the night. The speed of the boat combined with the light breeze was cooling me down and I closed my eyes briefly to savour the moment. *You're almost done, Green, you're almost there.* After a while the shadowy outline of the Star of Guangzhou became visible and I adjusted my course for where I knew the gangway to be.

Gradually the ominous bulk of the ship grew larger and larger until I dropped the revs and cruised alongside its rusted hull. I attached the small boat to the hanging gangway exactly the same way I had done the previous night. I opened my bag and retrieved my head torch which I strapped to my forehead. My next problem was how to get the dead weight of Carlos from the boat onto the gangway. It was something I hadn't thought through properly and I sat for a few minutes wondering how best to do it. Any mistake I made would see him drop him in the water and drown within minutes. That was something I could not allow to happen. It would be far too quick for a man like him. I wrapped the rope tighter around the metal ring on the side of the boat until it was only inches from the gangway. Next I pulled the lifeless lump that was Carlos to the front of the boat and dumped the upper half of his torso onto the gangway. Carefully I stepped over his body and onto the gangway before turning around and dragging him by the arms until his whole body lay on the metal mesh of the surface. *One more lift Green, only one more and you're done. Go on just get it over with.* I saw his eyes once again in the light of my head torch as I propped him up against the railing to the side of the gangway. They stared at me with a mixture of confusion and fear. I reached for his left arm and bent down to lift him into a fireman's lift for the final time.

My lower back screamed at me as white hot pain shot down my spine. There was a precarious moment where I thought I might stumble forward and drop him over the side of the railing but I managed to stabilise my footing and get into the upright position. The paralysed man grunted and I thought I felt him dribble down my back as I started the steep climb to the deck. After a few minutes I arrived to find the deck in exactly the same mess it had been on my last visit. Carefully I stepped through and over the rusted junk and broken glass until I arrived at the door of the twenty foot shipping container I had identified. I swung the heavy metal doors open and saw that the interior was as I had left it. It was completely empty and the wooden flooring was clean save for a few bird droppings. The corrugated metal of the interior walls was uniform except for the dented area to the rear which bulged inwards. I stepped through the door and walked two metres into the container before turning to my left and dropping to my knees. Once again the heavy man on my shoulder grunted involuntarily as I landed. Carefully I lowered his body and left him in a sitting position leaning against the wall of the container. Again I felt the urge to look him in the eyes but instead I got to my feet and headed for the gangway. As I made my way down the steep incline towards the small boat I realised that it was almost over. When I got to the boat I slung my bag over my shoulder and grabbed the three bottles of mineral water. A few minutes later and panting heavily, I arrived at the door of the container. I stepped inside, placed my bag and the water bottles on the floor, and sat with my back leaning on the metal wall opposite the slumped man. In the bright light of my head torch I saw his large bald head was flopped to one side. The folds of flesh on his neck were perspiring heavily as was his bulbous hairy stomach. He looked a pathetic sight in his boxer shorts with his stubby legs spread out in front of him and his arms to his sides. But it was his eyes that intrigued me most. They stared at me constantly. I wondered if he was fully conscious, or if he was still hallucinating from the ketamine. The dark, almost black, area of skin under each eye shone with perspiration. I held my hand out and waved slowly from left to right. His eyes followed the movement of my hand and I knew then that he understood what was happening to him. "So, Carlos," I said calmly, "here we are, just you and me, alone." I paused to look for a reaction but there was nothing. "I've been watching you, and I know what you've been doing. I saw you beating that waiter to death, the night of your party. Excellent party by the way. Thank you. I do enjoy your singing voice. I know all about your business Carlos. That's right. I have been to the factory where you load the surf boards with the cocaine. Oh, and I've been to the cave as well. Very impressive operation. I'm sure it's been extremely lucrative over the years." By that stage I was almost wishing he would show some kind of reaction to my words, but still it was only the eyes that watched me constantly." I was there when you killed your wife, Carlos.

I watched you and Tintin from the top of the cave. If I had only had a gun, I would have put you both out of your misery there and then, but unfortunately I didn't. How could you have done that Carlos?" I could feel the rage rising in me and the periphery of my vision started to turn red. My voice grew louder.

"How could you have murdered such a beautiful creature in cold blood like that? Your wife? Sure, she was in love with Richard, but you could have just accepted that and moved on. A man of means like yourself could surely find someone else? Instead you beat her until her arms broke and then shot her in the chest! What kind of a fucking monster are you?" I felt the tension and anger of the past days overwhelming me and I paused to look out the open door of the container to let it subside. After a while, I turned to face him again. The man I had imagined as a poisonous toad stared back at me blankly. He looked different by that stage. The sweat was running down his temples and onto his unshaven cheeks. The hairs of his shoulders, chest, and stomach were also matted with perspiration and I knew he was feeling the fear that Angelique had felt before she died. I made a conscious effort to lower my voice. "And what about the thousands of lives you have ruined around the world? Families ripped apart. Countless deaths from overdosing on your poison. Do you ever think about that Carlos? No, I guess you don't. Well, I have brought you here so you can have a long hard think about what you've done. Oh, and I've brought some of your products along as well. "I leant over and opened my bag to retrieve the packs of cocaine. I placed them on the wooden floor next to the three bottles of mineral water. "I know you were planning to kill Richard, and that's something I'm afraid I can't allow you to do. Now I'm sure you're going to get very hungry and thirsty in here, so I'm leaving you fifteen litres of water and ten kilograms of your white poison. Don't use it all at once."

I paused and looked at the evil little man slumped in front of me. The anger I had felt had turned to sadness and a feeling of acute nausea was building in my stomach. "So, this is it my friend," I said as I grabbed my bag and stood up, "I'm leaving you now. Enjoy your stay and good luck." I turned and walked out of the container while retrieving the heavy chain and padlock from my bag. I pulled the heavy door closed, leaving a gap of two inches to allow air to flow to the inside. Just as I was about to wrap the chain around the two thick steel bars that would secure the door, I paused. I dropped my head, closed my eyes, and thought about what I was about to do. In my mind I saw Angelique walking into the restaurant in Cape Town on the night I had first seen her. Her face radiant and lovely and full of happiness. I shook my head to get the vision from my mind, but it wouldn't go away. "No," I said out loud, "it's not enough." Red mist filled my vision as I swung the door open and stepped into the container again.

I knelt down beside the slumped man, grabbed his sweaty jowls with my left hand and looked him in the eyes. "It's time to go to sleep, Carlos," I growled through clenched teeth, "good night." My right fist crashed into the centre of his face with such force that I felt my two middle fingers break on impact. His head shot backwards and clanged loudly on the metal wall behind it. The red mist cleared as I watched his eyes roll backwards. I was certain he would be unconscious for some time. It was as if the pain in my right hand had liberated me and a feeling of quiet calm came over me as I walked out of the container for the last time. Slowly and methodically I wrapped the chain around the steel bars of the door. Like before I left a gap to allow the air to flow inside and I clicked the heavy padlock closed.

The feeling of calm stayed with me as I walked across the deck and down the gangway to the waiting boat. I tossed the set of three keys overboard and watched as they sank to the depths of the ocean. Using the filthy ropes, I raised the gangway to ten feet above the water line. This would prevent anyone from boarding the ship. Using the panga, I cut both ropes as high as I could and dropped them into the sea. The engine started on the first pull and before long I was speeding away from the ship towards Baya Beach with the night skyline of Stone Town to my right. I arrived to find the ever faithful Hassan waiting for me in his car under the banyan tree. "It's time to go Hassan," I said as I climbed into the car.

"Hakuna matata Mr Jason," he replied. We drove in silence down the sea front road, past the beautiful buildings of Stone Town, to the car park of the then quiet Explorers' Restaurant. Hassan accepted the wad of cash with grace and humility. I turned in my seat to face him. His wise old face looked back at mine openly and I held out my hand to him. He took my hand and shook it.

"This time, I promise, you will never see me again. Thank you Hassan." He smiled at me with his toothless grin. "Thank you Mr Jason and yes, I hope to never see you again." Despite the pain in my hand, the feeling of calm and serenity stayed with me all the way up the beach until I reached my hotel. I took a long cold shower and washed the sweat, salt, and polish from my body. With a white towel around my waist I opened the mini bar and took out a bottle of Safari beer. I walked out onto the patio and felt a cool breeze coming in from the Indian Ocean. In the far distance I could just make out the dim outline of the Star of Guangzhou in the moonlight. The ice cold liquid stung my throat as I drew deep from the bottle. I leant on the ornate wooden railing and looked out at the outline of the ship in the distance. In my mind, I felt like toasting Carlos da Costa. Then I decided it was the wrong thing to do.

I held the bottle up in the direction of the ship and spoke with a whisper. "Here's to you, Angelique."

CHAPTER EIGHTEEN

- MELTDOWN, DAY ONE

Carlos da Costa first stirred at around 4am. He was vaguely aware of having a blocked nose and he slowly shifted his position on the wooden floor of the container in an effort to clear it. He was having trouble with his thoughts which seemed random at the time. He was sure that he felt uncomfortable where he lay and was aware that the room he was in was stuffy and humid. The huge dose of ketamine was still coursing through his veins and it was only a few seconds before he sank back into a deep and troubled sleep. In his dreams he saw a malevolent dark figure crouching over him and looking him in the eyes. There were strange flashbacks and confusing memories in his mind. The smell of exhaust fumes and the sound of engines. Car engines, boat motors, and the sound of people talking quietly. Eventually the dreams faded away and he was once again surrounded by the dark and pleasant nothingness of sleep. He next stirred at 5.45am and rubbed the surface beneath the back of his right hand expecting to feel a satin sheet. Instead of the smooth sheet he felt something like tight-grained wood. Confused, he lay there with his eyes closed and tapped the strange surface with his knuckles while he tried to gather his thoughts. Slowly but surely he began to wake up. It felt right that the room he was sleeping in was dark, but he was slowly becoming aware that something was wrong. The room was warm and extremely uncomfortable. With great effort he opened his left eye and saw a thin sliver of vertical light. At that moment, he was overcome with what felt like the worst hangover ever. The seam of light wobbled from left to right and the headache that followed forced him to close his eye and lie still to wait for it to pass. He lay there, drifting in and out of consciousness for another half an hour before he dared to open his eyes again. The seam of light was brighter that time and he lay there looking at it for a few minutes. Slowly he raised his left hand and tried to bring it to his face in an effort to rub his eyes. His arm felt heavy and sluggish and when he eventually managed to raise his hand to his face he accidentally brushed it past his nose. A sharp pain shot into his brain and he immediately closed his eyes again to let it pass. The discomfort he was feeling was slowly waking him up and he began to realise that something was seriously wrong. He moved his feet up and down the surface of the container. There were no satin sheets, he was certain of that, and his limbs felt as heavy as lead. The next thing he became aware of was that his mouth was dry. So dry it was almost impossible to swallow. With a great effort he lifted his head from the floor of the container and opened his eyes again. This time everything was clearer. The sliver of light was brighter still and there was the sound of seagulls nearby. *What the fuck?* He thought. *Where the fuck am I?* There was no recollection of any drinking session or party and he was gradually becoming alarmed by the situation.

Slowly and with great effort he turned onto his back. His entire body ached as he moved and he was sure he felt corrugated metal behind his head. Fifteen minutes passed before he was finally able to prop himself up into a sitting position with his back leaning on the uncomfortable metal wall. He sat there with his eyes closed and his head resting on his chest. The throbbing in his head began to fade and finally he felt strong enough to have a good look at the strange surroundings. "What the fuck?" He whispered to himself as he looked around. The sliver of light was bright by then and finally the penny dropped. All around he could see the brown walls of a shipping container. He had been in business long enough with the drugs and the surfboards to know what the inside of a shipping container looked like. Then he saw the three bottles of mineral water in front of him. He knew that before he could begin to properly assess the situation he would need a drink from one of them. His mouth was so dry by that time he felt his tongue was stuck to the roof of his mouth. His wrists, elbows, and knees ached, and he groaned as he crawled slowly towards the water bottles. When he arrived he slumped down on his side and feebly opened one of the bottles with his left hand. The water was warm but it was a blessing and he drank a half litre, spilling some on his chest as he drank. He lay there with eyes closed once again and rubbed his chest where the water had spilled. *What the fuck? Am I naked? What the fuck is going on?* His hand travelled over his ample belly until he felt the boxer shorts. *A few more minutes, I lie here a few more minutes then I see what the fuck is going on.* It was as he lay there that the memories began to come back to him. His wife was dead. Tintin was missing and so was Richard. But then what? He remembered going to sleep in his bedroom and that was when things became blurry. Then he remembered the man who jumped on him while he slept. He had tried to fight him but there had been a sharp pain in his neck followed by a long period of darkness and light. Darkness and light and words. Angry words. The words had come from a voice he recognised but he could not put a face to the voice. It was all too confusing. Once again he gingerly touched his nose. The lightning bolt of pain he felt told him that it was broken and broken badly. He tried to inhale through his nose but found it impossible. Gently he inserted the index finger of his right hand into his right nostril. It was totally blocked with dried crusty blood, as was the left one. Already his mouth was dry again and he realised he would have to dig the dried blood from his nostrils before doing anything. He sat there with his eyes closed carefully removing the blood and mucous from his nose until the right nostril was clear enough to breathe through. He started to feel the strength returning to his mind and body and decided to try to stand up. Still his limbs felt heavy and sluggish but after a few attempts he managed to get onto his feet and stood there wobbling and looking at the slightly open door of the container. Using his right hand as support on the wall he waddled towards the opening.

The fresh morning air flowed through the narrow opening. It was a relief from the humid stuffiness of where he had been sitting. He leaned on the two sides of the doors and tried to push them open. It was then that he saw the chain and the padlock loosely wrapped around the two thick steel bars. *What the fuck?* Feeling dizzy and confused he decided to sit in the fresh air near the doors and try to go over the events of the previous night. It was as he sat there that it all started to come back to him. At first the memories were vague but they gradually became clearer. There had definitely been a man in his room, and that man had drugged him. The painful spot on the left hand side of his neck confirmed this. Then he remembered the dark and uncomfortable journey in the boot of a car followed by what had felt like a boat journey. All of these memories were interspersed with recollections of being carried around and dumped in various places. His body had been completely lifeless and he had been unable to move or speak at all. *What the fuck? Who the fuck could do this to Carlos da Costa? They would certainly die.* Then came the memories of the voice. The voice had spoken to him on a number of occasions. It was a man's voice and he knew he recognised it. "Bastard," he said out loud as the penny finally dropped. "Bastard!" Outside the container a seagull landed and walked around looking into the container curiously. It squawked a few times and this annoyed Carlos da Costa. Then he remembered the man talking to him as he sat in the container. It was the man who had come to the party with Richard. He remembered the voice and face clearly and he remembered the lecture he had been given as he sat there helpless in the container. "You think you fuck with Carlos da Costa? You fucking die!" he said loudly. The strength was coming back and he looked outside once again. The seagull was still there and it squawked loudly from the filthy steel deck. Angrily, he kicked at the steel door. There was a dull thud and a brief rattling of the chain. The bird shrieked and flew out of sight immediately.

He had no way of telling where he was or of telling the time but he guessed it from the light outside it was early morning. *Don't you worry. Today you will get out of here, and today you will fix the people who put you here. They will fucking suffer.* By 8.30am all of the strength had returned to his limbs and he began to explore his metal prison. He had hoped there would be some scrap steel or iron bars in the darkness to the rear of the container but to his great disappointment there was nothing. He began to hear the sound of distant boat engines and the horns of ships. It was at that time that the heat in the container started to become decidedly uncomfortable. He had scoured the entire length and breadth of the metal box for anything he could hit against the walls to attract attention but there was nothing. In the process he had also discovered the packages of tightly wrapped cocaine. Bastard!" he shouted.

"I find you Mr Man! Anywhere in the world, I fucking find you!" After a while he decided that the most comfortable place to be was near the doors. There was at least a source of fresh air and he would be able to repeatedly kick at the doors in an effort to weaken the chain and hopefully attract attention of nearby boats. He sat there, facing the doors, and kicked at them, alternating from his right to left foot. After half an hour his entire body was running with sweat and he was exhausted. He lay down on his right side with his face as close to the opening as he could get it and closed his eyes. Fear started to fill his mind as he lay there in the ever increasing heat of his metal tomb. He realised that what had happened to him was no random act of revenge. It was clearly a well-thought out and meticulously executed plan. The man who had put him in there had obviously been sure that he would not escape. As the heat intensified, the headache returned and his breathing became faster. He realised that if he continued kicking at the doors through the heat of the day he would likely pass out and might not wake up. *No, you lie here and try to relax. You think of a plan. You lie here and breathe nicely.*

By 11am the relentless equatorial sun was still rising in the cloudless sky over the Star of Guangzhou. The rusted orange metal of the outside of the container absorbed its rays and radiated them fiercely to the inside. Carlos da Costa was delirious by then. His entire body itched from the combination of sweat and the dust and grime that had come into contact with his skin since he had been abducted from his house. He had realised much earlier that the small amount of water he had would have to be carefully rationed if he was to survive for any great length of time. Every half an hour he allowed himself a small sip. Just enough to wet his mouth. He had tried to will himself to sleep but the combination of the headaches and the unimaginable heat were starting to drive him crazy. It was midday when Carlos da Costa finally started to scream. He felt like he was on some kind of a roller coaster. There were two specific emotions that raced through his mind. Fear and anger. The fear was primal. It was the basic and raw fear of dying. He felt his brain would boil and his body melt into the wood beneath him. "Mama!" he screamed as he tossed and turned on the sweat-soaked floor, "help me mama! Open the door please! Estou com medo!" After a while the delirium would take over and he lay there mumbling and snorting in a semi-conscious state. At times his strength would return and he would again try to kick at the metal doors. "Bastard! I fucking kill you all!" he shouted as his foot repeatedly banged against the searing corrugated metal. It was all in vain though as the chain and lock were too heavy and the level of noise being generated was nowhere near enough to be heard by anyone. This cycle of despair and rage continued until finally the interior of the container started to cool slightly at around 3pm.

This was when Carlos da Costa began to come to his senses and realise the gravity of the situation he found himself in. His right foot was swollen and bleeding slightly from being repeatedly pounded against the metal doors. Eventually he sat upright and stared out at the limited amount of deck and sky he could actually see.

The seagull that had landed near the container earlier that day returned and stood there cocking its head curiously and squawking at the strange noises from inside. Carlos da Costa sat there like a bull frog, motionless, and for a while he wondered if the bird was a friend or a foe. *Perhaps you are a messenger my friend? Maybe you bring me good news? Maybe you tell Tintin where I am and he come to get me?* Suddenly he found himself laughing quietly at the ridiculous thought. His laughter got louder and louder as he stared at the confused bird until it became hysterical. For a while the situation he found himself in didn't seem that bad and he sat there shaking his head, roaring and wheezing in great fits of mirth. But the euphoria was short lived and gradually the laughter turned into sobs as the terrifying reality of being trapped in a baking metal box returned. He sat there moaning and sobbing until the anger and rage returned. Once again he felt he was on a roller-coaster. The anger he felt gave him a sense of power and feeling that he had been badly wronged. *When you are angry you are strong my friend. Your strength will keep you alive until they find you. You stay angry and you survive.* Once again he decided to be proactive and got to his feet. As he stood he felt a sharp pain in his right foot from where he had been kicking at the doors. The pain only served to infuriate him further and he began screaming and pounding at the doors with his fists. The sound was like a giant bass drum, a dull thud, but anything seemed better than nothing and so he continued with eyes closed. All the while he imagined what he would do to punish the man who had brought him there. *Carrallio!! I kill you. I make you eat your fucking balls!!* Ten minutes later, fatigue and despair overtook him and he slumped to the floor. Wheezing for breath, he held his hands up to the light. Both were bleeding slightly and throbbing painfully. To his relief, the temperature in the container had dropped slightly. The water in the first bottle was almost finished but he was desperately thirsty and he greedily drank the last swallow. He lay there and realised that he had come dangerously close to madness that day. He told himself over and over that that must never happen again, that it was essential he stay focused and positive. *Those people who put you here, they want you to suffer like this. Bastards. You have to be better than them. You have to be more clever than them. Maybe they come to see if you are dead? They open container and you kill them. You bite their fucking noses off! No one can beat Carlos da Costa. No one. You better than them.* The afternoon cooled gradually and eventually he drifted off to sleep. The last thing he saw was the familiar seagull land outside the door of the container.

Hello my friend, you come to see me again. Hello my friend.

When he awoke there was no more sliver of light from the doors. Briefly he panicked as he realised that he could not even see his hands in front of his face. Eventually he noticed a few stars in the night sky through the gap in the doors and he moved his face as close as it would get to the opening. Carlos da Costa smelt the salty air from outside the container. He thanked God that it had cooled down to a manageable level. He got to his feet and walked to where he knew the water bottles lay. He picked up the second full bottle and the tightly wrapped package of cocaine and walked back to the doors. As he sat there he realised that he was not only thirsty but also incredibly hungry. He knew that the person who had put him there, that man from the party, had purposely put the cocaine in there to tempt him. *How did this man know so much? How had he circumvented all the security of the big house and seen everything he had claimed to have seen? Bastard!* The hunger pangs would not go away but he resisted the temptation to open the package. A few hours later he decided once again to get proactive and try to better his situation. Using his teeth he pierced the base of the empty two litre bottle and he carefully removed the bottom section. He was trying to fashion a trumpet of sorts. He could then attempt to shout through the bottle to try to attract the attention of nearby boats the next day. Still there was a chance, he hoped, that the person who had put him there might return during the night. Perhaps his punishment would be short lived. There were all sorts of possibilities running through his mind and he was becoming more optimistic as the interior of the container cooled. All around him was dead quiet. There were no sounds at all. No boats, no seagulls, no distant music, nothing. He wondered if the world had stopped around him permanently. This gave him a sense of dreadful loneliness as he had become reliant on the servitude and fear of all who surrounded him. He was alone for the first time in his life and he was afraid.

The mixture of fear and hunger and occasional optimism stayed with him until 11pm when he realised that he needed to defecate. *Filla da porta! Bastard! Who the fuck can humiliate Carlos da Costa like this?*

They die!! For a few hours he tried to put it off, to forget about it, but eventually nature took its course and he stood to try to find a suitable place to do his business. The only option was the rear of the container and he felt his way blindly through the darkness until he felt the jagged wall where the container had been damaged. Cursing loudly, he removed his boxer shorts and squatted down on the floor. The dehydration that his body was suffering had caused serious constipation and he groaned forlornly as he forced the stool from his backside. The sheer degradation and humiliation he felt as he squatted there reignited the rage he had felt repeatedly through the day.

The thick smell of faeces filled the stuffy space and he screamed as he ran back towards the fresh air of the door. His body slammed into the centre of the doors and instantly he bounced back and fell to the floor. He lay there, stunned and slightly winded. *You gotta keep your head Carlos, these people they want you to go mad like this. You have to be one step ahead of them. Maybe they come later to check on you. Maybe you offer them money. Millions. Then you kill them later. No problem. You gotta stay ahead and keep thinking.* Carlos da Costa shifted his body so he could breathe the night air instead of the stench that came from the back of the container. His brain was filled with a multitude of emotions and he lay there for hours staring at the stars he could see through the narrow gap of the doors. A long time later he drifted off into a troubled sleep.

CHAPTER NINETEEN

- MELTDOWN, DAY TWO

The time was 4am and Carlos da Costa was dreaming. He dreamt of his childhood in Lisbon and of how he would bully the other boys in the street and steal their sweets and pocket money. Although he knew he was an unpopular child he was happy in those old days. Not a lot had changed in his life since then and he still found he could get what he wanted from people by bullying them. He dreamt of his mother's cooking and the wonderful smells that would come from the small cramped kitchen in his parent's apartment. In his dream he saw his mother's smiling face as she passed him his dinner. She would always pile on the food and this had made him an extremely fat child. His father had been a sailor and as a result would be away from home for long periods of time. His mother had spoiled him in every respect, more so than any of the other boys on the street, and as a result they were all jealous. He had always been given the best toys, the best clothes, the best of everything. It was at 4.30am when the euphoria of the dream began to fade, and Carlos da Costa became aware that he was very uncomfortable where he lay. He opened his eyes and for a moment was confused at what he saw in front of him. The vertical sliver of pale light showed the debris and rubbish that lay on the deck of the ship and suddenly it all came back to him. Fear and panic filled his mind. All he wanted was to be asleep again and dreaming of his mother back in Lisbon. He closed his eyes and willed himself back to sleep, telling himself repeatedly that it had all been a terrible nightmare and that when he opened his eyes he would see her standing there in her black dress smiling at him. To see her leaning over and squeezing his chubby cheeks. But it was not to be. Terrified, he opened his eyes but the scene had not changed. It had been well over twenty four hours that he had been locked in his metal tomb and still there had been no sign of human life. No-one to bribe, no-one to sweet talk, no-one to kill. He was filthy dirty, itching all over, full of aches and pains, and still trapped in his metal prison. More importantly, he was thirsty. Thirsty and hungry. He glanced at the bottle of water and the packages of white powder that lay near him. *No, you no eat that stuff, it make you crazy. You drink water, little bit of water only, then you think, you stay calm.* It was morning and usually he would feel the need to urinate but there was no urge at all. The dehydration had set in and all he wanted was to drink from the bottle and eat something. The water was warm but deliciously wet as it entered his mouth and travelled down his throat. He had to fight the urge to drink the whole bottle and he sobbed as he closed the cap and placed it on the floor. *Não não não não não não! This can't be true, não please!* As he lay there, he realised that soon the heat would return. The walls of the container would burn to the touch and radiate inwards like a microwave oven. But there was still the water in the two bottles and the trumpet-like horn he had made from the empty one.

He lay there, oblivious to the stench of the faeces that emanated from the back of the container. The fear and despair he felt began to outweigh the hope. *Could he survive another day in the hell that he found himself?*

Would someone hear his shouts through the horn? Would he be saved? Would he ever get a chance to take revenge on the people that put him there? Had he been such a bad person? Had he deserved this terrible punishment? Drugs were surely a personal choice and he was simply a businessman who supplied a demand. Was that so bad? He remembered the delirium and the near madness of the previous day. The roasting heat that had sent him teetering on the brink of sanity.

There was nothing he could do except try to attract attention and conserve his energy and sanity during the terrible daylight hours. Plagued by thirst and ravenous hunger, he lay and waited. But it was not the heat that came first. It was the flies. Carlos da Costa noticed the first one at 7am and he swatted it away from his face in annoyance. But soon there were more and he began to hear them buzzing at the rear of the container. Then he remembered the awful humiliation of having to take a shit in the container the previous night. "Bastards!" he shouted. His voice was hoarse through his parched throat. Soon the interior of the container was alive with swarms of flies. They came in all shapes and sizes and colours. Carlos lay there filled with terror at the prospect of spending a day roasting in his metal box with a million shit-covered insects. Beads of sweat started to form on his face as the temperature rose. The buzzing of the flies drowned out all the comforting sounds of humanity he had heard the previous day. Gone were the sounds of the distant ship horns and boat motors. The temperature inside the container rose steadily and relentlessly and the buzzing of the flies grew louder and louder. Carlos da Costa knew in his heart that there was no way he would survive another day of the heat combined with the flies. Any sane person would be driven completely mad. Sweat began to pour from his body and the flies began landing all over his itching flesh. At that moment the seagull he had seen twice the previous day landed in its usual place near the door of the container. "Hello my friend," he said as he swatted flies from his face, "you come to see me again? Maybe you help me today?" The curious bird waddled around in the debris on the deck outside. It was then that Carlos had an idea. He had to keep trying to be proactive, to improve his situation and to survive. "Yes, yes," he said nodding at the bird. "you give me good idea. You help me today. Thank you my friend." Carlos sat up and immediately became aware of the millions of flies that had got into the metal box. The ceiling of the container was barely visible through the swarming clouds of insects that droned constantly in his ears. Carlos reached for the tightly wrapped package of cocaine. Carefully he dug his fingers into the top left corner and began tearing the top off around the edge.

His plan was get a large square of the plastic and cover the turd completely. He would use handfuls of the white powder from inside to weigh down the plastic and seal the edges. He hoped this would prevent any smell from emanating from the rear of the container and the flies would eventually leave. He nodded at the bird as he worked. "Thank you my friend. You help me today." Once he had successfully removed the top of the package he crawled to the rear of the container dragging the open package with him. The air was thick with the pungent stench and swarming with flies. They flew into his mouth, ears, and eyes as he went but he persevered until he arrived at the spot where he had defecated. In the dim light he saw the outline of the turd completely covered with flies and immediately covered it with the plastic. Quickly he took handfuls of the fine white powder and placed it on the edges of the plastic until it was completely sealed. Choking and spluttering he scrambled on all fours back to the doors of the container. He lay there for some time with his eyes and mouth closed. His left hand covered his nose and his right ear lay on his shoulder. His right hand covered his ear all in an attempt to escape the horror of the flies. An hour passed and Carlos was sure the maddening drone of the flies began to subside. In fact they had indeed begun to leave the container but that was of no comfort to him. The heat inside the container intensified with every passing minute. Outside the sky was a glorious blue and the sun rose steadily and shone with ever increasing intensity onto the rusted deck of the Star of Guangzhou. Carlos da Costa lay as still as he could with his face close to the narrow opening. He knew from the previous day that he had to try to keep calm and conserve water at all costs. He knew that any sudden movements or exertion would waste valuable calories and endanger his chances of survival and rescue.

He had decided that he would refrain from using the plastic horn he had made until the day began to cool down. But all of his careful planning and attempts at being proactive were in vain. By midday Carlos da Costa felt he was roasting in the pits of hell and the delirium of the previous day returned with a vengeance. Once again he was overwhelmed by the agonising ferocity of the furnace inside the container and he began to moan weakly. The moans would quickly turn into cracked screams of agony and despair and he tossed and turned violently before slipping into unconsciousness. Very little sweat came from his body as he lay there and when he awoke at 3pm he realised that he had come close to death. Outside, the sun was steadily making its way down to the west and the inside of the container was slowly starting to cool. Sobbing and mumbling, he reached for the second water bottle that was by then two thirds finished. The warm liquid reminded him of the crystal clear fresh water lakes of Switzerland as he sipped it carefully through his cracked lips. Fatigue overcame him and once again he fell into a deep, dreamless sleep.

He was suddenly awoken at 4.30pm by the horn of a nearby ship. He sat bolt upright and reached for the plastic horn he had made from the water bottle. "Help!" he shouted as loud as he could through the opening. The bottle amplified the sound to some extent but the dehydration and lack of food had left his voice croaky and weak. He repeated the exercise for a good half hour until, in a fit of anger and despair, he tossed the bottle to the side and slumped back down to the floor. Carlos da Costa lay there weeping and praying for forgiveness. He acknowledged the wrongs he had done throughout his life and he begged God to spare him from the dreadful hell he found himself in. He resolved that if he was to ever escape he would immediately sell his worldly possessions and donate everything to a worthy cause. The repetitive whispering of his prayers stopped suddenly when he heard a scratching sound outside the doors of the container. He opened his eyes to see the familiar sight of the seagull cocking its head curiously and looking at him. "Hello my friend," he said, "you come to see me again, thank you my friend." It was as he lay there staring at the bird that he noticed the open packet of cocaine nearby. The intense hunger he had felt had returned by then and he stared at the white powder suspiciously for a while. *Just a taste. You are starving, just a small taste. At least it is something to put in the stomach. Not a lot. Just a taste.* Using his left hand he dabbed his index finger into the white powder. The humidity had made the upper layer of the powder thicker, almost paste like. It stuck to his finger easily and he brought it up to his face to study it. *All this shit just because of some drugs? All because of this white powder?* He quickly put the finger in his mouth and sucked on it. Immediately he noticed the distinct, clinical, almost surgical taste of pure cocaine. It was not unpleasant. He rubbed it around his mouth and gums using his tongue and was instantly aware that it had an extremely strong numbing effect on anything it came into contact with. He lay back on his side with his face near the opening and looked out. The seagull was still there, waddling around in the rusted debris. "Não problem," he attempted to say but the words were garbled by his highly anaesthetised mouth. "Não problem my friend," he tried again but it was no good, the words came out indistinct and nonsensical. Again and again he tried to say the words and failed. For some strange reason he found this to be hilarious and he began to giggle like a little boy. The laughter grew louder and continued for a few minutes, but this time it did not end with tears. When he had finished, Carlos da Costa realised that he was no longer feeling hungry. Gone were the desperate aching pangs that had plagued him for so long. He felt his spirits had been lifted and his mind rejuvenated. The terrible fear and despair he had suffered since he had been locked in the container were gone and almost forgotten. Those feelings were replaced by a new found sense of energy and ingenuity.

Gone were the aches and pains in his body, the terrible itchiness he had felt all over his skin. The flies were gone, the container was cooling down nicely, and everything seemed to be better than before. Feeling pleasantly surprised he sat up and looked around him. *I find a way. I think of a way out. I make a plan which will work for me, and I make a plan tonight. Yes, that's what I do. Tonight!* Carlos da Costa had no idea that his descent into true madness had begun in earnest. He got up on his feet and studied the scene outside angling his head so as to see as much as possible. Rusted hunks of metal lay all around and there was no sight of sea or land. He put his hand to his chin and in deep concentration began pacing the length of the container being careful to avoid the spot where he had defecated. All the while he mumbled to himself as he imagined his escape and plotted and planned his future. The cocaine he had ingested was working its magic and his mind raced with hundreds of possibilities. Gone were the weeping repentant prayers and resolutions of earlier and he found himself once again planning revenge on the cruel man who had put him there. "Carralio! Bastard!" he whispered as he paced the thirty foot metal box. In his mind he praised himself for his ingenuity. The fact that he had fashioned the horn from the empty water bottle and succeeded in getting rid of the nightmare of the flies earlier.

He felt that he was on a roll and that it was imperative for him to keep the positive thoughts and actions. In the distance he heard the horn of a ship. With a spring in his step he made his way to the doors and started shouting through the horn. "Hello!" he called, "can anyone hear me? Help!" His voice seemed louder and more powerful than the last time he had tried and this gave him hope. Suddenly he began to hear all manner of sounds. There were the deep sound of ships' horns, the buzzing of boat motors, and even what he thought sounded like the repetitive drumbeat of music. *There are people all around me. Someone must hear me! I must continue.* And so he stood there for the next forty minutes as he watched the sun gradually move down through the sky. Every thirty seconds he would repeat the same call. "Hello! Can anyone hear me? Help!" Eventually his voice became hoarse again and he began to feel unsteady on his feet. *I sit down and continue. I no give up!* It was as he sat that the effects of the cocaine began to wane and he felt the anxiety and despair returning.

Slowly he placed his horn on the floor next to where he sat and stared at the deck outside. He was once again desperately thirsty and he glanced worriedly at the second bottle of water which by then was only one third full. *Just one sip. Just one sip is all you need. Take it.* Carefully he opened the bottle and brought the neck to his mouth. The warm liquid soothed his mouth and he kept it there, breathing through his broken but clear nose for a good three minutes. With the water in his mouth he lay down and closed his eyes.

Once again in his mind he imagined cascades of cold sparking spring water flowing over moss-covered rocks in some babbling brook. But his mouth and body were by then so dehydrated that the volume of water in his mouth began to diminish along with his hope and positivity. After a while he succumbed and swallowed what was left of the water. He closed his eyes and turned to lie on his side. Once again he felt the itchiness on his filthy skin. It was all over, from his head to his feet. There was no single part of his flesh that was immune. He felt the aches and pains return all over his body and a throbbing in his head. It was nothing new, but this time it came with a heightened sense of despair and paranoia. *Were there actual living things crawling on his skin or was he imagining it? Would he be scared of the darkness that was steadily coming? Would his friend the seagull be there to talk to through the night? Were there hidden cameras in the dark corners of the container watching his every move? Were the sounds he had heard earlier real or had they been a figment of his imagination?* So many questions. So many fears and worries. More than before. He opened his eyes and immediately saw the open package of cocaine. *It helps me. I no feel hungry anymore and it helps me. Keeps my mind thinking good thoughts. Good thoughts that will keep me alive. Good thoughts that will get me out of this shit hole.* Without pausing he licked the index finger of his left hand and dabbed it into the pasty surface of the white powder. Deeper this time. It came out covered to the second knuckle with a thick coating of powder which he put straight into his mouth. The familiar bitter, chemical taste, and the simple action of putting something semi-solid into his body comforted him and he lay there once again swirling the powder around his teeth, his gums, and all around his mouth. He lay there in the fading light, opening and closing his then completely numb mouth and stared at the scene outside the doors. It was only a matter of minutes before all the fears, all the aches, all the worries and feelings of paranoia began to recede. The cycle had begun again and he sat upright with renewed enthusiasm and gusto. His mind began to tick faster and faster with thoughts of escape and plans for the future. There was no way he was going to die in this shit box. No fucking way. He was Carlos da Costa. The most powerful man in Zanzibar, if not the whole of Tanzania. Feared, respected and loved. There was no chance he would end his days like this. No chance. But Carlos da Costa had no idea that in a surprisingly short space of time, he had become addicted to his own product. Once again he began pacing the length of the container back and forth. The interior felt cool and manageable in his mind and he began to see his predicament as a mere challenge to be overcome. He told himself repeatedly to keep thinking of plans, ways to weaken the chain or the lock on the doors. The cocaine was once again coursing through his veins, raising his heart rate, and speeding his mind along nicely. He began humming tunes from his favourite bands and singers. Frank Sinatra, Elvis Presley, Dean Martin.

He found that it cheered him up and at the same time he could plan his escape and eventual revenge. He planned holidays to cooler climes and imagined all of the wonderful drinks he would consume. And so he paced his metal prison, humming and singing, and occasionally swearing out loud. Eventually he brought an imaginary microphone to his mouth and began giving a performance. His voice felt strong and vibrant and he peeked out into the fading light occasionally to see if his friend the seagull was there to enjoy the show. In reality, it was a pitiful sight but Carlos da Costa was too far gone to know or care. As he sang he danced lightly on his feet, closed his eyes and imagined his backing band playing behind him. In-between songs he would thank his imaginary audience for the applause and bow before introducing the next one. But it was only one hour until the itchiness, the physical pain, the fatigue and the headaches returned. They returned with a new, greater paranoia. An almost unimaginable sense of fear and despair. Once again he lay on the floor, his head near the opening and stared out into the night. "My friend," he called, "my friend, are you there? Please come and talk to me. I am scared my friend, please come!" The seagull never came and Carlos da Costa was left alone with ever increasing fear and panic. He lay there, filthy, and completely stupefied. Rigid with terror until the moon rose into the night sky and shone a milky beam of light through the gap in the doors. In that light he saw the open package of white powder and he knew what he had to do. He needed to recreate that feeling of invincibility and power from before. That sense of well-being and security that came with a simple dab of a finger. He took a swig of water from the bottle and wet his finger before plunging it deep into the powder. The cycle had begun again and it continued all through the night. There was no sleeping, only the peaks and troughs, the songs and the sobbing, the panic and the bravado until the first rays of sunlight fell on the deck of the Star of Guangzhou.

CHAPTER TWENTY

- MELTDOWN, DAY THREE

By that stage it was 5am, but fatigue was the last thing on Carlos da Costa's mind. Instead he sat there, dabbing his finger into the white powder repeatedly and taking small sips of water. In his mind the sunlight was no threat. It was a blessing as he knew the sounds of humanity would soon return and his chances of rescue would increase. Impatiently he got up and paced the length of the container, stopping to cock an ear at the doors every few minutes. He had found by that stage that he needed to eat a little more powder every half an hour as opposed to every hour. It seemed that the headaches and fear came around faster but it posed no problem at all as the first packet of cocaine was still full. It would, in his mind, last a lifetime for one person and would keep him on top of things until his rescue. A rescue he felt sure would come at any time. All the previous night he had plotted and planned his escape. He decided he would use a combination of the horn he had made and kicking at the doors. At least by doing that he figured that it would generate some noise and have the effect of hopefully weakening the chain or the lock. All feelings of hunger were gone and he felt sure that with the help of the drugs, he would make it through the day without a problem. In his racing mind he saw thousands of possible scenarios that would lead to his rescue and he repeatedly visualised his triumphant return to civilisation and normality. He would be a hero, Carlos the benevolent. Father of Zanzibar, creator of employment, thrower of lavish parties and entertainer par excellence. In his drug-addled mind Carlos da Costa felt more positive about his situation that day than since he had found himself in the abandoned metal box. He had no idea that his heart was straining and pumping a great deal faster than it ever had done in his life and that his breathing had become hard and fast. As he picked up his horn he failed to notice that his hands were shaking uncontrollably. He was only focused on one thing and that was his escape. Even his dwindling water supply was of no concern to him, such was his absolute certainty that today would be the day he would get out. He found himself with an uncontrollable urge to grind his teeth and articulate his mouth and jaw. It caused him no discomfort however, and he found it had the effect of focusing his mind on the task at hand. Soon after he heard the comforting sound of boat engines in the distance and he decided to resume his calls for help. He stood there at the doors of the container and began shouting through his horn. His voice was croaky and strange sounding but in his mind he felt it was loud enough to be heard.

After fifteen minutes of doing this, he placed the horn on the floor and began slamming the doors open and shut.

There was a metallic clanging sound with each push and he consoled himself with the knowledge that even thick chains like the ones that held him there would be steadily weakening with each attempt. It was only half an hour before Carlos da Costa began to feel a tingling sensation in his arms and face. It was not unpleasant at first but it began to worry him when he found it hard to breathe. Telling himself he had exerted too much energy he sat down once again. *You need to pace yourself,* he told himself. The tingling sensation began to subside and Carlos lay on his side to relax for a while. He tried to close his eyes but there were far too many thoughts racing through his mind. He lay there, mumbling, and grinding his teeth furiously, until the heat began to return once again.

The sun rose steadily through a perfect blue sky above Stone Town harbour. The tourists began to filter into the various restaurants of their hotels for chilled fruit juice and cooked breakfasts. Far out to sea on the rusted deck of the Star of Guangzhou, in an old shipping container, a bad man lay. His fat, filthy body had begun itching again and the throbbing in his head was fast and intense. By then there was no sweat at all coming from his body, and after an extended period of time his eyes opened suddenly. They looked as if they might pop out of his rotund head and they were filled with abject terror. Carlos da Costa was hallucinating and it was only 9am. On his filthy flesh he saw insects. Thousands of crawling, hissing, insects. They crawled over his belly and legs and neck and face leaving their filth behind them. They crawled into his pants and over his groin. Onto his face and into his nose and eyes. Screaming, he leapt to his feet and began scratching frantically all over his body. The insects seemed to disappear where he had scratched but would instantly reappear somewhere else on his body. Carlos da Costa realised that his mind was playing tricks on him and immediately sat down next to the open package of cocaine. He plunged two fingers of his left hand deep into the powder and immediately swallowed the drug. With his eyes closed he sat there mumbling and cursing until soon, just like before, the bad feelings began to subside and the world seemed a better place. Gone were the imaginary hissing, clicking insects that had only just been crawling all over him. Cautiously he scanned the now light interior of the container. *Não, they were gone, thank the lord.* Carlos da Costa began to sing a tune. "Tall and tan and young and lovely, the girl from Ipanema goes walking and when she passes each one she passes goes 'ah.' " He had no idea that his blood pressure had reached dangerous levels and every single organ in his body was screaming under the strain. The constant dosing with ever increasing amounts of cocaine had pushed his mind far past any concept of reality and he sat there, swaying back and forth, staring out at one single point and singing his song in some bizarre cabaret of death.

His mind raced at a thousand miles an hour and for some time he imagined he was no longer confined in his steel tomb. Instead he saw what was like a series of photographs and videos from his past flash before him. The need for more of the drug came twice in the next hour until at 10am he regained enough focus to continue trying with the horn and the banging of the doors. As he stood he felt incredibly tingly and light-headed. It was not an unpleasant feeling and the steadily rising temperature in the container didn't seem to feel as dreadful as it had done the previous days. He began shouting through the plastic horn but this time with more frequency than before. In his now completely insane mind, his voice sounded like it was not his own. It felt like there was another person doing all the work and he was able to stand back and watch the proceedings as they happened. This did not displease him as he was used to delegating and he felt like he was having a rest. In reality Carlos da Costa was shaking violently as he stood at the door. The croaky calls for help came every five seconds followed by a violent push at the chained steel doors. Blood dripped from his now mangled hands and formed dark pools on the wooden floor. His jugular veins pumped furiously beneath the grimy skin of his neck as did the veins in his temples. The capillaries in his right eye had all burst and he blinked frantically as he stared out at the deck of the ship. He had consumed almost half of the last remaining bottle of water and it was 10.50am when his legs failed him and he collapsed in a heap on the floor. In his mind he felt that he should persevere. It puzzled him slightly that his legs had suddenly failed. *You rest for a while then you continue.* Carlos da Costa's mind drifted away into another series of flashed hallucinations. The temperature inside the container rose and rose and he lay there completely delirious. Occasionally he would call out in some unintelligible language and then proceed to mumble for a minute or so before becoming still again.

In his stupor he had no idea that a combination of terrible things were about to begin. It was at exactly 12 midday when the series of flashing images he had been seeing began to recede and were replaced by glowing deep red light. It pulsated with ever-increasing brightness and was accompanied by what sounded like white noise that grew louder and louder with each passing second. Then, slowly but surely he heard the hissing and scratching of the insects. It sounded like they were far away at first and they might pass by and go away. But they didn't. Thirty seconds later his mad, bloodshot eyes opened in a flash. His terrifying hallucinations were now mingled with whatever was left of reality and he saw the insects coming through the gap in the door in their millions. The entire deck of the ship was crawling with them and they clicked and hissed and piled up as they scrambled over each other in an effort to get through the small gap of the container doors. Carlos da Costa shrieked in terror and leapt to his feet.

As he looked down he saw his lower legs change colour to a shiny brown as the insects began to climb his body. Wide-eyed and wailing with blind panic he raced across the length of the container to escape them and in the process the top right of his head collided with the jagged steel of the damaged corner of the container. He stood there, briefly stunned with a bell like sound ringing in his head. Strips of flesh were peeled back from his head from the impact revealing the white bone of his skull. Blood poured profusely from the messy wounds, completely blinding his right eye and covering his face. Still, he felt no pain and his only concern was that of the insects. Through his left eye he saw them still pouring through the doors in their millions. They crawled over the remaining water bottle and the open package of white powder. Carlos da Costa knew he had to brave them and get back to his salvation. In some dark corner of his confused mind a final vestige of sanity told him he had to eat some more of the drug and drink some water. Wailing in abject terror he stumbled forward and in the process he slipped on the plastic he had placed on top of his turd. He landed on top of it squarely and winded himself badly in the process. With his good eye he saw the insects steadily making their way towards him across the floor. Completely oblivious to where he had landed he writhed around on the floor in an effort to get up. In the process of doing so he smeared his entire back and shoulders with his own faeces. Eventually he made it to his hands and knees, and he knew that he was about to make the most terrifying journey of his life. Yelping and panting frantically he began to crawl through the millions of imagined insects. They crawled up his arms and bit and tickled his body as they went. After what seemed an eternity he arrived at the open package. With his blood-soaked right hand he scooped huge portions of the white powder into his mouth. In his mind there was only one way to get rid of the insects and that was it. He ate with such speed that the powder went up his broken nose and covered his chest and his entire face until he resembled some bloody clown from a cheap horror movie. Unable to swallow such a huge amount of the drug, he reached for the remaining water and gulped down a large portion. Carlos da Costa closed his eyes and waited for the horror of the insects to pass. Every second felt like an hour and eventually the scratching, clicking and hissing began to subside. Stunned and mildly optimistic he opened his eyes. Sure enough the insects had gone but something had changed. The air in the container appeared slightly misty to him and there was a strange electronic buzzing sound in his ears. It grew louder and louder with every second. The obscene amount of cocaine he had eaten was being rapidly digested by his empty stomach. It surged through his blood stream like a steam train, travelling to every organ in his body and pushing them to breaking point. He had no idea that the vessels in his brain carried his death and he was seconds away from a massive intracranial haemorrhage.

Blind rage began to fill his mind and body and, as he stood, he let out an inhuman sound from his mouth.

The dreadful sound grew louder and louder until it sounded like some warped banshee scream. An unimaginable strength filled every muscle of his body and somewhere deep in what was left of his mind, something told him to run. From above Carlos da Costa's body resembled a bloody, shit-covered pinball as he sprinted about bouncing off the burning steel walls of the container. Still the terrible screaming continued as did the dull thuds of his heavy frame as it collided with every surface. Blood and white powder and faeces covered his body leaving streaks and stains on the walls as he ran and bounced as if being repelled by some invisible electric force. It was thirty seconds later when Carlos da Costa's legs stopped working. The banshee screaming stopped at the same time, and he fell in the centre of the container without holding up his arms to break his fall. A huge accumulation of blood had burst through the walls of a major vessel in his brain causing him to suffer a massive stroke. The last thing Carlos da Costa saw was the thin seam of light that was the doors of the container. Outside on the rusted deck a seagull landed and cocked its head inquisitively at the sounds from within. Carlos da Costa tried to speak but found he was unable to. Within seconds his vision began to fade into darkness from the corners of his good eye. The vision grew smaller and smaller until it was a tiny pinprick in the darkness. Soon the tiny dot of light disappeared as well, and Carlos da Costa lay dead. Dead in a metal box, on the deck of the Star of Guangzhou, in the port of Stone Town, on the island of Zanzibar.

THE END

Dear reader.

I'm guessing if you are seeing this it means you have finished this book. If so I really hope you enjoyed it. I would like to ask you to please take a minute to leave a review on Amazon & Goodreads. Your reviews are essential and help me to reach new readers. Why not come and say hi on my Facebook page which you can find here https://www.facebook.com/pg/gordonwallisauthor. There are a lot more books in the Jason Green series and you can find the next one by clicking here : https://geni.us/WPdF

Made in the USA
Middletown, DE
20 January 2022

59236571R00255